Everything Old
WRITTEN BY
Thom Zahler

ART BY
Andy Price

Queen For One Less Day
WRITTEN BY
Thom Zahler

ART BY
Andy Price

Applewood Follies
WRITTEN BY
Ted Anderson

ART BY
Tony Fleecs

Tempest's Tale
WRITTEN BY
Jeremy Whitley

ART BY
Andy Price

COLORS BY
Heather Breckel

LETTERS BY
Neil Uyetake

SERIES EDITS BY
Bobby Curnow

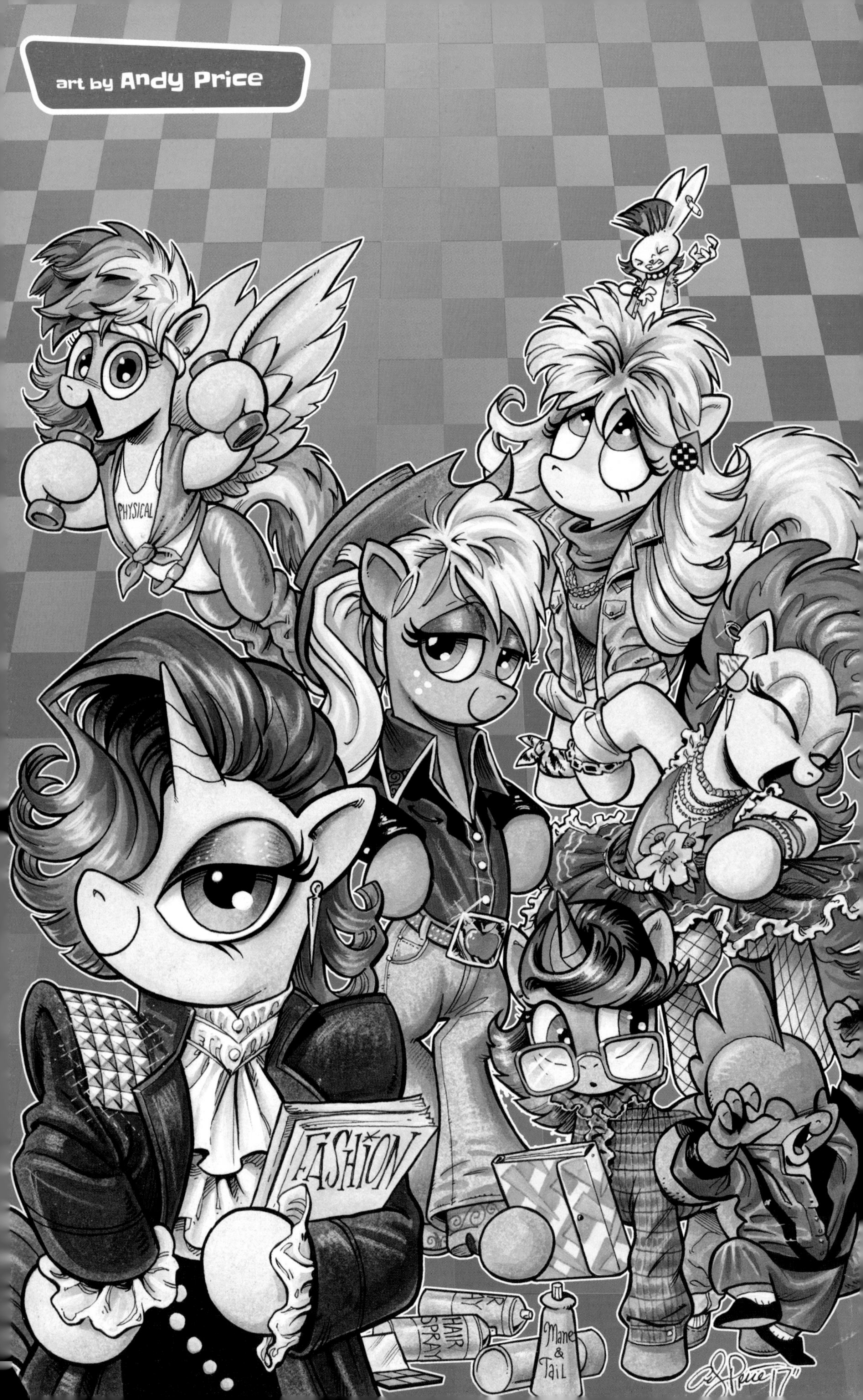
PHYSICAL
FASHION
HAIR SPRAY
Mane & Tail
art by Andy Price

My Little Pony
Friendship is Magic

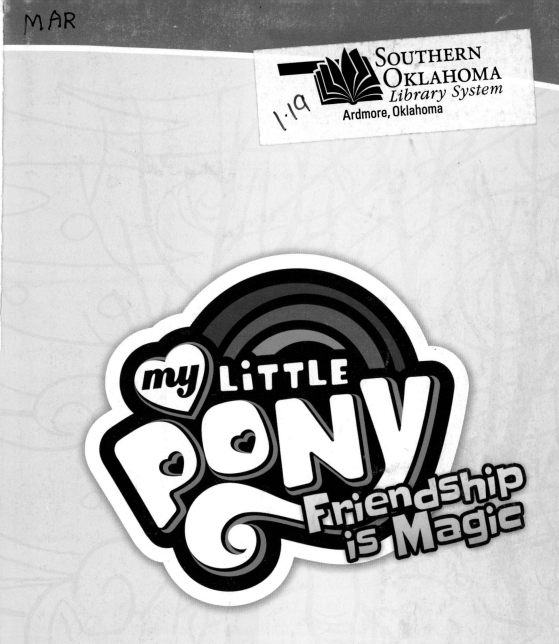

COLLECTION EDITS BY
Justin Eisinger and Alonzo Simon

COLLECTION DESIGN BY
Neil Uyetake

PUBLISHER
Greg Goldstein

COVER BY
Andy Price

Special thanks to Meghan McCarthy, Eliza Hart, Ed Lane, Beth Artale, and Michael Kelly.

For international rights, contact licensing@idwpublishing.com

ISBN: 978-1-68405-357-5

21 20 19 18   1 2 3 4

Greg Goldstein, President & Publisher • John Barber, Editor-in-Chief • Robbie Robbins, EVP/Sr. Art Director • Cara Morrison, Chief Financial Officer • Matthew Ruzicka, Chief Accounting Officer • Anita Frazier, SVP of Sales and Marketing • David Hedgecock, Associate Publisher • Jerry Bennington, VP of New Product Development • Lorelei Bunjes, VP of Digital Services • Justin Eisinger, Editorial Director, Graphic Novels & Collections • Eric Moss, Sr. Director, Licensing & Business Development

Ted Adams, Founder & CEO of IDW Media Holdings

Facebook: facebook.com/idwpublishing • Twitter: @idwpublishing • YouTube: youtube.com/idwpublishing
Tumblr: tumblr.com/idwpublishing • Instagram: instagram.com/idwpublishing

Originally published as MY LITTLE PONY: FRIENDSHIP IS MAGIC issues #64–68.

www.IDWPUBLISHING.com

PHANTOM OF THE STABLEHOUSE ON BRIDLEWAY

West 42ND

FIFTH Ave

Mira's DEL

7

SILVER

HOTEL

NO CART PARKING 6 AM - 6 PM

UPTOWN

SHOES MacLEOD AN

KEENS STE

TAXI
CHAPIN TAXI Co.

MANEHATTAN, FLUTTERSHY! *MANEHATTAN!* AREN'T YOU *EXCITED* TO BE HEADING BACK TO THE CENTER OF *CULTURE AND ART* IN EQUESTRIA?

I *CAN'T WAIT* TO TAP BACK INTO THE ART AND DESIGN ENERGY IN THE CITY!

I'D BE *MORE* EXCITED IF I WEREN'T HEADED THERE FOR THE *ANIMAL SHELTER SYMPOSIUM.* THIS IS THE FIRST TIME I'LL BE MEETING OTHER SHELTER DIRECTORS.

GOAT FANCY

Everything Old

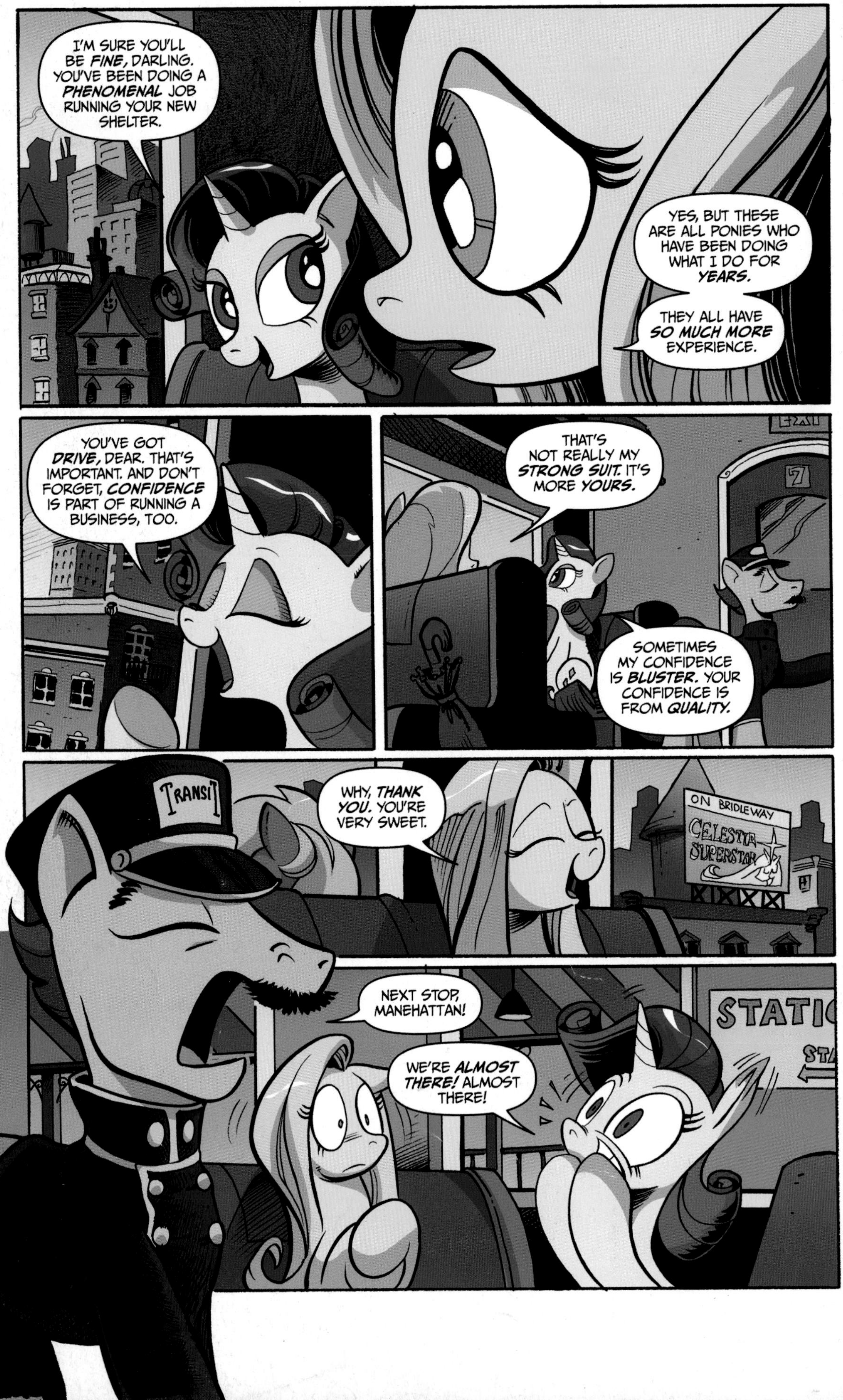
I'M SURE YOU'LL BE *FINE,* DARLING. YOU'VE BEEN DOING A *PHENOMENAL* JOB RUNNING YOUR NEW SHELTER.
YES, BUT THESE ARE ALL PONIES WHO HAVE BEEN DOING WHAT I DO FOR *YEARS.*
THEY ALL HAVE *SO MUCH MORE* EXPERIENCE.
YOU'VE GOT *DRIVE,* DEAR. THAT'S IMPORTANT. AND DON'T FORGET, *CONFIDENCE* IS PART OF RUNNING A BUSINESS, TOO.
THAT'S NOT REALLY MY *STRONG SUIT.* IT'S MORE *YOURS.*
SOMETIMES MY CONFIDENCE IS *BLUSTER.* YOUR CONFIDENCE IS FROM *QUALITY.*
WHY, *THANK YOU.* YOU'RE VERY SWEET.
ON BRIDLEWAY
CELESTIA SUPERSTAR
NEXT STOP, MANEHATTAN!
WE'RE *ALMOST THERE!* ALMOST THERE!

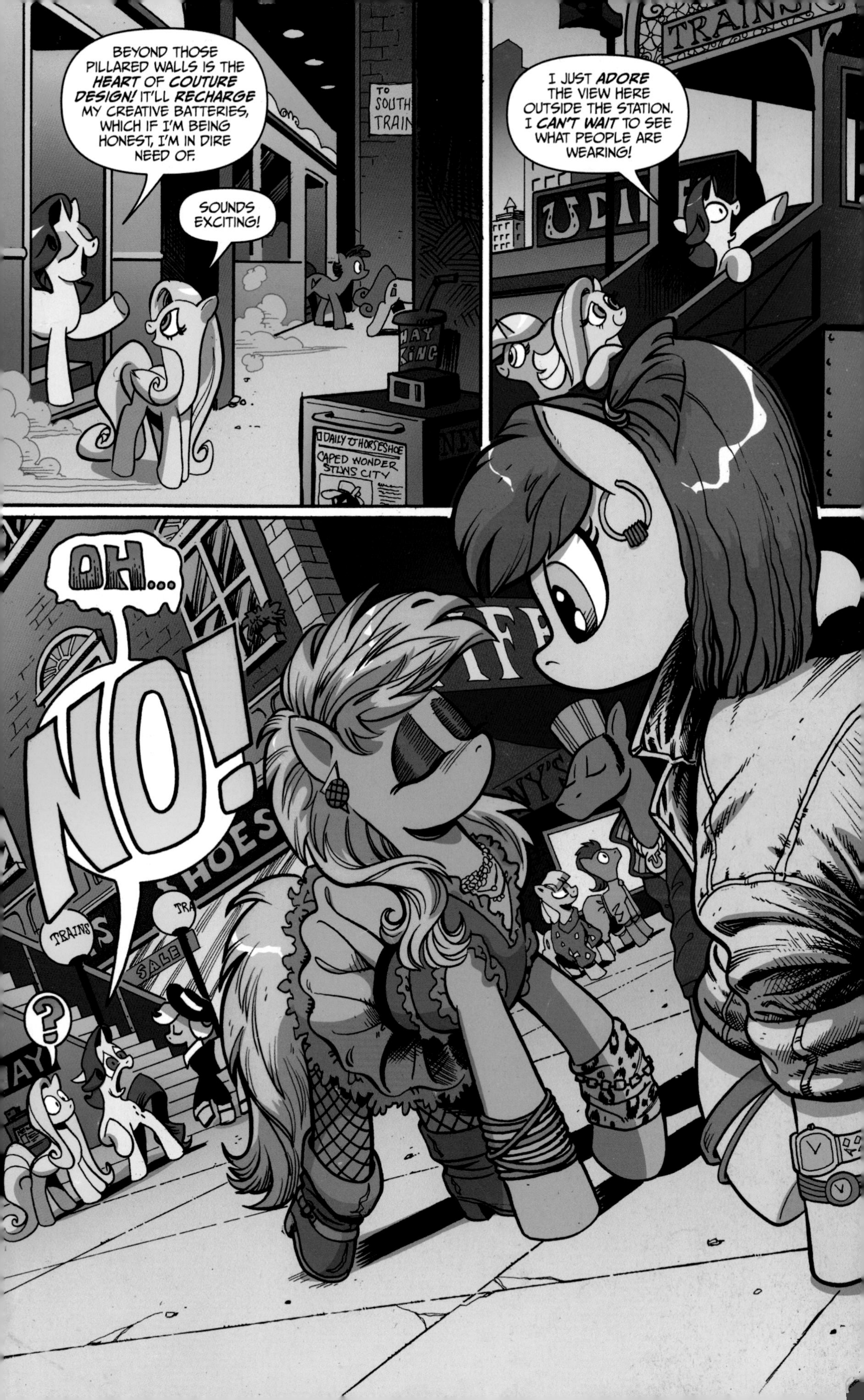
BEYOND THOSE PILLARED WALLS IS THE HEART OF COUTURE DESIGN! IT'LL RECHARGE MY CREATIVE BATTERIES, WHICH IF I'M BEING HONEST, I'M IN DIRE NEED OF.
SOUNDS EXCITING!
TO SOUTH TRAIN
DAILY HORSESHOE
CAPED WONDER STUNS CITY
TRAIN
I JUST ADORE THE VIEW HERE OUTSIDE THE STATION. I CAN'T WAIT TO SEE WHAT PEOPLE ARE WEARING!
OH...
NO!
?
SHOES
TRAINS
SALE

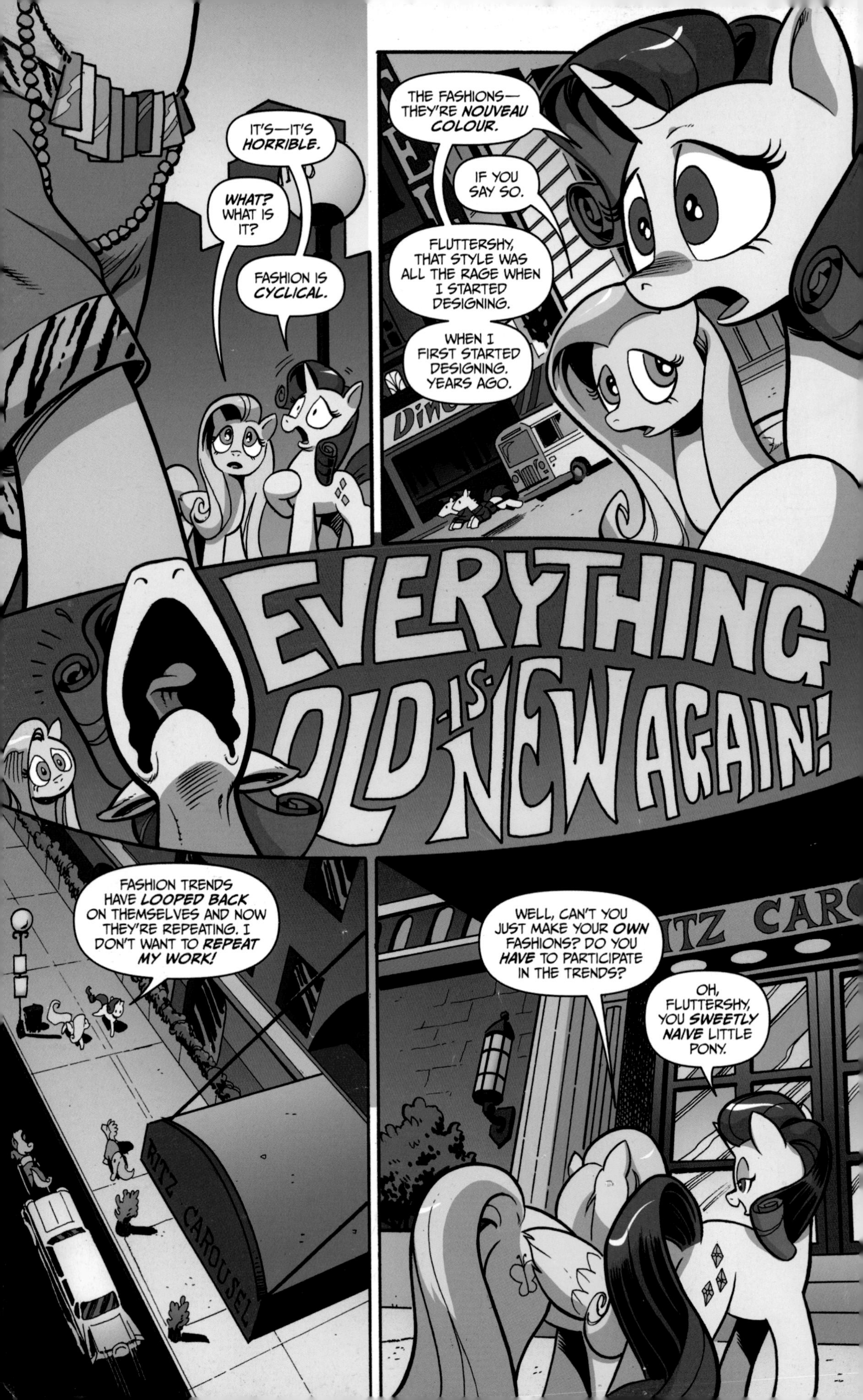
IT'S—IT'S HORRIBLE.
WHAT? WHAT IS IT?
FASHION IS CYCLICAL.
THE FASHIONS—THEY'RE NOUVEAU COLOUR.
IF YOU SAY SO.
FLUTTERSHY, THAT STYLE WAS ALL THE RAGE WHEN I STARTED DESIGNING.
WHEN I FIRST STARTED DESIGNING. YEARS AGO.
EVERYTHING OLD-IS-NEW AGAIN!
FASHION TRENDS HAVE LOOPED BACK ON THEMSELVES AND NOW THEY'RE REPEATING. I DON'T WANT TO REPEAT MY WORK!
RITZ CAROUSEL
WELL, CAN'T YOU JUST MAKE YOUR OWN FASHIONS? DO YOU HAVE TO PARTICIPATE IN THE TRENDS?
OH, FLUTTERSHY, YOU SWEETLY NAIVE LITTLE PONY.

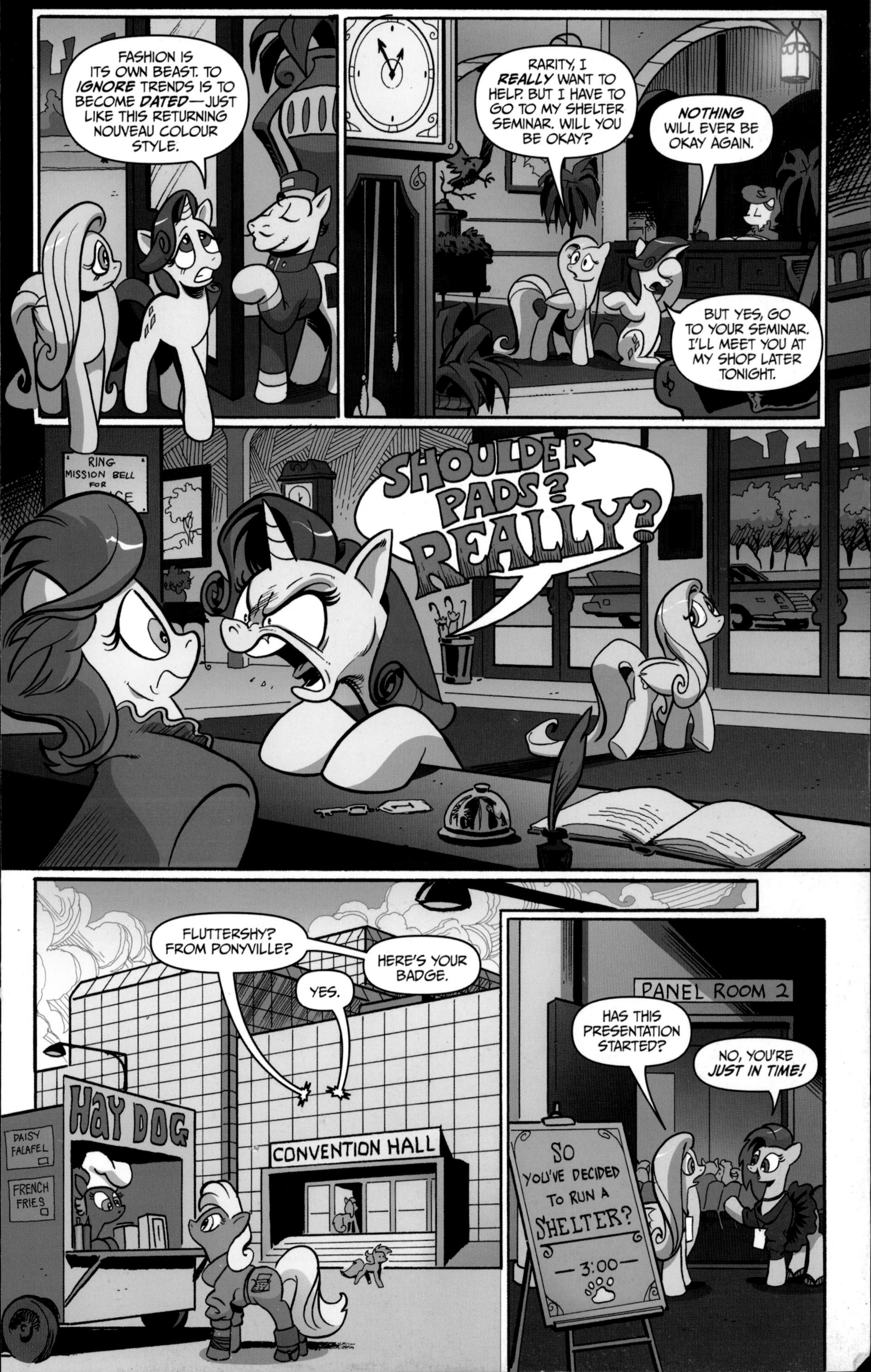

FASHION IS ITS OWN BEAST. TO IGNORE TRENDS IS TO BECOME DATED—JUST LIKE THIS RETURNING NOUVEAU COLOUR STYLE.
RARITY, I REALLY WANT TO HELP. BUT I HAVE TO GO TO MY SHELTER SEMINAR. WILL YOU BE OKAY?
NOTHING WILL EVER BE OKAY AGAIN.
BUT YES, GO TO YOUR SEMINAR. I'LL MEET YOU AT MY SHOP LATER TONIGHT.
RING MISSION BELL FOR
SHOULDER PADS? REALLY?
FLUTTERSHY? FROM PONYVILLE?
YES.
HERE'S YOUR BADGE.
HAY DOG
DAISY FALAFEL
FRENCH FRIES
CONVENTION HALL
PANEL ROOM 2
HAS THIS PRESENTATION STARTED?
NO, YOU'RE JUST IN TIME!
SO YOU'VE DECIDED TO RUN A SHELTER?
3:00

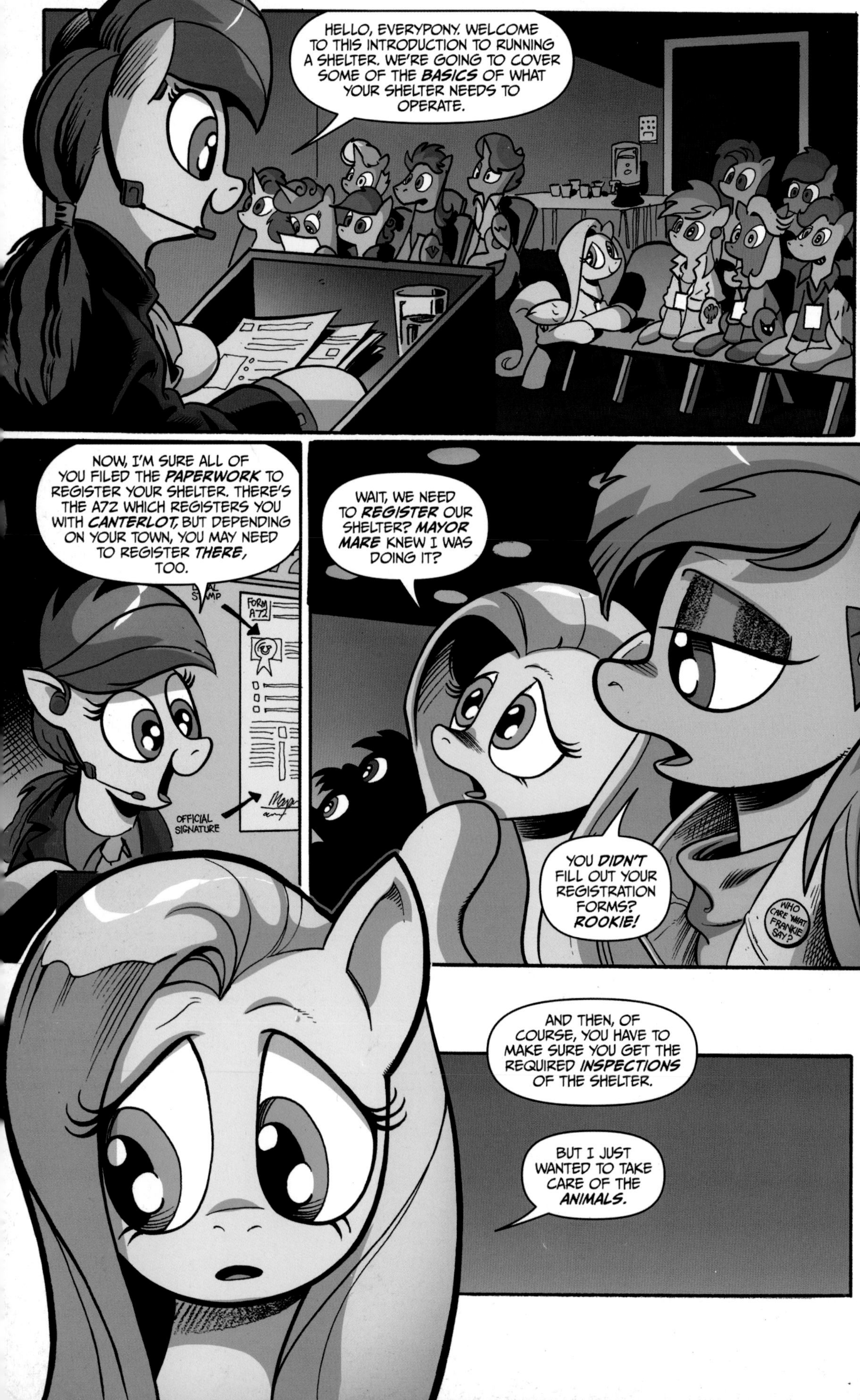
HELLO, EVERYPONY. WELCOME TO THIS INTRODUCTION TO RUNNING A SHELTER. WE'RE GOING TO COVER SOME OF THE *BASICS* OF WHAT YOUR SHELTER NEEDS TO OPERATE.
NOW, I'M SURE ALL OF YOU FILED THE *PAPERWORK* TO REGISTER YOUR SHELTER. THERE'S THE A72 WHICH REGISTERS YOU WITH *CANTERLOT,* BUT DEPENDING ON YOUR TOWN, YOU MAY NEED TO REGISTER *THERE,* TOO.
FORM A72
OFFICIAL SIGNATURE
WAIT, WE NEED TO *REGISTER* OUR SHELTER? *MAYOR MARE* KNEW I WAS DOING IT?
YOU *DIDN'T* FILL OUT YOUR REGISTRATION FORMS? *ROOKIE!*
WHO CARE WHAT FRANKIE SAY?
AND THEN, OF COURSE, YOU HAVE TO MAKE SURE YOU GET THE REQUIRED *INSPECTIONS* OF THE SHELTER.
BUT I JUST WANTED TO TAKE CARE OF THE *ANIMALS.*

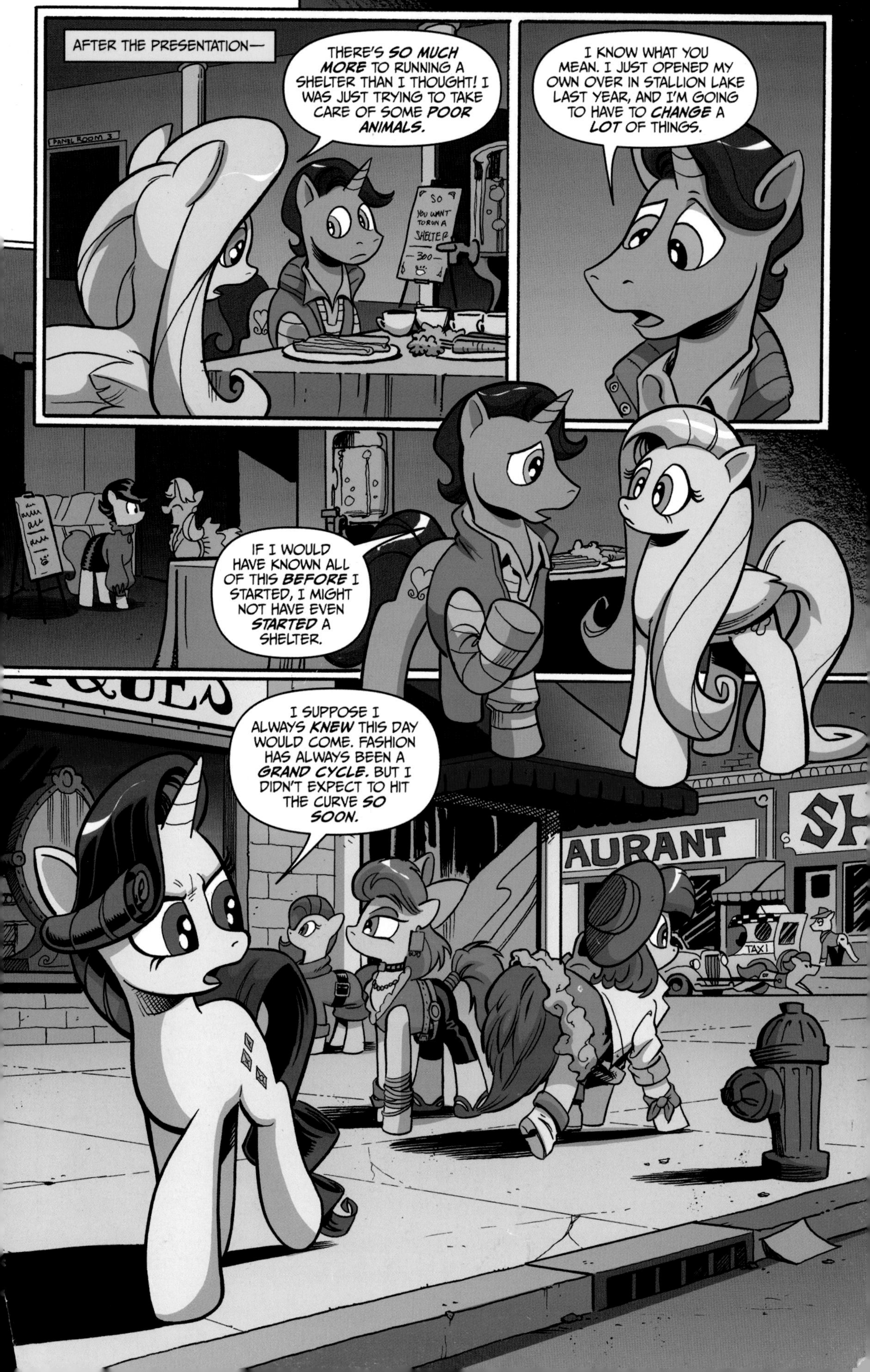
AFTER THE PRESENTATION—
THERE'S SO MUCH MORE TO RUNNING A SHELTER THAN I THOUGHT! I WAS JUST TRYING TO TAKE CARE OF SOME POOR ANIMALS.
PANEL ROOM 3
SO YOU WANT TO RUN A SHELTER? —300—
I KNOW WHAT YOU MEAN. I JUST OPENED MY OWN OVER IN STALLION LAKE LAST YEAR, AND I'M GOING TO HAVE TO CHANGE A LOT OF THINGS.
IF I WOULD HAVE KNOWN ALL OF THIS BEFORE I STARTED, I MIGHT NOT HAVE EVEN STARTED A SHELTER.
I SUPPOSE I ALWAYS KNEW THIS DAY WOULD COME. FASHION HAS ALWAYS BEEN A GRAND CYCLE. BUT I DIDN'T EXPECT TO HIT THE CURVE SO SOON.
AURANT
TAXI

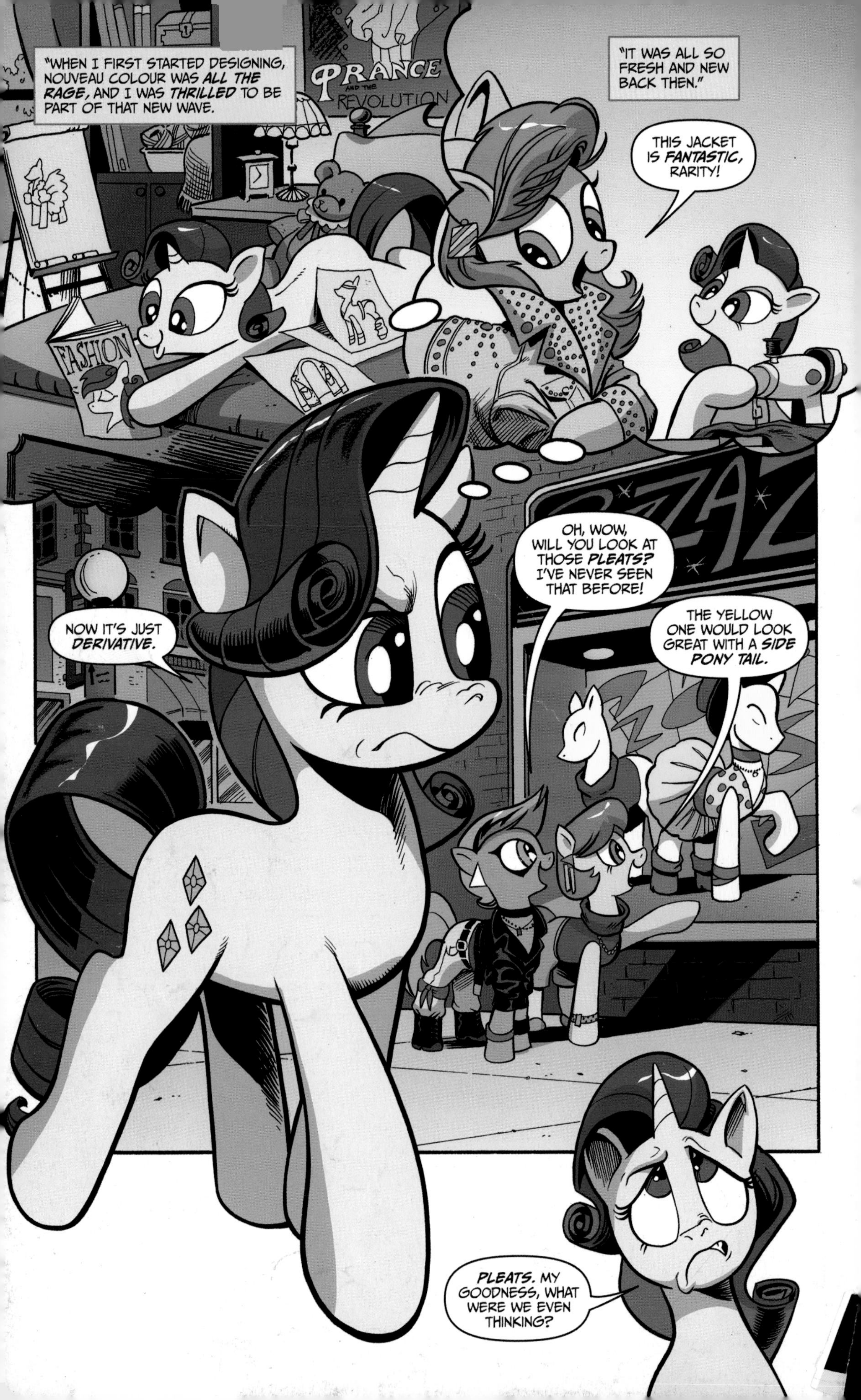
"WHEN I FIRST STARTED DESIGNING, NOUVEAU COLOUR WAS ALL THE RAGE, AND I WAS THRILLED TO BE PART OF THAT NEW WAVE.
PRANCE AND THE REVOLUTION
"IT WAS ALL SO FRESH AND NEW BACK THEN."
THIS JACKET IS FANTASTIC, RARITY!
FASHION
OH, WOW, WILL YOU LOOK AT THOSE PLEATS? I'VE NEVER SEEN THAT BEFORE!
NOW IT'S JUST DERIVATIVE.
THE YELLOW ONE WOULD LOOK GREAT WITH A SIDE PONY TAIL.
PLEATS. MY GOODNESS, WHAT WERE WE EVEN THINKING?

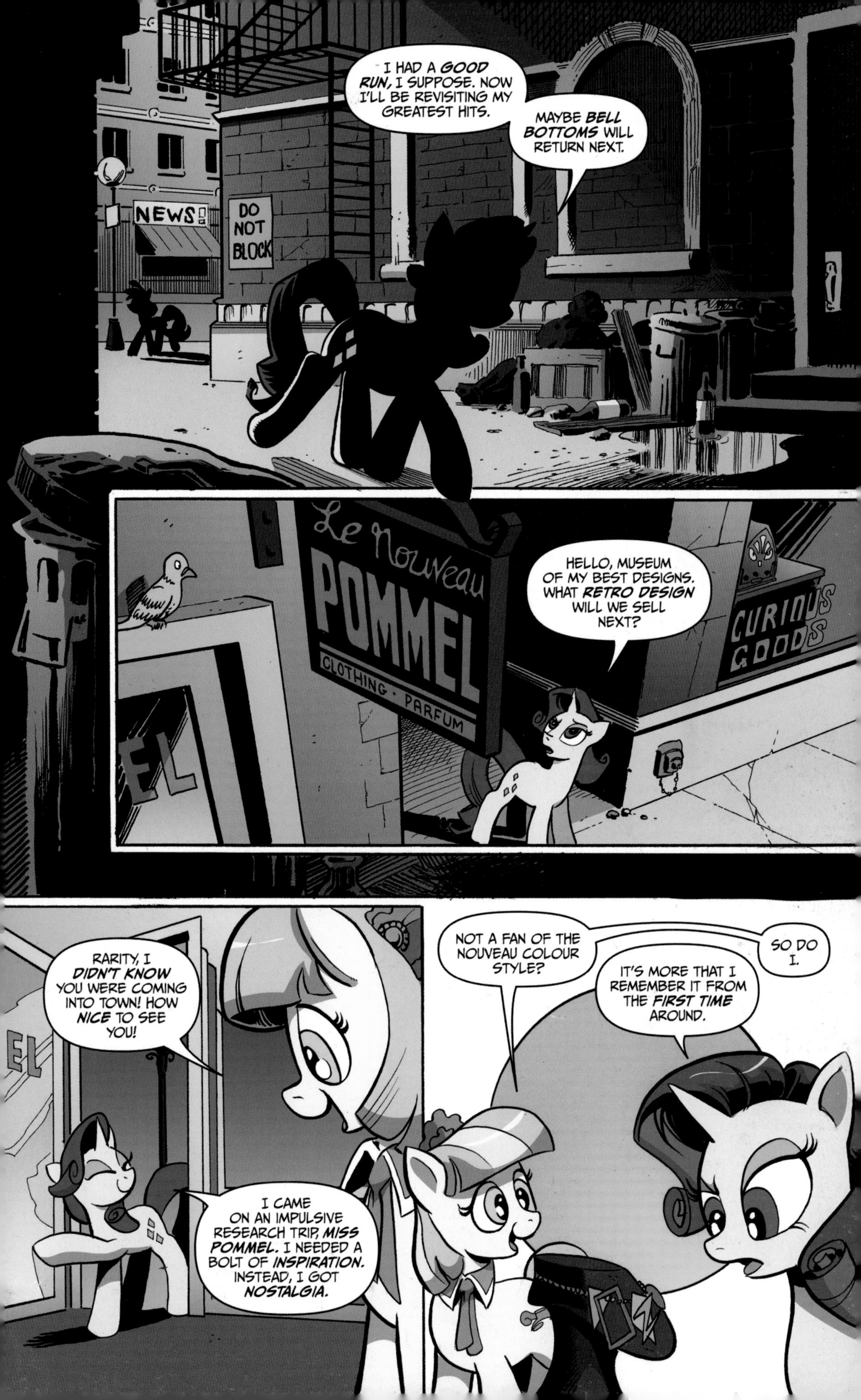
I HAD A GOOD RUN, I SUPPOSE. NOW I'LL BE REVISITING MY GREATEST HITS.
MAYBE BELL BOTTOMS WILL RETURN NEXT.
NEWS
DO NOT BLOCK
Le Nouveau POMMEL CLOTHING · PARFUM
CURIOUS GOODS
HELLO, MUSEUM OF MY BEST DESIGNS. WHAT RETRO DESIGN WILL WE SELL NEXT?
RARITY, I DIDN'T KNOW YOU WERE COMING INTO TOWN! HOW NICE TO SEE YOU!
I CAME ON AN IMPULSIVE RESEARCH TRIP, MISS POMMEL. I NEEDED A BOLT OF INSPIRATION. INSTEAD, I GOT NOSTALGIA.
NOT A FAN OF THE NOUVEAU COLOUR STYLE?
SO DO I.
IT'S MORE THAT I REMEMBER IT FROM THE FIRST TIME AROUND.

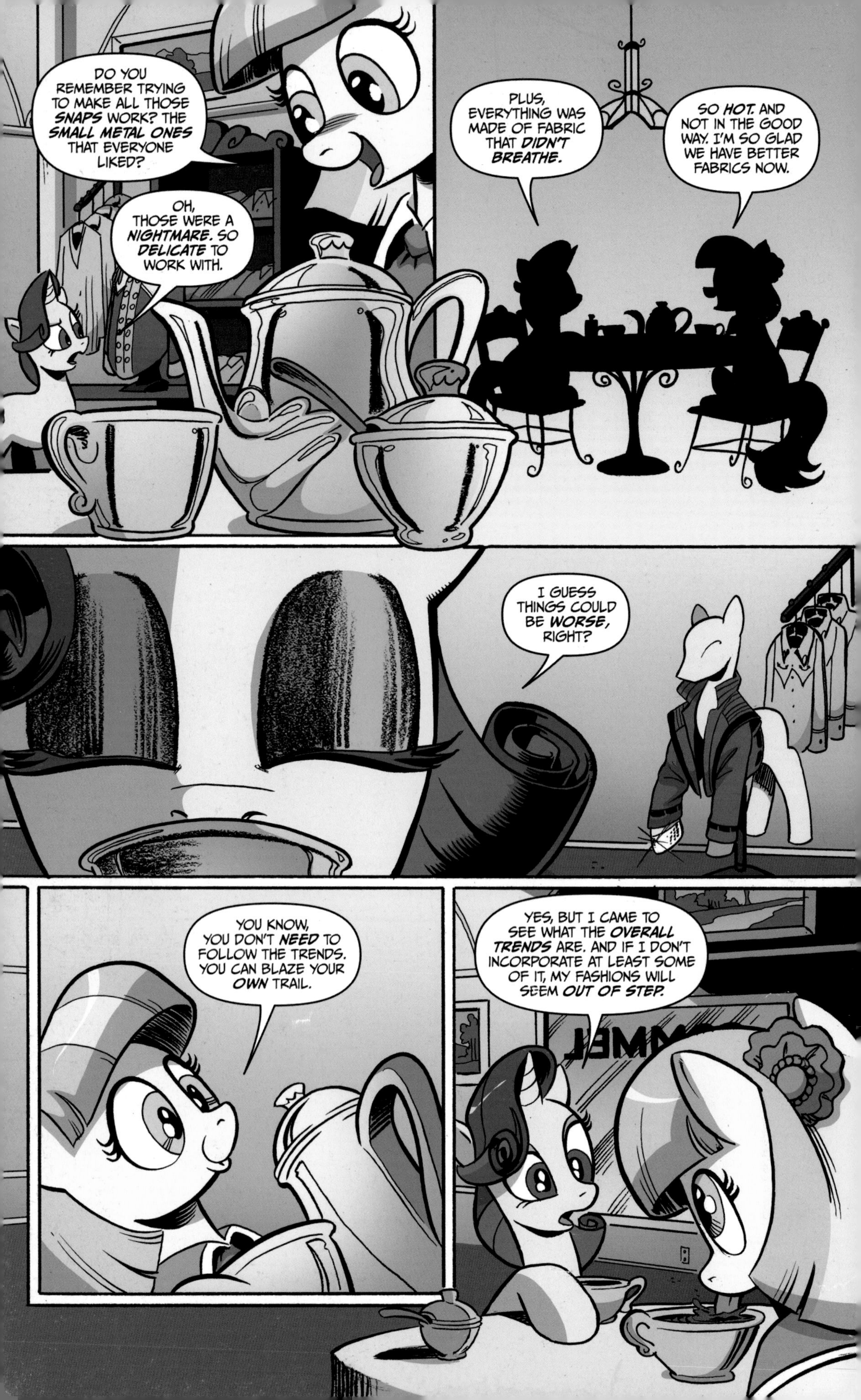
DO YOU REMEMBER TRYING TO MAKE ALL THOSE SNAPS WORK? THE SMALL METAL ONES THAT EVERYONE LIKED?
OH, THOSE WERE A NIGHTMARE. SO DELICATE TO WORK WITH.
PLUS, EVERYTHING WAS MADE OF FABRIC THAT DIDN'T BREATHE.
SO HOT. AND NOT IN THE GOOD WAY. I'M SO GLAD WE HAVE BETTER FABRICS NOW.
I GUESS THINGS COULD BE WORSE, RIGHT?
YOU KNOW, YOU DON'T NEED TO FOLLOW THE TRENDS. YOU CAN BLAZE YOUR OWN TRAIL.
YES, BUT I CAME TO SEE WHAT THE OVERALL TRENDS ARE. AND IF I DON'T INCORPORATE AT LEAST SOME OF IT, MY FASHIONS WILL SEEM OUT OF STEP.

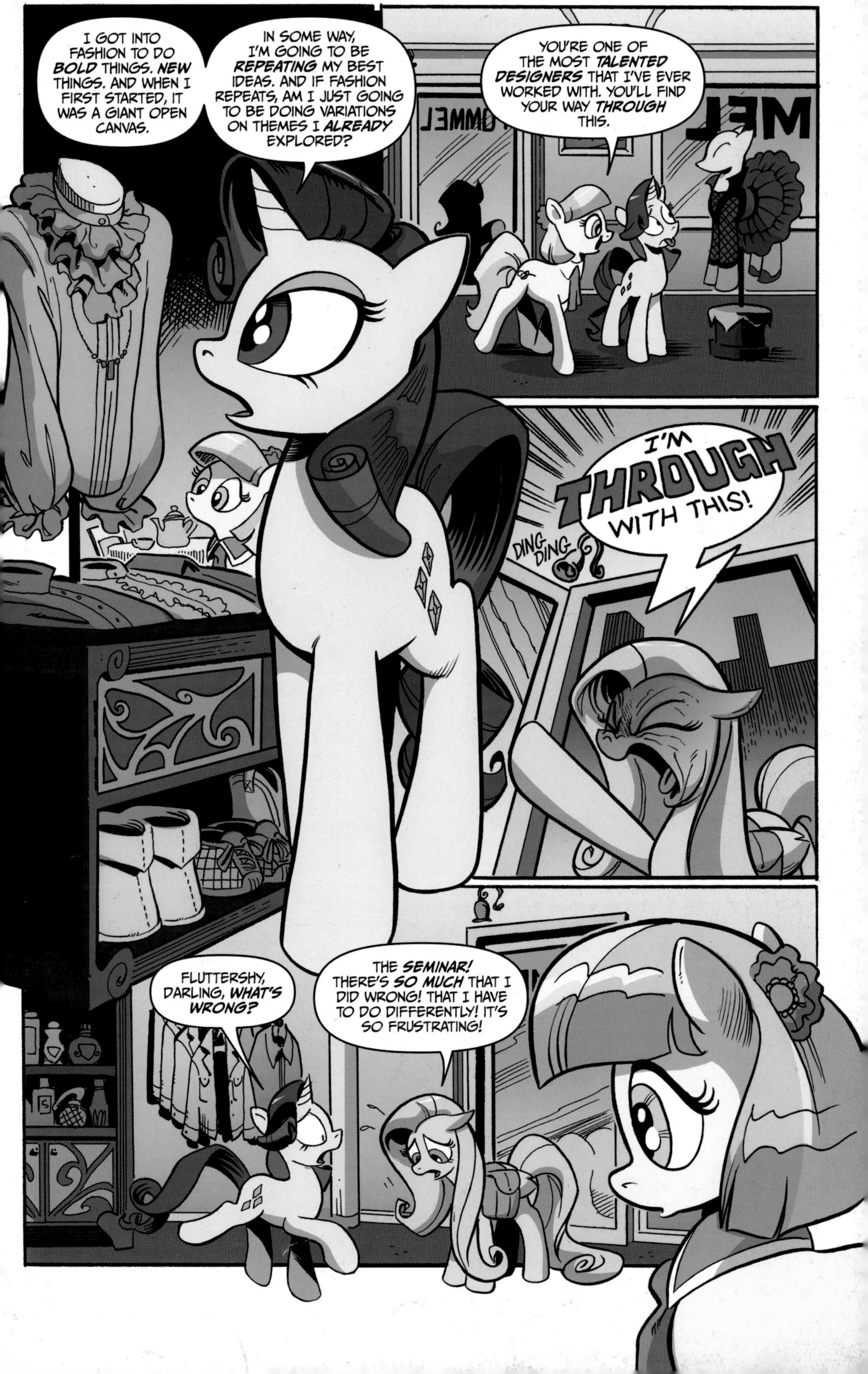
I GOT INTO FASHION TO DO BOLD THINGS. NEW THINGS. AND WHEN I FIRST STARTED, IT WAS A GIANT OPEN CANVAS.
IN SOME WAY, I'M GOING TO BE REPEATING MY BEST IDEAS. AND IF FASHION REPEATS, AM I JUST GOING TO BE DOING VARIATIONS ON THEMES I ALREADY EXPLORED?
YOU'RE ONE OF THE MOST TALENTED DESIGNERS THAT I'VE EVER WORKED WITH. YOU'LL FIND YOUR WAY THROUGH THIS.
I'M THROUGH WITH THIS!
DING DING
FLUTTERSHY, DARLING, WHAT'S WRONG?
THE SEMINAR! THERE'S SO MUCH THAT I DID WRONG! THAT I HAVE TO DO DIFFERENTLY! IT'S SO FRUSTRATING!

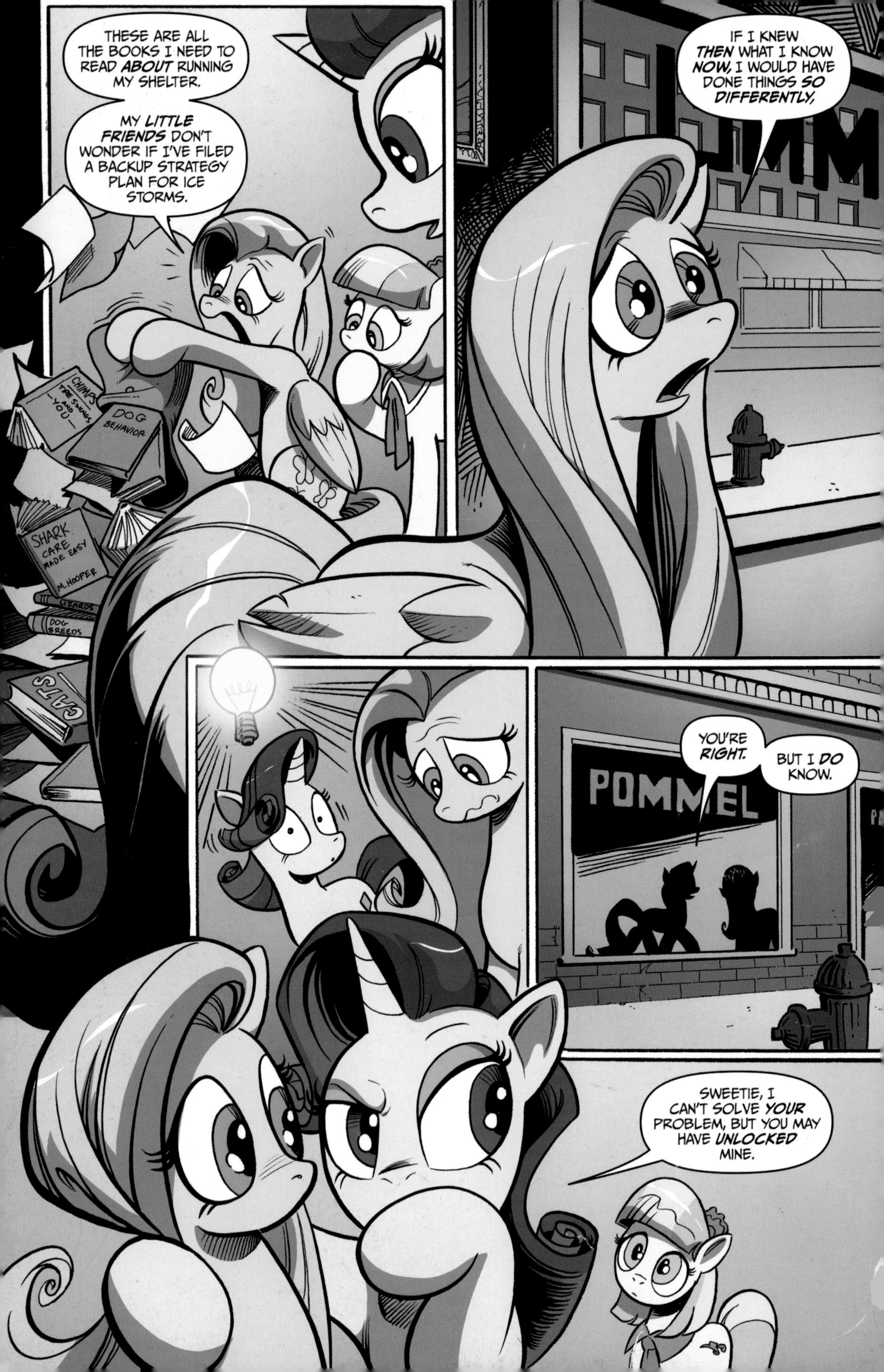
THESE ARE ALL THE BOOKS I NEED TO READ ABOUT RUNNING MY SHELTER.
MY LITTLE FRIENDS DON'T WONDER IF I'VE FILED A BACKUP STRATEGY PLAN FOR ICE STORMS.
CHIMPS THE SWINGS AND YOU
DOG BEHAVIOR
SHARK CARE MADE EASY M. HOOPER
LIZARDS
DOG BREEDS
CATS
IF I KNEW THEN WHAT I KNOW NOW, I WOULD HAVE DONE THINGS SO DIFFERENTLY,
POMMEL
YOU'RE RIGHT.
BUT I DO KNOW.
SWEETIE, I CAN'T SOLVE YOUR PROBLEM, BUT YOU MAY HAVE UNLOCKED MINE.

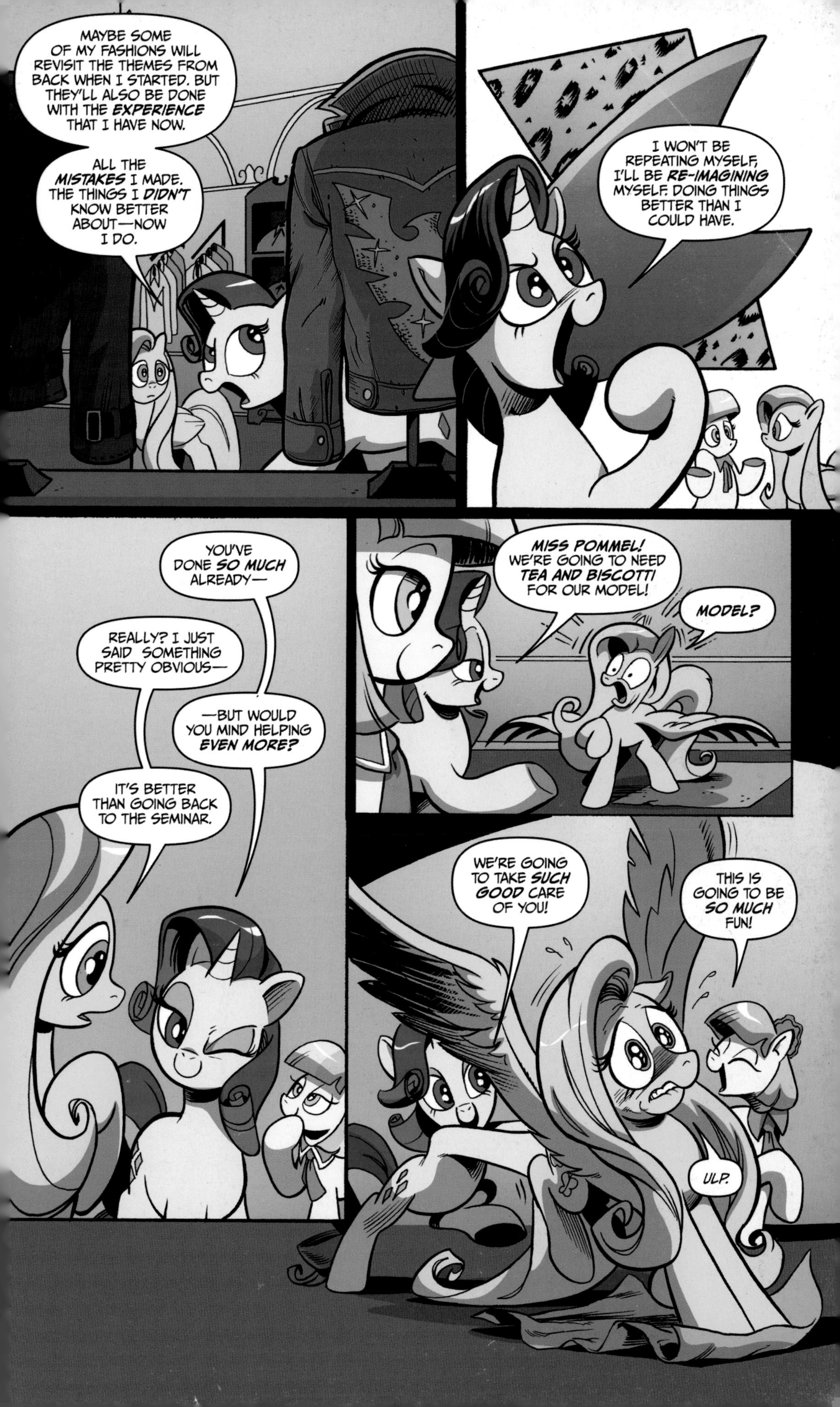
MAYBE SOME OF MY FASHIONS WILL REVISIT THE THEMES FROM BACK WHEN I STARTED. BUT THEY'LL ALSO BE DONE WITH THE EXPERIENCE THAT I HAVE NOW.
ALL THE MISTAKES I MADE. THE THINGS I DIDN'T KNOW BETTER ABOUT—NOW I DO.
I WON'T BE REPEATING MYSELF, I'LL BE RE-IMAGINING MYSELF. DOING THINGS BETTER THAN I COULD HAVE.
YOU'VE DONE SO MUCH ALREADY—
REALLY? I JUST SAID SOMETHING PRETTY OBVIOUS—
—BUT WOULD YOU MIND HELPING EVEN MORE?
IT'S BETTER THAN GOING BACK TO THE SEMINAR.
MISS POMMEL! WE'RE GOING TO NEED TEA AND BISCOTTI FOR OUR MODEL!
MODEL?
WE'RE GOING TO TAKE SUCH GOOD CARE OF YOU!
THIS IS GOING TO BE SO MUCH FUN!
ULP.

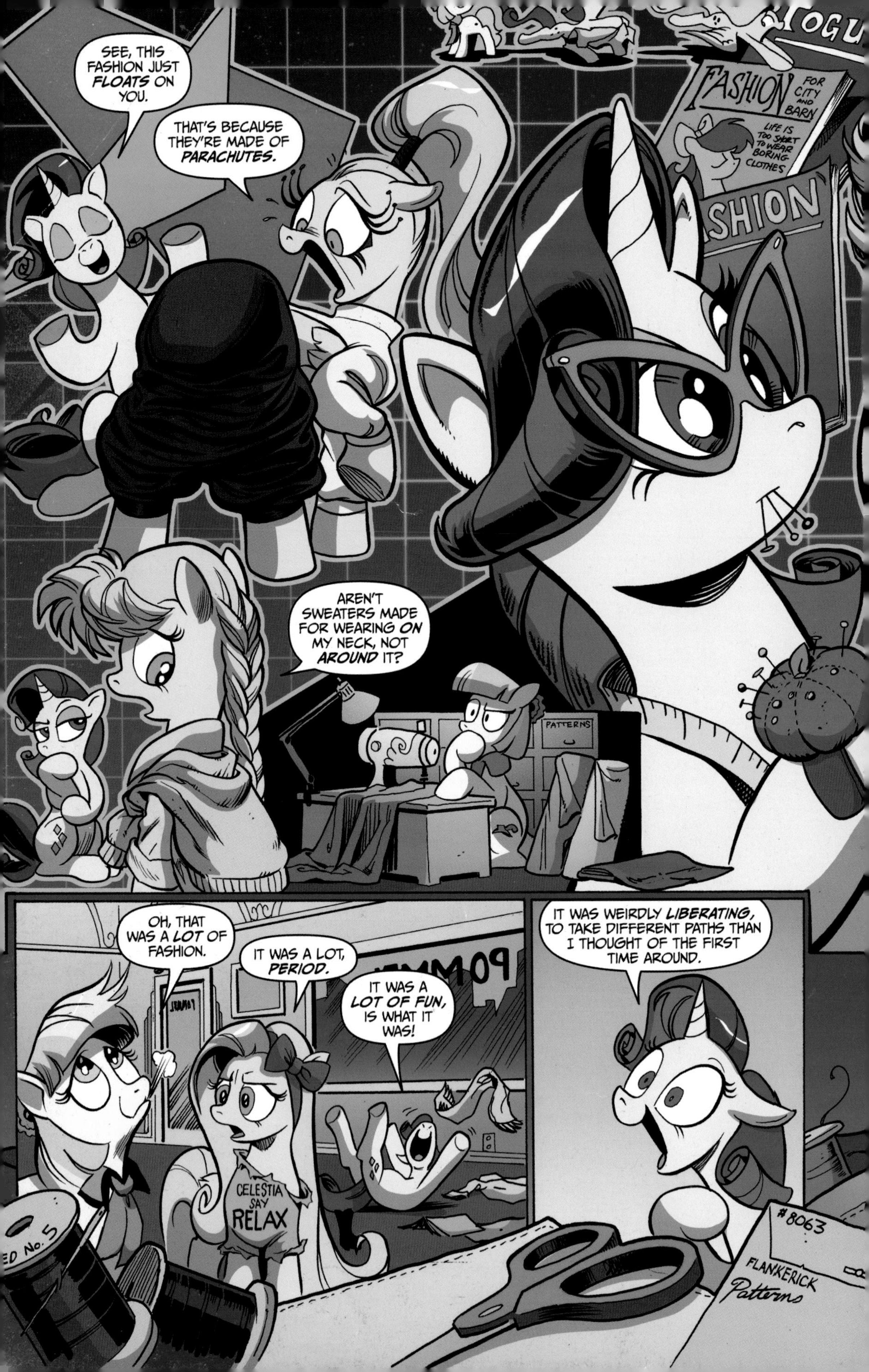

OGU
FASHION FOR CITY AND BARN
LIFE IS TOO SHORT TO WEAR BORING CLOTHES
SHION
SEE, THIS FASHION JUST *FLOATS* ON YOU.
THAT'S BECAUSE THEY'RE MADE OF *PARACHUTES.*
AREN'T SWEATERS MADE FOR WEARING *ON* MY NECK, NOT *AROUND* IT?
PATTERNS
OH, THAT WAS A *LOT* OF FASHION.
IT WAS A LOT, *PERIOD.*
IT WAS A *LOT OF FUN,* IS WHAT IT WAS!
CELESTIA SAY RELAX
ED No. 5
IT WAS WEIRDLY *LIBERATING,* TO TAKE DIFFERENT PATHS THAN I THOUGHT OF THE FIRST TIME AROUND.
#8063
FLANKERICK Patterns

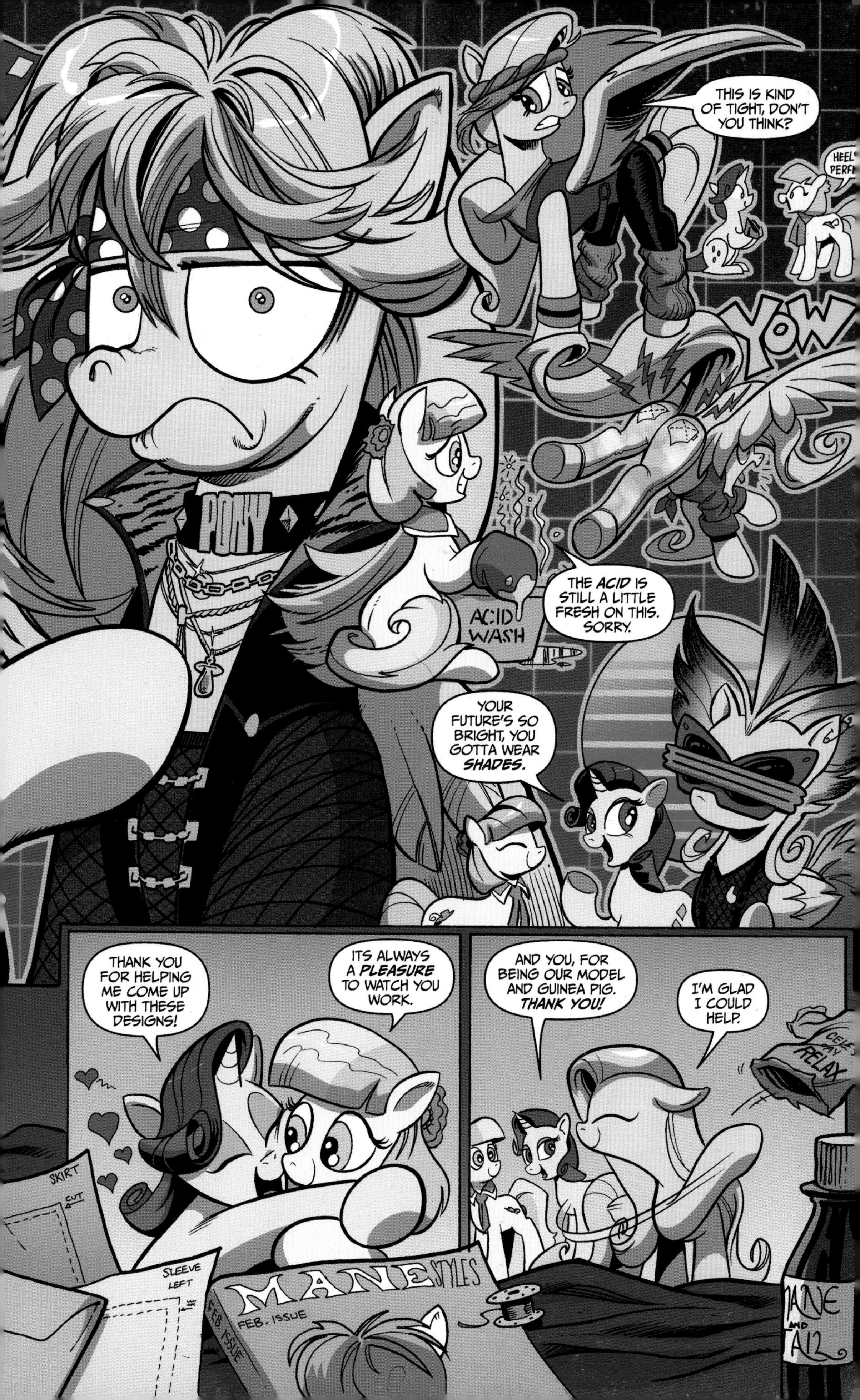
PONY
THIS IS KIND OF TIGHT, DON'T YOU THINK?
YOW
ACID WASH
THE *ACID* IS STILL A LITTLE FRESH ON THIS. SORRY.
YOUR FUTURE'S SO BRIGHT, YOU GOTTA WEAR ***SHADES.***
THANK YOU FOR HELPING ME COME UP WITH THESE DESIGNS!
ITS ALWAYS A ***PLEASURE*** TO WATCH YOU WORK.
SKIRT
CUT
SLEEVE
LEFT
MANE STYLES
FEB. ISSUE
FEB. ISSUE
AND YOU, FOR BEING OUR MODEL AND GUINEA PIG. ***THANK YOU!***
I'M GLAD I COULD HELP.
RELAX

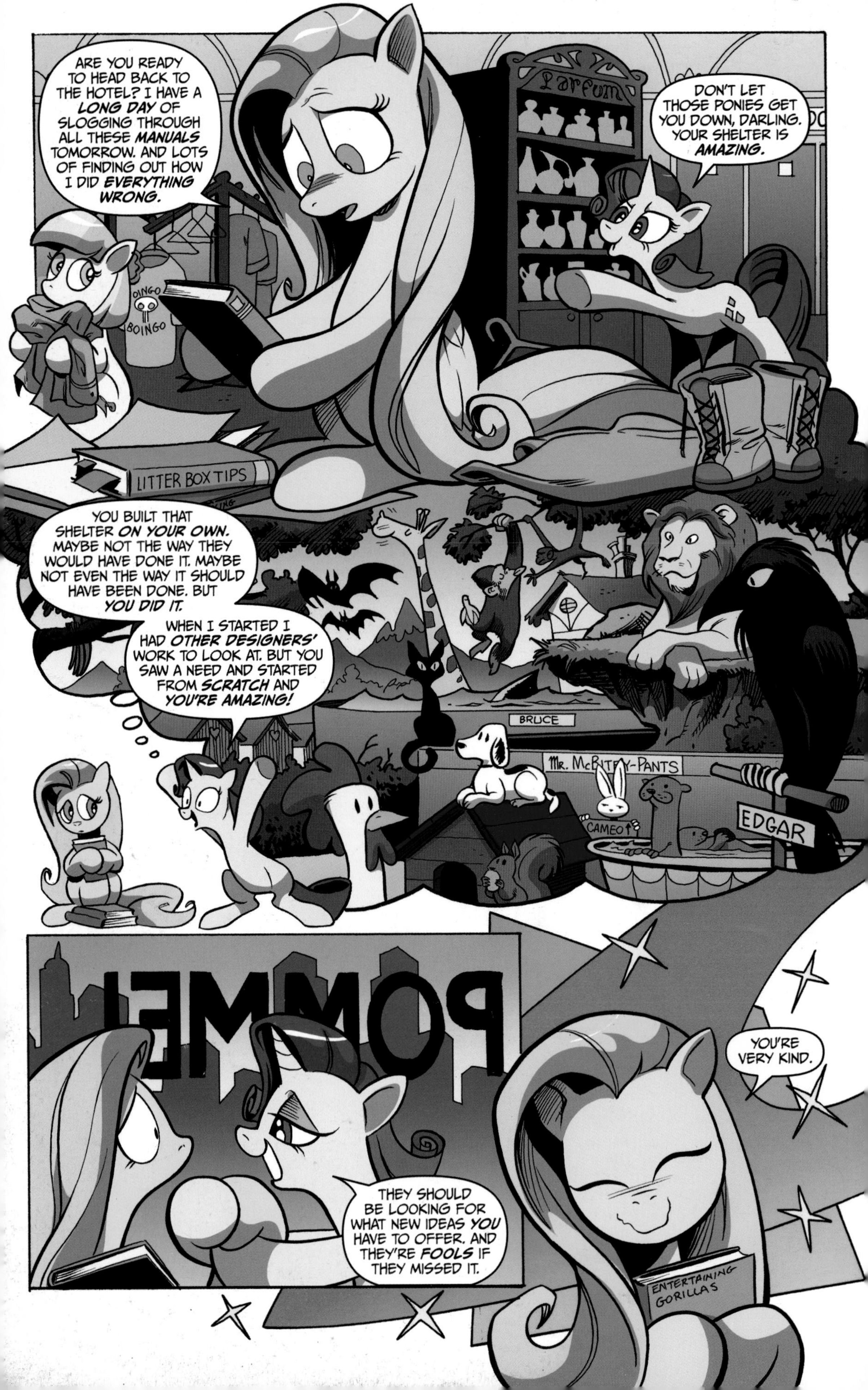

ARE YOU READY TO HEAD BACK TO THE HOTEL? I HAVE A LONG DAY OF SLOGGING THROUGH ALL THESE MANUALS TOMORROW. AND LOTS OF FINDING OUT HOW I DID EVERYTHING WRONG.
Parfum
DON'T LET THOSE PONIES GET YOU DOWN, DARLING. YOUR SHELTER IS AMAZING.
OINGO BOINGO
LITTER BOX TIPS
YOU BUILT THAT SHELTER ON YOUR OWN. MAYBE NOT THE WAY THEY WOULD HAVE DONE IT. MAYBE NOT EVEN THE WAY IT SHOULD HAVE BEEN DONE. BUT YOU DID IT.
WHEN I STARTED I HAD OTHER DESIGNERS' WORK TO LOOK AT. BUT YOU SAW A NEED AND STARTED FROM SCRATCH AND YOU'RE AMAZING!
BRUCE
CAMEO
EDGAR
THEY SHOULD BE LOOKING FOR WHAT NEW IDEAS YOU HAVE TO OFFER. AND THEY'RE FOOLS IF THEY MISSED IT.
YOU'RE VERY KIND.
ENTERTAINING GORILLAS

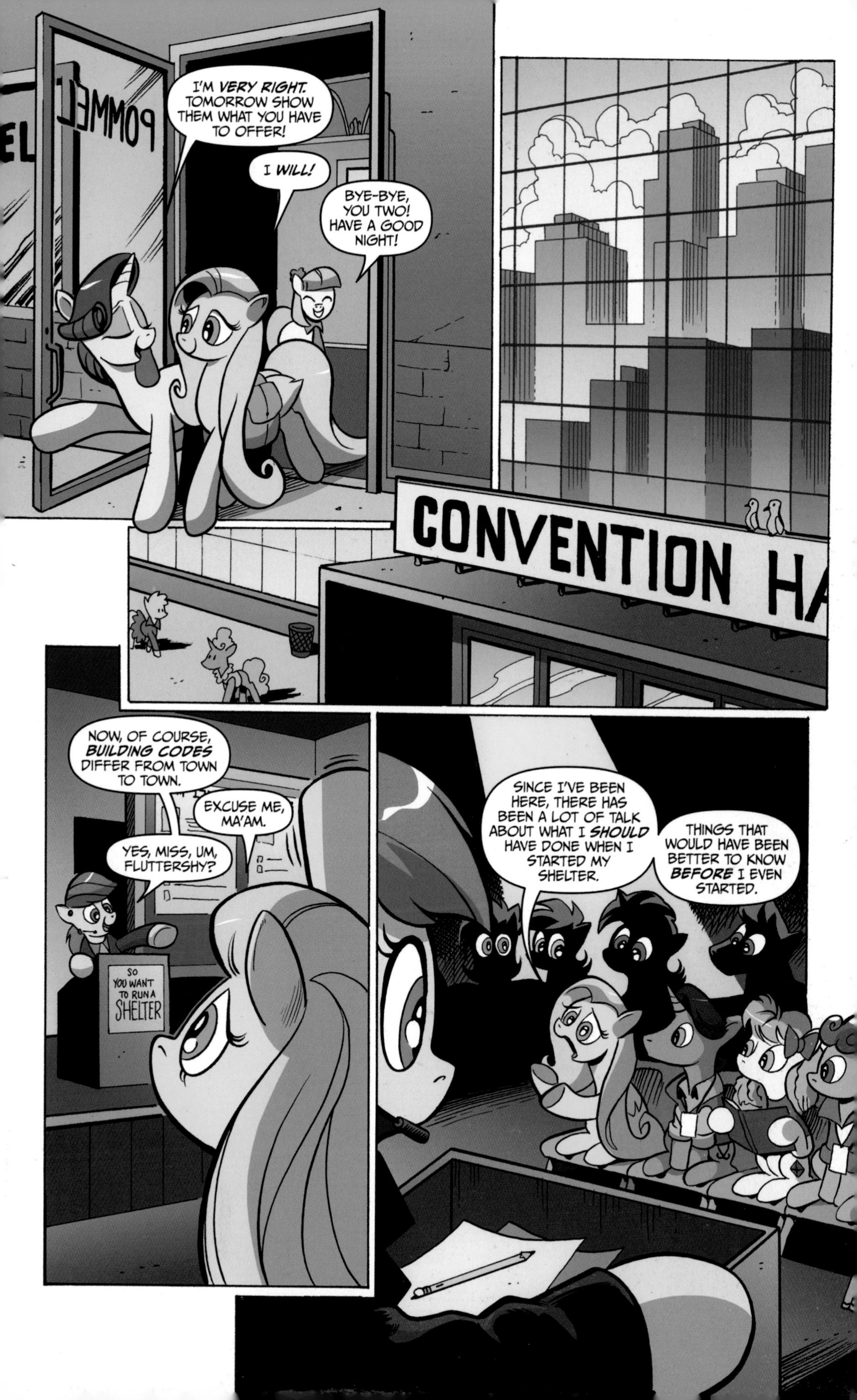
POMMEL
I'M VERY RIGHT. TOMORROW SHOW THEM WHAT YOU HAVE TO OFFER!
I WILL!
BYE-BYE, YOU TWO! HAVE A GOOD NIGHT!
CONVENTION HA
NOW, OF COURSE, BUILDING CODES DIFFER FROM TOWN TO TOWN.
EXCUSE ME, MA'AM.
YES, MISS, UM, FLUTTERSHY?
SO YOU WANT TO RUN A SHELTER
SINCE I'VE BEEN HERE, THERE HAS BEEN A LOT OF TALK ABOUT WHAT I SHOULD HAVE DONE WHEN I STARTED MY SHELTER.
THINGS THAT WOULD HAVE BEEN BETTER TO KNOW BEFORE I EVEN STARTED.

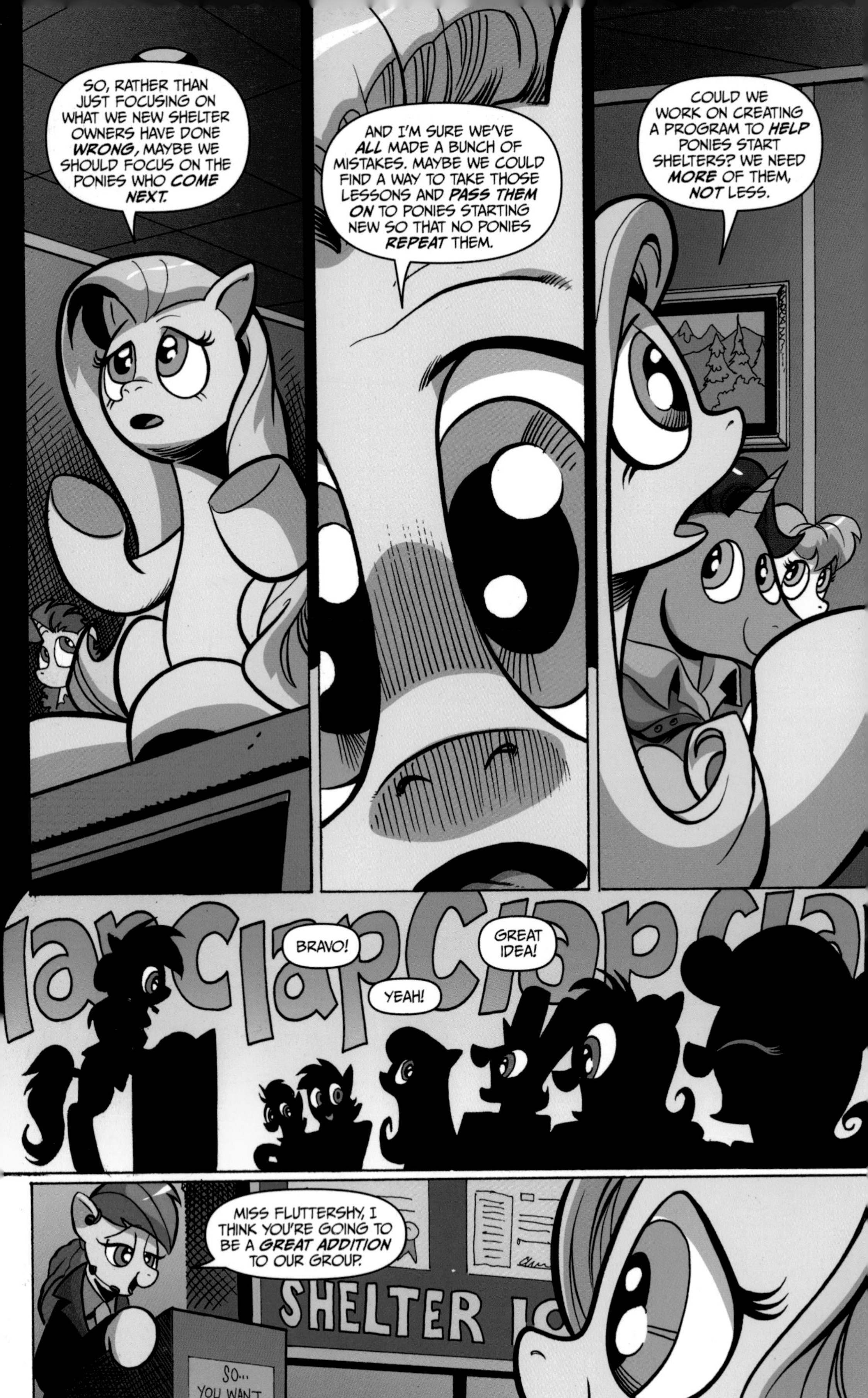
SO, RATHER THAN JUST FOCUSING ON WHAT WE NEW SHELTER OWNERS HAVE DONE WRONG, MAYBE WE SHOULD FOCUS ON THE PONIES WHO COME NEXT.
AND I'M SURE WE'VE ALL MADE A BUNCH OF MISTAKES. MAYBE WE COULD FIND A WAY TO TAKE THOSE LESSONS AND PASS THEM ON TO PONIES STARTING NEW SO THAT NO PONIES REPEAT THEM.
COULD WE WORK ON CREATING A PROGRAM TO HELP PONIES START SHELTERS? WE NEED MORE OF THEM, NOT LESS.
BRAVO!
YEAH!
GREAT IDEA!
MISS FLUTTERSHY, I THINK YOU'RE GOING TO BE A GREAT ADDITION TO OUR GROUP.
SHELTER
SO... YOU WANT

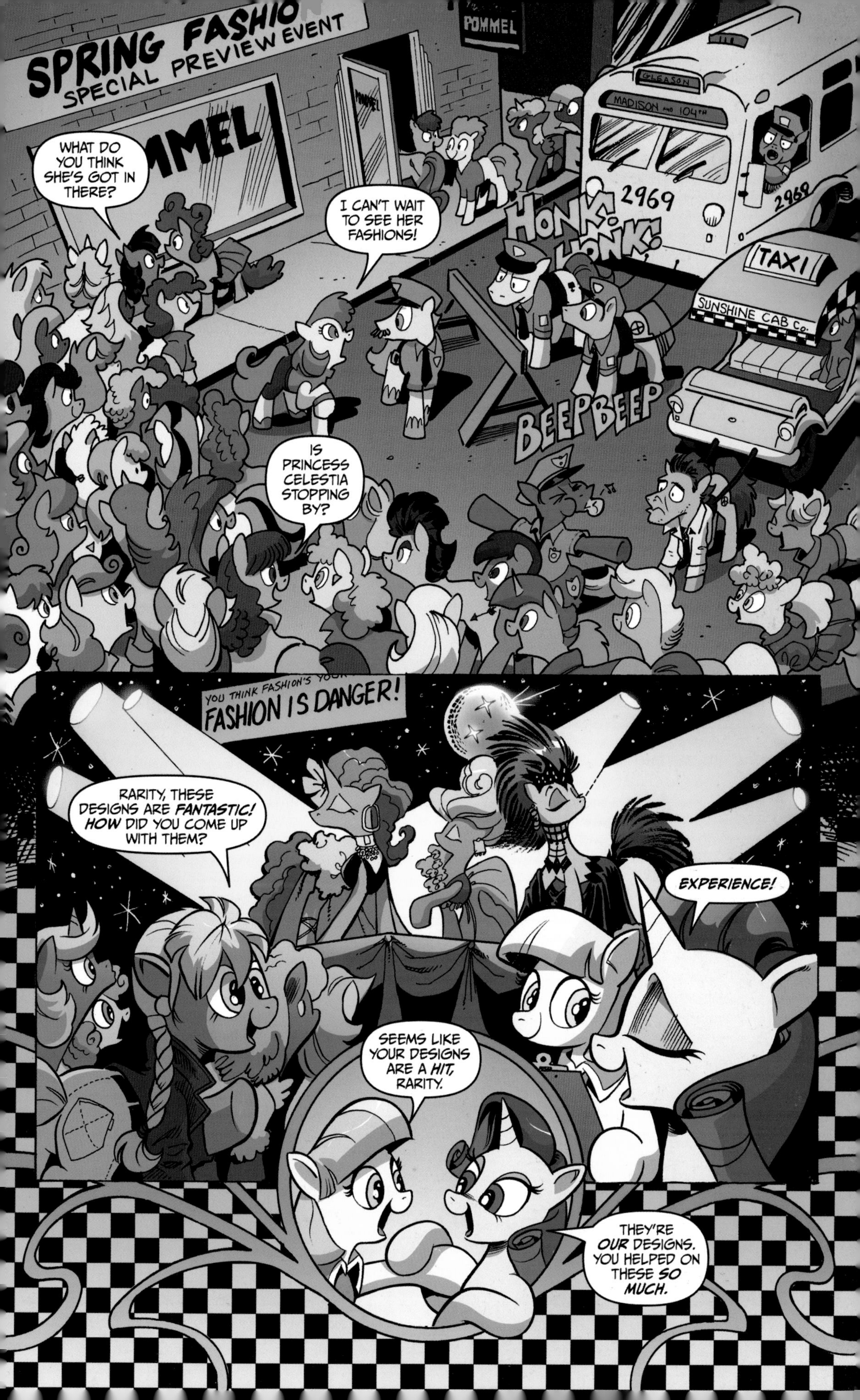
SPRING FASHIO
SPECIAL PREVIEW EVENT
POMMEL
MMEL
GLEASON
MADISON AND 104TH
2969
WHAT DO YOU THINK SHE'S GOT IN THERE?
I CAN'T WAIT TO SEE HER FASHIONS!
HONK! HONK!
TAXI
SUNSHINE CAB Co.
BEEPBEEP
IS PRINCESS CELESTIA STOPPING BY?
FASHION IS DANGER!
RARITY, THESE DESIGNS ARE *FANTASTIC!* *HOW* DID YOU COME UP WITH THEM?
EXPERIENCE!
SEEMS LIKE YOUR DESIGNS ARE A *HIT,* RARITY.
THEY'RE *OUR* DESIGNS. YOU HELPED ON THESE *SO MUCH.*

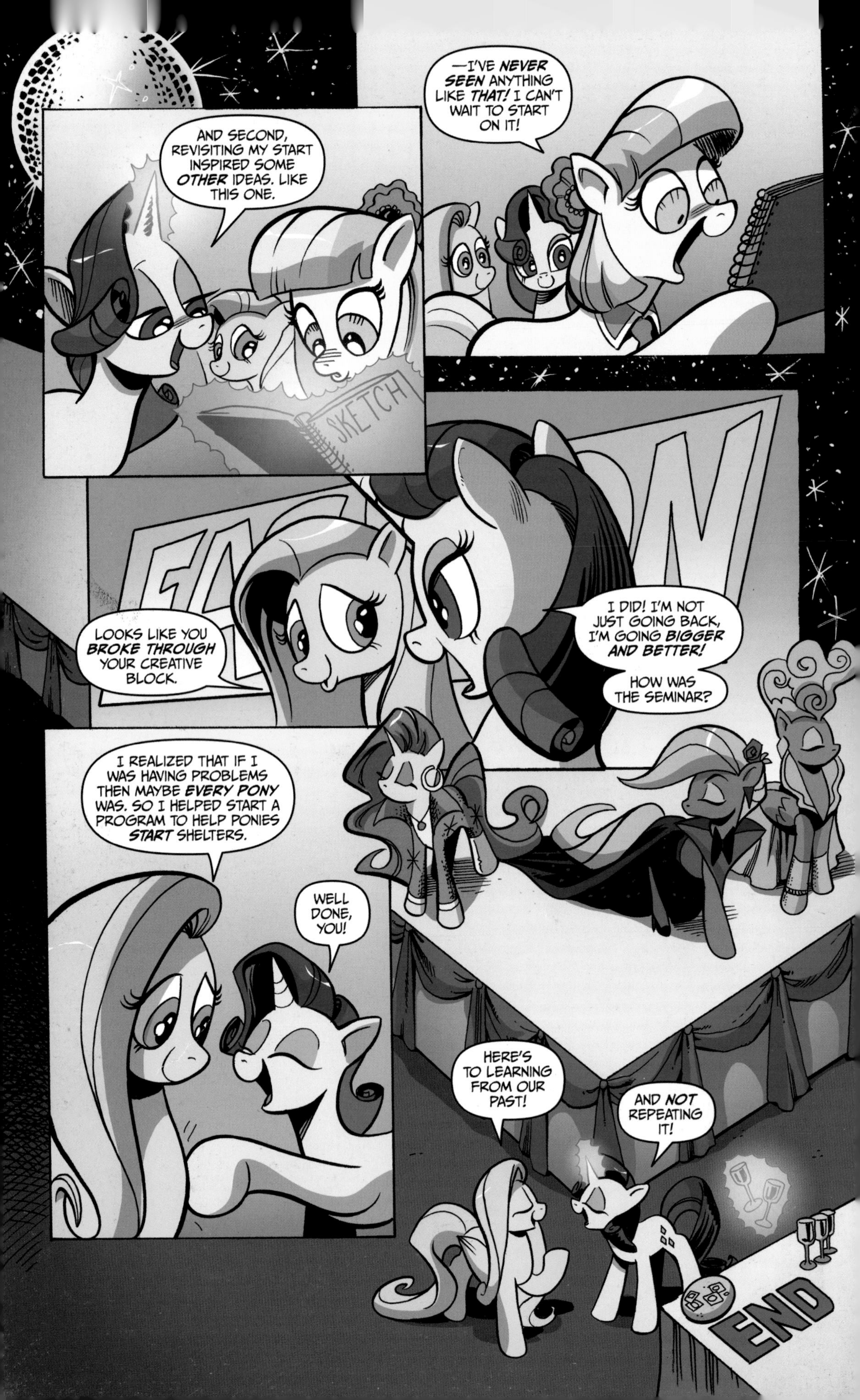
AND SECOND, REVISITING MY START INSPIRED SOME OTHER IDEAS. LIKE THIS ONE.
SKETCH
—I'VE NEVER SEEN ANYTHING LIKE THAT! I CAN'T WAIT TO START ON IT!
LOOKS LIKE YOU BROKE THROUGH YOUR CREATIVE BLOCK.
I DID! I'M NOT JUST GOING BACK, I'M GOING BIGGER AND BETTER!
HOW WAS THE SEMINAR?
I REALIZED THAT IF I WAS HAVING PROBLEMS THEN MAYBE EVERY PONY WAS. SO I HELPED START A PROGRAM TO HELP PONIES START SHELTERS.
WELL DONE, YOU!
HERE'S TO LEARNING FROM OUR PAST!
AND NOT REPEATING IT!
END

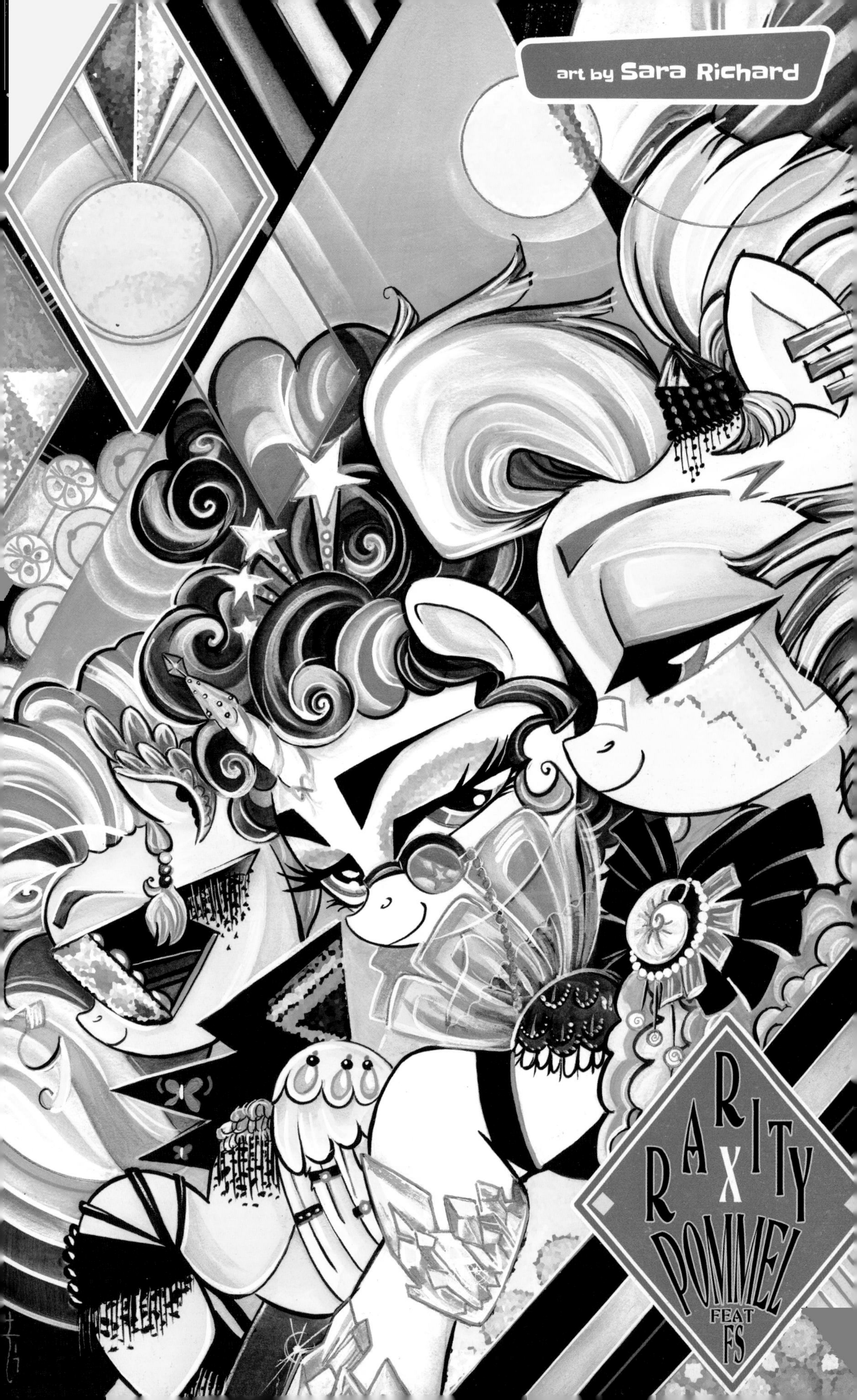
art by Sara Richard
RARITY
X
POMMEL
FEAT
FS

art by Andy Price

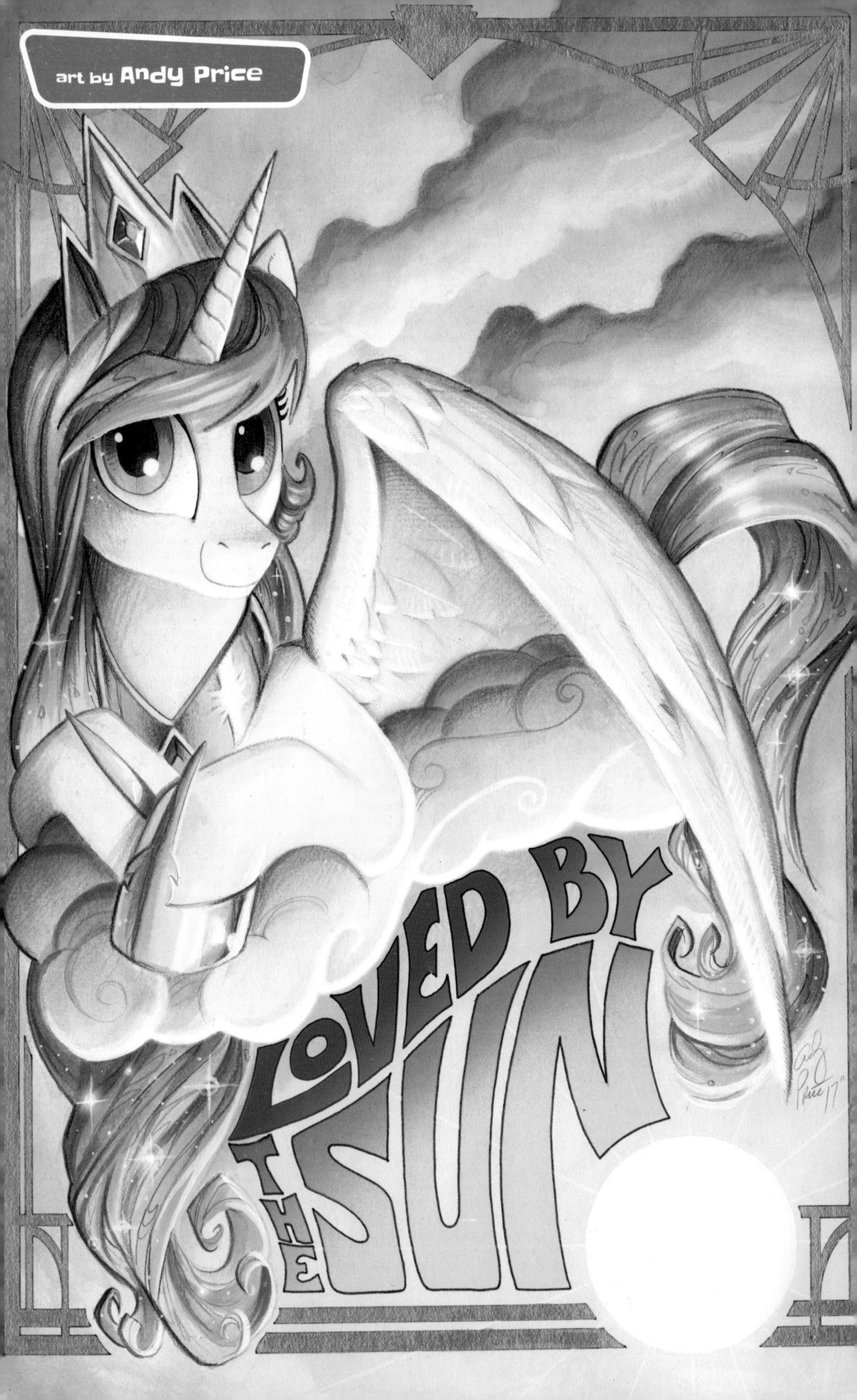
LOVED BY THE SUN

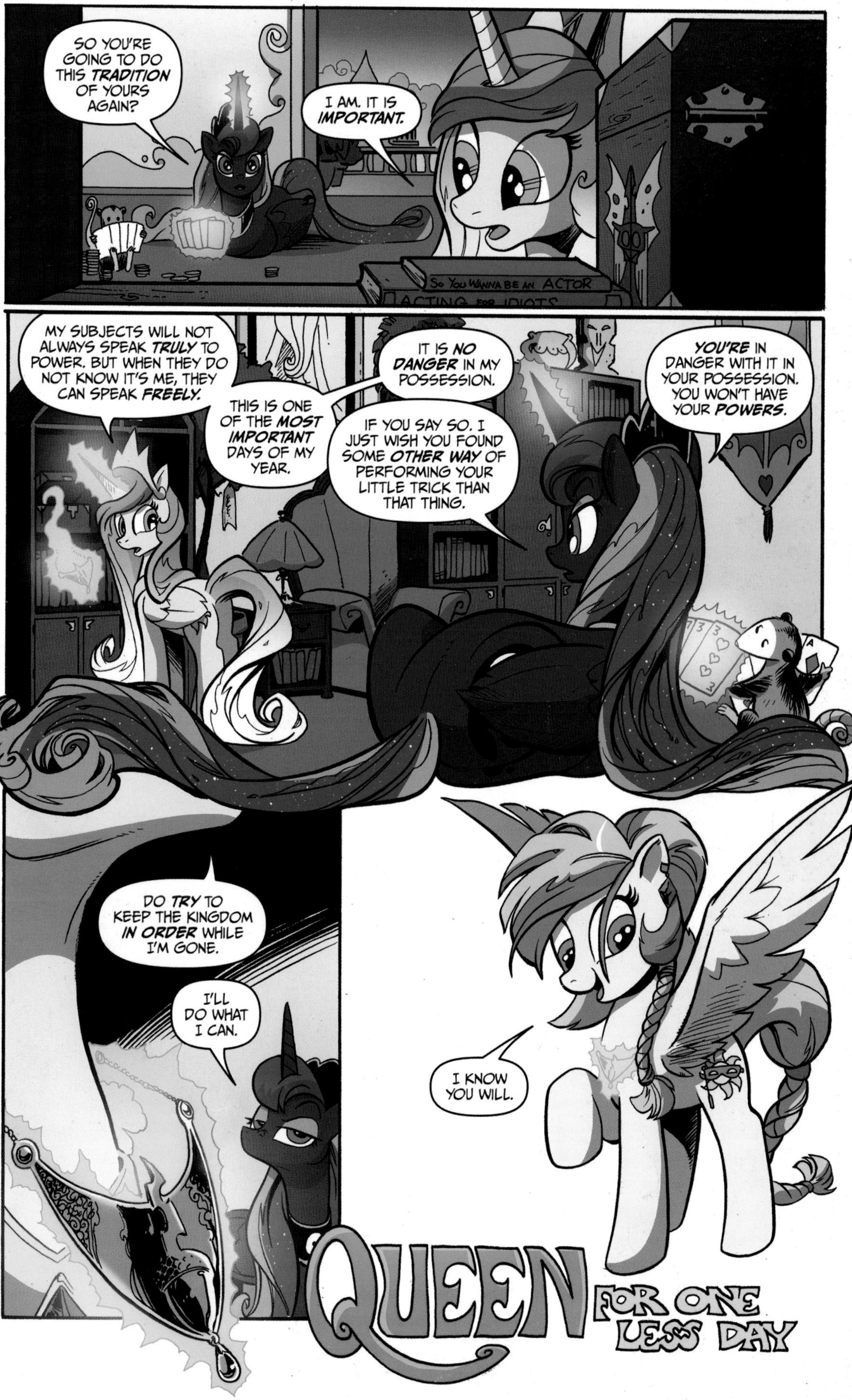

SO YOU'RE GOING TO DO THIS TRADITION OF YOURS AGAIN?
I AM. IT IS IMPORTANT.
So You Wanna be an ACTOR
MY SUBJECTS WILL NOT ALWAYS SPEAK TRULY TO POWER. BUT WHEN THEY DO NOT KNOW IT'S ME, THEY CAN SPEAK FREELY.
THIS IS ONE OF THE MOST IMPORTANT DAYS OF MY YEAR.
IT IS NO DANGER IN MY POSSESSION.
YOU'RE IN DANGER WITH IT IN YOUR POSSESSION. YOU WON'T HAVE YOUR POWERS.
IF YOU SAY SO. I JUST WISH YOU FOUND SOME OTHER WAY OF PERFORMING YOUR LITTLE TRICK THAN THAT THING.
DO TRY TO KEEP THE KINGDOM IN ORDER WHILE I'M GONE.
I'LL DO WHAT I CAN.
I KNOW YOU WILL.
QUEEN FOR ONE LESS DAY

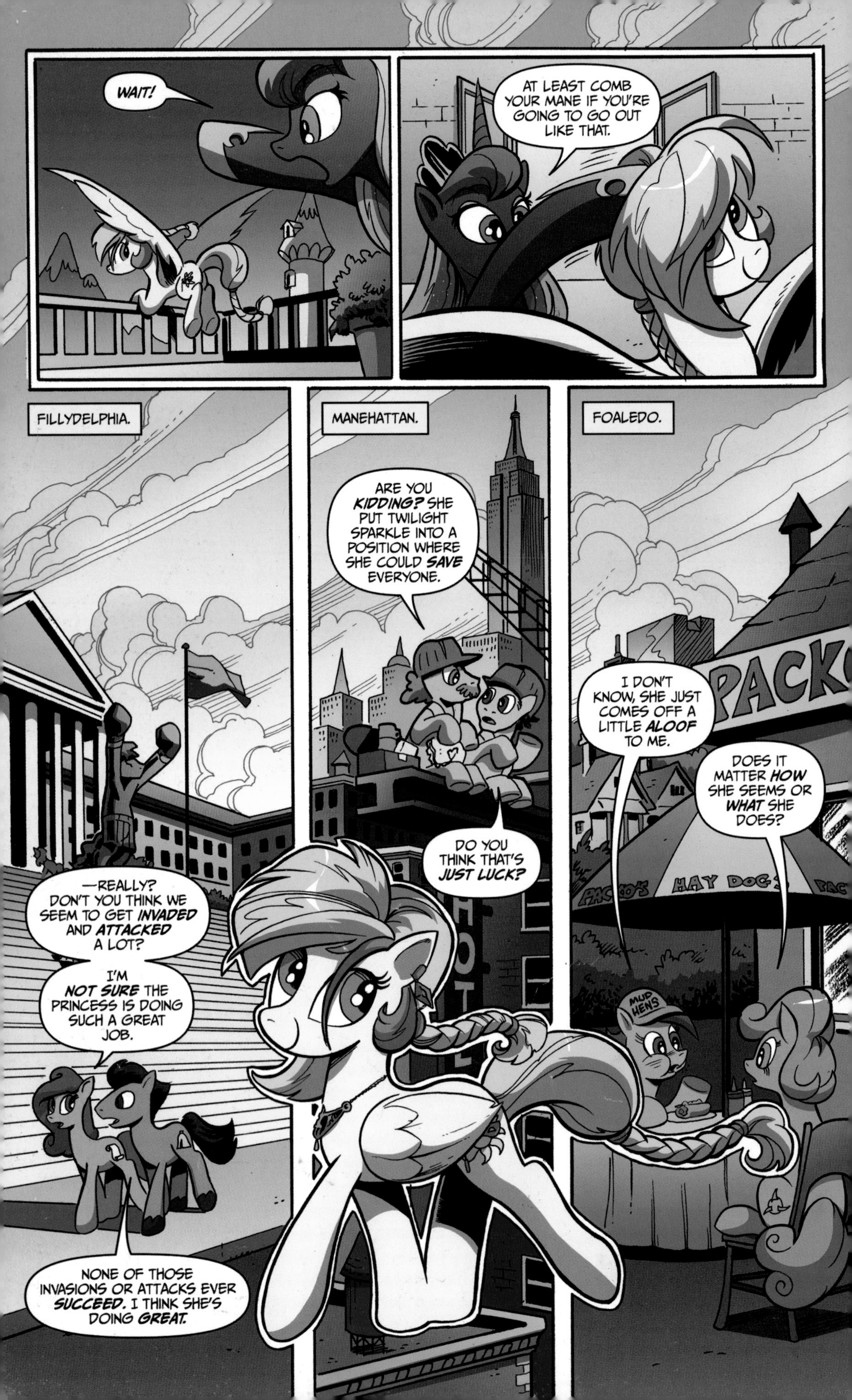
WAIT!
AT LEAST COMB YOUR MANE IF YOU'RE GOING TO GO OUT LIKE THAT.
FILLYDELPHIA.
—REALLY? DON'T YOU THINK WE SEEM TO GET INVADED AND ATTACKED A LOT?
I'M NOT SURE THE PRINCESS IS DOING SUCH A GREAT JOB.
NONE OF THOSE INVASIONS OR ATTACKS EVER SUCCEED. I THINK SHE'S DOING GREAT.
MANEHATTAN.
ARE YOU KIDDING? SHE PUT TWILIGHT SPARKLE INTO A POSITION WHERE SHE COULD SAVE EVERYONE.
DO YOU THINK THAT'S JUST LUCK?
FOALEDO.
PACK
I DON'T KNOW, SHE JUST COMES OFF A LITTLE ALOOF TO ME.
DOES IT MATTER HOW SHE SEEMS OR WHAT SHE DOES?
PACKO'S HAY DOGS
MUD HENS

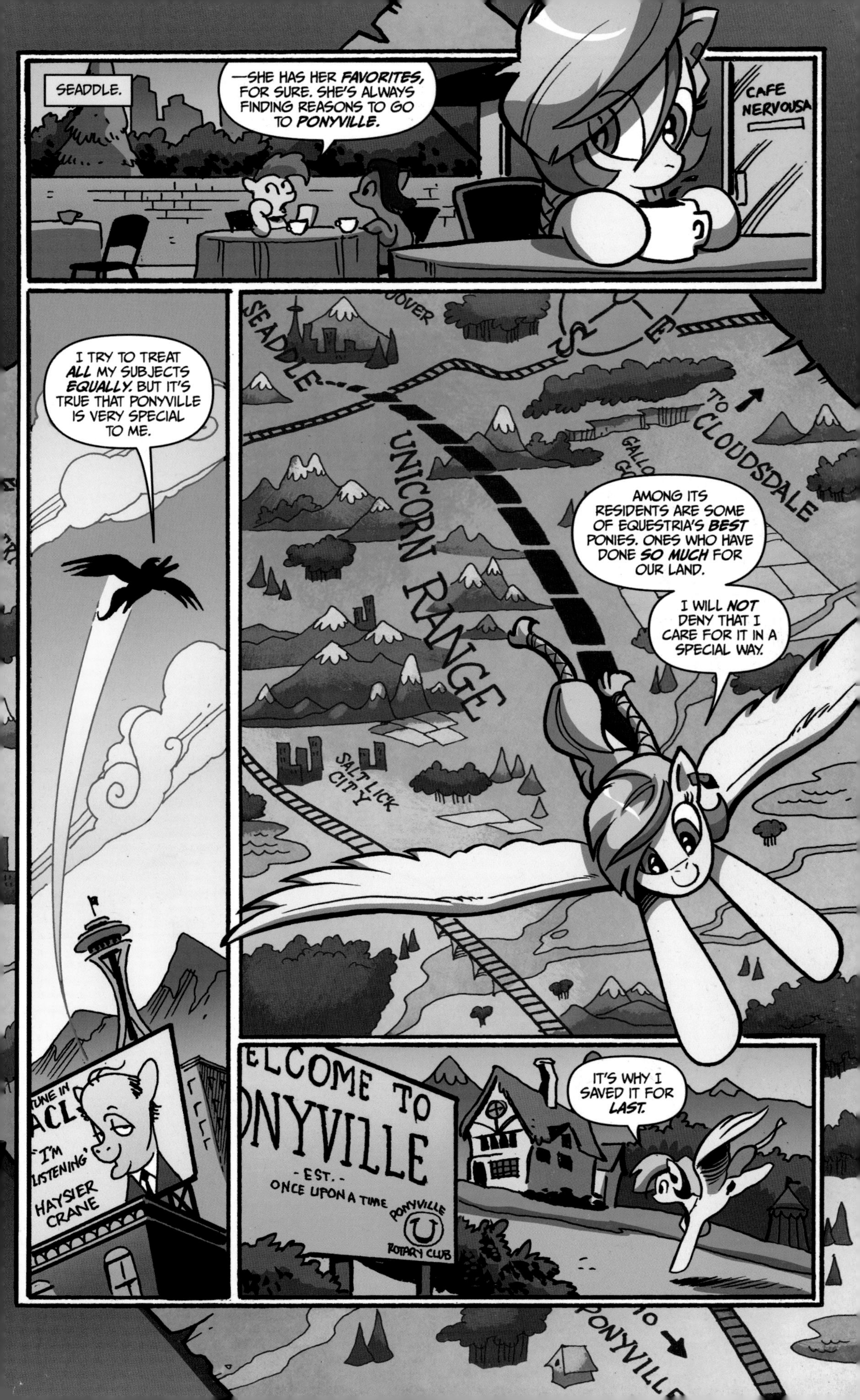
SEADDLE.
—SHE HAS HER FAVORITES, FOR SURE. SHE'S ALWAYS FINDING REASONS TO GO TO PONYVILLE.
CAFE NERVOUSA
I TRY TO TREAT ALL MY SUBJECTS EQUALLY. BUT IT'S TRUE THAT PONYVILLE IS VERY SPECIAL TO ME.
SEADDLE
UNICORN RANGE
SALT LICK CITY
TO CLOUDSDALE
AMONG ITS RESIDENTS ARE SOME OF EQUESTRIA'S BEST PONIES. ONES WHO HAVE DONE SO MUCH FOR OUR LAND.
I WILL NOT DENY THAT I CARE FOR IT IN A SPECIAL WAY.
'I'M LISTENING'
HAYSIER CRANE
ELCOME TO
ONYVILLE
- EST. -
ONCE UPON A TIME
PONYVILLE ROTARY CLUB
IT'S WHY I SAVED IT FOR LAST.

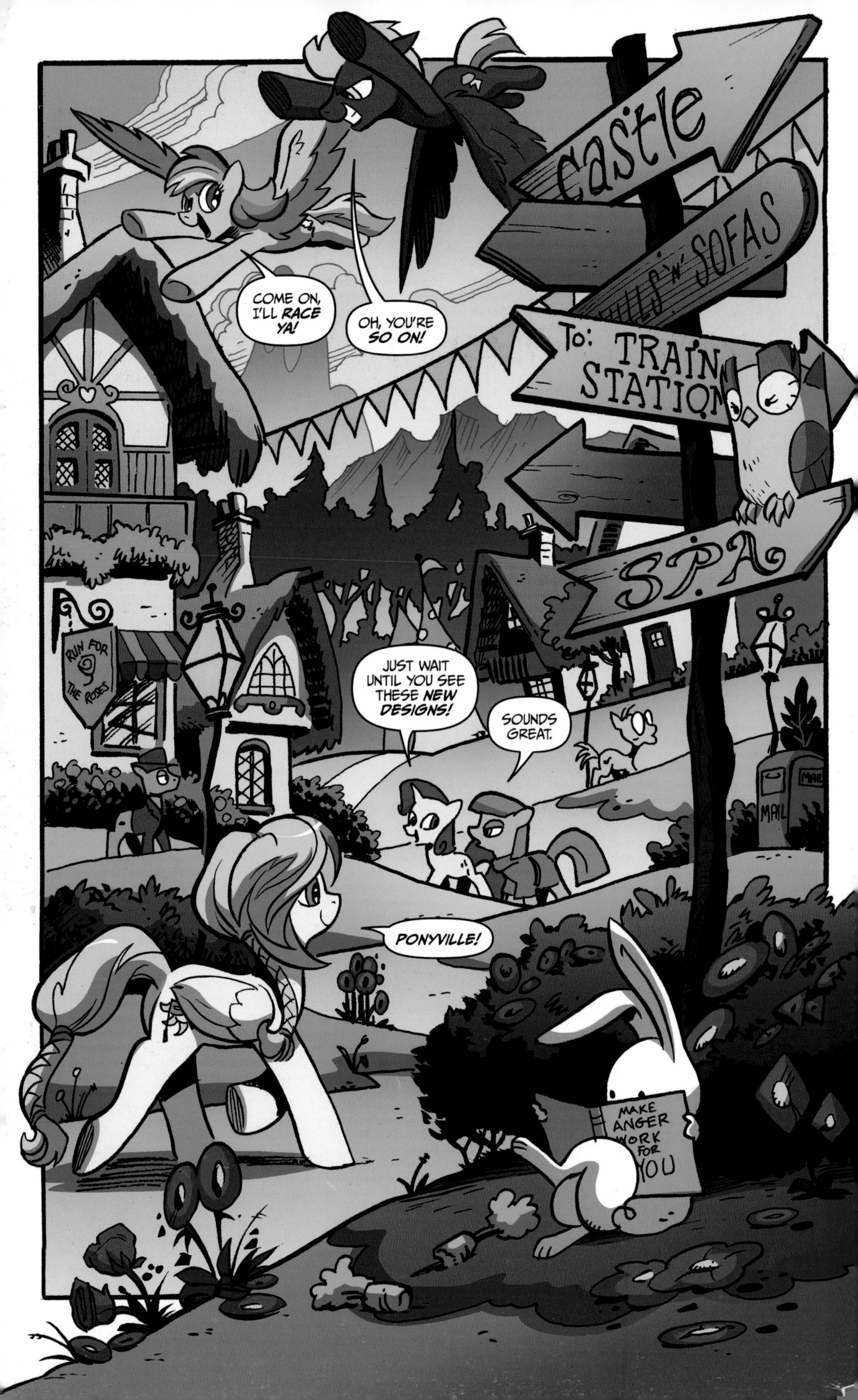

CASTLE
...LLS 'N' SOFAS
TO: TRAIN STATION
SPA
COME ON, I'LL RACE YA!
OH, YOU'RE SO ON!
RUN FOR THE ROSES
JUST WAIT UNTIL YOU SEE THESE NEW DESIGNS!
SOUNDS GREAT.
MAIL
MAIL
PONYVILLE!
MAKE ANGER WORK FOR YOU

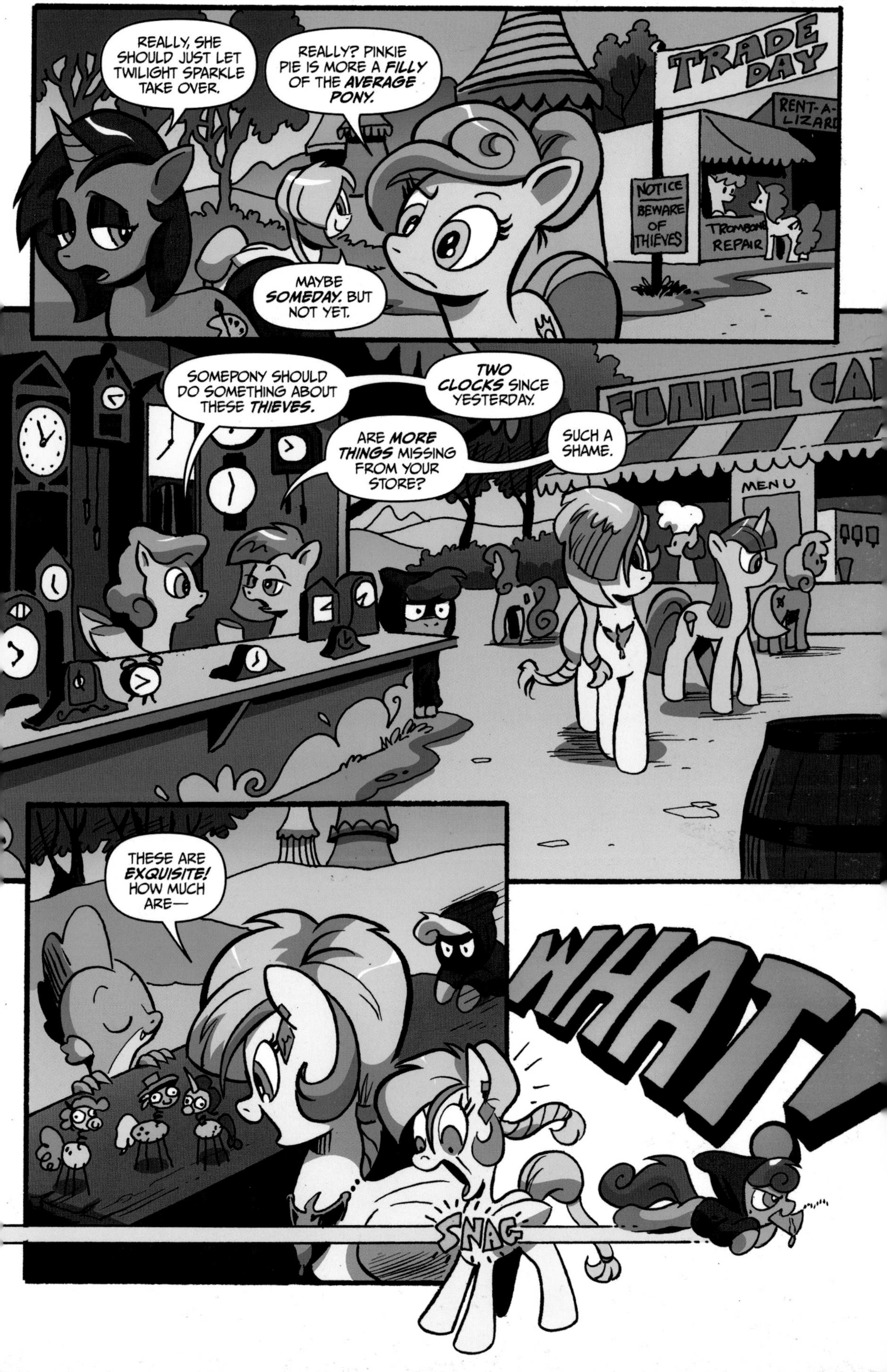
REALLY, SHE SHOULD JUST LET TWILIGHT SPARKLE TAKE OVER.
REALLY? PINKIE PIE IS MORE A FILLY OF THE AVERAGE PONY.
TRADE DAY
RENT-A-LIZARD
NOTICE BEWARE OF THIEVES
TROMBONE REPAIR
MAYBE SOMEDAY. BUT NOT YET.
SOMEPONY SHOULD DO SOMETHING ABOUT THESE THIEVES.
TWO CLOCKS SINCE YESTERDAY.
ARE MORE THINGS MISSING FROM YOUR STORE?
SUCH A SHAME.
MENU
THESE ARE EXQUISITE! HOW MUCH ARE—
WHAT!
SNAG

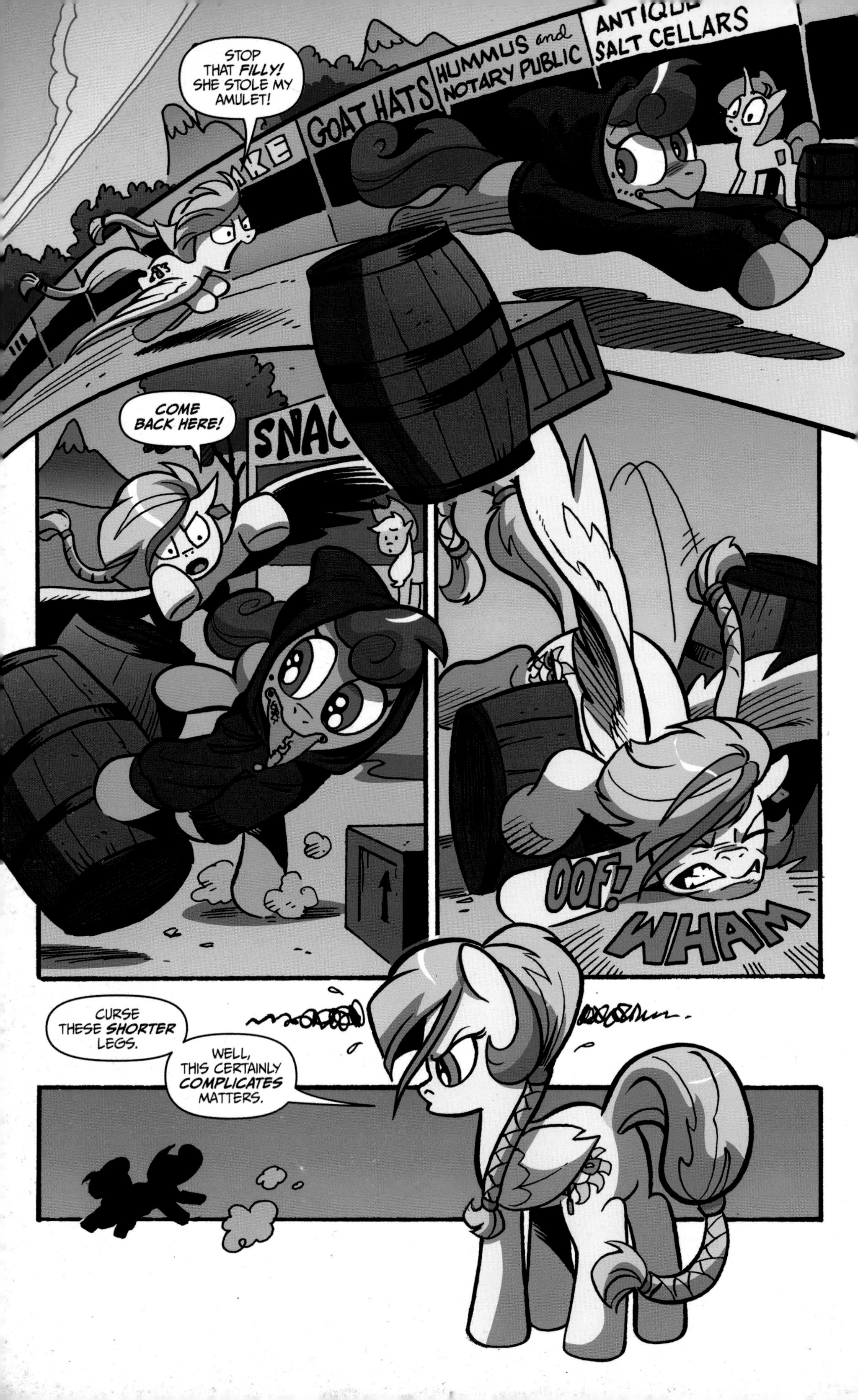
ANTIQUE SALT CELLARS
HUMMUS and NOTARY PUBLIC
GOAT HATS
STOP THAT FILLY! SHE STOLE MY AMULET!
COME BACK HERE!
OOF!
WHAM
CURSE THESE SHORTER LEGS.
WELL, THIS CERTAINLY COMPLICATES MATTERS.

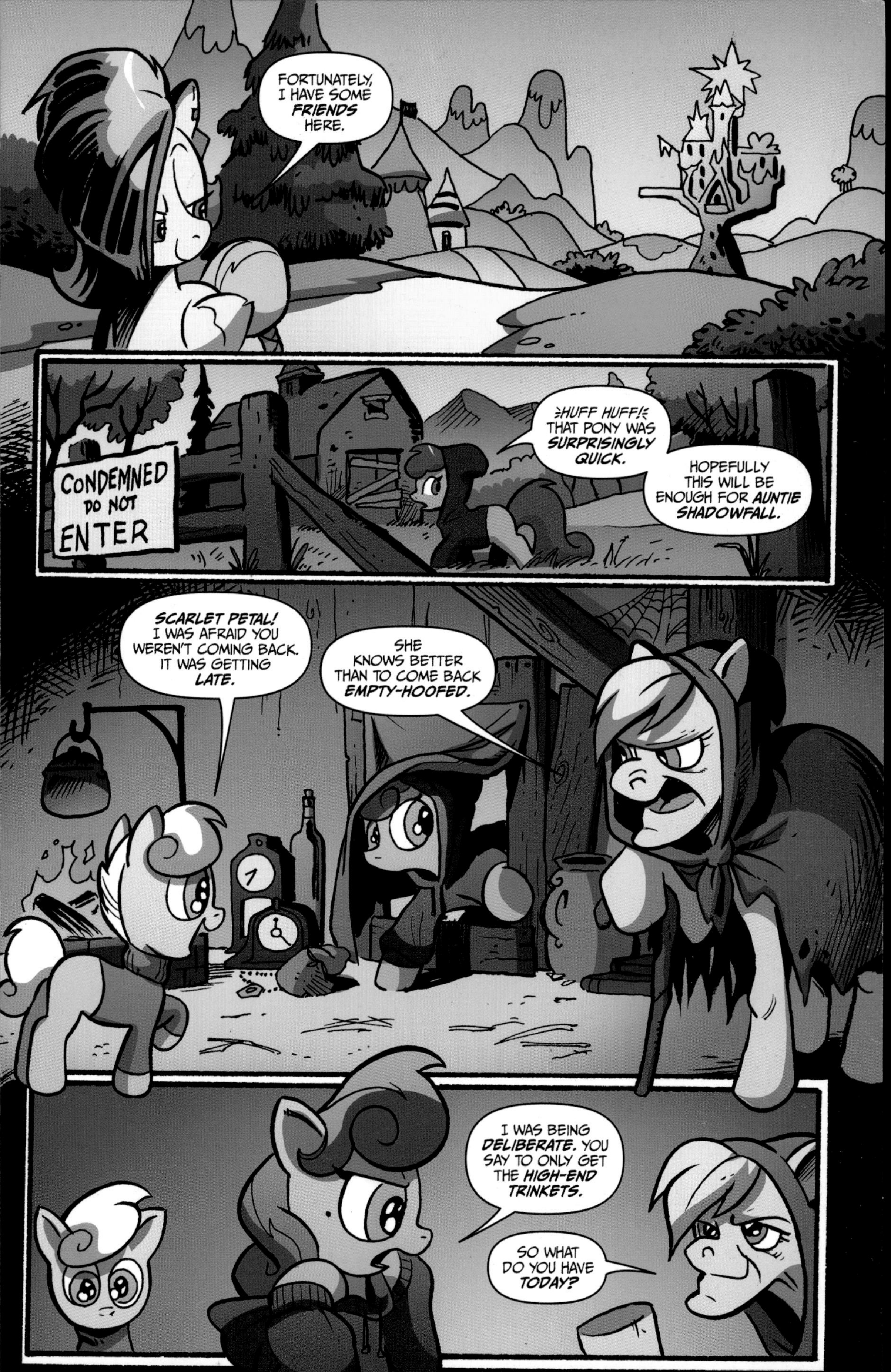
FORTUNATELY, I HAVE SOME FRIENDS HERE.
CONDEMNED DO NOT ENTER
HUFF HUFF! THAT PONY WAS SURPRISINGLY QUICK.
HOPEFULLY THIS WILL BE ENOUGH FOR AUNTIE SHADOWFALL.
SCARLET PETAL! I WAS AFRAID YOU WEREN'T COMING BACK. IT WAS GETTING LATE.
SHE KNOWS BETTER THAN TO COME BACK EMPTY-HOOFED.
I WAS BEING DELIBERATE. YOU SAY TO ONLY GET THE HIGH-END TRINKETS.
SO WHAT DO YOU HAVE TODAY?

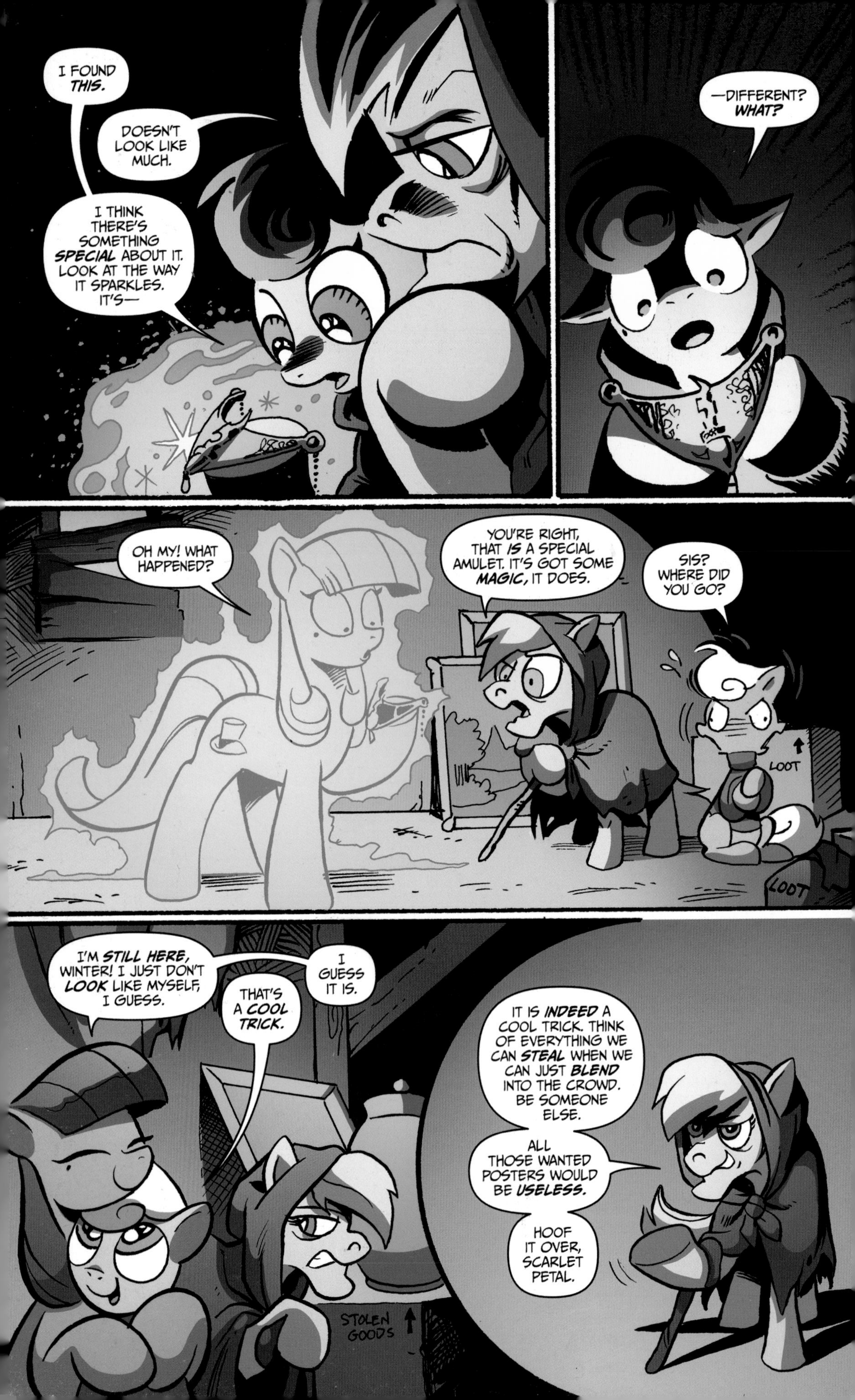
I FOUND THIS.
DOESN'T LOOK LIKE MUCH.
I THINK THERE'S SOMETHING SPECIAL ABOUT IT. LOOK AT THE WAY IT SPARKLES. IT'S—
—DIFFERENT? WHAT?
OH MY! WHAT HAPPENED?
YOU'RE RIGHT, THAT IS A SPECIAL AMULET. IT'S GOT SOME MAGIC, IT DOES.
SIS? WHERE DID YOU GO?
LOOT
LOOT
I'M STILL HERE, WINTER! I JUST DON'T LOOK LIKE MYSELF, I GUESS.
THAT'S A COOL TRICK.
I GUESS IT IS.
IT IS INDEED A COOL TRICK. THINK OF EVERYTHING WE CAN STEAL WHEN WE CAN JUST BLEND INTO THE CROWD. BE SOMEONE ELSE.
ALL THOSE WANTED POSTERS WOULD BE USELESS.
HOOF IT OVER, SCARLET PETAL.
STOLEN GOODS

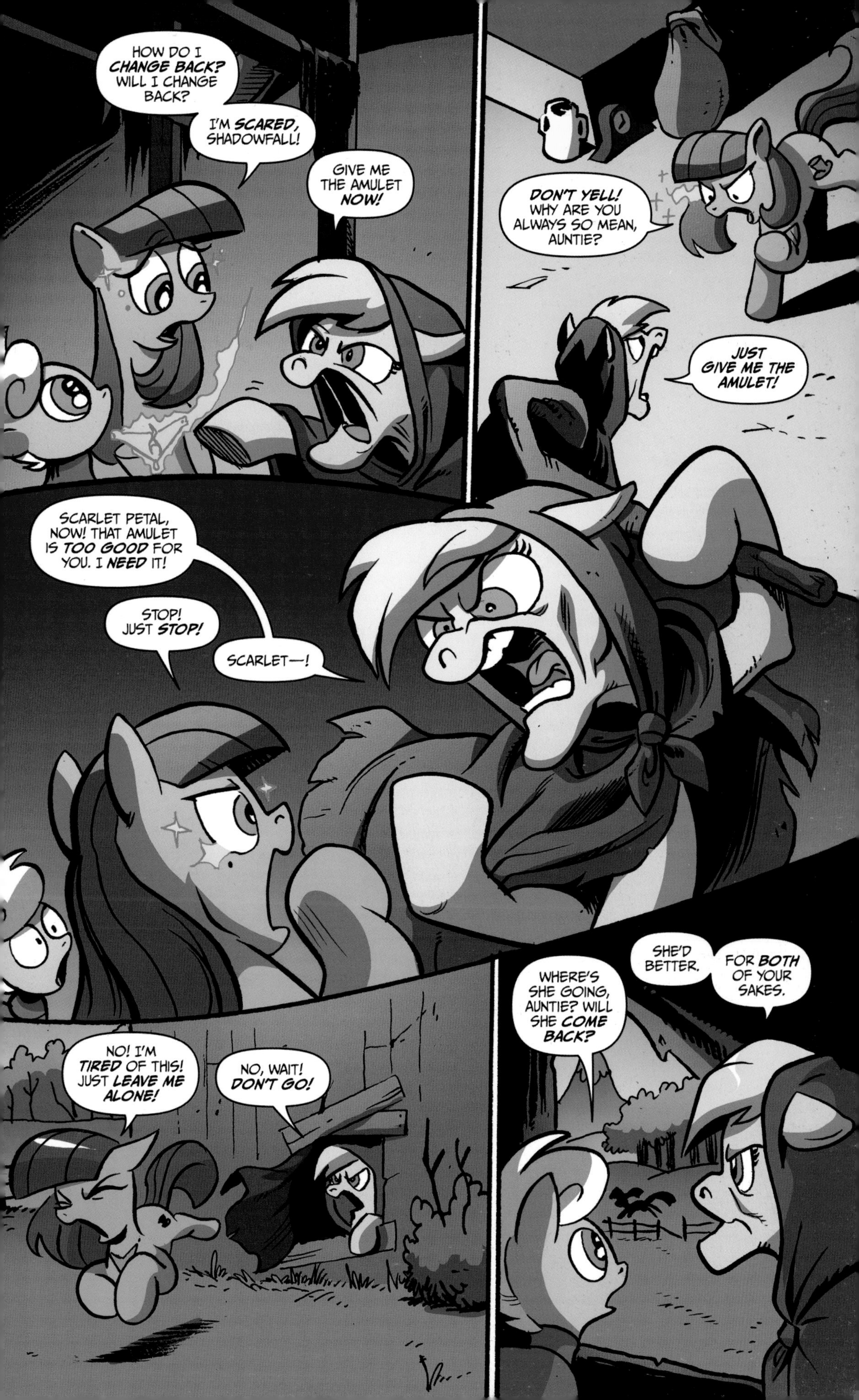
HOW DO I CHANGE BACK? WILL I CHANGE BACK?
I'M SCARED, SHADOWFALL!
GIVE ME THE AMULET NOW!
DON'T YELL! WHY ARE YOU ALWAYS SO MEAN, AUNTIE?
JUST GIVE ME THE AMULET!
SCARLET PETAL, NOW! THAT AMULET IS TOO GOOD FOR YOU. I NEED IT!
STOP! JUST STOP!
SCARLET—!
NO! I'M TIRED OF THIS! JUST LEAVE ME ALONE!
NO, WAIT! DON'T GO!
WHERE'S SHE GOING, AUNTIE? WILL SHE COME BACK?
SHE'D BETTER.
FOR BOTH OF YOUR SAKES.

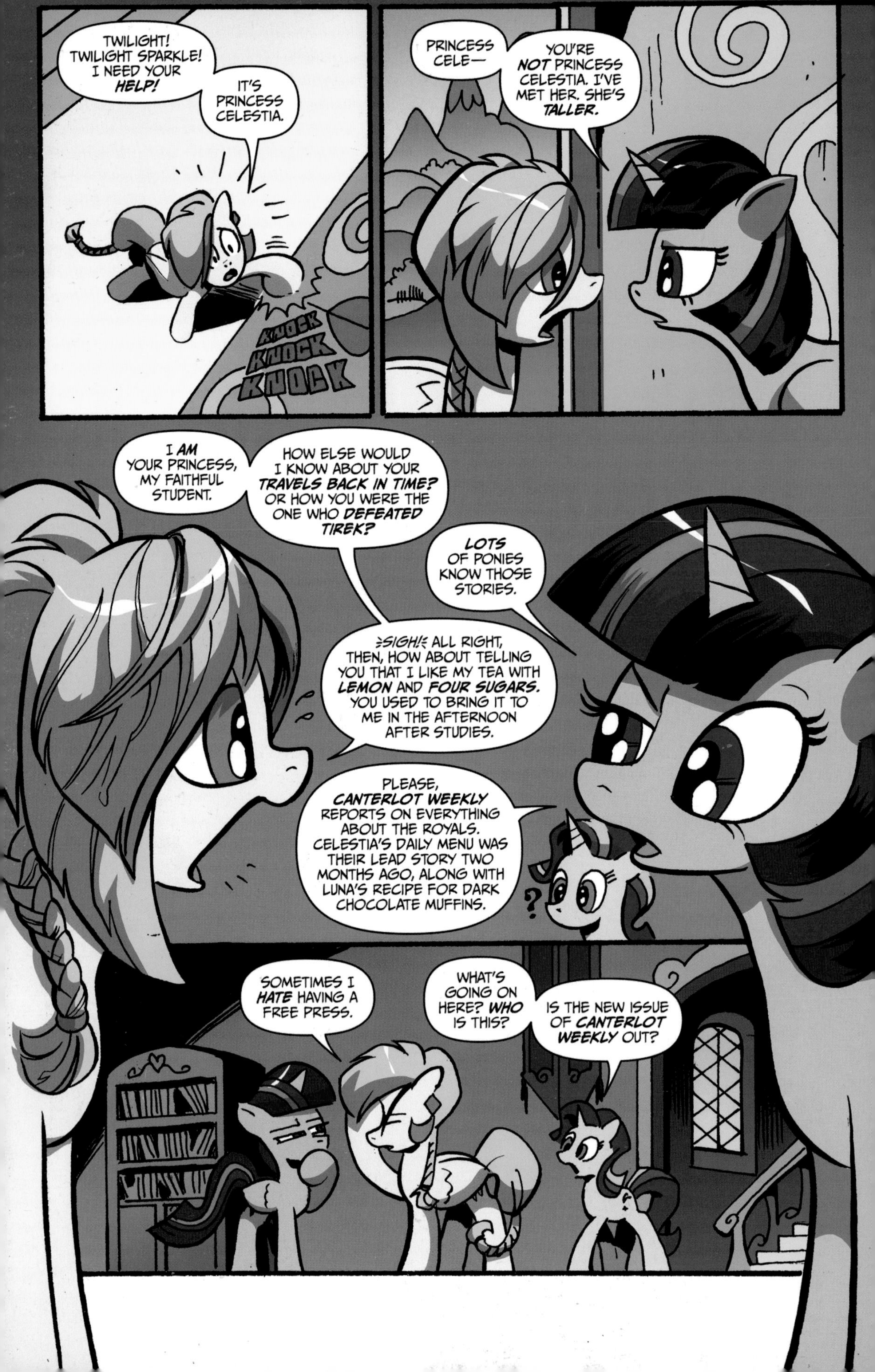
TWILIGHT! TWILIGHT SPARKLE! I NEED YOUR HELP!
IT'S PRINCESS CELESTIA.
KNOCK KNOCK KNOCK
PRINCESS CELE—
YOU'RE NOT PRINCESS CELESTIA. I'VE MET HER. SHE'S TALLER.
I AM YOUR PRINCESS, MY FAITHFUL STUDENT.
HOW ELSE WOULD I KNOW ABOUT YOUR TRAVELS BACK IN TIME? OR HOW YOU WERE THE ONE WHO DEFEATED TIREK?
LOTS OF PONIES KNOW THOSE STORIES.
SIGH! ALL RIGHT, THEN, HOW ABOUT TELLING YOU THAT I LIKE MY TEA WITH LEMON AND FOUR SUGARS. YOU USED TO BRING IT TO ME IN THE AFTERNOON AFTER STUDIES.
PLEASE, CANTERLOT WEEKLY REPORTS ON EVERYTHING ABOUT THE ROYALS. CELESTIA'S DAILY MENU WAS THEIR LEAD STORY TWO MONTHS AGO, ALONG WITH LUNA'S RECIPE FOR DARK CHOCOLATE MUFFINS.
?
SOMETIMES I HATE HAVING A FREE PRESS.
WHAT'S GOING ON HERE? WHO IS THIS?
IS THE NEW ISSUE OF CANTERLOT WEEKLY OUT?

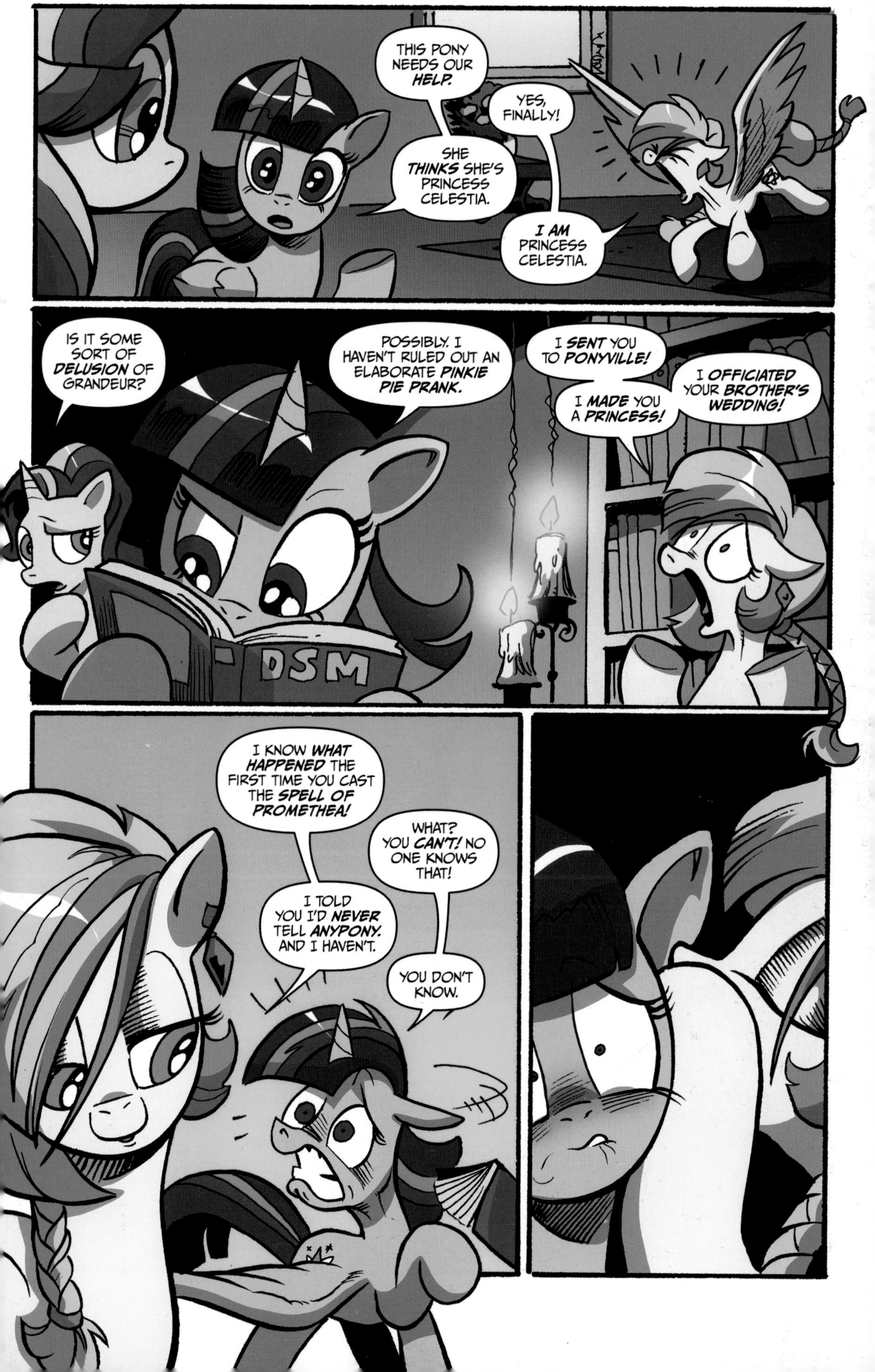
THIS PONY NEEDS OUR HELP.
YES, FINALLY!
SHE THINKS SHE'S PRINCESS CELESTIA.
I AM PRINCESS CELESTIA.
IS IT SOME SORT OF DELUSION OF GRANDEUR?
POSSIBLY. I HAVEN'T RULED OUT AN ELABORATE PINKIE PIE PRANK.
I SENT YOU TO PONYVILLE!
I MADE YOU A PRINCESS!
I OFFICIATED YOUR BROTHER'S WEDDING!
DSM
I KNOW WHAT HAPPENED THE FIRST TIME YOU CAST THE SPELL OF PROMETHEA!
WHAT? YOU CAN'T! NO ONE KNOWS THAT!
I TOLD YOU I'D NEVER TELL ANYPONY. AND I HAVEN'T.
YOU DON'T KNOW.

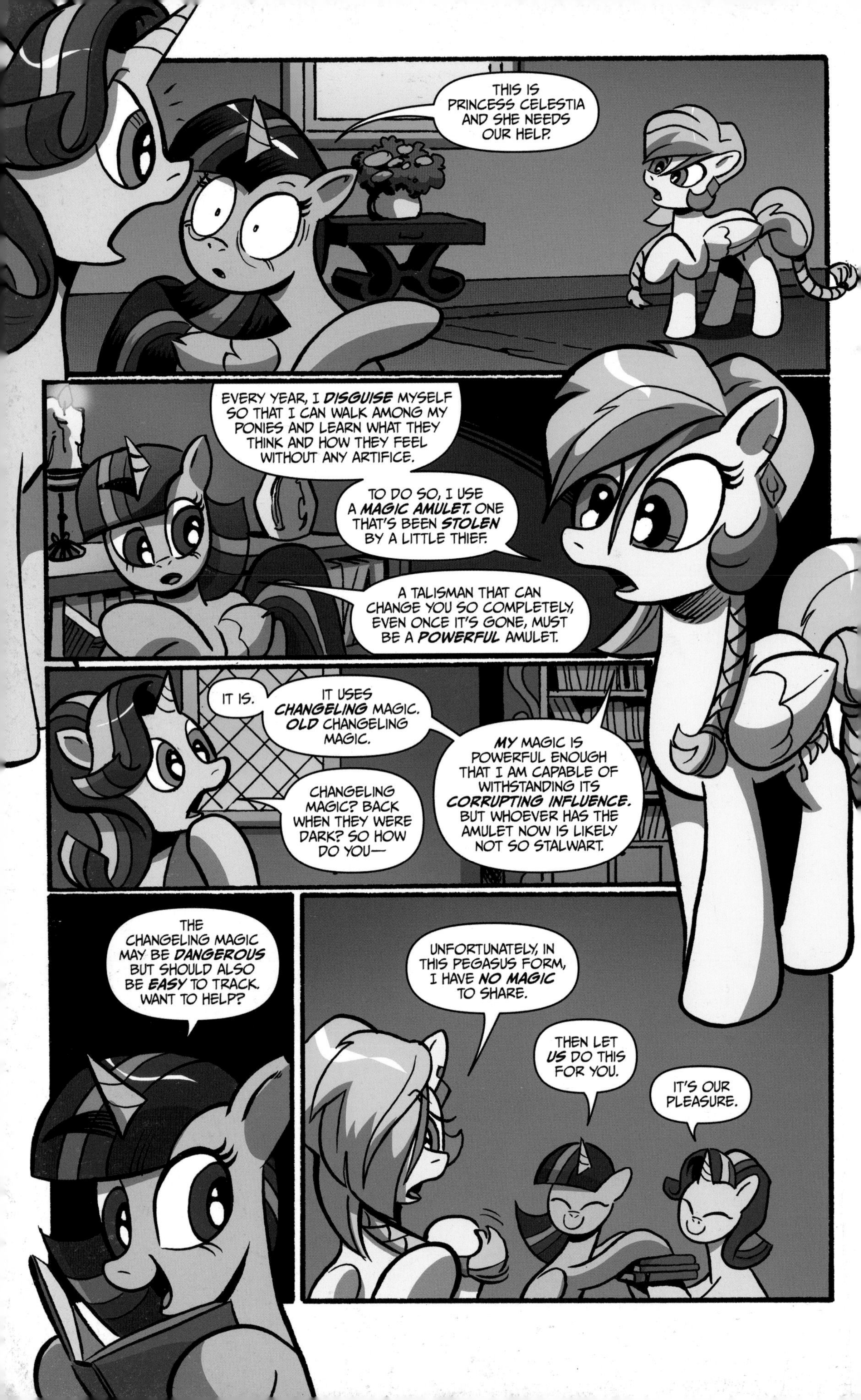
THIS IS PRINCESS CELESTIA AND SHE NEEDS OUR HELP.
EVERY YEAR, I DISGUISE MYSELF SO THAT I CAN WALK AMONG MY PONIES AND LEARN WHAT THEY THINK AND HOW THEY FEEL WITHOUT ANY ARTIFICE.
TO DO SO, I USE A MAGIC AMULET. ONE THAT'S BEEN STOLEN BY A LITTLE THIEF.
A TALISMAN THAT CAN CHANGE YOU SO COMPLETELY, EVEN ONCE IT'S GONE, MUST BE A POWERFUL AMULET.
IT IS.
IT USES CHANGELING MAGIC. OLD CHANGELING MAGIC.
CHANGELING MAGIC? BACK WHEN THEY WERE DARK? SO HOW DO YOU—
MY MAGIC IS POWERFUL ENOUGH THAT I AM CAPABLE OF WITHSTANDING ITS CORRUPTING INFLUENCE. BUT WHOEVER HAS THE AMULET NOW IS LIKELY NOT SO STALWART.
THE CHANGELING MAGIC MAY BE DANGEROUS BUT SHOULD ALSO BE EASY TO TRACK. WANT TO HELP?
UNFORTUNATELY, IN THIS PEGASUS FORM, I HAVE NO MAGIC TO SHARE.
THEN LET US DO THIS FOR YOU.
IT'S OUR PLEASURE.

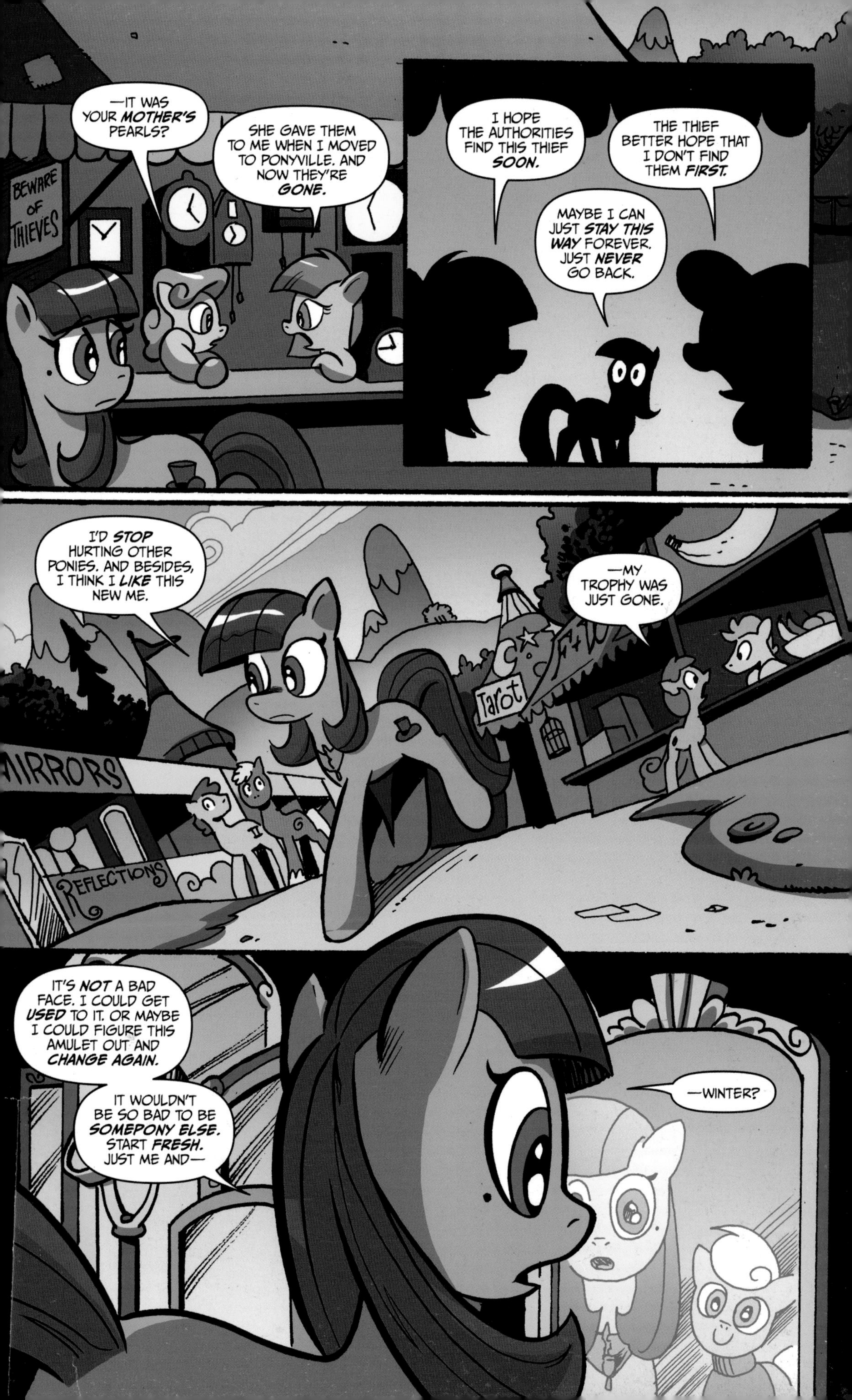
—IT WAS YOUR MOTHER'S PEARLS?
SHE GAVE THEM TO ME WHEN I MOVED TO PONYVILLE. AND NOW THEY'RE GONE.
BEWARE OF THIEVES
I HOPE THE AUTHORITIES FIND THIS THIEF SOON.
THE THIEF BETTER HOPE THAT I DON'T FIND THEM FIRST.
MAYBE I CAN JUST STAY THIS WAY FOREVER. JUST NEVER GO BACK.
I'D STOP HURTING OTHER PONIES. AND BESIDES, I THINK I LIKE THIS NEW ME.
—MY TROPHY WAS JUST GONE.
Tarot
MIRRORS
REFLECTIONS
IT'S NOT A BAD FACE. I COULD GET USED TO IT. OR MAYBE I COULD FIGURE THIS AMULET OUT AND CHANGE AGAIN.
IT WOULDN'T BE SO BAD TO BE SOMEPONY ELSE. START FRESH. JUST ME AND—
—WINTER?

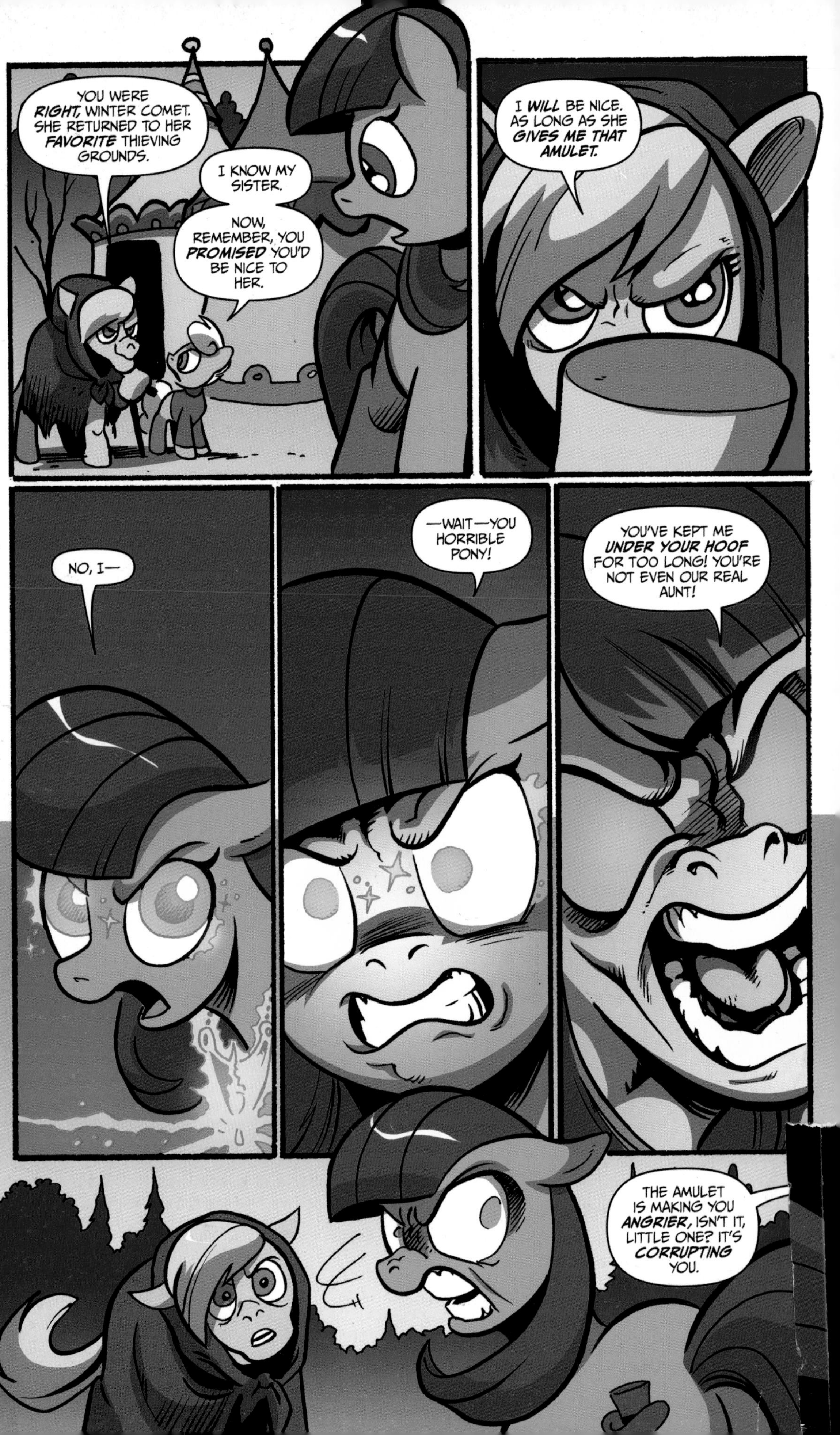
YOU WERE RIGHT, WINTER COMET. SHE RETURNED TO HER FAVORITE THIEVING GROUNDS.
I KNOW MY SISTER.
NOW, REMEMBER, YOU PROMISED YOU'D BE NICE TO HER.
I WILL BE NICE. AS LONG AS SHE GIVES ME THAT AMULET.
NO, I—
—WAIT—YOU HORRIBLE PONY!
YOU'VE KEPT ME UNDER YOUR HOOF FOR TOO LONG! YOU'RE NOT EVEN OUR REAL AUNT!
THE AMULET IS MAKING YOU ANGRIER, ISN'T IT, LITTLE ONE? IT'S CORRUPTING YOU.

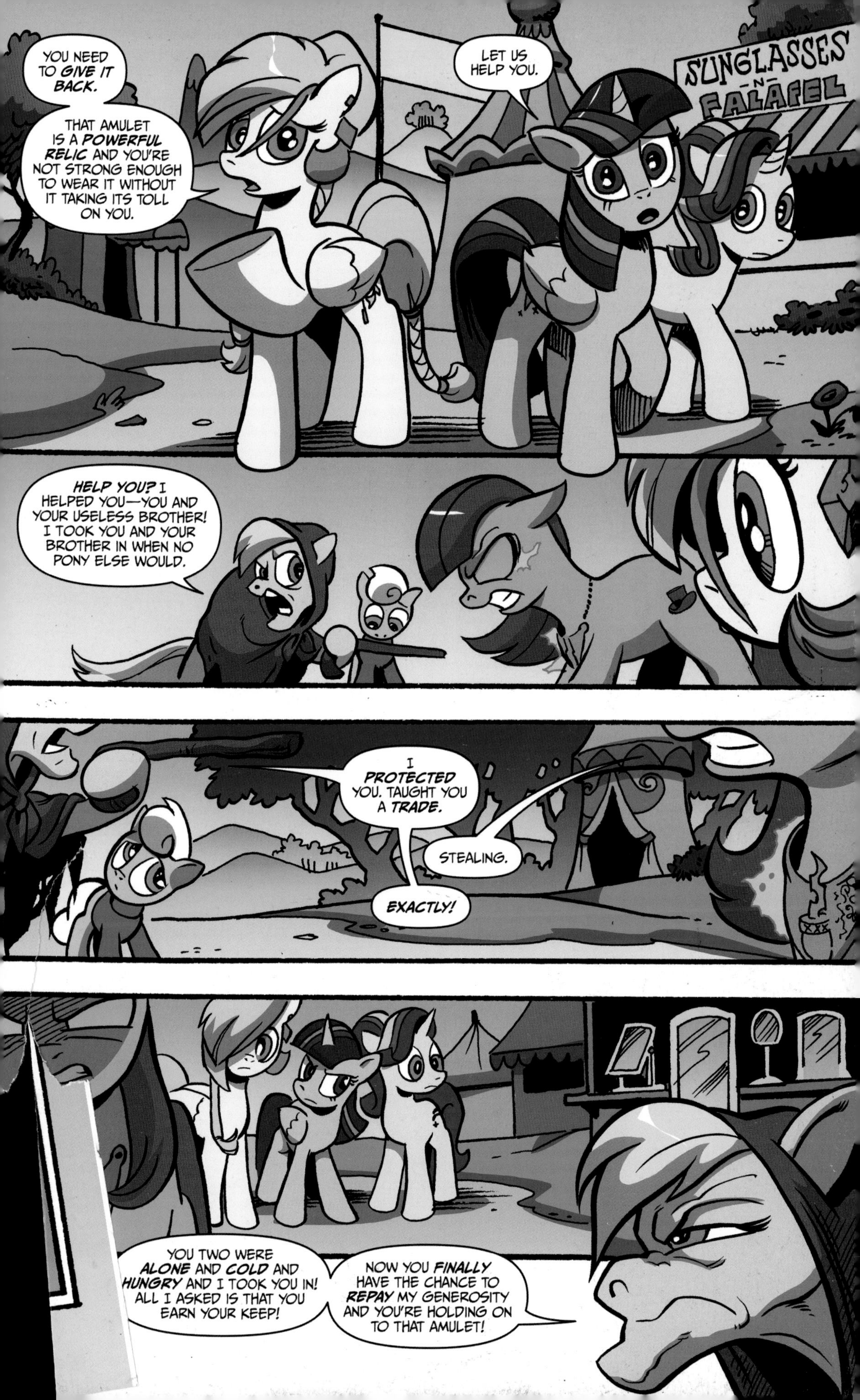

SUNGLASSES -N- FALAFEL
YOU NEED TO GIVE IT BACK.
THAT AMULET IS A POWERFUL RELIC AND YOU'RE NOT STRONG ENOUGH TO WEAR IT WITHOUT IT TAKING ITS TOLL ON YOU.
LET US HELP YOU.
HELP YOU? I HELPED YOU—YOU AND YOUR USELESS BROTHER! I TOOK YOU AND YOUR BROTHER IN WHEN NO PONY ELSE WOULD.
I PROTECTED YOU. TAUGHT YOU A TRADE.
STEALING.
EXACTLY!
YOU TWO WERE ALONE AND COLD AND HUNGRY AND I TOOK YOU IN! ALL I ASKED IS THAT YOU EARN YOUR KEEP!
NOW YOU FINALLY HAVE THE CHANCE TO REPAY MY GENEROSITY AND YOU'RE HOLDING ON TO THAT AMULET!

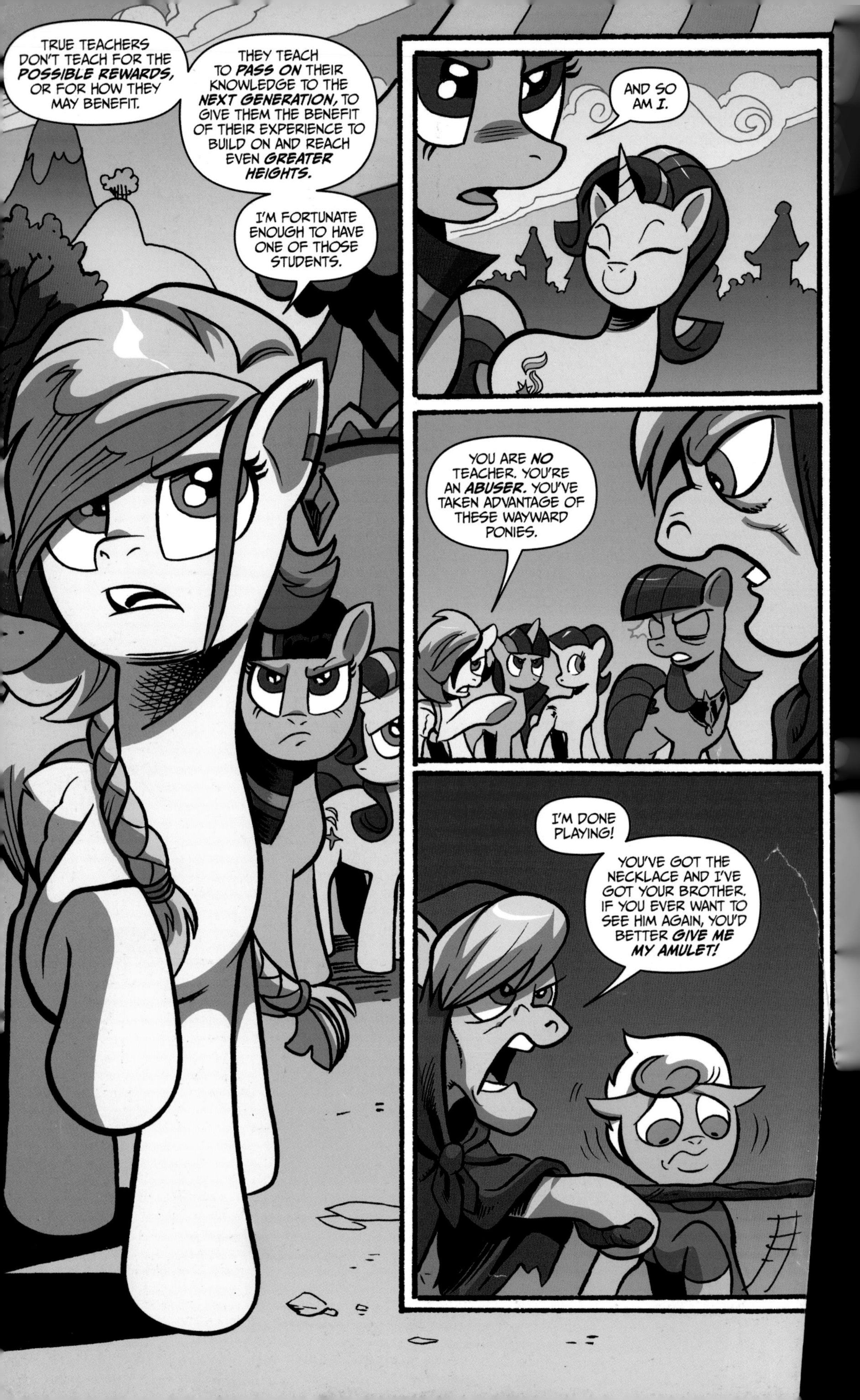

TRUE TEACHERS DON'T TEACH FOR THE POSSIBLE REWARDS, OR FOR HOW THEY MAY BENEFIT.
THEY TEACH TO PASS ON THEIR KNOWLEDGE TO THE NEXT GENERATION, TO GIVE THEM THE BENEFIT OF THEIR EXPERIENCE TO BUILD ON AND REACH EVEN GREATER HEIGHTS.
I'M FORTUNATE ENOUGH TO HAVE ONE OF THOSE STUDENTS.
AND SO AM I.
YOU ARE NO TEACHER. YOU'RE AN ABUSER. YOU'VE TAKEN ADVANTAGE OF THESE WAYWARD PONIES.
I'M DONE PLAYING!
YOU'VE GOT THE NECKLACE AND I'VE GOT YOUR BROTHER. IF YOU EVER WANT TO SEE HIM AGAIN, YOU'D BETTER GIVE ME MY AMULET!

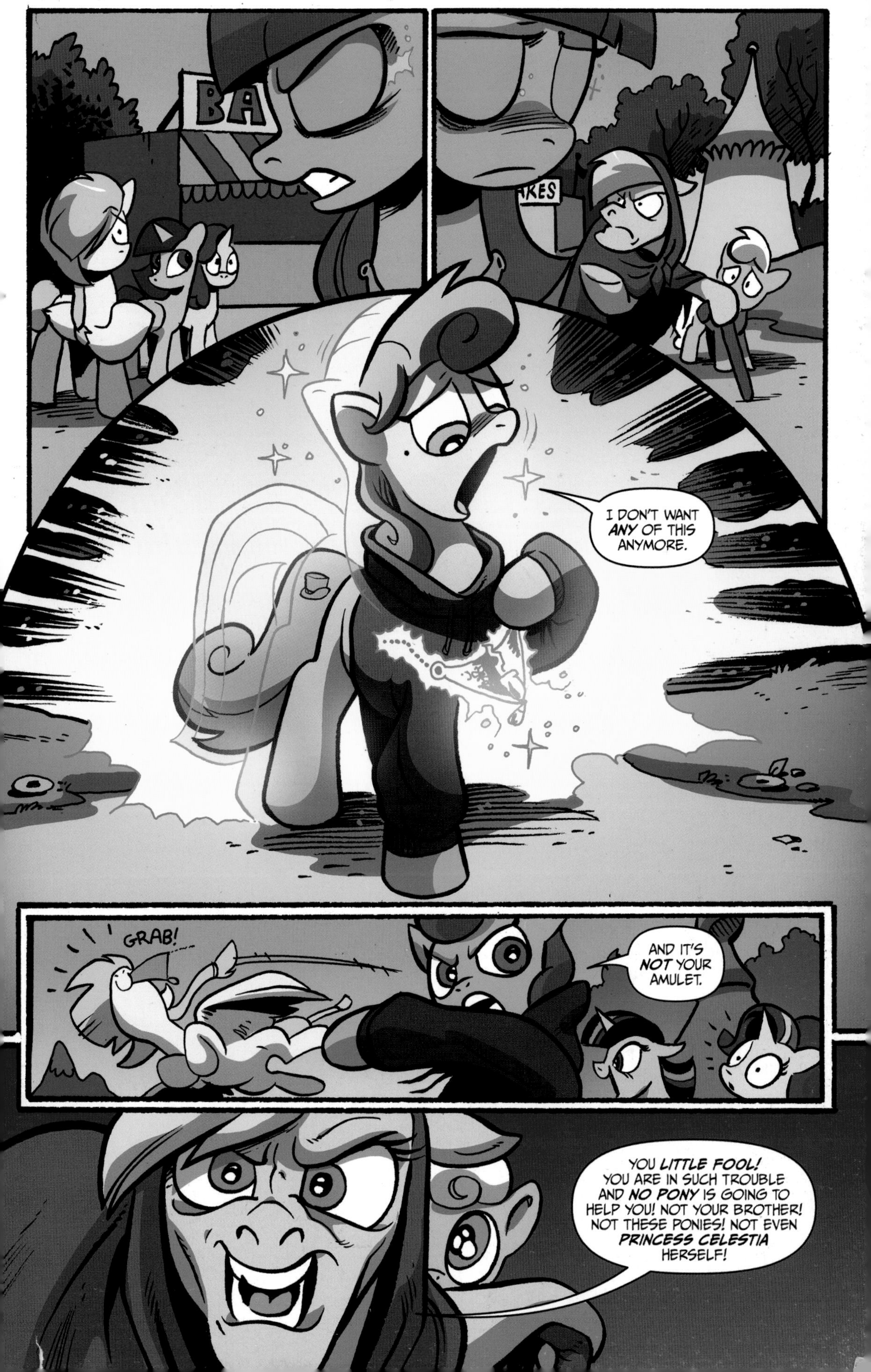
BA
AKES
I DON'T WANT ANY OF THIS ANYMORE.
GRAB!
AND IT'S NOT YOUR AMULET.
YOU LITTLE FOOL! YOU ARE IN SUCH TROUBLE AND NO PONY IS GOING TO HELP YOU! NOT YOUR BROTHER! NOT THESE PONIES! NOT EVEN PRINCESS CELESTIA HERSELF!

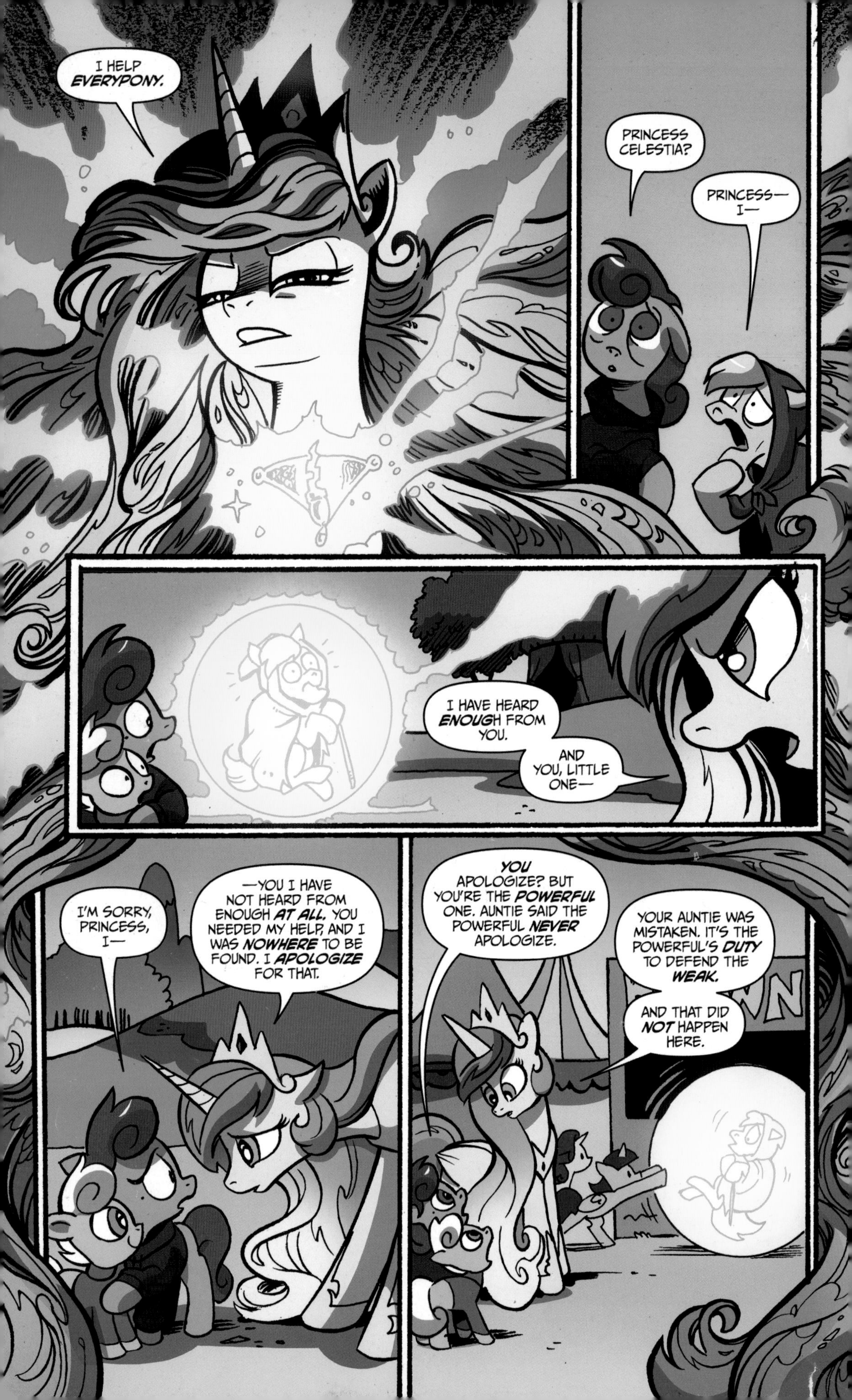
I HELP *EVERYPONY.*
PRINCESS CELESTIA?
PRINCESS— I—
I HAVE HEARD *ENOUGH* FROM YOU.
AND YOU, LITTLE ONE—
I'M SORRY, PRINCESS, I—
—YOU I HAVE NOT HEARD FROM ENOUGH *AT ALL.* YOU NEEDED MY HELP, AND I WAS *NOWHERE* TO BE FOUND. I *APOLOGIZE* FOR THAT.
YOU APOLOGIZE? BUT YOU'RE THE *POWERFUL* ONE. AUNTIE SAID THE POWERFUL *NEVER* APOLOGIZE.
YOUR AUNTIE WAS MISTAKEN. IT'S THE POWERFUL'S *DUTY* TO DEFEND THE *WEAK.*
AND THAT DID *NOT* HAPPEN HERE.

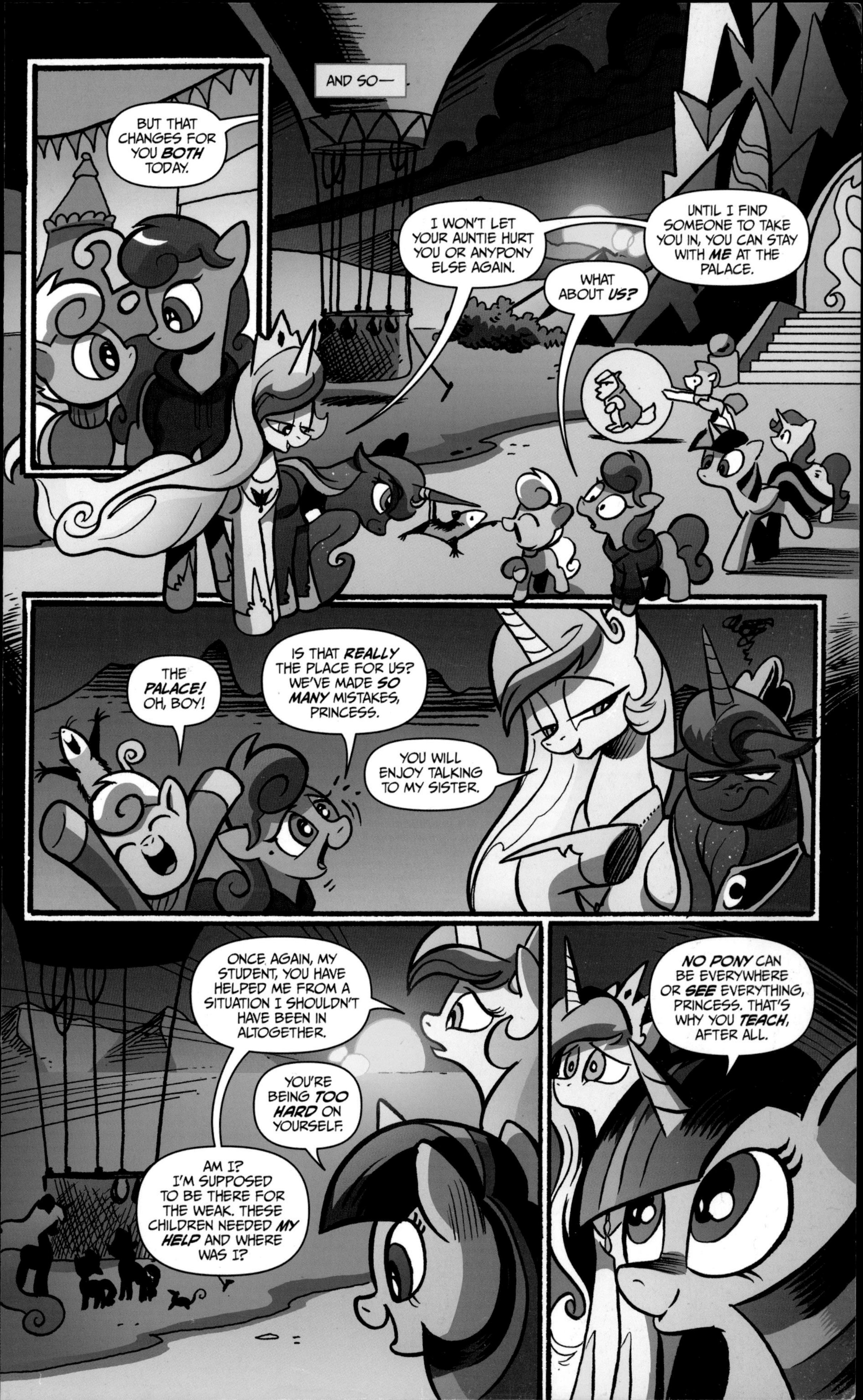
AND SO—
BUT THAT CHANGES FOR YOU **BOTH** TODAY.
I WON'T LET YOUR AUNTIE HURT YOU OR ANYPONY ELSE AGAIN.
UNTIL I FIND SOMEONE TO TAKE YOU IN, YOU CAN STAY WITH **ME** AT THE PALACE.
WHAT ABOUT **US?**
THE **PALACE!** OH, BOY!
IS THAT **REALLY** THE PLACE FOR US? WE'VE MADE **SO MANY** MISTAKES, PRINCESS.
YOU WILL ENJOY TALKING TO MY SISTER.
ONCE AGAIN, MY STUDENT, YOU HAVE HELPED ME FROM A SITUATION I SHOULDN'T HAVE BEEN IN ALTOGETHER.
YOU'RE BEING **TOO HARD** ON YOURSELF.
AM I? I'M SUPPOSED TO BE THERE FOR THE WEAK. THESE CHILDREN NEEDED **MY HELP** AND WHERE WAS I?
NO PONY CAN BE EVERYWHERE OR **SEE** EVERYTHING, PRINCESS. THAT'S WHY YOU **TEACH**, AFTER ALL.

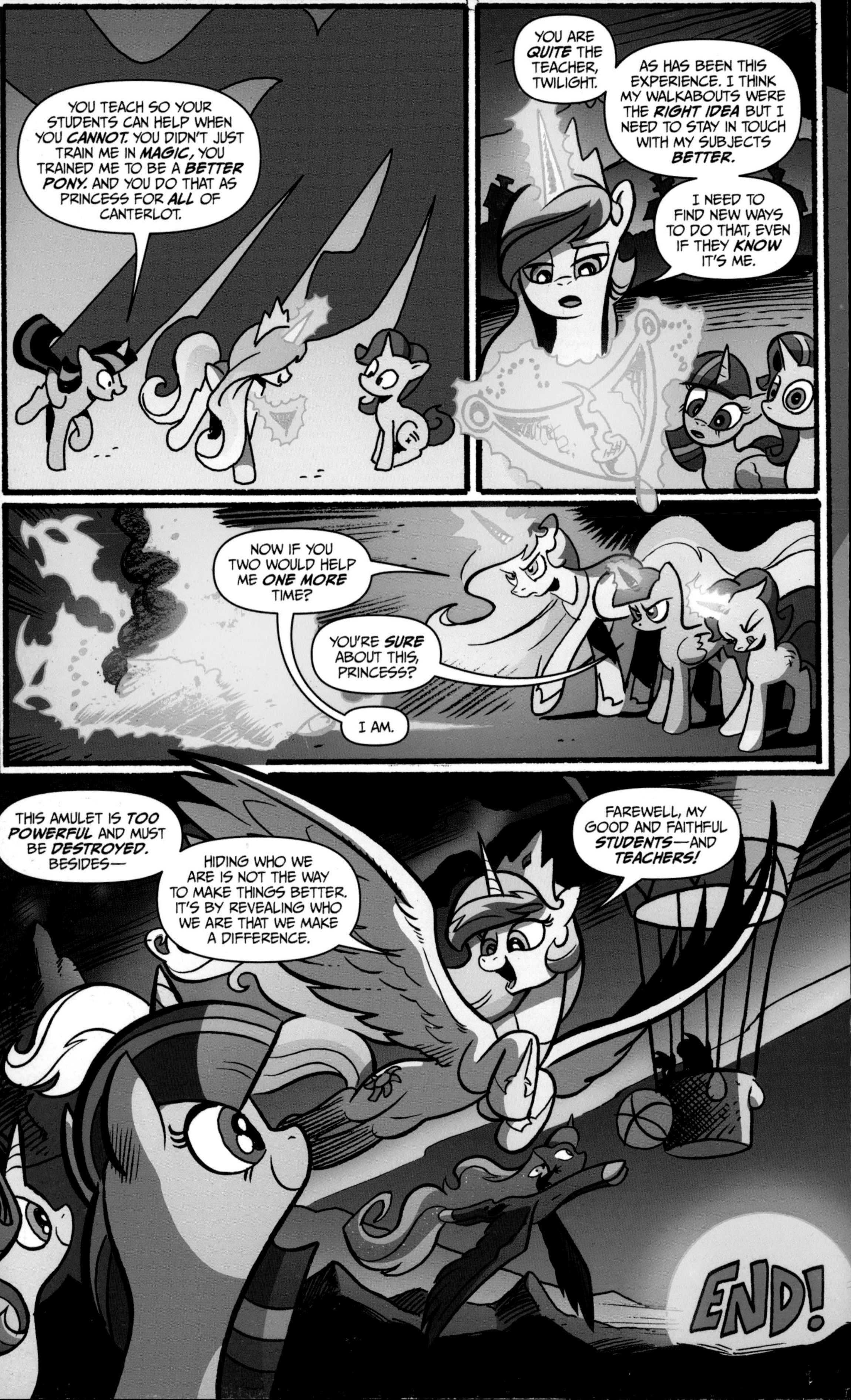
YOU TEACH SO YOUR STUDENTS CAN HELP WHEN YOU CANNOT. YOU DIDN'T JUST TRAIN ME IN MAGIC, YOU TRAINED ME TO BE A BETTER PONY. AND YOU DO THAT AS PRINCESS FOR ALL OF CANTERLOT.
YOU ARE QUITE THE TEACHER, TWILIGHT.
AS HAS BEEN THIS EXPERIENCE. I THINK MY WALKABOUTS WERE THE RIGHT IDEA BUT I NEED TO STAY IN TOUCH WITH MY SUBJECTS BETTER.
I NEED TO FIND NEW WAYS TO DO THAT, EVEN IF THEY KNOW IT'S ME.
NOW IF YOU TWO WOULD HELP ME ONE MORE TIME?
YOU'RE SURE ABOUT THIS, PRINCESS?
I AM.
THIS AMULET IS TOO POWERFUL AND MUST BE DESTROYED. BESIDES—
HIDING WHO WE ARE IS NOT THE WAY TO MAKE THINGS BETTER. IT'S BY REVEALING WHO WE ARE THAT WE MAKE A DIFFERENCE.
FAREWELL, MY GOOD AND FAITHFUL STUDENTS—AND TEACHERS!
END!

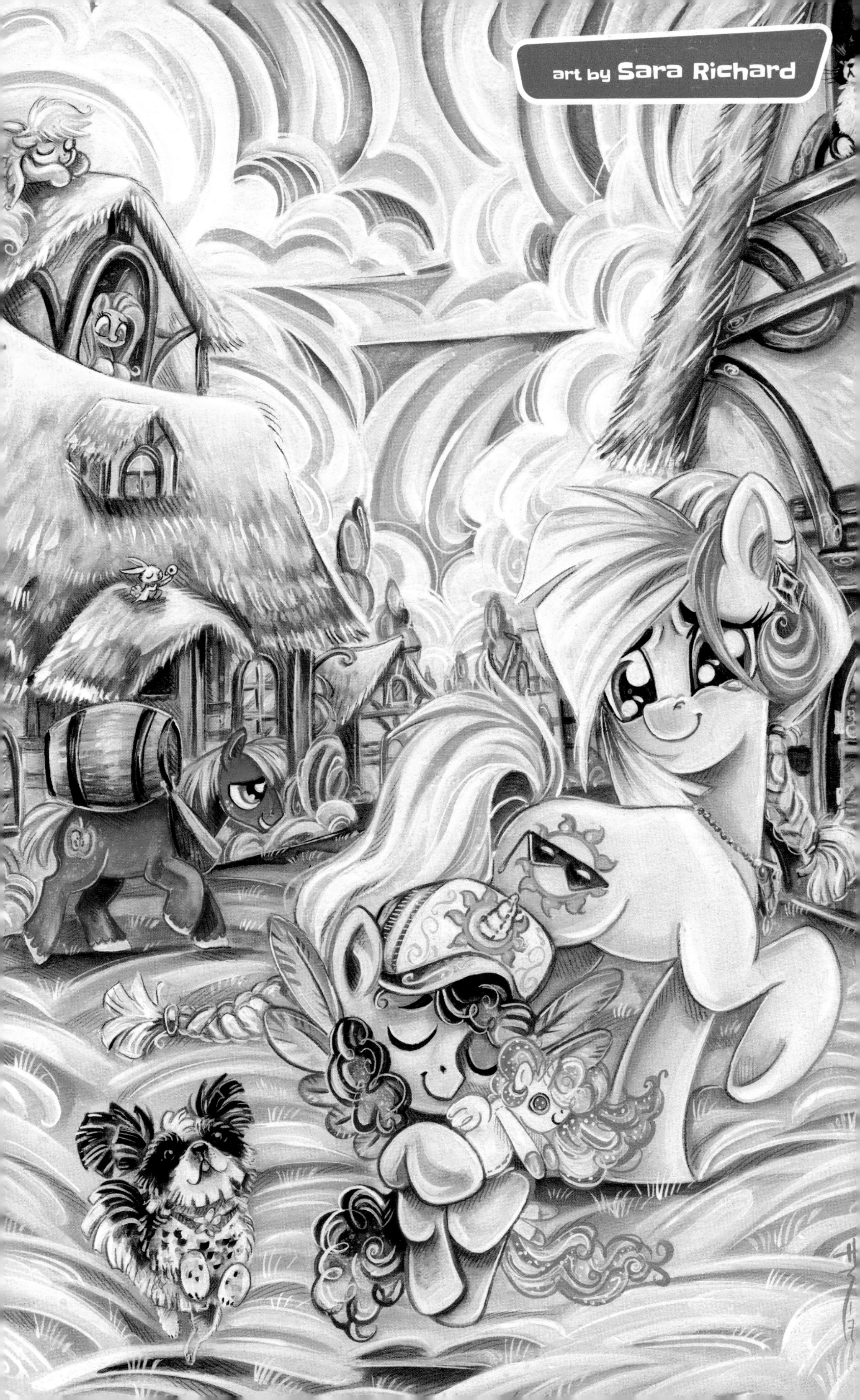
art by Sara Richard

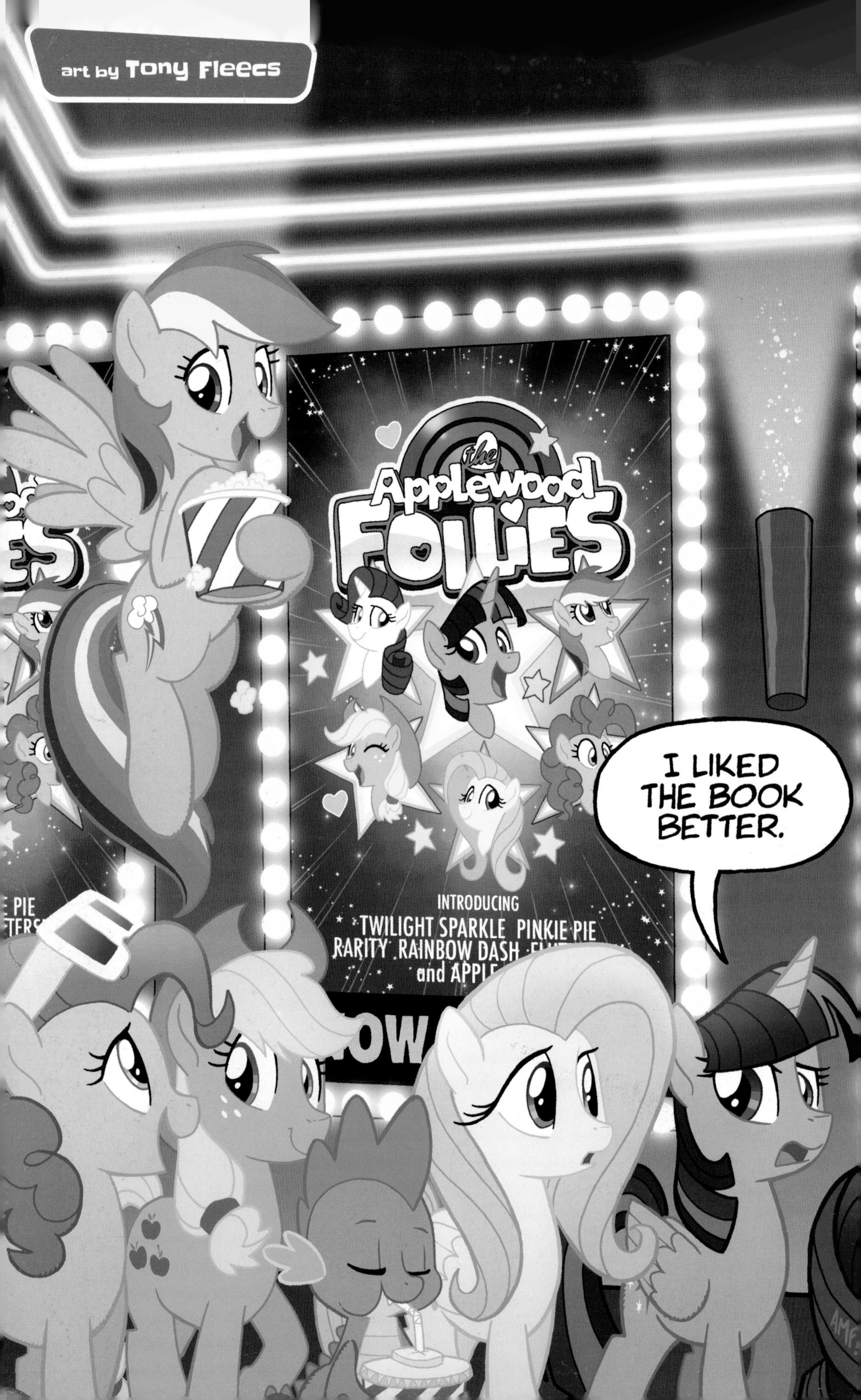
art by Tony Fleecs
the Applewood Follies
INTRODUCING
TWILIGHT SPARKLE PINKIE PIE
RARITY RAINBOW DASH
I LIKED THE BOOK BETTER.

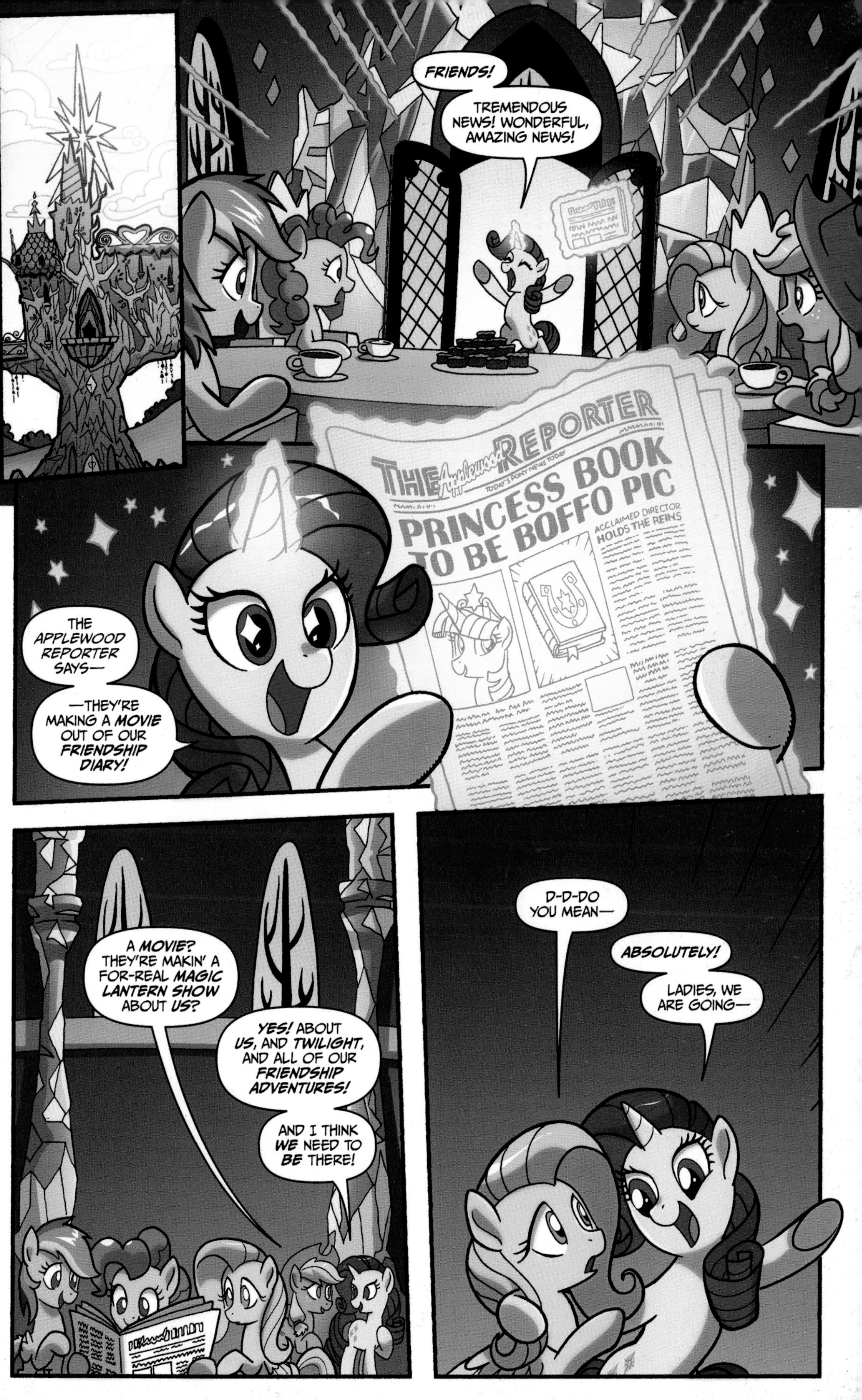
FRIENDS!
TREMENDOUS NEWS! WONDERFUL, AMAZING NEWS!
THE Applewood REPORTER
TODAY'S PONY NEWS TODAY
PRINCESS BOOK TO BE BOFFO PIC
ACCLAIMED DIRECTOR HOLDS THE REINS
THE APPLEWOOD REPORTER SAYS—
—THEY'RE MAKING A MOVIE OUT OF OUR FRIENDSHIP DIARY!
A MOVIE? THEY'RE MAKIN' A FOR-REAL MAGIC LANTERN SHOW ABOUT US?
YES! ABOUT US, AND TWILIGHT, AND ALL OF OUR FRIENDSHIP ADVENTURES!
AND I THINK WE NEED TO BE THERE!
D-D-DO YOU MEAN—
ABSOLUTELY!
LADIES, WE ARE GOING—

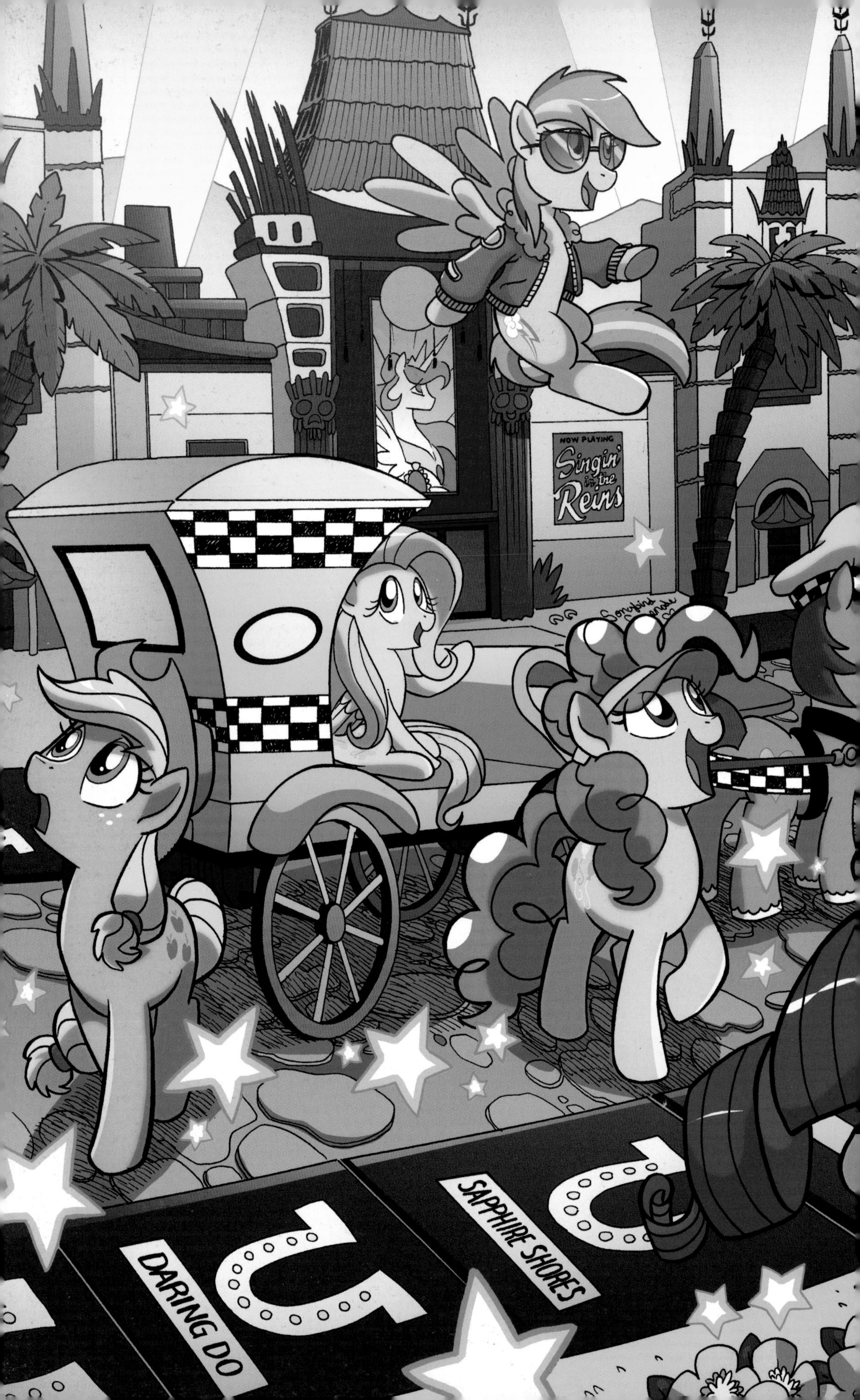
NOW PLAYING
Singin' in the Reins
SAPPHIRE SHORES
DARING DO

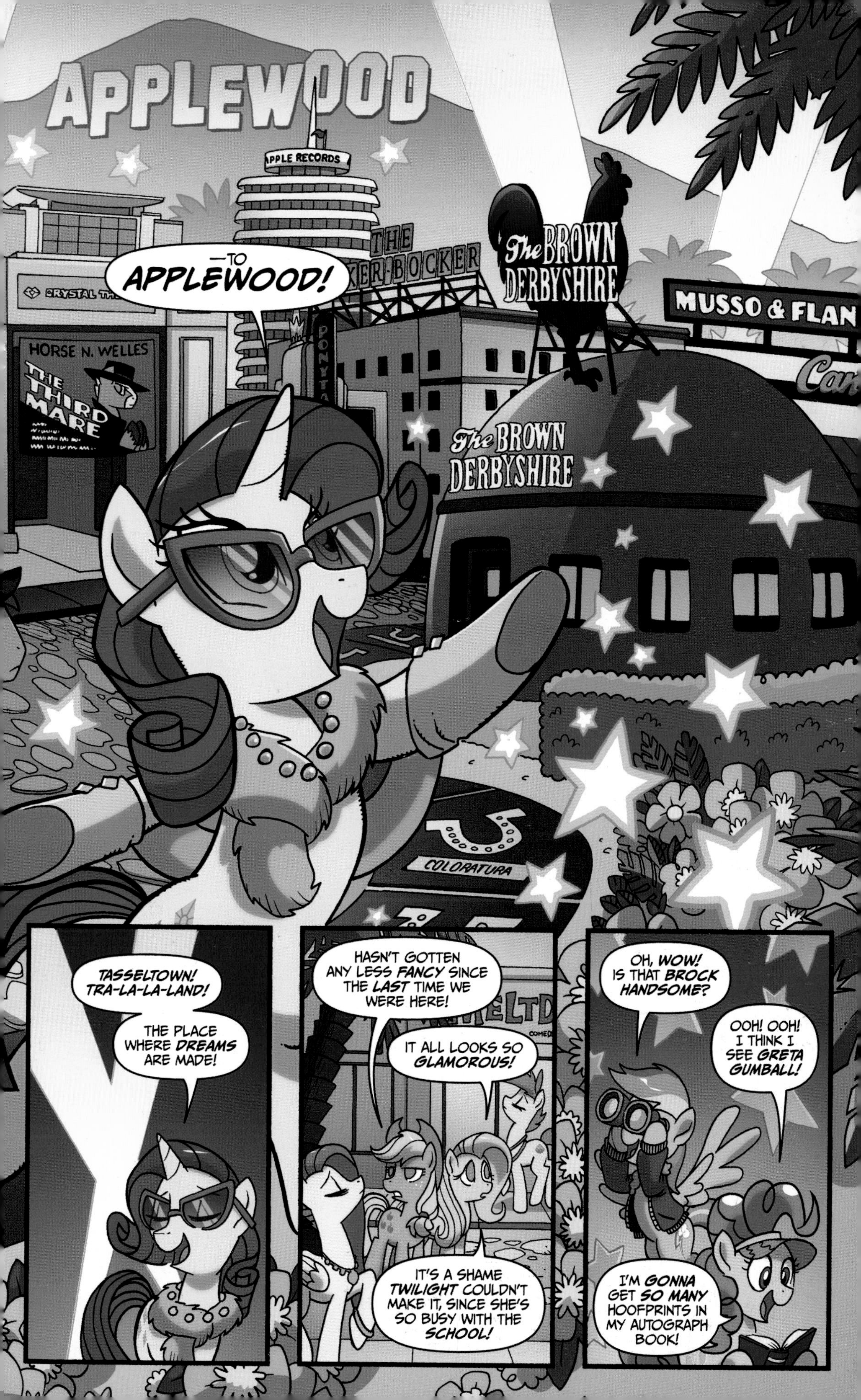
APPLEWOOD
APPLE RECORDS
THE
CRYSTAL THE
HORSE N. WELLES
THE THIRD MARE
The BROWN DERBYSHIRE
MUSSO & FLAN
—TO APPLEWOOD!
The BROWN DERBYSHIRE
COLORATURA
TASSELTOWN! TRA-LA-LA-LAND!
THE PLACE WHERE DREAMS ARE MADE!
HASN'T GOTTEN ANY LESS FANCY SINCE THE LAST TIME WE WERE HERE!
IT ALL LOOKS SO GLAMOROUS!
IT'S A SHAME TWILIGHT COULDN'T MAKE IT, SINCE SHE'S SO BUSY WITH THE SCHOOL!
OH, WOW! IS THAT BROCK HANDSOME?
OOH! OOH! I THINK I SEE GRETA GUMBALL!
I'M GONNA GET SO MANY HOOFPRINTS IN MY AUTOGRAPH BOOK!

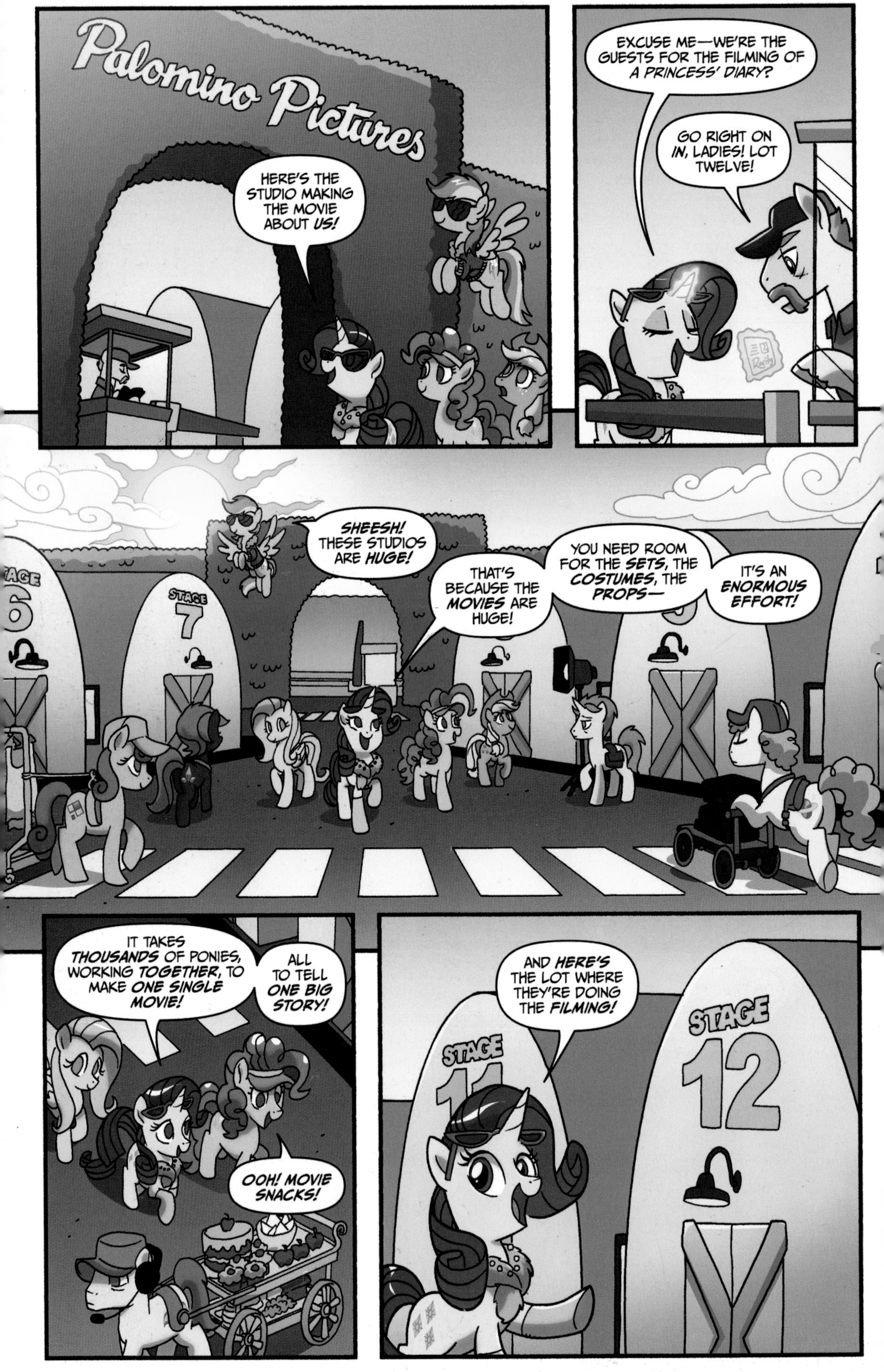
Palomino Pictures
HERE'S THE STUDIO MAKING THE MOVIE ABOUT *US!*
EXCUSE ME—WE'RE THE GUESTS FOR THE FILMING OF *A PRINCESS' DIARY?*
GO RIGHT ON *IN,* LADIES! LOT TWELVE!
STAGE 7
SHEESH! THESE STUDIOS ARE ***HUGE!***
THAT'S BECAUSE THE ***MOVIES*** ARE HUGE!
YOU NEED ROOM FOR THE ***SETS,*** THE ***COSTUMES,*** THE ***PROPS—***
IT'S AN ***ENORMOUS*** EFFORT!
IT TAKES ***THOUSANDS*** OF PONIES, WORKING ***TOGETHER,*** TO MAKE ***ONE SINGLE MOVIE!***
ALL TO TELL ***ONE BIG STORY!***
OOH! MOVIE SNACKS!
AND ***HERE'S*** THE LOT WHERE THEY'RE DOING THE ***FILMING!***
STAGE
STAGE 12

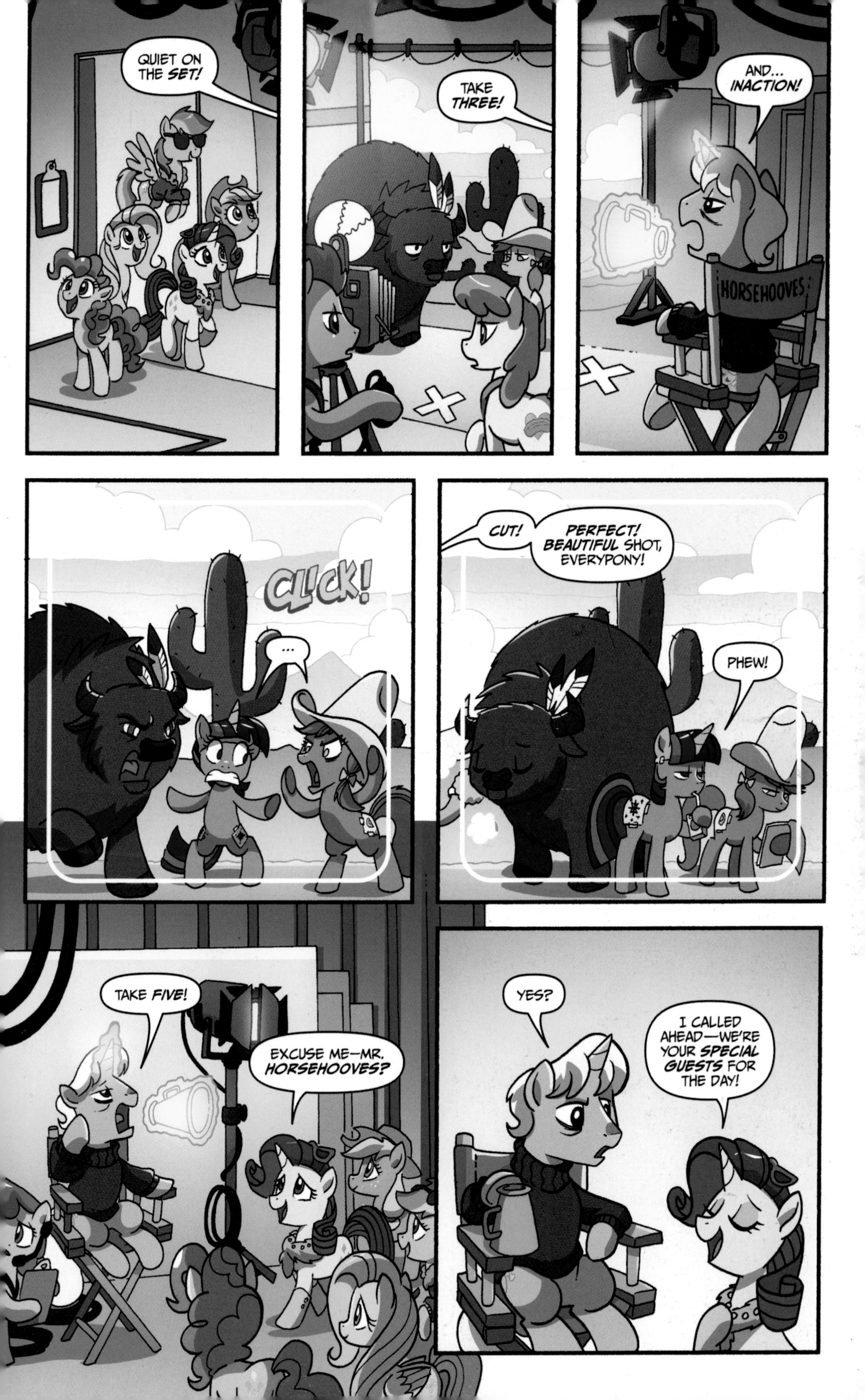

QUIET ON THE SET!
TAKE THREE!
AND... INACTION!
HORSEHOOVES
CLICK!
...
CUT!
PERFECT! BEAUTIFUL SHOT, EVERYPONY!
PHEW!
TAKE FIVE!
EXCUSE ME—MR. HORSEHOOVES?
YES?
I CALLED AHEAD—WE'RE YOUR SPECIAL GUESTS FOR THE DAY!

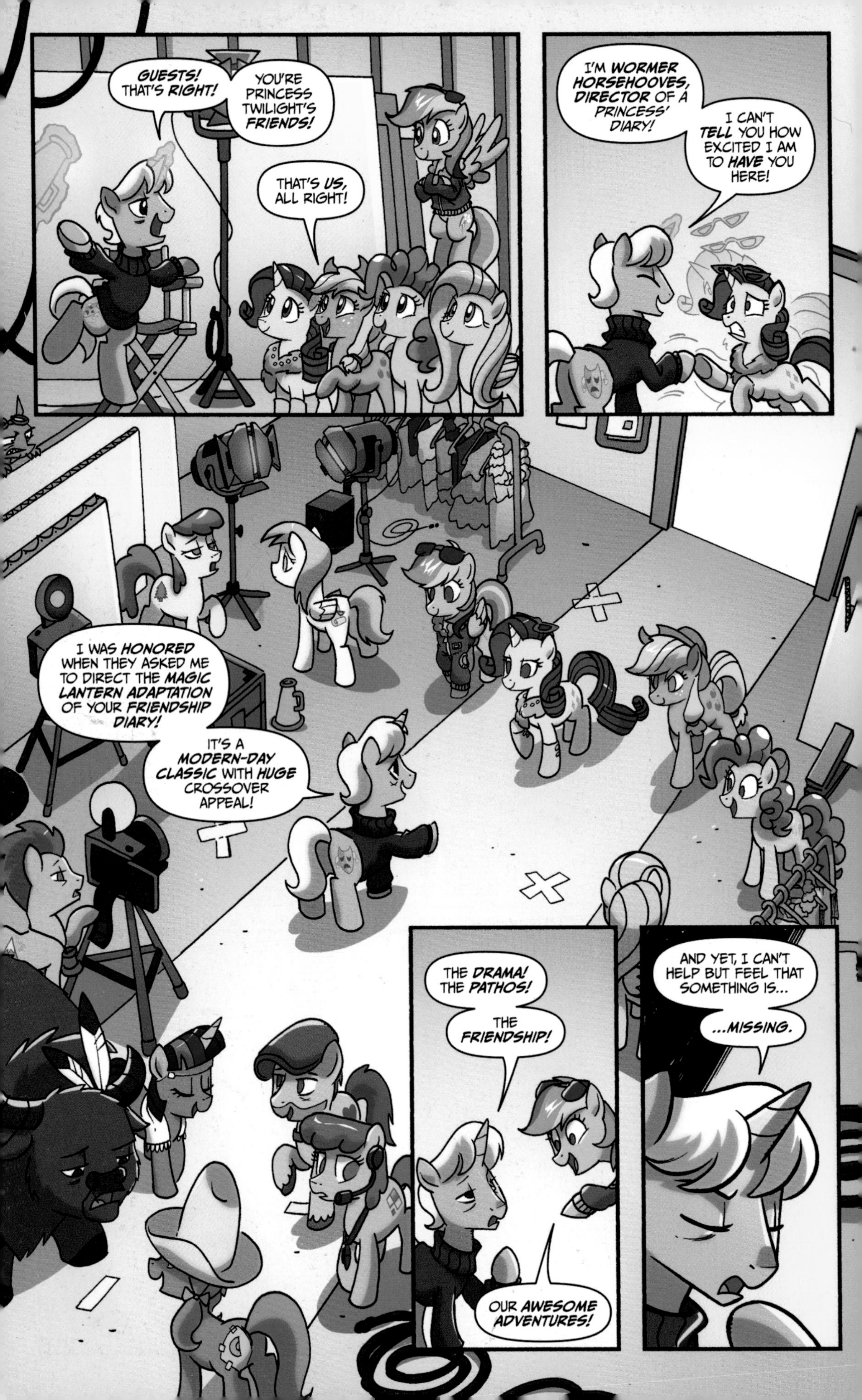
GUESTS! THAT'S RIGHT!
YOU'RE PRINCESS TWILIGHT'S FRIENDS!
THAT'S US, ALL RIGHT!
I'M WORMER HORSEHOOVES, DIRECTOR OF A PRINCESS' DIARY!
I CAN'T TELL YOU HOW EXCITED I AM TO HAVE YOU HERE!
I WAS HONORED WHEN THEY ASKED ME TO DIRECT THE MAGIC LANTERN ADAPTATION OF YOUR FRIENDSHIP DIARY!
IT'S A MODERN-DAY CLASSIC WITH HUGE CROSSOVER APPEAL!
THE DRAMA! THE PATHOS!
THE FRIENDSHIP!
OUR AWESOME ADVENTURES!
AND YET, I CAN'T HELP BUT FEEL THAT SOMETHING IS...
...MISSING.

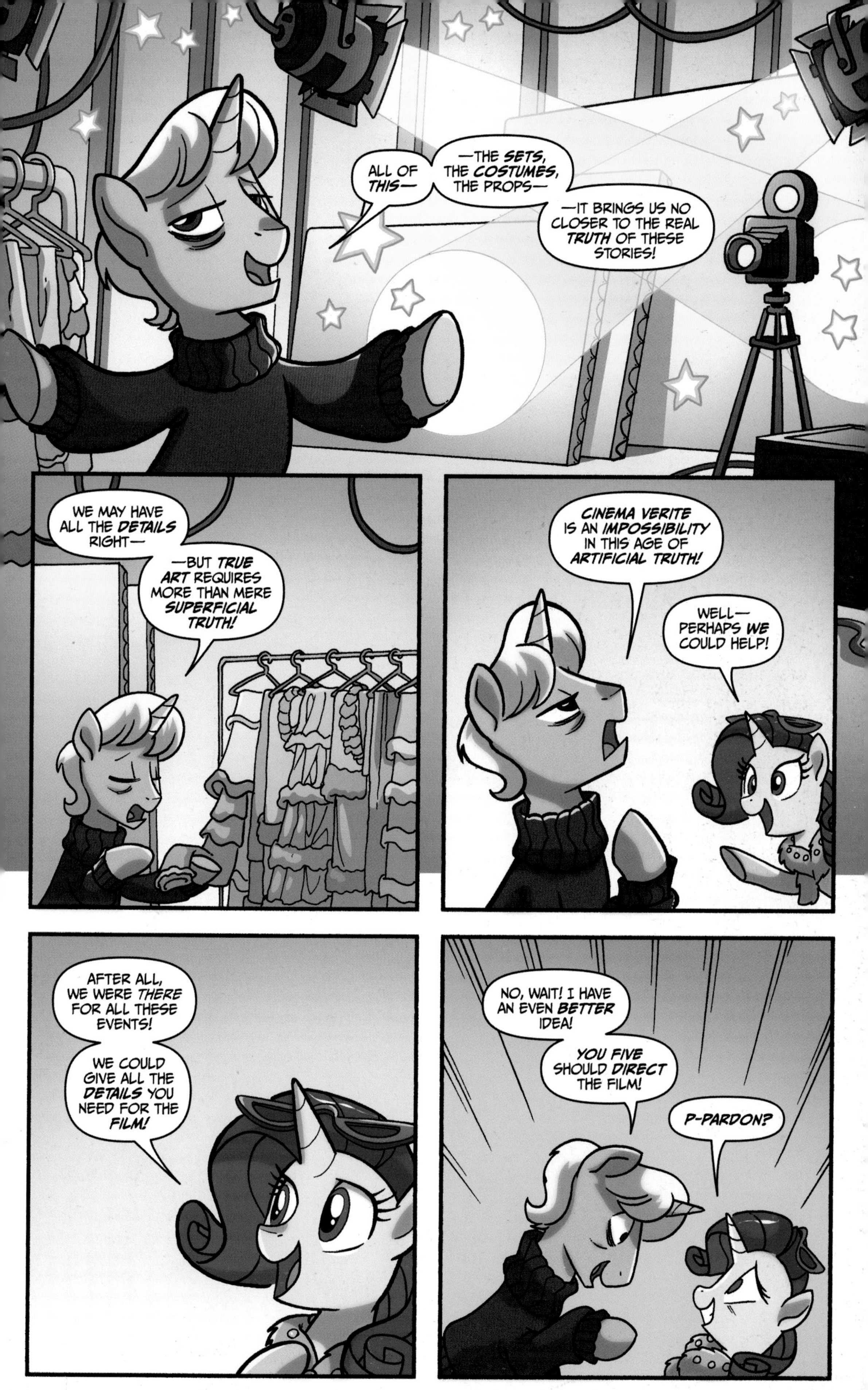
ALL OF THIS—
—THE SETS, THE COSTUMES, THE PROPS—
—IT BRINGS US NO CLOSER TO THE REAL TRUTH OF THESE STORIES!
WE MAY HAVE ALL THE DETAILS RIGHT—
—BUT TRUE ART REQUIRES MORE THAN MERE SUPERFICIAL TRUTH!
CINEMA VERITE IS AN IMPOSSIBILITY IN THIS AGE OF ARTIFICIAL TRUTH!
WELL— PERHAPS WE COULD HELP!
AFTER ALL, WE WERE THERE FOR ALL THESE EVENTS!
WE COULD GIVE ALL THE DETAILS YOU NEED FOR THE FILM!
NO, WAIT! I HAVE AN EVEN BETTER IDEA!
YOU FIVE SHOULD DIRECT THE FILM!
P-PARDON?

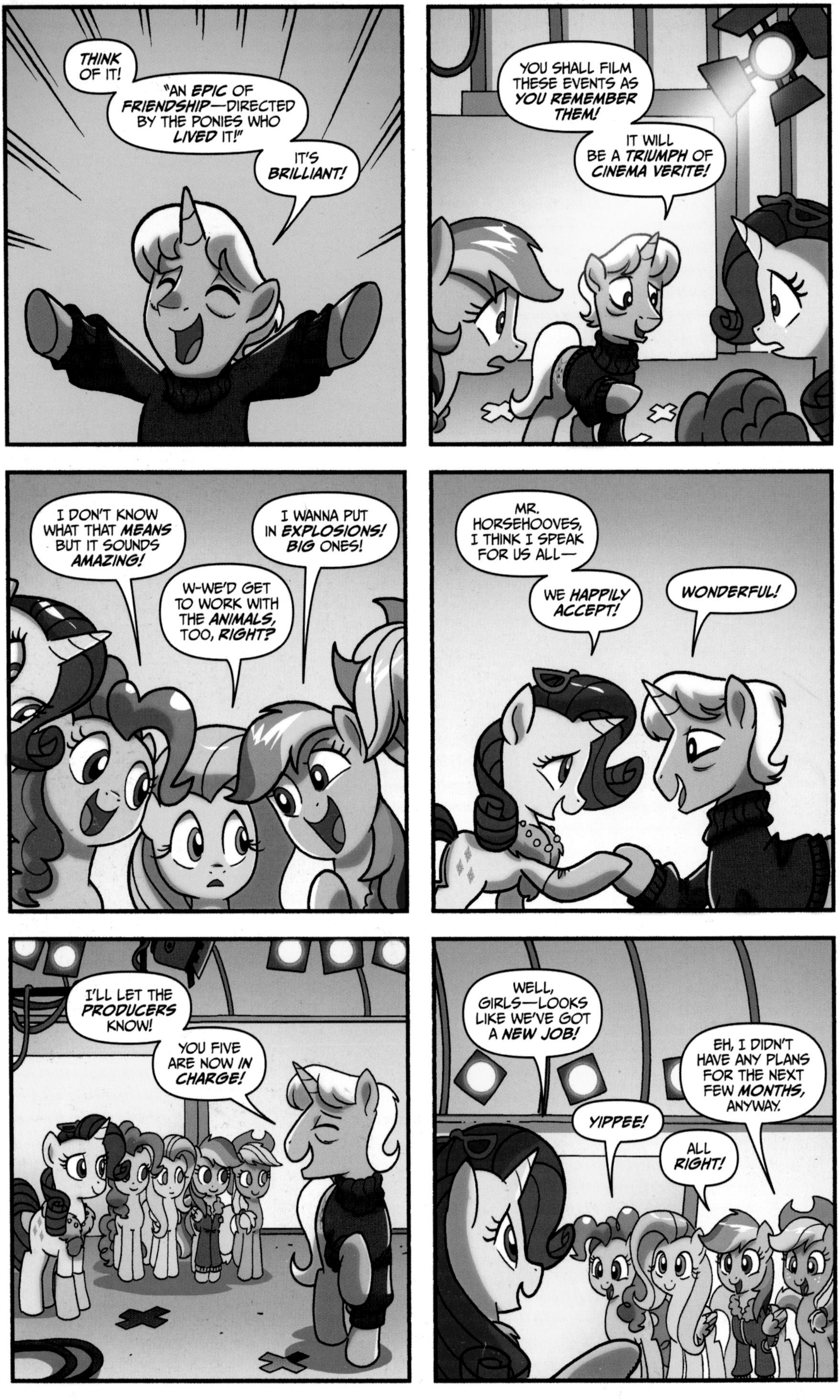
THINK OF IT!
"AN EPIC OF FRIENDSHIP—DIRECTED BY THE PONIES WHO LIVED IT!"
IT'S BRILLIANT!
YOU SHALL FILM THESE EVENTS AS YOU REMEMBER THEM!
IT WILL BE A TRIUMPH OF CINEMA VERITE!
I DON'T KNOW WHAT THAT MEANS BUT IT SOUNDS AMAZING!
W-WE'D GET TO WORK WITH THE ANIMALS, TOO, RIGHT?
I WANNA PUT IN EXPLOSIONS! BIG ONES!
MR. HORSEHOOVES, I THINK I SPEAK FOR US ALL—
WE HAPPILY ACCEPT!
WONDERFUL!
I'LL LET THE PRODUCERS KNOW!
YOU FIVE ARE NOW IN CHARGE!
WELL, GIRLS—LOOKS LIKE WE'VE GOT A NEW JOB!
YIPPEE!
ALL RIGHT!
EH, I DIDN'T HAVE ANY PLANS FOR THE NEXT FEW MONTHS, ANYWAY.

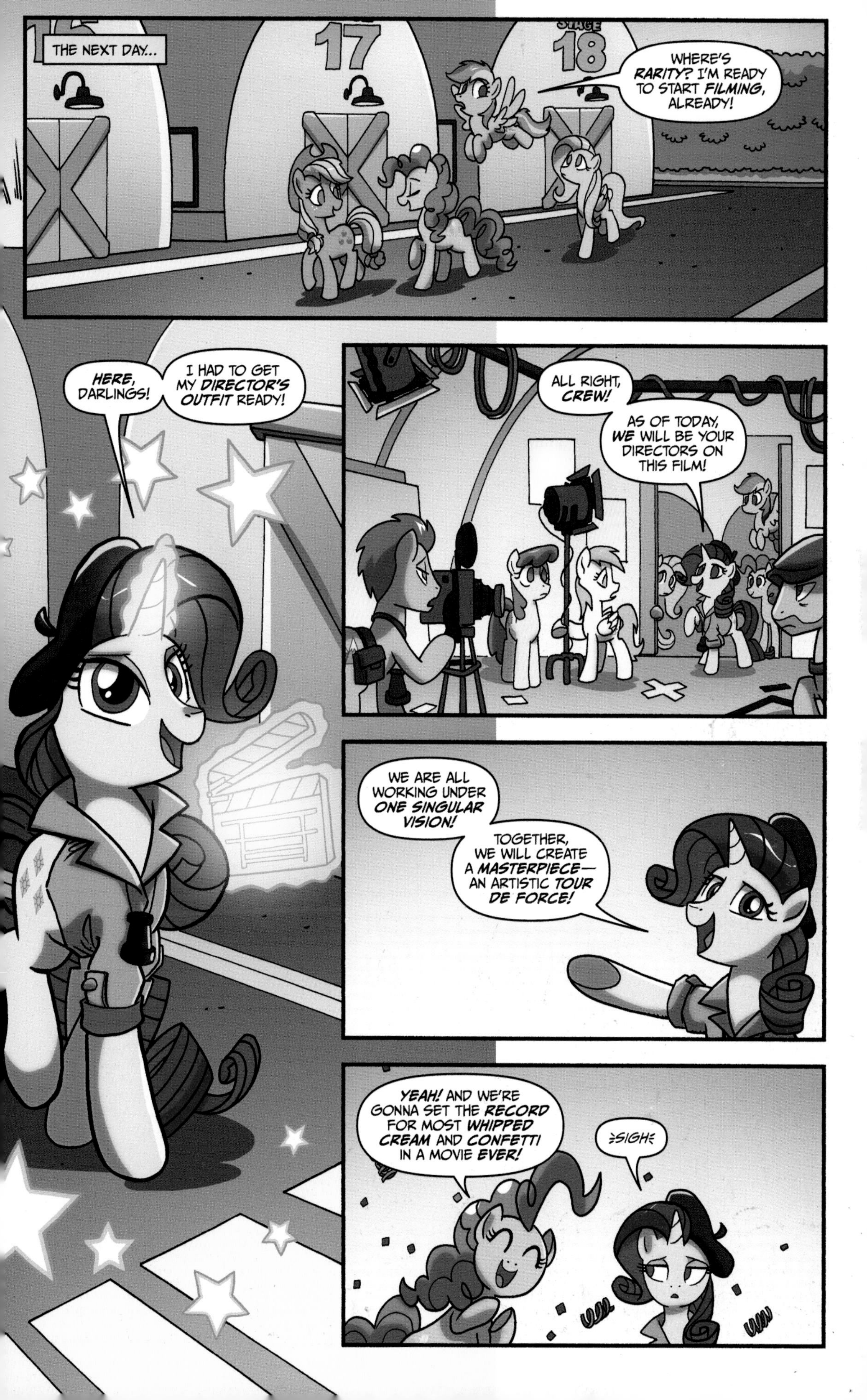
17
STAGE 18
THE NEXT DAY...
WHERE'S RARITY? I'M READY TO START FILMING, ALREADY!
HERE, DARLINGS!
I HAD TO GET MY DIRECTOR'S OUTFIT READY!
ALL RIGHT, CREW!
AS OF TODAY, WE WILL BE YOUR DIRECTORS ON THIS FILM!
WE ARE ALL WORKING UNDER ONE SINGULAR VISION!
TOGETHER, WE WILL CREATE A MASTERPIECE— AN ARTISTIC TOUR DE FORCE!
YEAH! AND WE'RE GONNA SET THE RECORD FOR MOST WHIPPED CREAM AND CONFETTI IN A MOVIE EVER!
SIGH

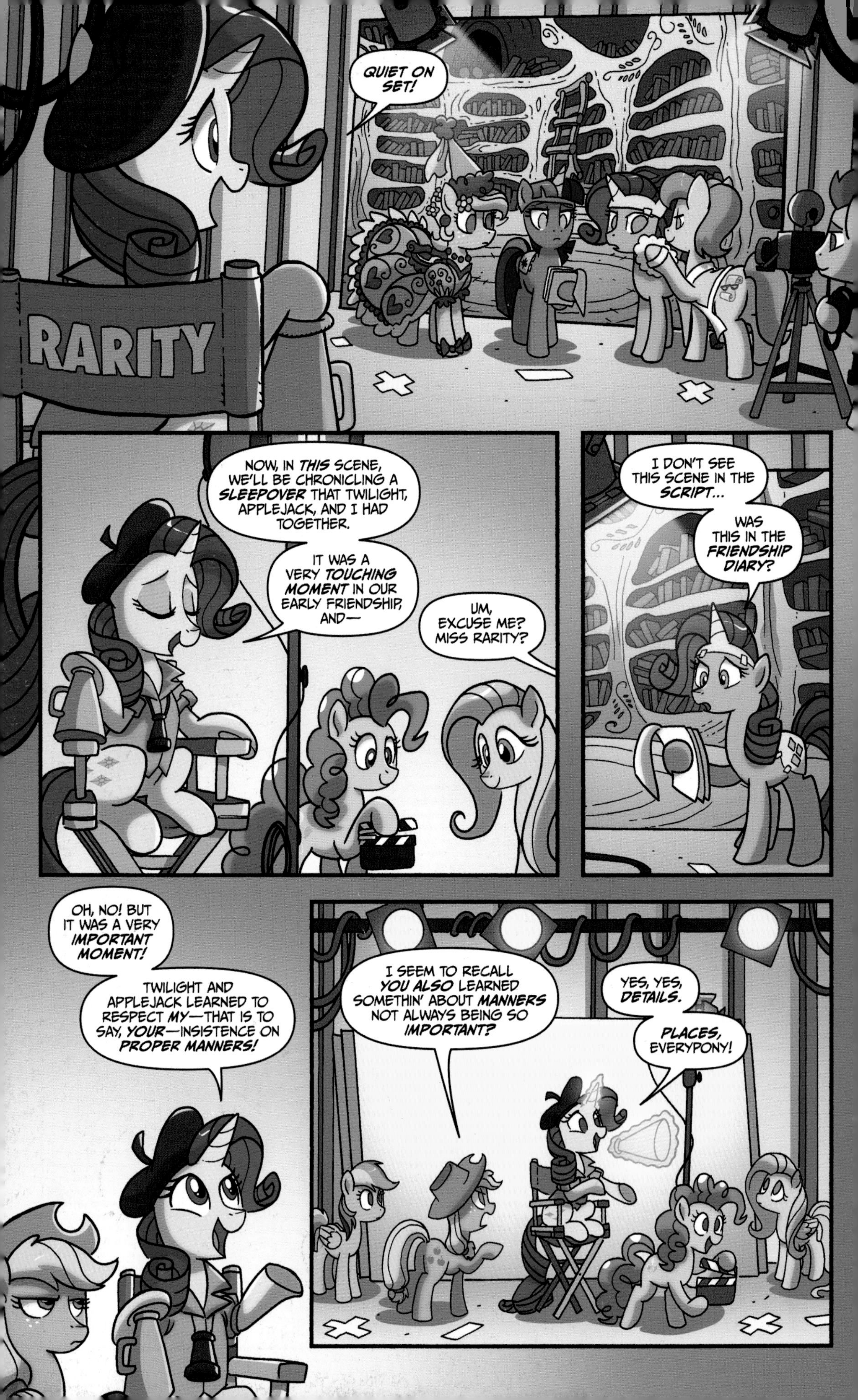
QUIET ON SET!
RARITY
NOW, IN THIS SCENE, WE'LL BE CHRONICLING A SLEEPOVER THAT TWILIGHT, APPLEJACK, AND I HAD TOGETHER.
IT WAS A VERY TOUCHING MOMENT IN OUR EARLY FRIENDSHIP, AND—
UM, EXCUSE ME? MISS RARITY?
I DON'T SEE THIS SCENE IN THE SCRIPT...
WAS THIS IN THE FRIENDSHIP DIARY?
OH, NO! BUT IT WAS A VERY IMPORTANT MOMENT!
TWILIGHT AND APPLEJACK LEARNED TO RESPECT MY—THAT IS TO SAY, YOUR—INSISTENCE ON PROPER MANNERS!
I SEEM TO RECALL YOU ALSO LEARNED SOMETHIN' ABOUT MANNERS NOT ALWAYS BEING SO IMPORTANT?
YES, YES, DETAILS.
PLACES, EVERYPONY!

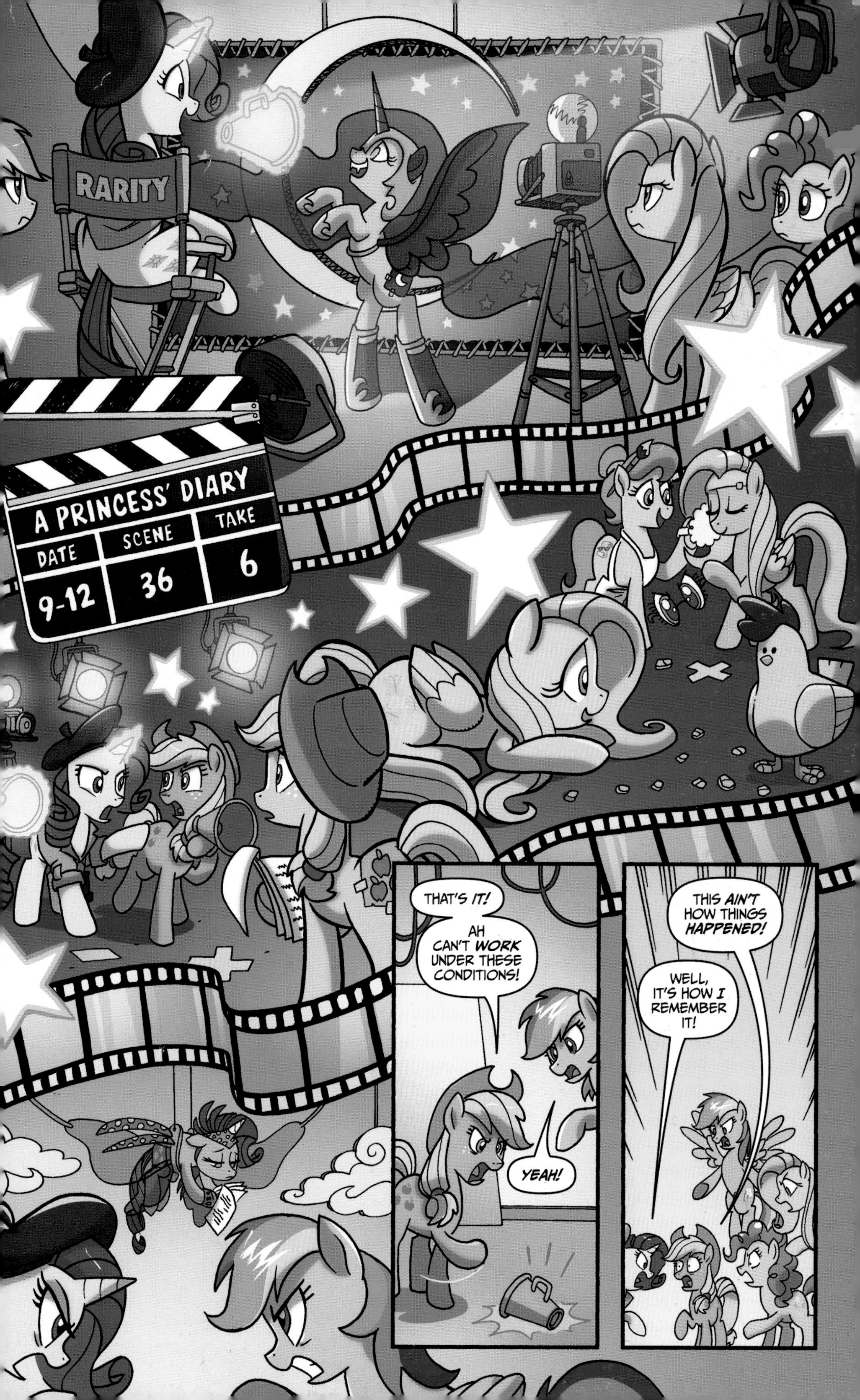
RARITY
A PRINCESS' DIARY
SCENE
TAKE
DATE
9-12
36
6
THAT'S IT!
AH CAN'T WORK UNDER THESE CONDITIONS!
YEAH!
THIS AIN'T HOW THINGS HAPPENED!
WELL, IT'S HOW I REMEMBER IT!

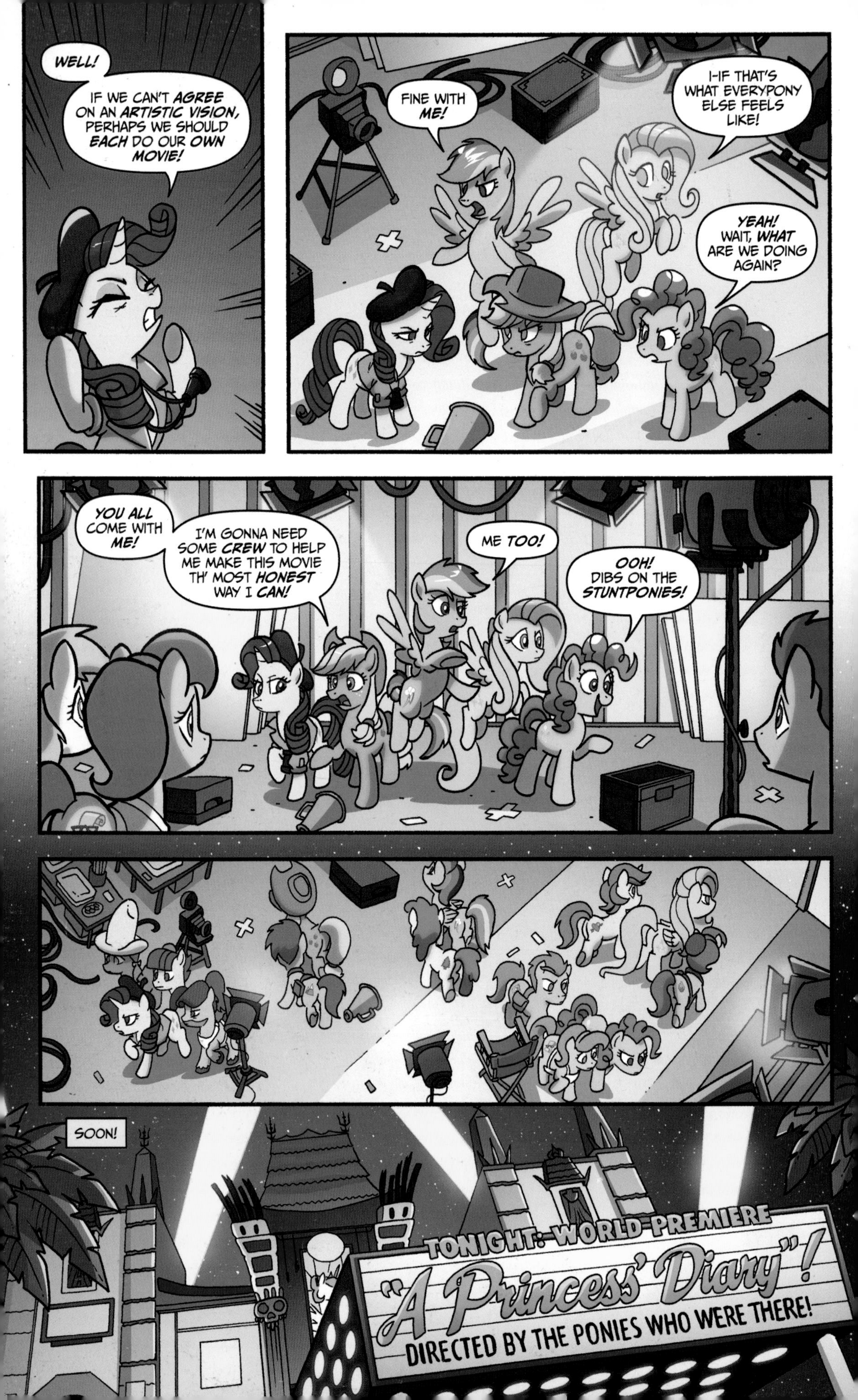

WELL!
IF WE CAN'T AGREE ON AN ARTISTIC VISION, PERHAPS WE SHOULD EACH DO OUR OWN MOVIE!
FINE WITH ME!
I-IF THAT'S WHAT EVERYPONY ELSE FEELS LIKE!
YEAH! WAIT, WHAT ARE WE DOING AGAIN?
YOU ALL COME WITH ME!
I'M GONNA NEED SOME CREW TO HELP ME MAKE THIS MOVIE TH' MOST HONEST WAY I CAN!
ME TOO!
OOH! DIBS ON THE STUNTPONIES!
SOON!
TONIGHT: WORLD PREMIERE
"A Princess' Diary"!
DIRECTED BY THE PONIES WHO WERE THERE!

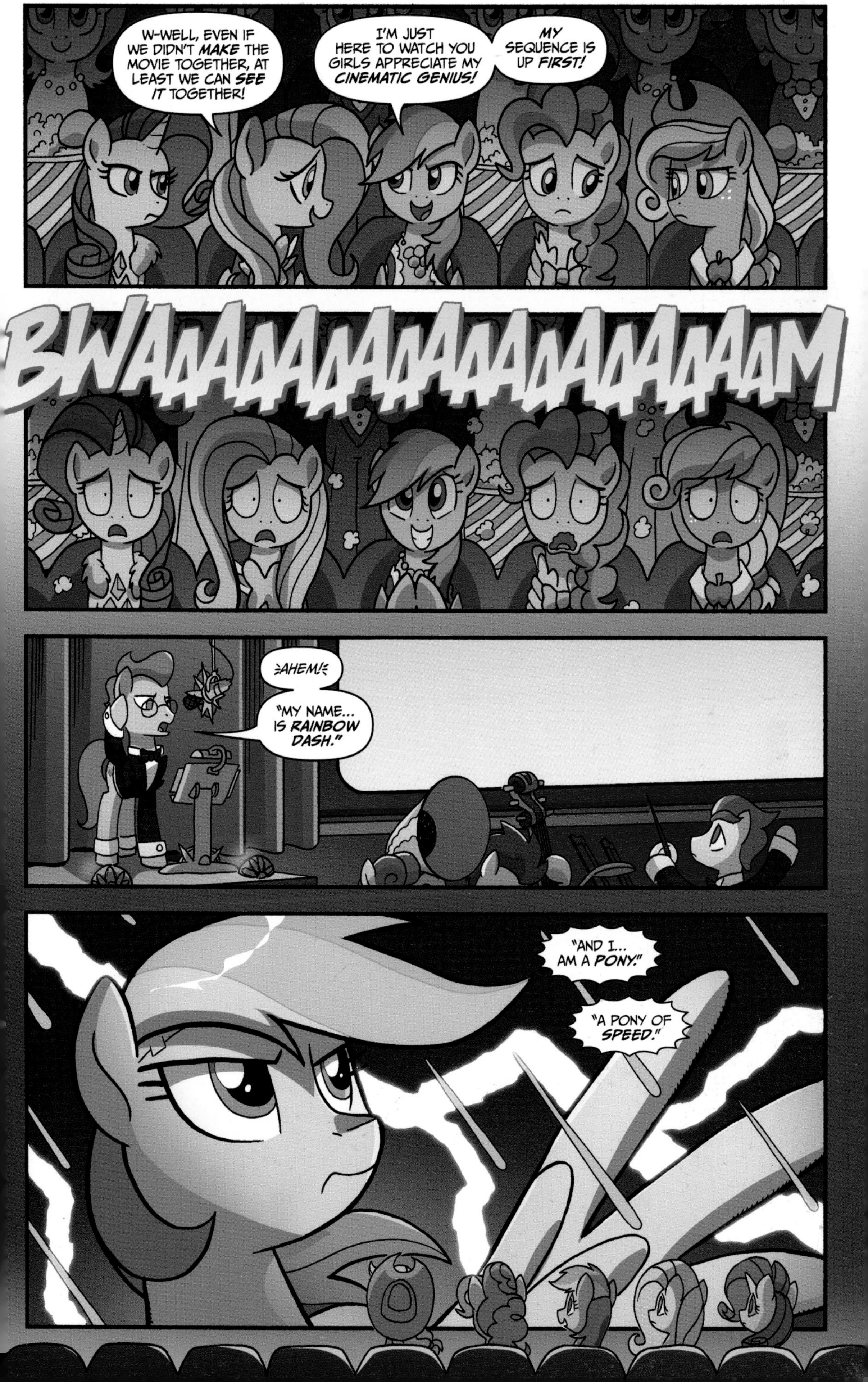
W-WELL, EVEN IF WE DIDN'T MAKE THE MOVIE TOGETHER, AT LEAST WE CAN SEE IT TOGETHER!
I'M JUST HERE TO WATCH YOU GIRLS APPRECIATE MY CINEMATIC GENIUS!
MY SEQUENCE IS UP FIRST!
BWAAAAAAAAAAAAAAAAAAM
AHEM!
"MY NAME... IS RAINBOW DASH."
"AND I... AM A PONY."
"A PONY OF SPEED."

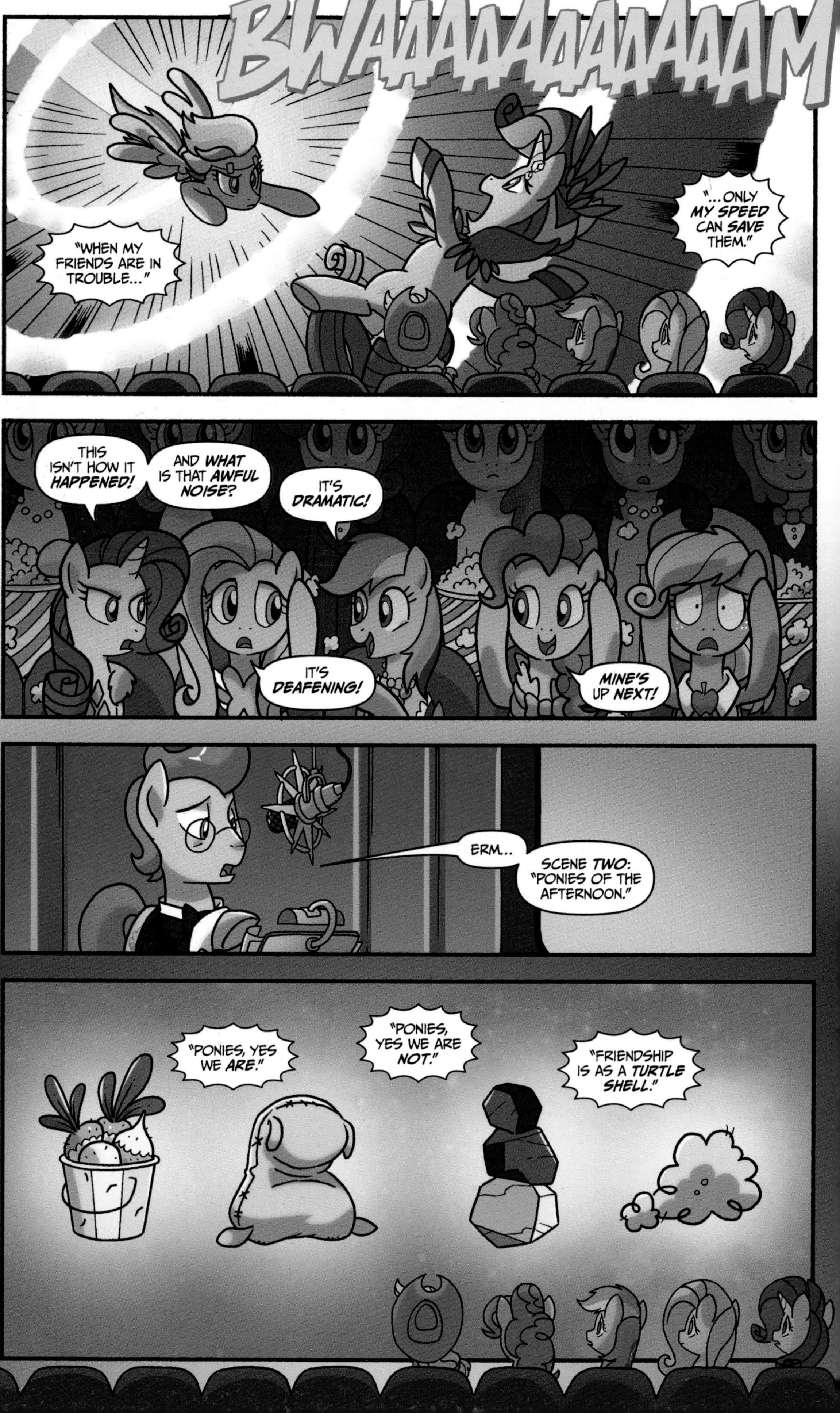
BWAAAAAAAAAAAAM
"WHEN MY FRIENDS ARE IN TROUBLE..."
"...ONLY MY SPEED CAN SAVE THEM."
THIS ISN'T HOW IT HAPPENED!
AND WHAT IS THAT AWFUL NOISE?
IT'S DRAMATIC!
IT'S DEAFENING!
MINE'S UP NEXT!
ERM...
SCENE TWO: "PONIES OF THE AFTERNOON."
"PONIES, YES WE ARE."
"PONIES, YES WE ARE NOT."
"FRIENDSHIP IS AS A TURTLE SHELL."

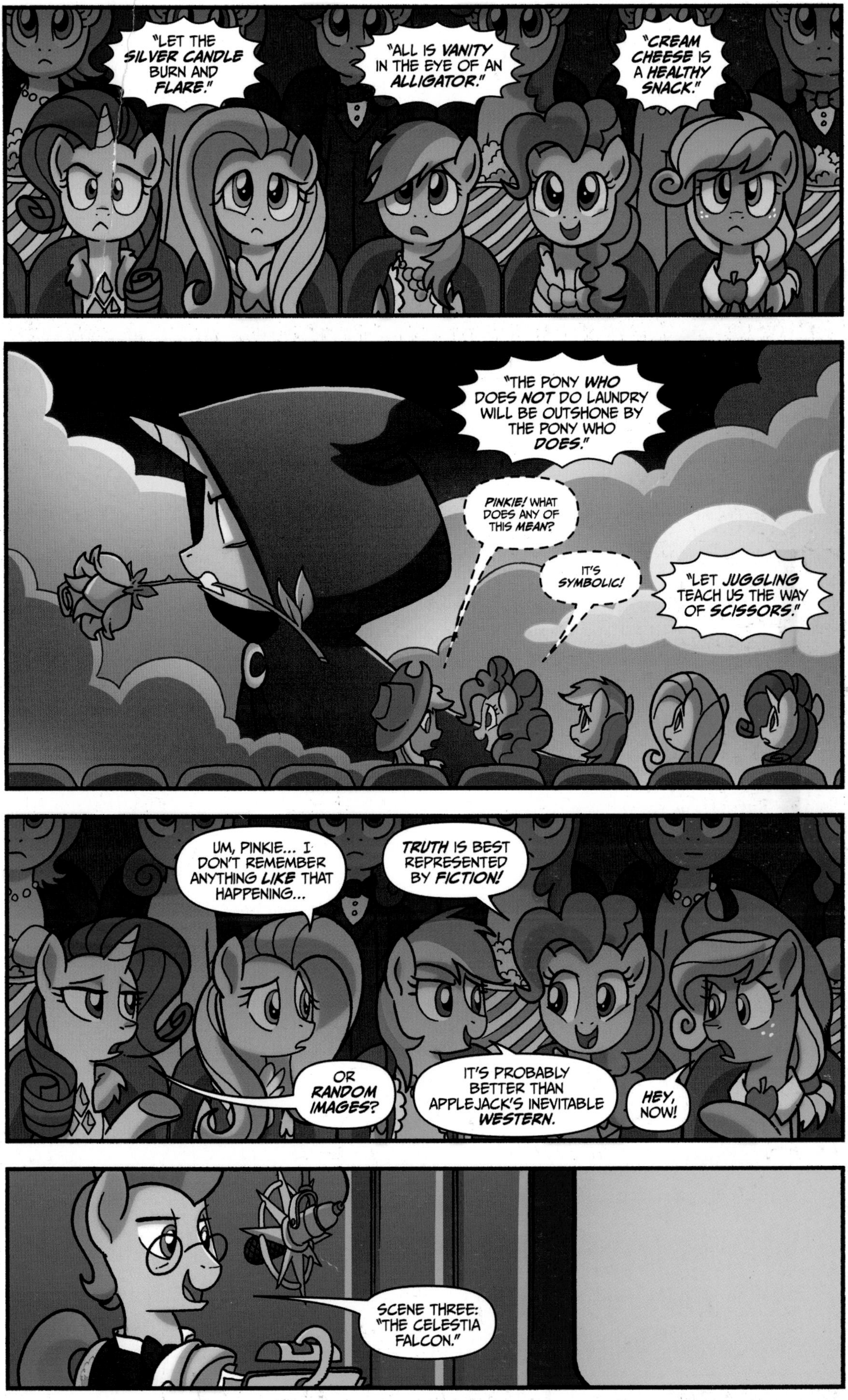
"LET THE SILVER CANDLE BURN AND FLARE."
"ALL IS VANITY IN THE EYE OF AN ALLIGATOR."
"CREAM CHEESE IS A HEALTHY SNACK."
"THE PONY WHO DOES NOT DO LAUNDRY WILL BE OUTSHONE BY THE PONY WHO DOES."
PINKIE! WHAT DOES ANY OF THIS MEAN?
IT'S SYMBOLIC!
"LET JUGGLING TEACH US THE WAY OF SCISSORS."
UM, PINKIE... I DON'T REMEMBER ANYTHING LIKE THAT HAPPENING...
TRUTH IS BEST REPRESENTED BY FICTION!
OR RANDOM IMAGES?
IT'S PROBABLY BETTER THAN APPLEJACK'S INEVITABLE WESTERN.
HEY, NOW!
SCENE THREE: "THE CELESTIA FALCON."

"THE PRINCESS' *BIRD* HAD GONE MISSING, AND EVERY *GUMSHOE* IN *PONYVILLE* WAS POUNDING THE PAVEMENT FOR IT."

"BUT I HAD A *HUNCH*."

"THE DAME WAS TRYING TO PULL ONE OVER ON ME—"

"—BUT I KNEW IT WAS JUST AN *ACT*."

"*NOPONY* WAS *THAT* INNOCENT."

H-HEY!

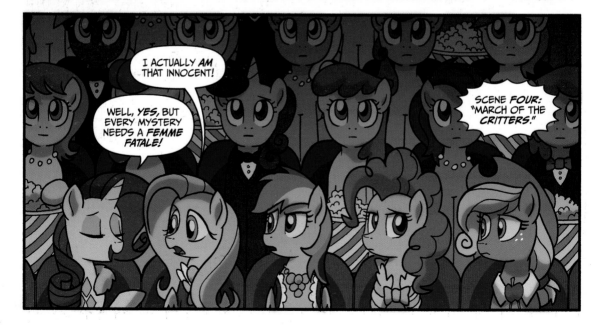

I ACTUALLY *AM* THAT INNOCENT!

WELL, *YES*, BUT EVERY MYSTERY NEEDS A *FEMME FATALE*!

SCENE *FOUR*: "MARCH OF THE *CRITTERS*."

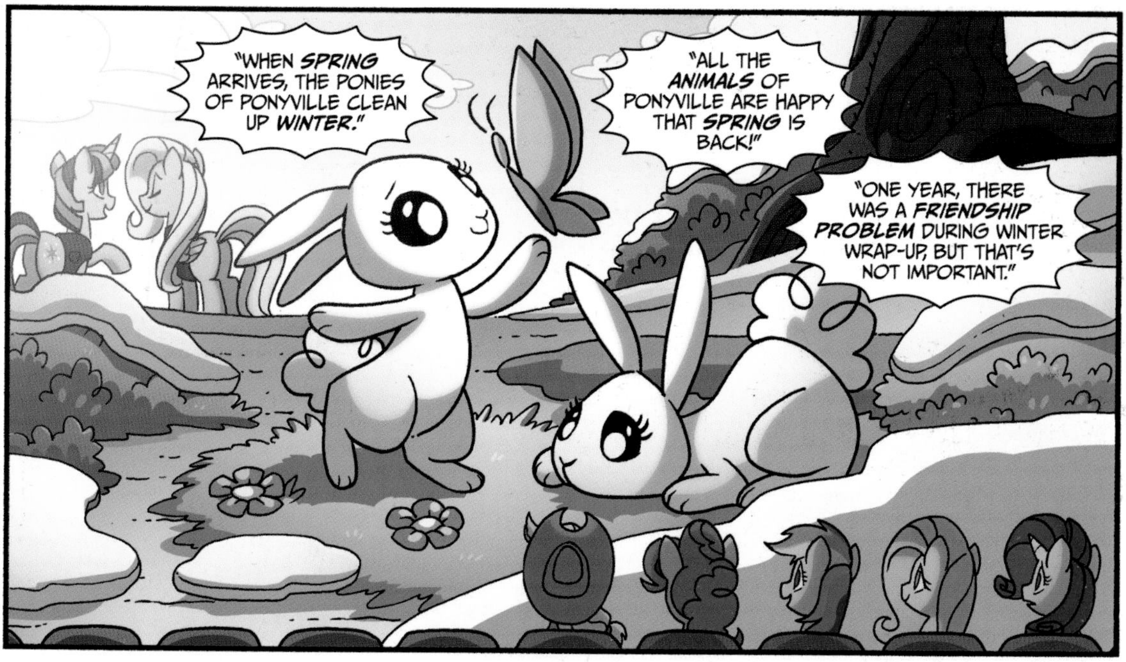
"WHEN SPRING ARRIVES, THE PONIES OF PONYVILLE CLEAN UP WINTER."
"ALL THE ANIMALS OF PONYVILLE ARE HAPPY THAT SPRING IS BACK!"
"ONE YEAR, THERE WAS A FRIENDSHIP PROBLEM DURING WINTER WRAP-UP, BUT THAT'S NOT IMPORTANT."

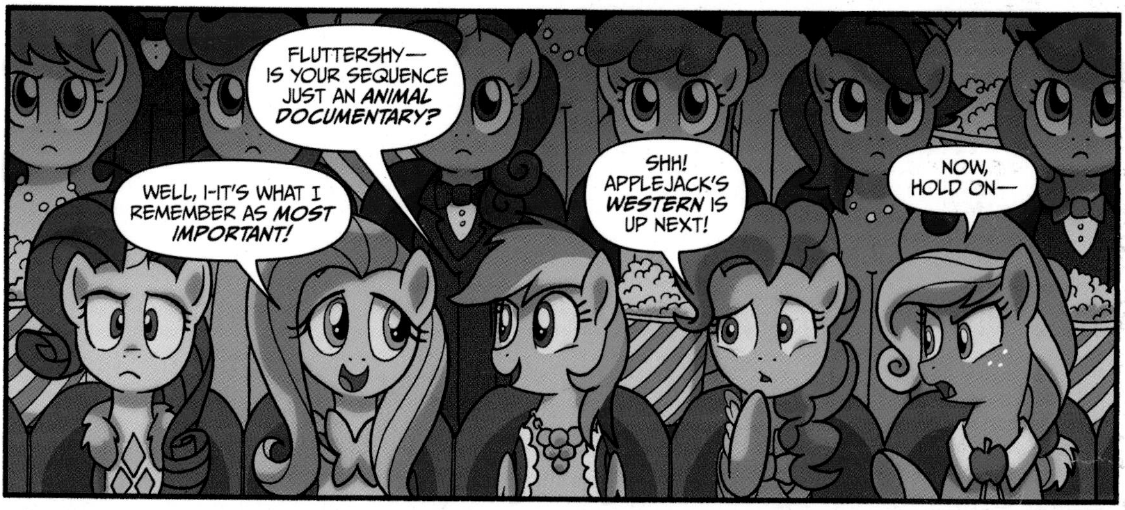
FLUTTERSHY— IS YOUR SEQUENCE JUST AN ANIMAL DOCUMENTARY?
WELL, I-IT'S WHAT I REMEMBER AS MOST IMPORTANT!
SHH! APPLEJACK'S WESTERN IS UP NEXT!
NOW, HOLD ON—

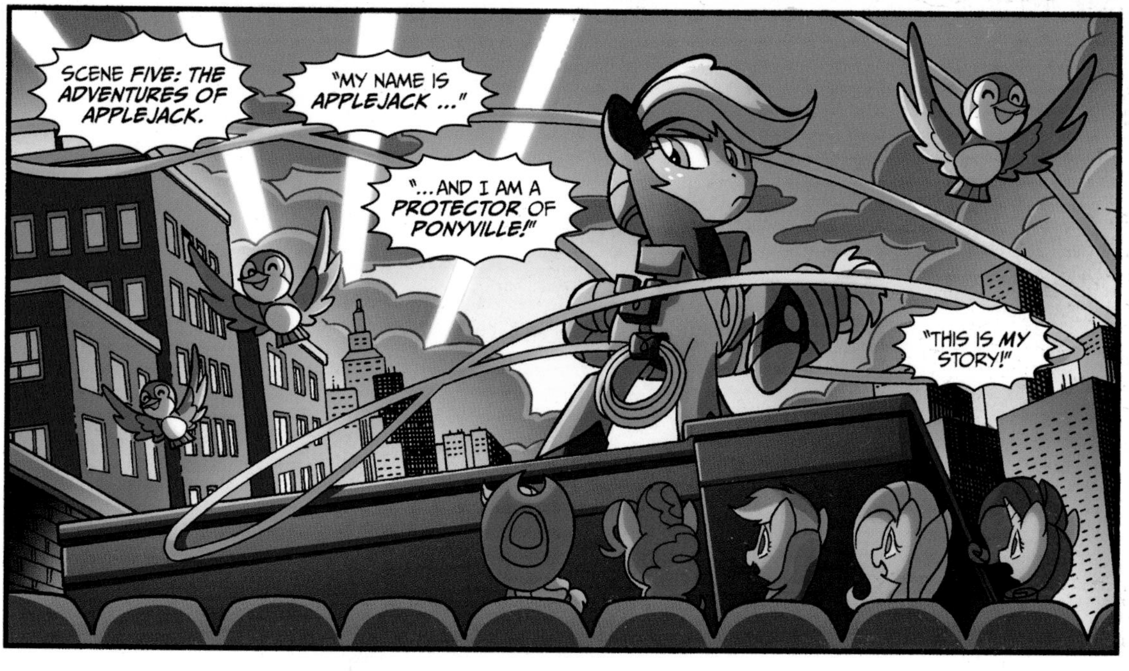
SCENE FIVE: THE ADVENTURES OF APPLEJACK.
"MY NAME IS APPLEJACK ..."
"...AND I AM A PROTECTOR OF PONYVILLE!"
"THIS IS MY STORY!"

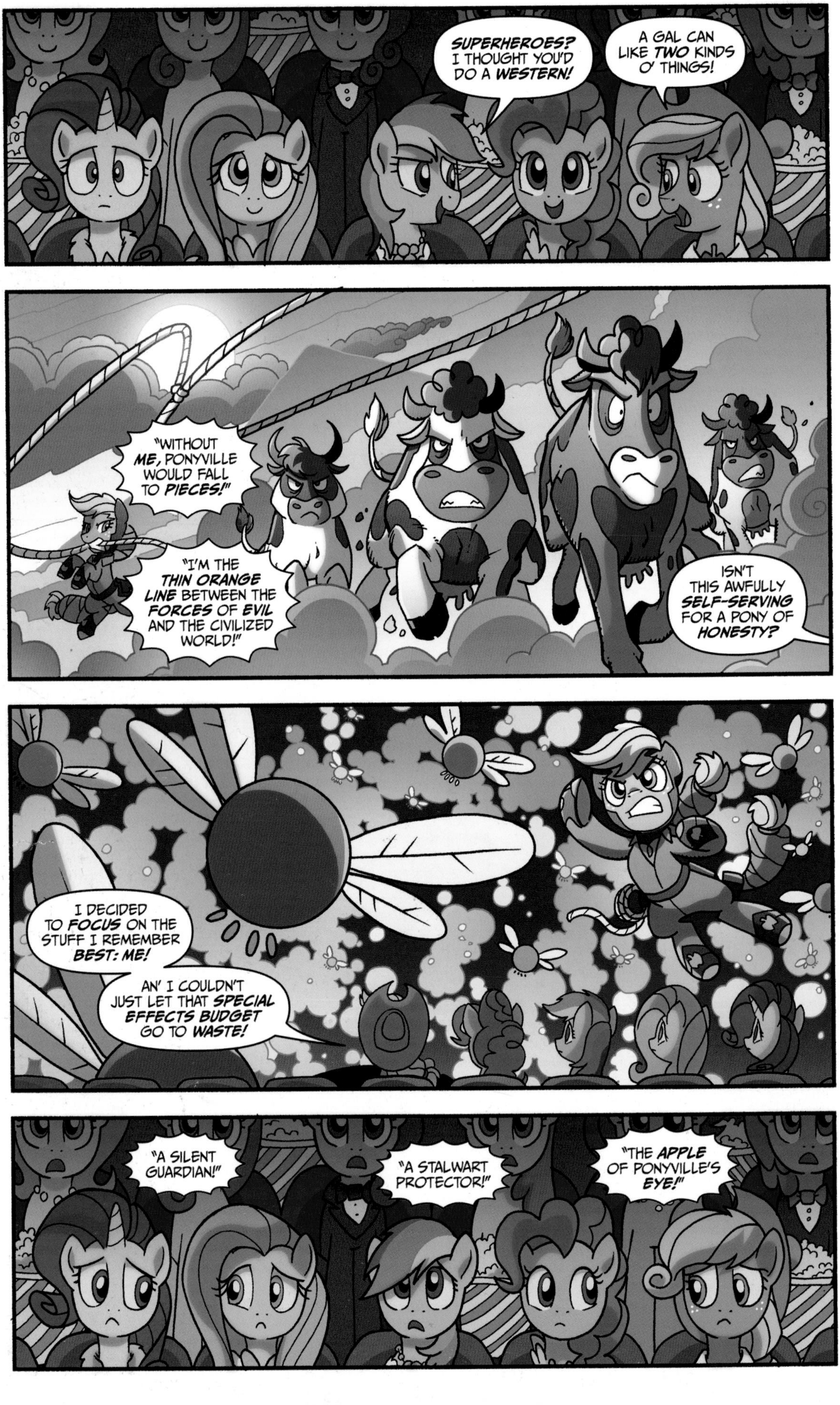
SUPERHEROES? I THOUGHT YOU'D DO A WESTERN!
A GAL CAN LIKE TWO KINDS O' THINGS!
"WITHOUT ME, PONYVILLE WOULD FALL TO PIECES!"
"I'M THE THIN ORANGE LINE BETWEEN THE FORCES OF EVIL AND THE CIVILIZED WORLD!"
ISN'T THIS AWFULLY SELF-SERVING FOR A PONY OF HONESTY?
I DECIDED TO FOCUS ON THE STUFF I REMEMBER BEST: ME!
AN' I COULDN'T JUST LET THAT SPECIAL EFFECTS BUDGET GO TO WASTE!
"A SILENT GUARDIAN!"
"A STALWART PROTECTOR!"
"THE APPLE OF PONYVILLE'S EYE!"

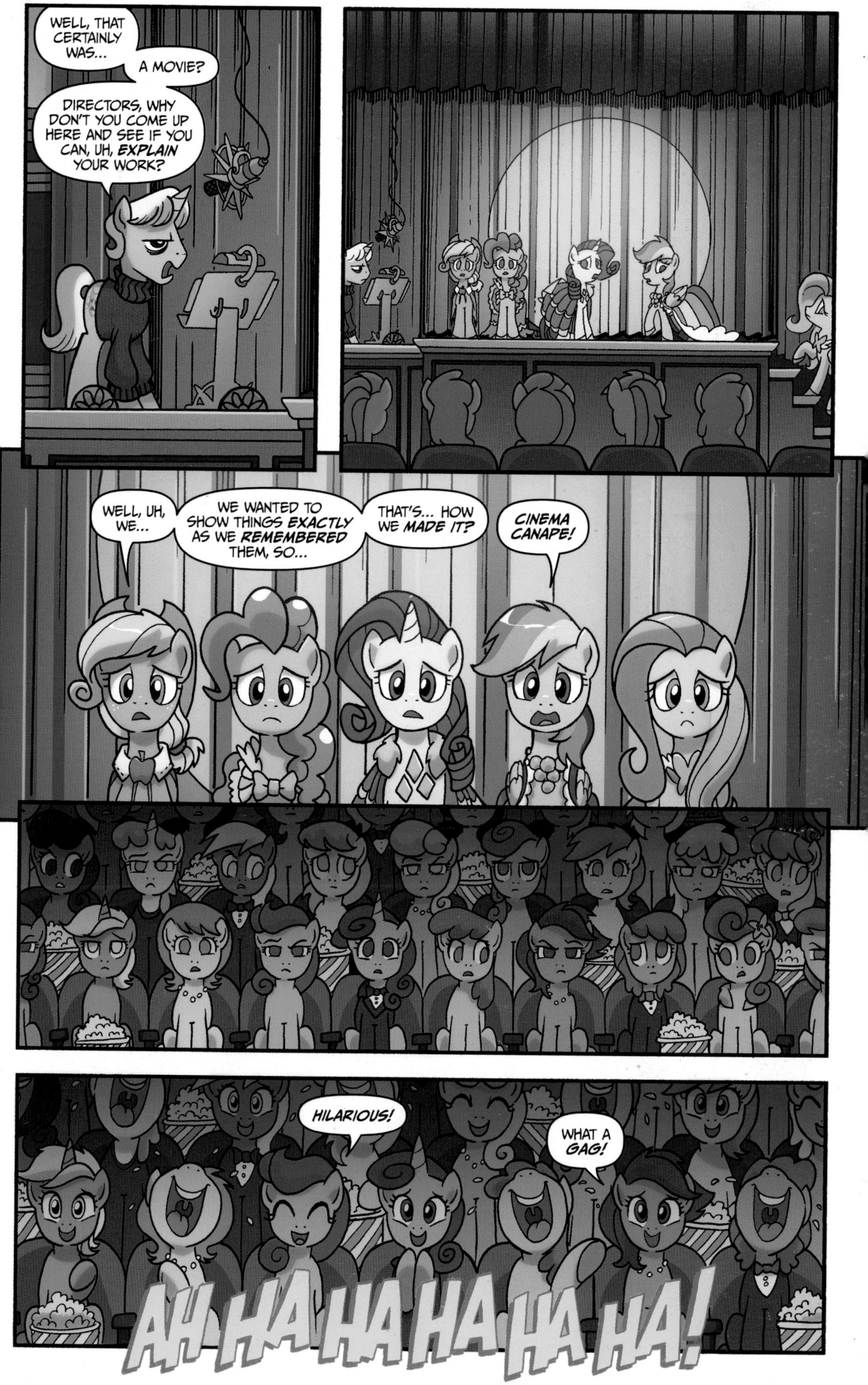
WELL, THAT CERTAINLY WAS...
A MOVIE?
DIRECTORS, WHY DON'T YOU COME UP HERE AND SEE IF YOU CAN, UH, EXPLAIN YOUR WORK?
WELL, UH, WE...
WE WANTED TO SHOW THINGS EXACTLY AS WE REMEMBERED THEM, SO...
THAT'S... HOW WE MADE IT?
CINEMA CANAPE!
HILARIOUS!
WHAT A GAG!
AH HA HA HA HA HA HA!

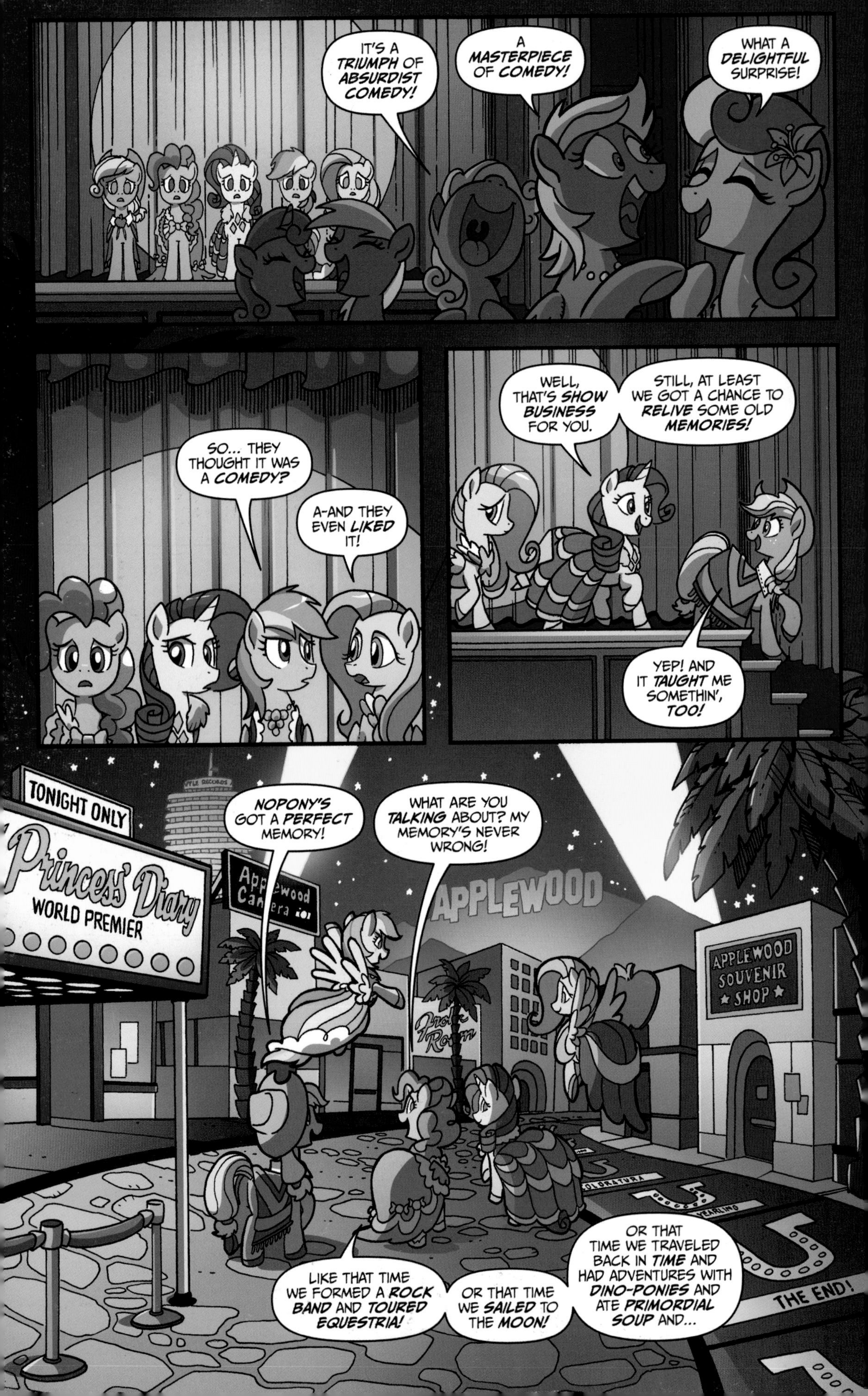
IT'S A TRIUMPH OF ABSURDIST COMEDY!
A MASTERPIECE OF COMEDY!
WHAT A DELIGHTFUL SURPRISE!
SO... THEY THOUGHT IT WAS A COMEDY?
A-AND THEY EVEN LIKED IT!
WELL, THAT'S SHOW BUSINESS FOR YOU.
STILL, AT LEAST WE GOT A CHANCE TO RELIVE SOME OLD MEMORIES!
YEP! AND IT TAUGHT ME SOMETHIN', TOO!
TONIGHT ONLY
Princess' Diary
WORLD PREMIER
APPLEWOOD
APPLEWOOD SOUVENIR ★ SHOP ★
NOPONY'S GOT A PERFECT MEMORY!
WHAT ARE YOU TALKING ABOUT? MY MEMORY'S NEVER WRONG!
LIKE THAT TIME WE FORMED A ROCK BAND AND TOURED EQUESTRIA!
OR THAT TIME WE SAILED TO THE MOON!
OR THAT TIME WE TRAVELED BACK IN TIME AND HAD ADVENTURES WITH DINO-PONIES AND ATE PRIMORDIAL SOUP AND...
COLORATURA
YEARLING
THE END!

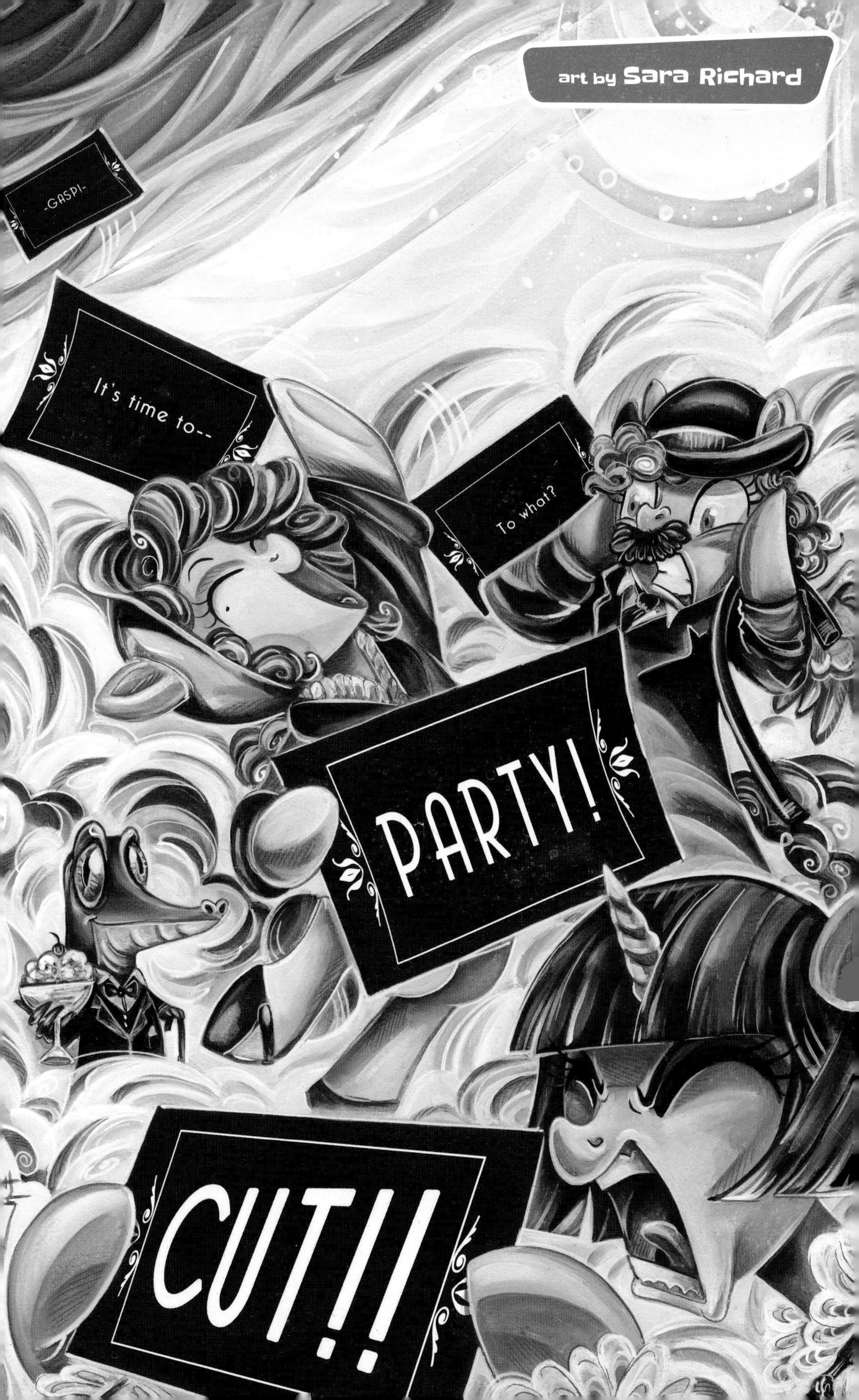
art by Sara Richard
-GASP!-
It's time to--
To what?
PARTY!
CUT!!

art by Andy Price

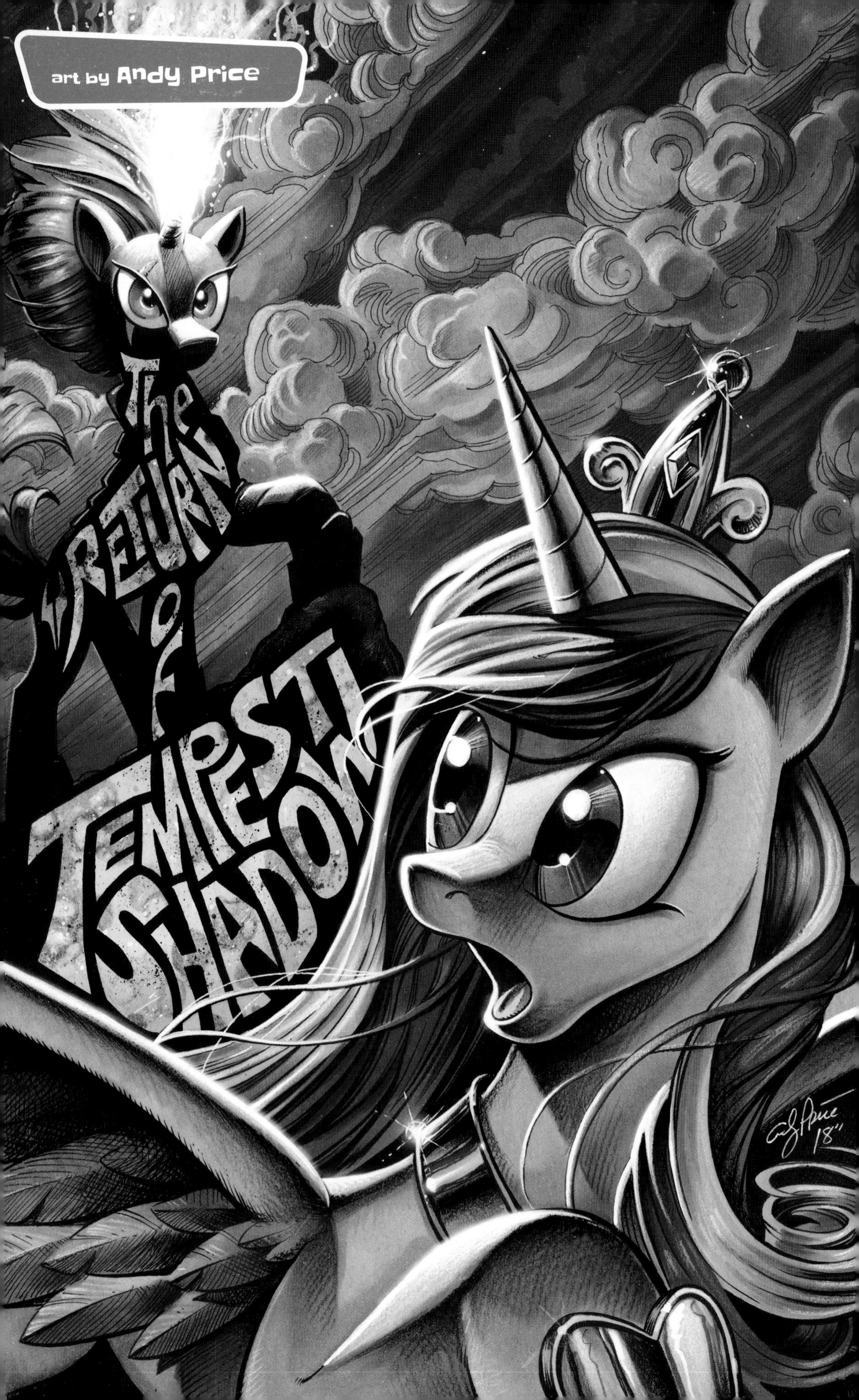
The Return of Tempest Shadow

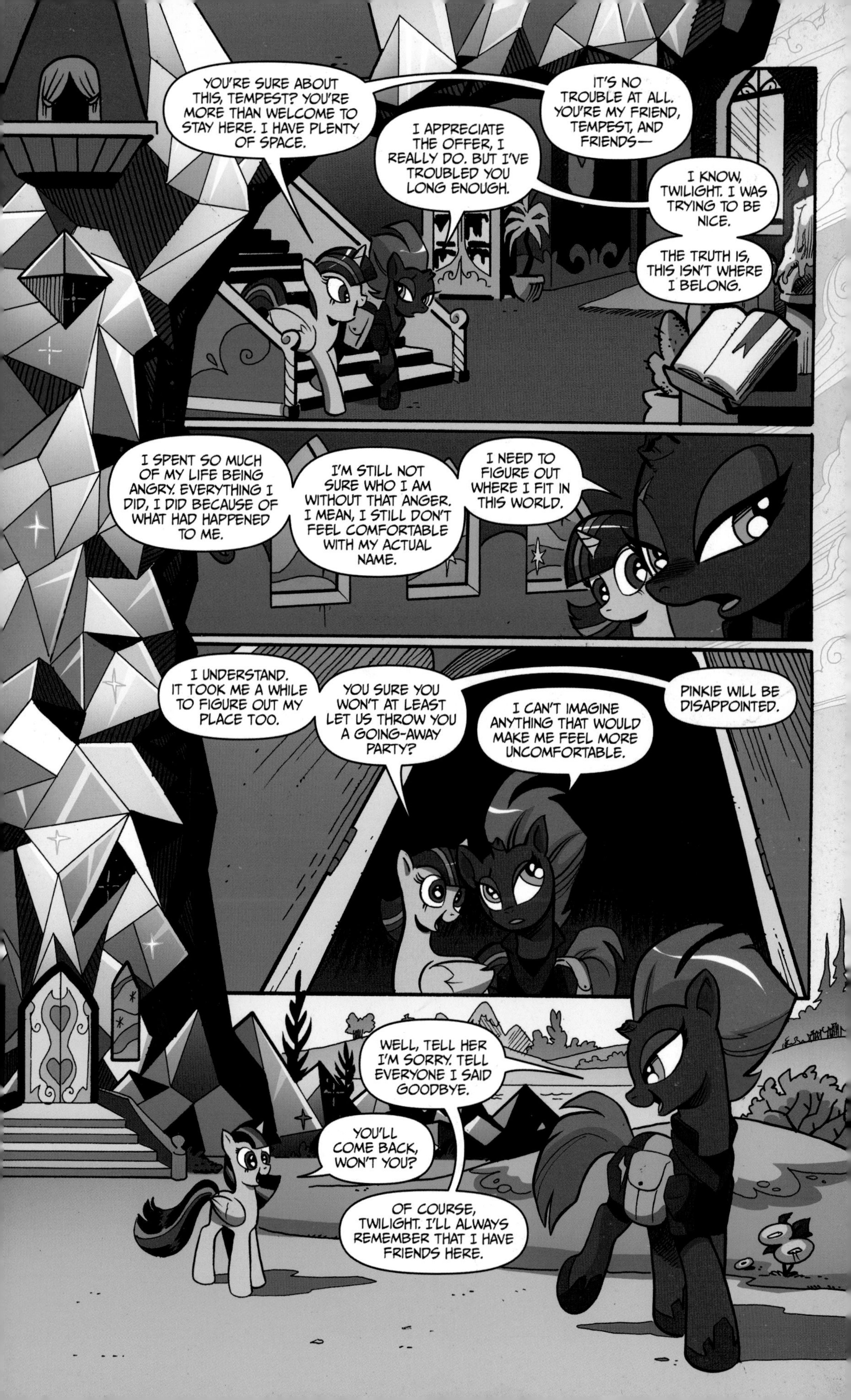
YOU'RE SURE ABOUT THIS, TEMPEST? YOU'RE MORE THAN WELCOME TO STAY HERE. I HAVE PLENTY OF SPACE.
I APPRECIATE THE OFFER, I REALLY DO. BUT I'VE TROUBLED YOU LONG ENOUGH.
IT'S NO TROUBLE AT ALL. YOU'RE MY FRIEND, TEMPEST, AND FRIENDS—
I KNOW, TWILIGHT. I WAS TRYING TO BE NICE.
THE TRUTH IS, THIS ISN'T WHERE I BELONG.
I SPENT SO MUCH OF MY LIFE BEING ANGRY. EVERYTHING I DID, I DID BECAUSE OF WHAT HAD HAPPENED TO ME.
I'M STILL NOT SURE WHO I AM WITHOUT THAT ANGER. I MEAN, I STILL DON'T FEEL COMFORTABLE WITH MY ACTUAL NAME.
I NEED TO FIGURE OUT WHERE I FIT IN THIS WORLD.
I UNDERSTAND. IT TOOK ME A WHILE TO FIGURE OUT MY PLACE TOO.
YOU SURE YOU WON'T AT LEAST LET US THROW YOU A GOING-AWAY PARTY?
I CAN'T IMAGINE ANYTHING THAT WOULD MAKE ME FEEL MORE UNCOMFORTABLE.
PINKIE WILL BE DISAPPOINTED.
WELL, TELL HER I'M SORRY. TELL EVERYONE I SAID GOODBYE.
YOU'LL COME BACK, WON'T YOU?
OF COURSE, TWILIGHT. I'LL ALWAYS REMEMBER THAT I HAVE FRIENDS HERE.

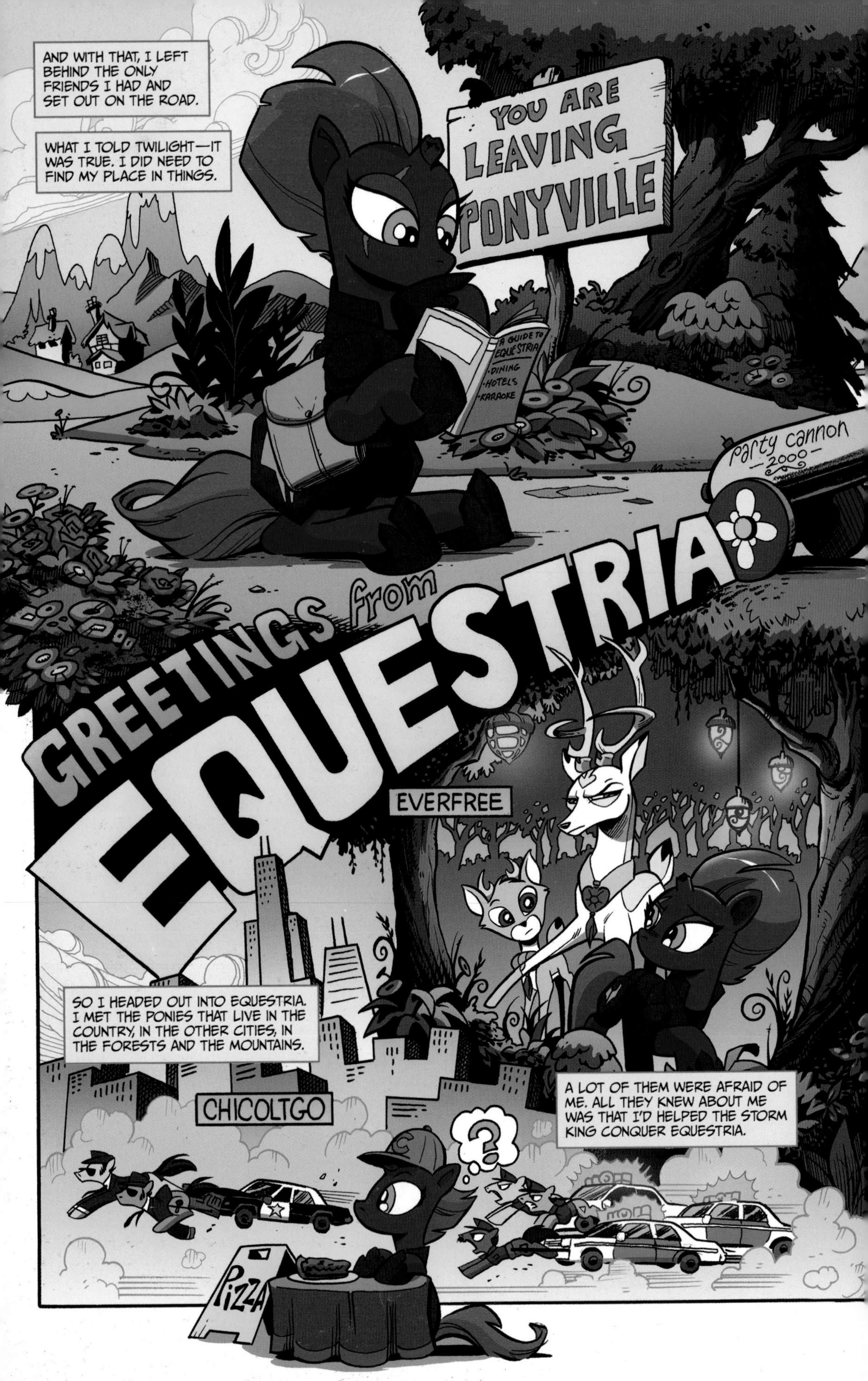

AND WITH THAT, I LEFT BEHIND THE ONLY FRIENDS I HAD AND SET OUT ON THE ROAD.
WHAT I TOLD TWILIGHT—IT WAS TRUE. I DID NEED TO FIND MY PLACE IN THINGS.
YOU ARE LEAVING PONYVILLE
A GUIDE TO EQUESTRIA
•DINING •HOTELS •KARAOKE
Party cannon 2000
GREETINGS from EQUESTRIA
EVERFREE
SO I HEADED OUT INTO EQUESTRIA. I MET THE PONIES THAT LIVE IN THE COUNTRY, IN THE OTHER CITIES, IN THE FORESTS AND THE MOUNTAINS.
CHICOLTGO
A LOT OF THEM WERE AFRAID OF ME. ALL THEY KNEW ABOUT ME WAS THAT I'D HELPED THE STORM KING CONQUER EQUESTRIA.
?
PIZZA

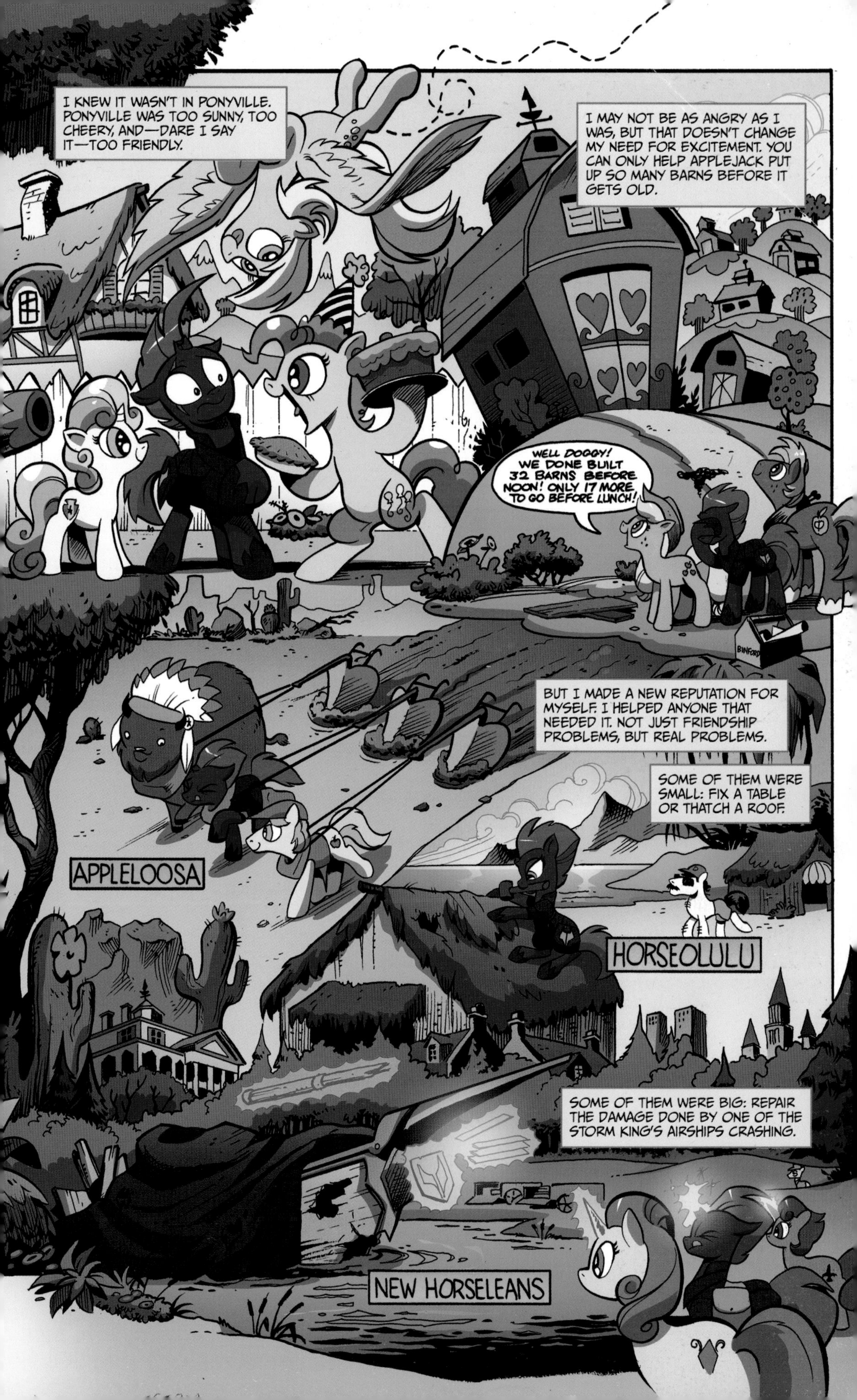
I KNEW IT WASN'T IN PONYVILLE. PONYVILLE WAS TOO SUNNY, TOO CHEERY, AND—DARE I SAY IT—TOO FRIENDLY.
I MAY NOT BE AS ANGRY AS I WAS, BUT THAT DOESN'T CHANGE MY NEED FOR EXCITEMENT. YOU CAN ONLY HELP APPLEJACK PUT UP SO MANY BARNS BEFORE IT GETS OLD.
WELL DOGGY! WE DONE BUILT 32 BARNS BEFORE NOON! ONLY 17 MORE TO GO BEFORE LUNCH!
BINFORD
BUT I MADE A NEW REPUTATION FOR MYSELF. I HELPED ANYONE THAT NEEDED IT. NOT JUST FRIENDSHIP PROBLEMS, BUT REAL PROBLEMS.
SOME OF THEM WERE SMALL: FIX A TABLE OR THATCH A ROOF.
APPLELOOSA
HORSEOLULU
SOME OF THEM WERE BIG: REPAIR THE DAMAGE DONE BY ONE OF THE STORM KING'S AIRSHIPS CRASHING.
NEW HORSELEANS

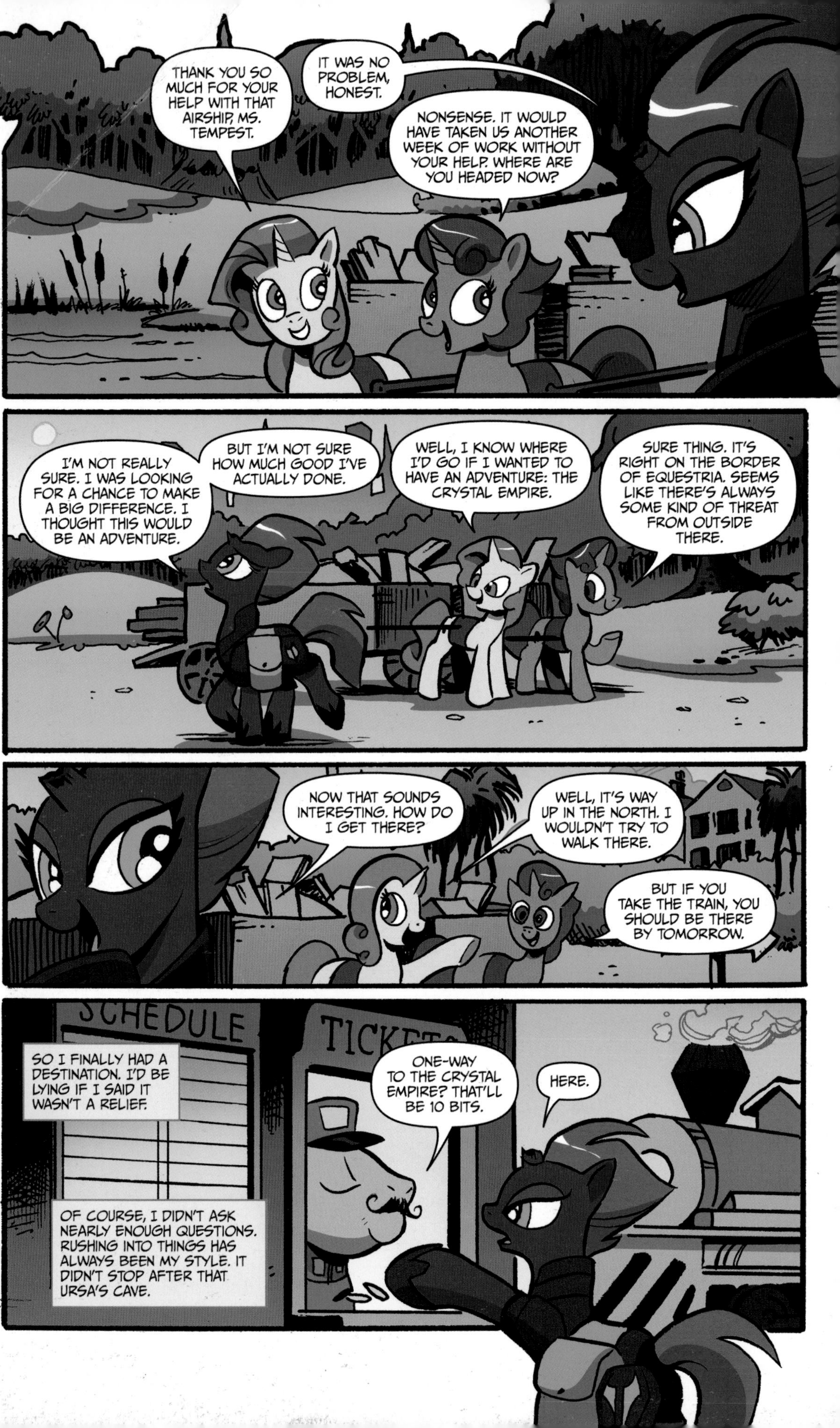
THANK YOU SO MUCH FOR YOUR HELP WITH THAT AIRSHIP, MS. TEMPEST.
IT WAS NO PROBLEM, HONEST.
NONSENSE. IT WOULD HAVE TAKEN US ANOTHER WEEK OF WORK WITHOUT YOUR HELP. WHERE ARE YOU HEADED NOW?
I'M NOT REALLY SURE. I WAS LOOKING FOR A CHANCE TO MAKE A BIG DIFFERENCE. I THOUGHT THIS WOULD BE AN ADVENTURE.
BUT I'M NOT SURE HOW MUCH GOOD I'VE ACTUALLY DONE.
WELL, I KNOW WHERE I'D GO IF I WANTED TO HAVE AN ADVENTURE: THE CRYSTAL EMPIRE.
SURE THING. IT'S RIGHT ON THE BORDER OF EQUESTRIA. SEEMS LIKE THERE'S ALWAYS SOME KIND OF THREAT FROM OUTSIDE THERE.
NOW THAT SOUNDS INTERESTING. HOW DO I GET THERE?
WELL, IT'S WAY UP IN THE NORTH. I WOULDN'T TRY TO WALK THERE.
BUT IF YOU TAKE THE TRAIN, YOU SHOULD BE THERE BY TOMORROW.
SCHEDULE
TICKETS
SO I FINALLY HAD A DESTINATION. I'D BE LYING IF I SAID IT WASN'T A RELIEF.
ONE-WAY TO THE CRYSTAL EMPIRE? THAT'LL BE 10 BITS.
HERE.
OF COURSE, I DIDN'T ASK NEARLY ENOUGH QUESTIONS. RUSHING INTO THINGS HAS ALWAYS BEEN MY STYLE. IT DIDN'T STOP AFTER THAT URSA'S CAVE.

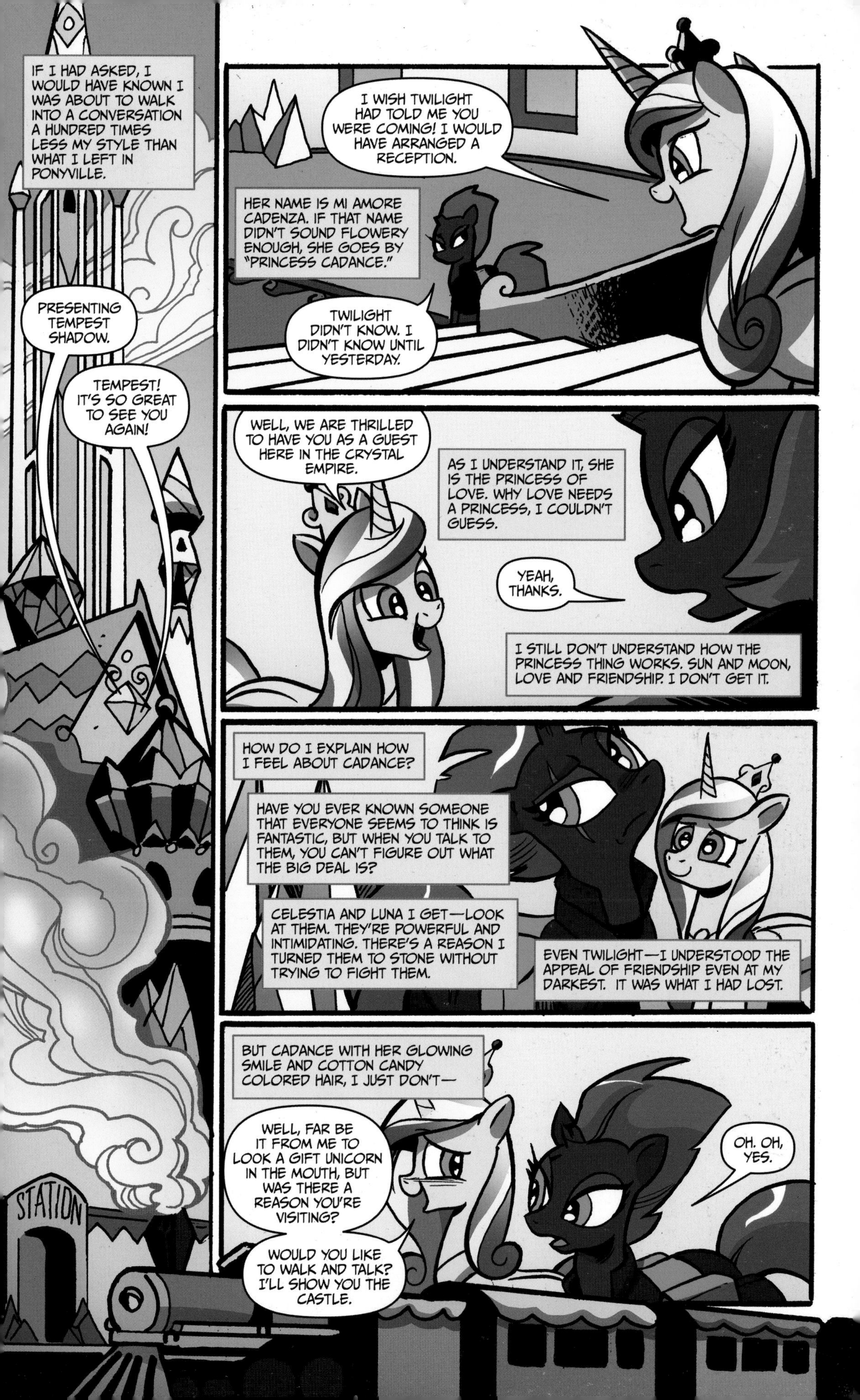

IF I HAD ASKED, I WOULD HAVE KNOWN I WAS ABOUT TO WALK INTO A CONVERSATION A HUNDRED TIMES LESS MY STYLE THAN WHAT I LEFT IN PONYVILLE.
PRESENTING TEMPEST SHADOW.
TEMPEST! IT'S SO GREAT TO SEE YOU AGAIN!
STATION
I WISH TWILIGHT HAD TOLD ME YOU WERE COMING! I WOULD HAVE ARRANGED A RECEPTION.
HER NAME IS MI AMORE CADENZA. IF THAT NAME DIDN'T SOUND FLOWERY ENOUGH, SHE GOES BY "PRINCESS CADANCE."
TWILIGHT DIDN'T KNOW. I DIDN'T KNOW UNTIL YESTERDAY.
WELL, WE ARE THRILLED TO HAVE YOU AS A GUEST HERE IN THE CRYSTAL EMPIRE.
AS I UNDERSTAND IT, SHE IS THE PRINCESS OF LOVE. WHY LOVE NEEDS A PRINCESS, I COULDN'T GUESS.
YEAH, THANKS.
I STILL DON'T UNDERSTAND HOW THE PRINCESS THING WORKS. SUN AND MOON, LOVE AND FRIENDSHIP. I DON'T GET IT.
HOW DO I EXPLAIN HOW I FEEL ABOUT CADANCE?
HAVE YOU EVER KNOWN SOMEONE THAT EVERYONE SEEMS TO THINK IS FANTASTIC, BUT WHEN YOU TALK TO THEM, YOU CAN'T FIGURE OUT WHAT THE BIG DEAL IS?
CELESTIA AND LUNA I GET—LOOK AT THEM. THEY'RE POWERFUL AND INTIMIDATING. THERE'S A REASON I TURNED THEM TO STONE WITHOUT TRYING TO FIGHT THEM.
EVEN TWILIGHT—I UNDERSTOOD THE APPEAL OF FRIENDSHIP EVEN AT MY DARKEST. IT WAS WHAT I HAD LOST.
BUT CADANCE WITH HER GLOWING SMILE AND COTTON CANDY COLORED HAIR, I JUST DON'T—
WELL, FAR BE IT FROM ME TO LOOK A GIFT UNICORN IN THE MOUTH, BUT WAS THERE A REASON YOU'RE VISITING?
OH. OH, YES.
WOULD YOU LIKE TO WALK AND TALK? I'LL SHOW YOU THE CASTLE.

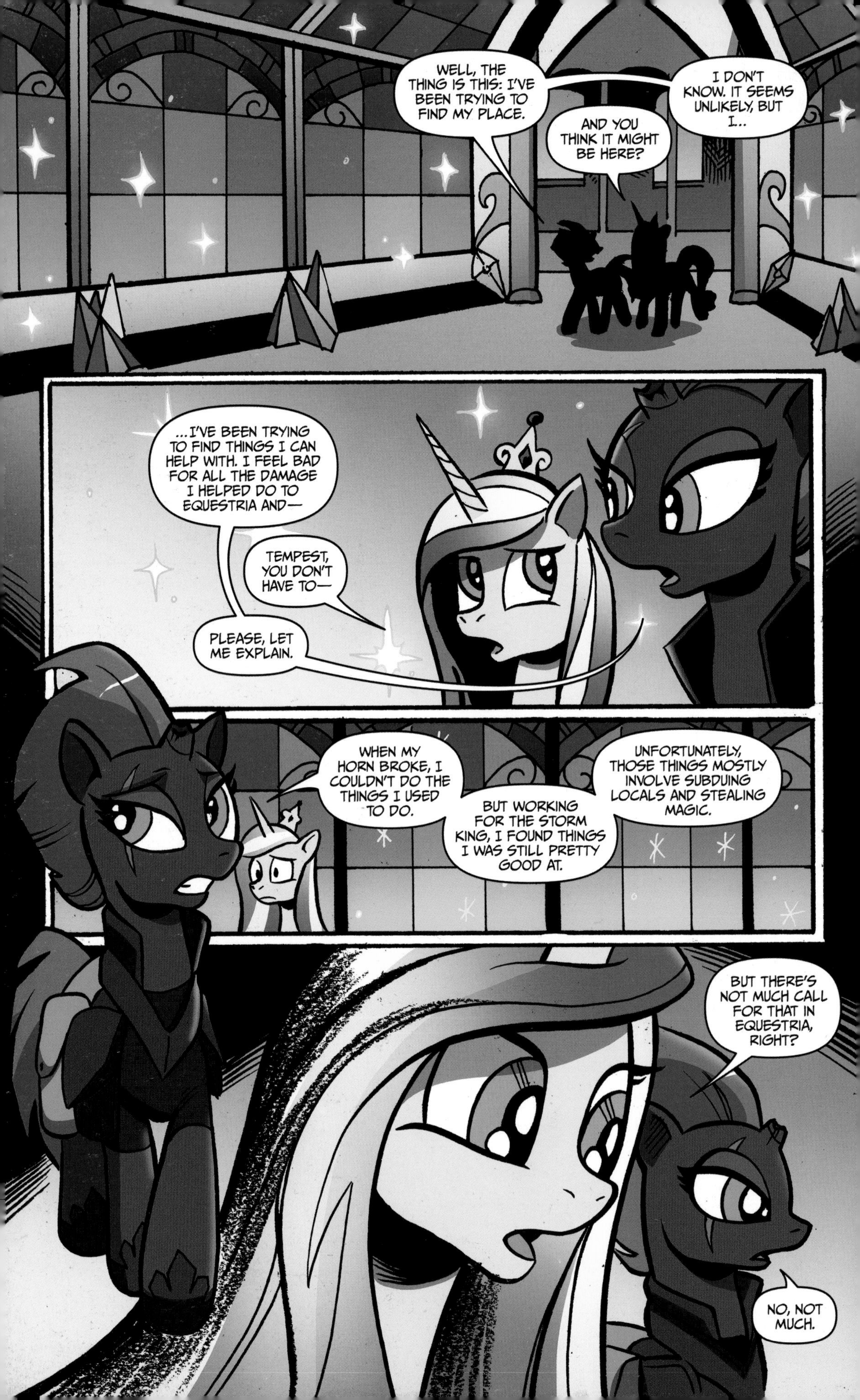
WELL, THE THING IS THIS: I'VE BEEN TRYING TO FIND MY PLACE.
AND YOU THINK IT MIGHT BE HERE?
I DON'T KNOW. IT SEEMS UNLIKELY, BUT I...
...I'VE BEEN TRYING TO FIND THINGS I CAN HELP WITH. I FEEL BAD FOR ALL THE DAMAGE I HELPED DO TO EQUESTRIA AND—
TEMPEST, YOU DON'T HAVE TO—
PLEASE, LET ME EXPLAIN.
WHEN MY HORN BROKE, I COULDN'T DO THE THINGS I USED TO DO.
BUT WORKING FOR THE STORM KING, I FOUND THINGS I WAS STILL PRETTY GOOD AT.
UNFORTUNATELY, THOSE THINGS MOSTLY INVOLVE SUBDUING LOCALS AND STEALING MAGIC.
BUT THERE'S NOT MUCH CALL FOR THAT IN EQUESTRIA, RIGHT?
NO, NOT MUCH.

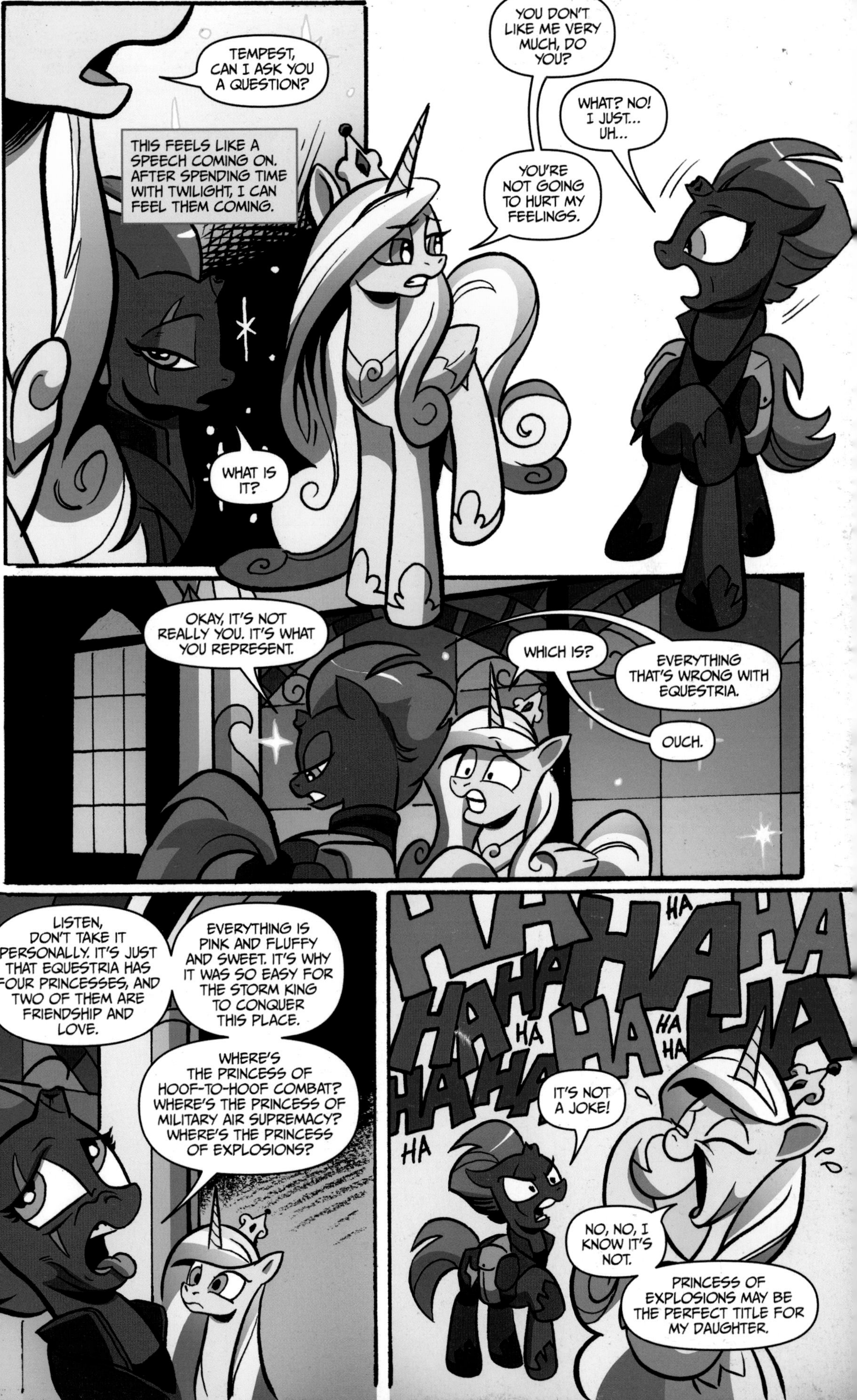
TEMPEST, CAN I ASK YOU A QUESTION?
THIS FEELS LIKE A SPEECH COMING ON. AFTER SPENDING TIME WITH TWILIGHT, I CAN FEEL THEM COMING.
WHAT IS IT?
YOU DON'T LIKE ME VERY MUCH, DO YOU?
WHAT? NO! I JUST... UH...
YOU'RE NOT GOING TO HURT MY FEELINGS.
OKAY, IT'S NOT REALLY YOU. IT'S WHAT YOU REPRESENT.
WHICH IS?
EVERYTHING THAT'S WRONG WITH EQUESTRIA.
OUCH.
LISTEN, DON'T TAKE IT PERSONALLY. IT'S JUST THAT EQUESTRIA HAS FOUR PRINCESSES, AND TWO OF THEM ARE FRIENDSHIP AND LOVE.
EVERYTHING IS PINK AND FLUFFY AND SWEET. IT'S WHY IT WAS SO EASY FOR THE STORM KING TO CONQUER THIS PLACE.
WHERE'S THE PRINCESS OF HOOF-TO-HOOF COMBAT? WHERE'S THE PRINCESS OF MILITARY AIR SUPREMACY? WHERE'S THE PRINCESS OF EXPLOSIONS?
HA HA HA HA HA HA HA HA HA HA HA HA HA HA HA
IT'S NOT A JOKE!
NO, NO, I KNOW IT'S NOT.
PRINCESS OF EXPLOSIONS MAY BE THE PERFECT TITLE FOR MY DAUGHTER.

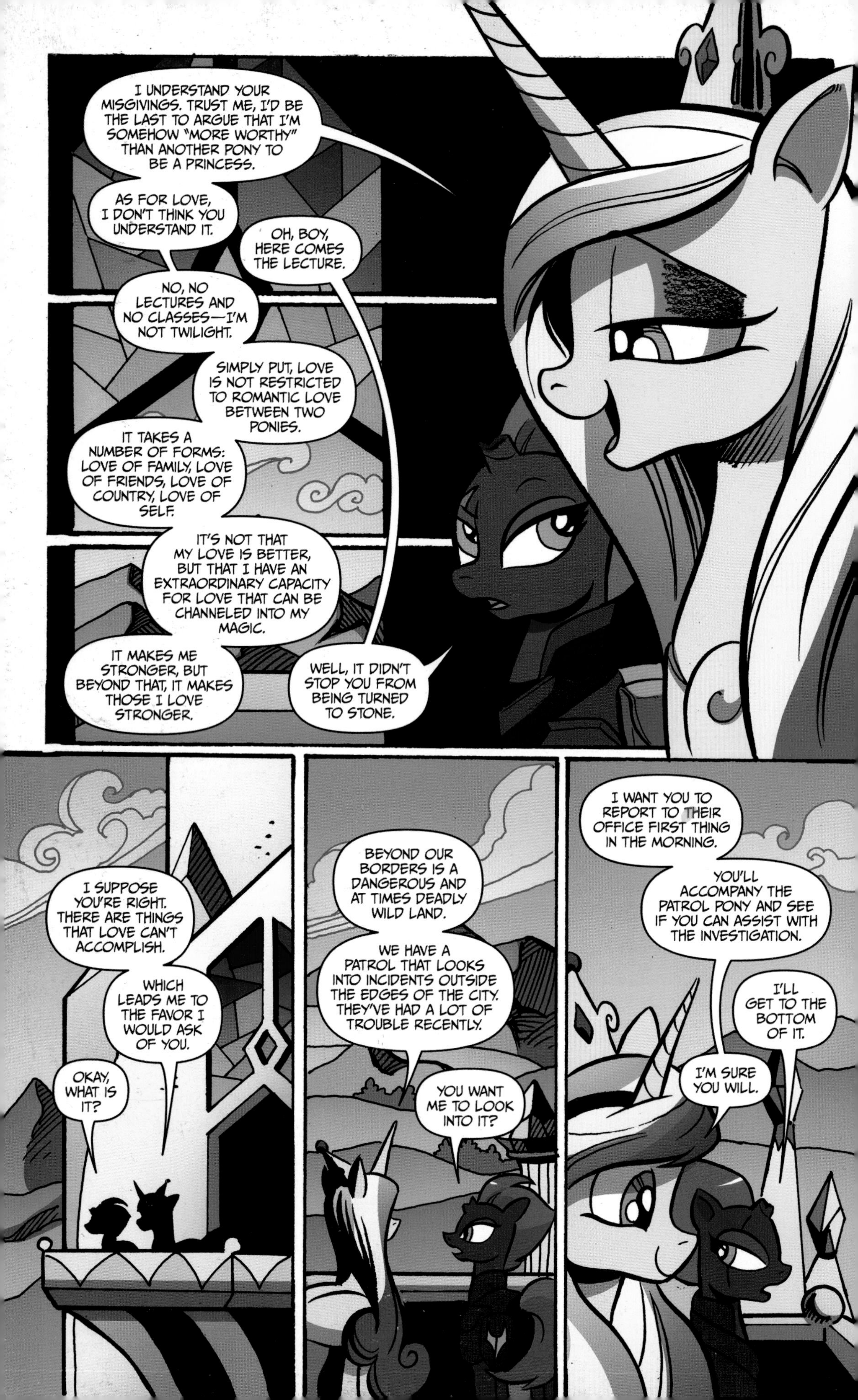
I UNDERSTAND YOUR MISGIVINGS. TRUST ME, I'D BE THE LAST TO ARGUE THAT I'M SOMEHOW "MORE WORTHY" THAN ANOTHER PONY TO BE A PRINCESS.
AS FOR LOVE, I DON'T THINK YOU UNDERSTAND IT.
OH, BOY, HERE COMES THE LECTURE.
NO, NO LECTURES AND NO CLASSES—I'M NOT TWILIGHT.
SIMPLY PUT, LOVE IS NOT RESTRICTED TO ROMANTIC LOVE BETWEEN TWO PONIES.
IT TAKES A NUMBER OF FORMS: LOVE OF FAMILY, LOVE OF FRIENDS, LOVE OF COUNTRY, LOVE OF SELF.
IT'S NOT THAT MY LOVE IS BETTER, BUT THAT I HAVE AN EXTRAORDINARY CAPACITY FOR LOVE THAT CAN BE CHANNELED INTO MY MAGIC.
IT MAKES ME STRONGER, BUT BEYOND THAT, IT MAKES THOSE I LOVE STRONGER.
WELL, IT DIDN'T STOP YOU FROM BEING TURNED TO STONE.
I SUPPOSE YOU'RE RIGHT. THERE ARE THINGS THAT LOVE CAN'T ACCOMPLISH.
WHICH LEADS ME TO THE FAVOR I WOULD ASK OF YOU.
OKAY, WHAT IS IT?
BEYOND OUR BORDERS IS A DANGEROUS AND AT TIMES DEADLY WILD LAND.
WE HAVE A PATROL THAT LOOKS INTO INCIDENTS OUTSIDE THE EDGES OF THE CITY. THEY'VE HAD A LOT OF TROUBLE RECENTLY.
YOU WANT ME TO LOOK INTO IT?
I WANT YOU TO REPORT TO THEIR OFFICE FIRST THING IN THE MORNING.
YOU'LL ACCOMPANY THE PATROL PONY AND SEE IF YOU CAN ASSIST WITH THE INVESTIGATION.
I'LL GET TO THE BOTTOM OF IT.
I'M SURE YOU WILL.

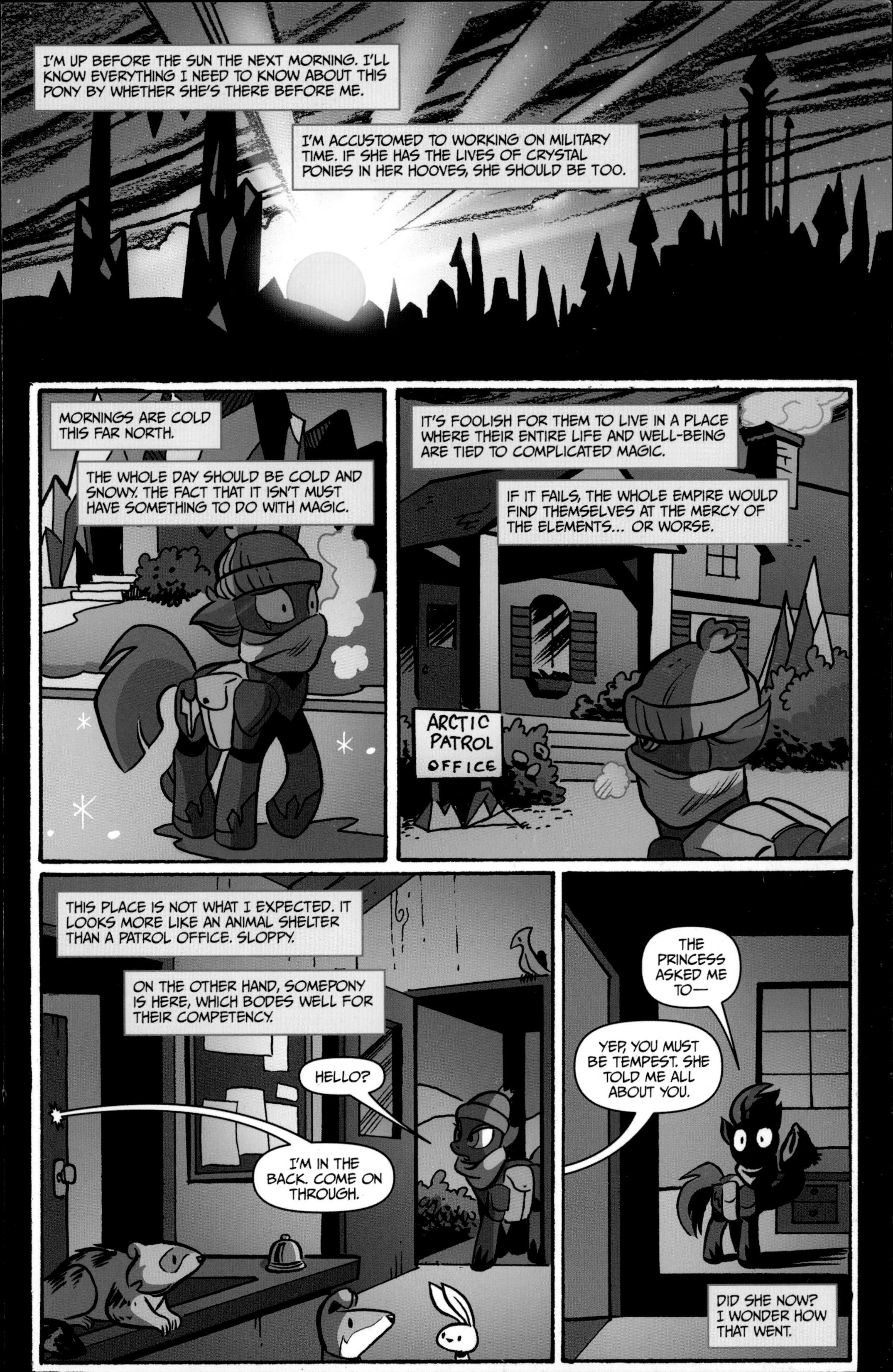
I'M UP BEFORE THE SUN THE NEXT MORNING. I'LL KNOW EVERYTHING I NEED TO KNOW ABOUT THIS PONY BY WHETHER SHE'S THERE BEFORE ME.
I'M ACCUSTOMED TO WORKING ON MILITARY TIME. IF SHE HAS THE LIVES OF CRYSTAL PONIES IN HER HOOVES, SHE SHOULD BE TOO.
MORNINGS ARE COLD THIS FAR NORTH.
THE WHOLE DAY SHOULD BE COLD AND SNOWY. THE FACT THAT IT ISN'T MUST HAVE SOMETHING TO DO WITH MAGIC.
IT'S FOOLISH FOR THEM TO LIVE IN A PLACE WHERE THEIR ENTIRE LIFE AND WELL-BEING ARE TIED TO COMPLICATED MAGIC.
IF IT FAILS, THE WHOLE EMPIRE WOULD FIND THEMSELVES AT THE MERCY OF THE ELEMENTS... OR WORSE.
ARCTIC PATROL OFFICE
THIS PLACE IS NOT WHAT I EXPECTED. IT LOOKS MORE LIKE AN ANIMAL SHELTER THAN A PATROL OFFICE. SLOPPY.
ON THE OTHER HAND, SOMEPONY IS HERE, WHICH BODES WELL FOR THEIR COMPETENCY.
HELLO?
I'M IN THE BACK. COME ON THROUGH.
THE PRINCESS ASKED ME TO—
YEP, YOU MUST BE TEMPEST. SHE TOLD ME ALL ABOUT YOU.
DID SHE NOW? I WONDER HOW THAT WENT.

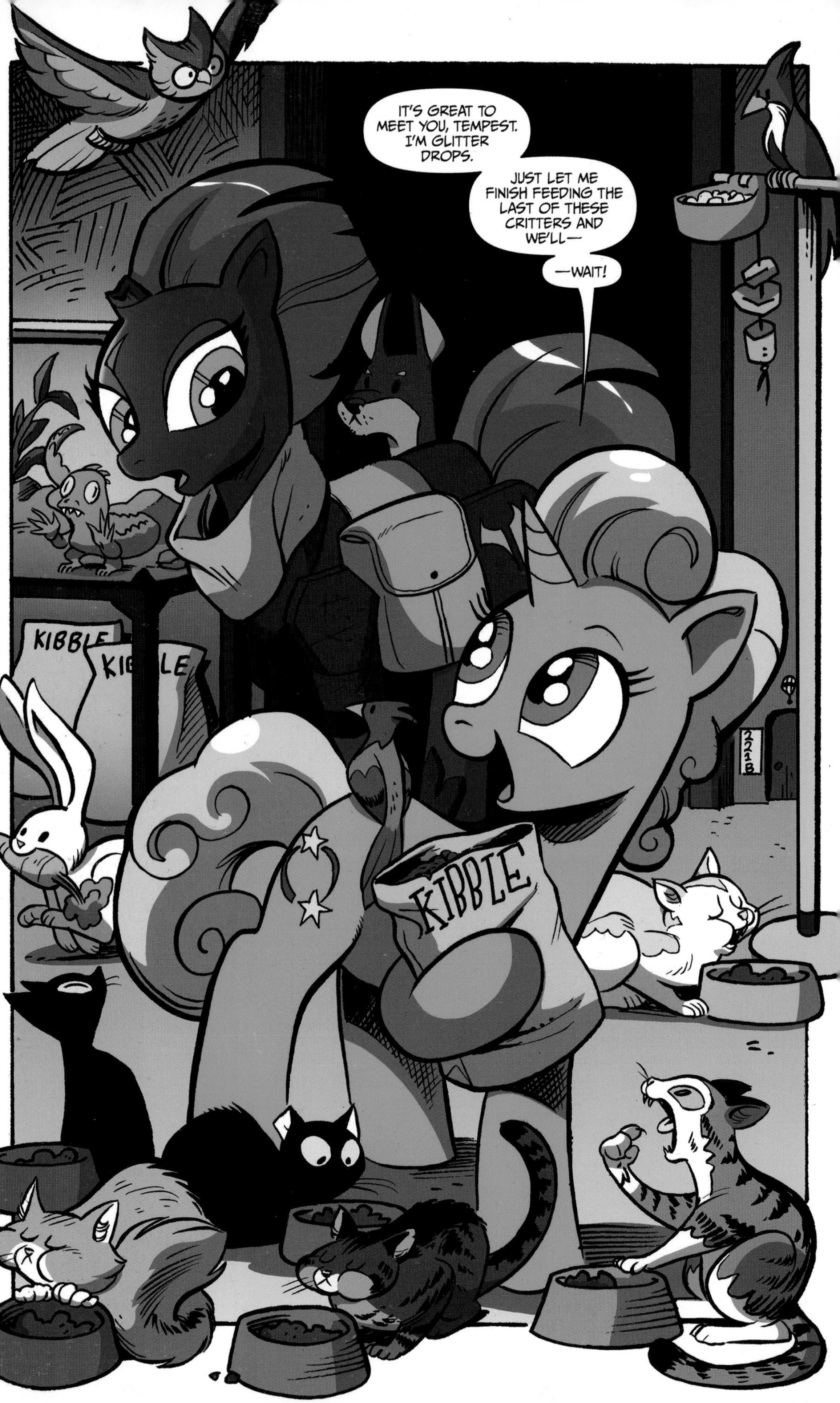
IT'S GREAT TO MEET YOU, TEMPEST. I'M GLITTER DROPS.
JUST LET ME FINISH FEEDING THE LAST OF THESE CRITTERS AND WE'LL—
—WAIT!
KIBBLE

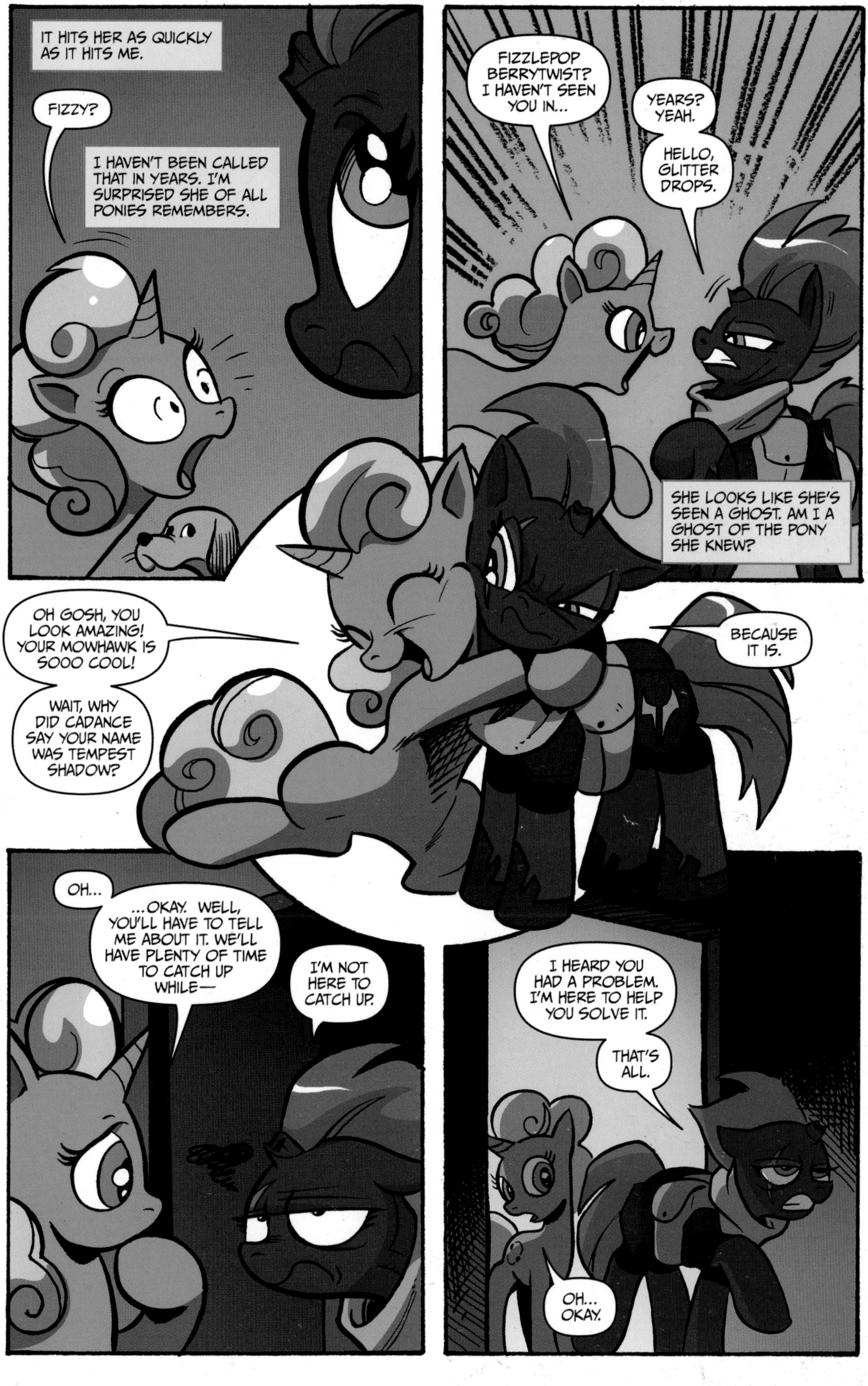
IT HITS HER AS QUICKLY AS IT HITS ME.
FIZZY?
I HAVEN'T BEEN CALLED THAT IN YEARS. I'M SURPRISED SHE OF ALL PONIES REMEMBERS.
FIZZLEPOP BERRYTWIST? I HAVEN'T SEEN YOU IN...
YEARS? YEAH.
HELLO, GLITTER DROPS.
SHE LOOKS LIKE SHE'S SEEN A GHOST. AM I A GHOST OF THE PONY SHE KNEW?
OH GOSH, YOU LOOK AMAZING! YOUR MOWHAWK IS SOOO COOL!
WAIT, WHY DID CADANCE SAY YOUR NAME WAS TEMPEST SHADOW?
BECAUSE IT IS.
OH...
...OKAY. WELL, YOU'LL HAVE TO TELL ME ABOUT IT. WE'LL HAVE PLENTY OF TIME TO CATCH UP WHILE—
I'M NOT HERE TO CATCH UP.
I HEARD YOU HAD A PROBLEM. I'M HERE TO HELP YOU SOLVE IT.
THAT'S ALL.
OH... OKAY.

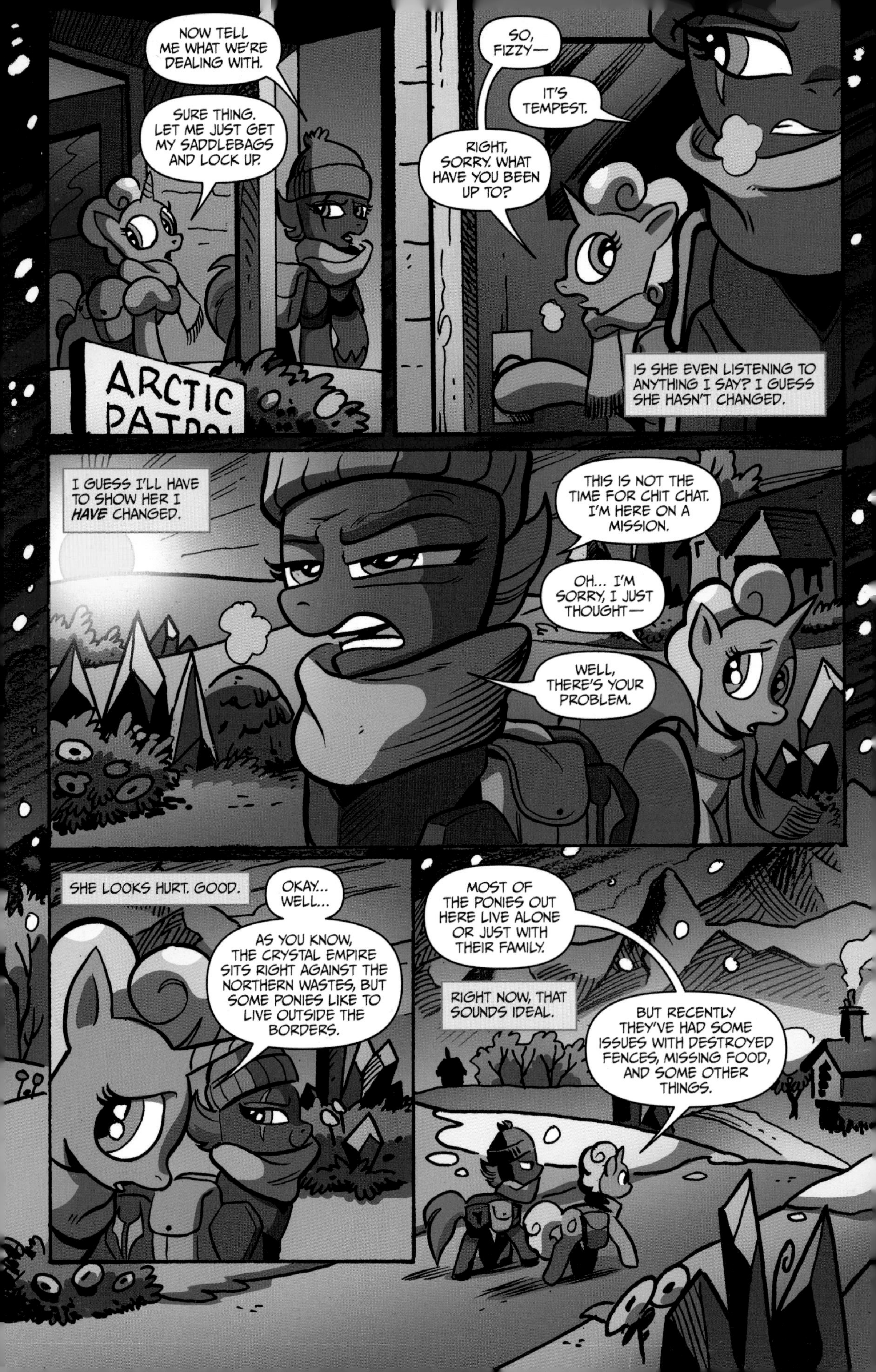
NOW TELL ME WHAT WE'RE DEALING WITH.
SURE THING. LET ME JUST GET MY SADDLEBAGS AND LOCK UP.
ARCTIC PATRO
SO, FIZZY—
IT'S TEMPEST.
RIGHT, SORRY. WHAT HAVE YOU BEEN UP TO?
IS SHE EVEN LISTENING TO ANYTHING I SAY? I GUESS SHE HASN'T CHANGED.
I GUESS I'LL HAVE TO SHOW HER I *HAVE* CHANGED.
THIS IS NOT THE TIME FOR CHIT CHAT. I'M HERE ON A MISSION.
OH... I'M SORRY, I JUST THOUGHT—
WELL, THERE'S YOUR PROBLEM.
SHE LOOKS HURT. GOOD.
OKAY... WELL...
AS YOU KNOW, THE CRYSTAL EMPIRE SITS RIGHT AGAINST THE NORTHERN WASTES, BUT SOME PONIES LIKE TO LIVE OUTSIDE THE BORDERS.
MOST OF THE PONIES OUT HERE LIVE ALONE OR JUST WITH THEIR FAMILY.
RIGHT NOW, THAT SOUNDS IDEAL.
BUT RECENTLY THEY'VE HAD SOME ISSUES WITH DESTROYED FENCES, MISSING FOOD, AND SOME OTHER THINGS.

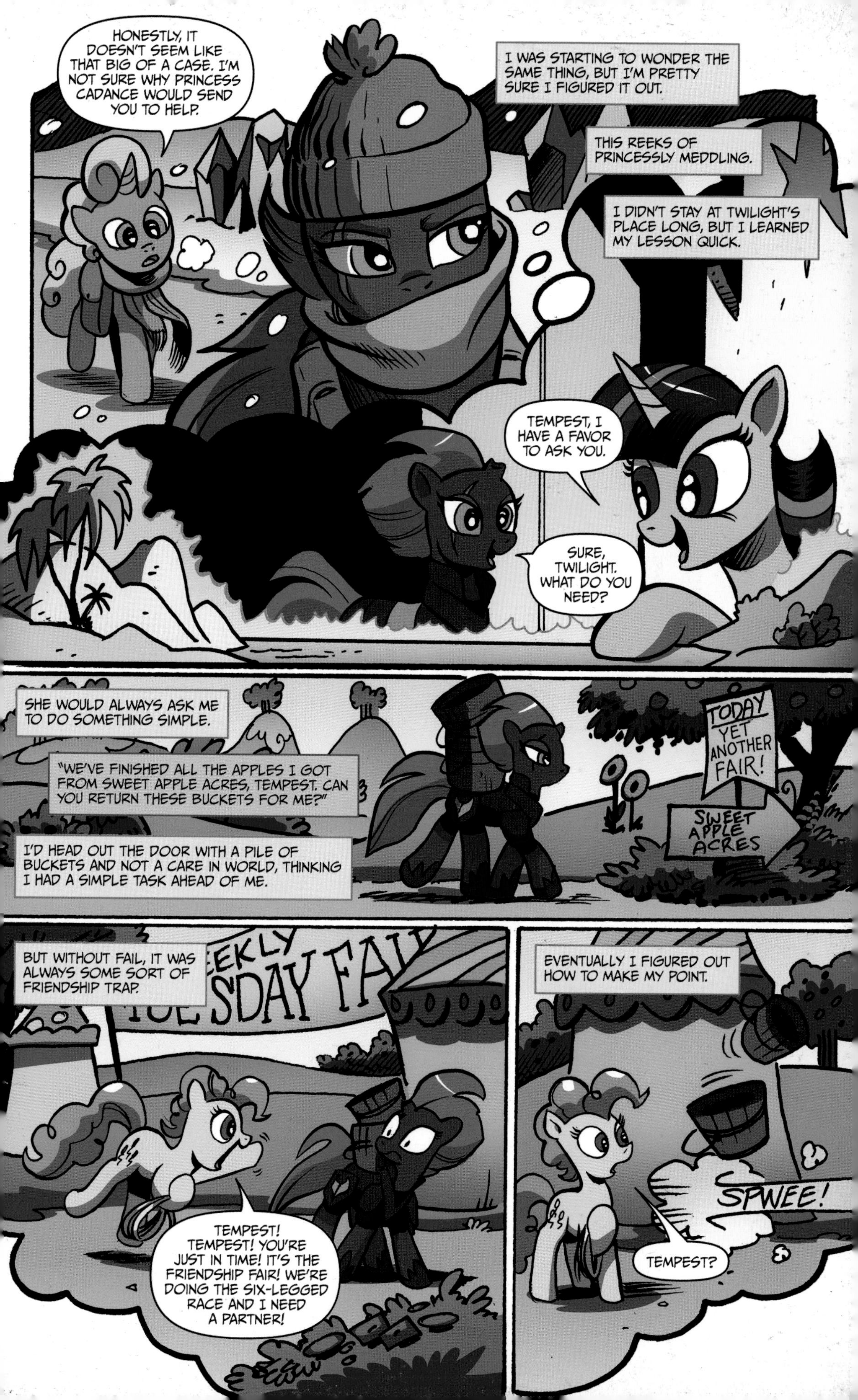

HONESTLY, IT DOESN'T SEEM LIKE THAT BIG OF A CASE. I'M NOT SURE WHY PRINCESS CADANCE WOULD SEND YOU TO HELP.
I WAS STARTING TO WONDER THE SAME THING, BUT I'M PRETTY SURE I FIGURED IT OUT.
THIS REEKS OF PRINCESSLY MEDDLING.
I DIDN'T STAY AT TWILIGHT'S PLACE LONG, BUT I LEARNED MY LESSON QUICK.
TEMPEST, I HAVE A FAVOR TO ASK YOU.
SURE, TWILIGHT. WHAT DO YOU NEED?
SHE WOULD ALWAYS ASK ME TO DO SOMETHING SIMPLE.
"WE'VE FINISHED ALL THE APPLES I GOT FROM SWEET APPLE ACRES, TEMPEST. CAN YOU RETURN THESE BUCKETS FOR ME?"
I'D HEAD OUT THE DOOR WITH A PILE OF BUCKETS AND NOT A CARE IN WORLD, THINKING I HAD A SIMPLE TASK AHEAD OF ME.
TODAY YET ANOTHER FAIR!
SWEET APPLE ACRES
BUT WITHOUT FAIL, IT WAS ALWAYS SOME SORT OF FRIENDSHIP TRAP.
TEMPEST! TEMPEST! YOU'RE JUST IN TIME! IT'S THE FRIENDSHIP FAIR! WE'RE DOING THE SIX-LEGGED RACE AND I NEED A PARTNER!
EVENTUALLY I FIGURED OUT HOW TO MAKE MY POINT.
SPWEE!
TEMPEST?

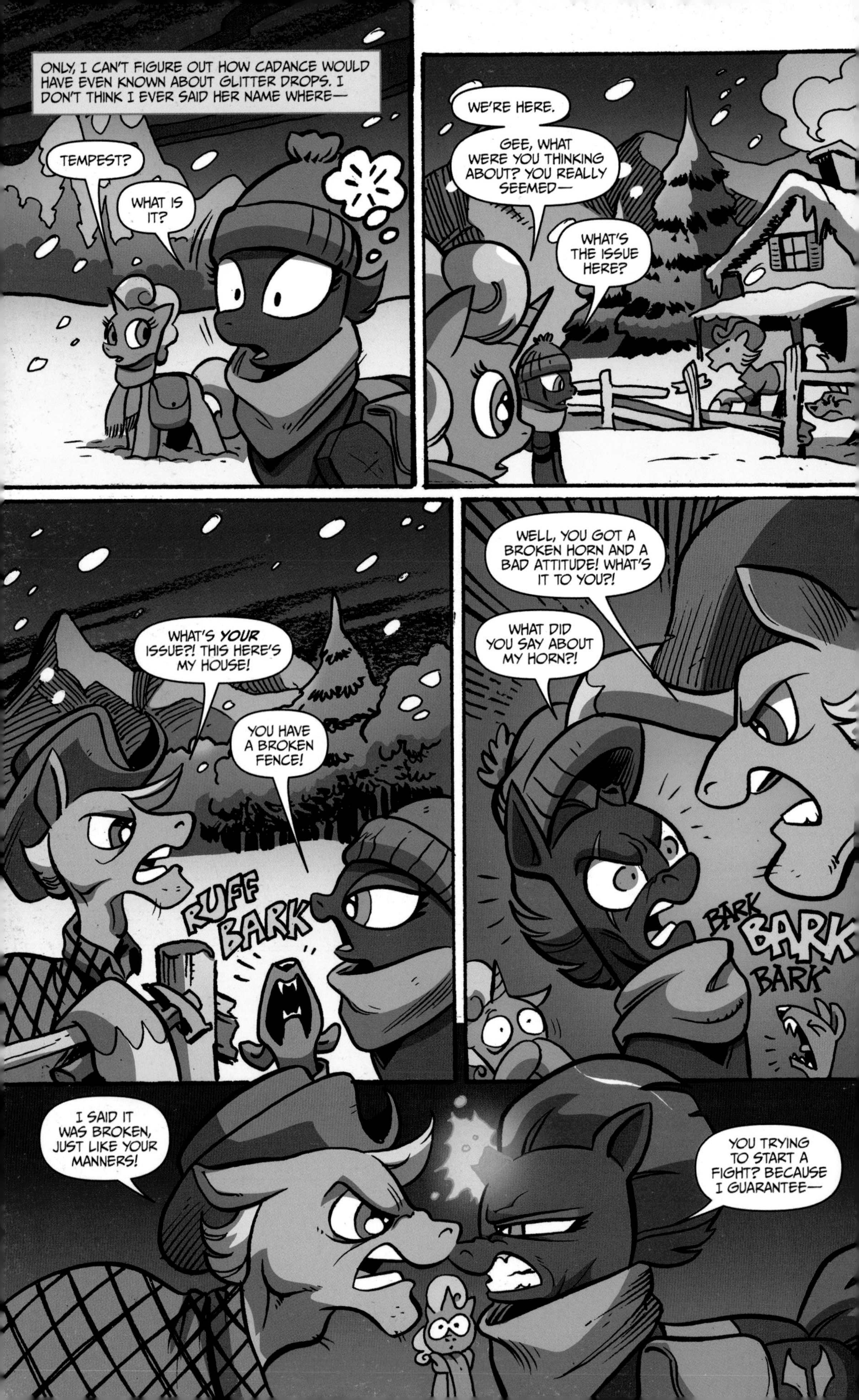
ONLY, I CAN'T FIGURE OUT HOW CADANCE WOULD HAVE EVEN KNOWN ABOUT GLITTER DROPS. I DON'T THINK I EVER SAID HER NAME WHERE—
TEMPEST?
WHAT IS IT?
WE'RE HERE.
GEE, WHAT WERE YOU THINKING ABOUT? YOU REALLY SEEMED—
WHAT'S THE ISSUE HERE?
WHAT'S *YOUR* ISSUE?! THIS HERE'S MY HOUSE!
YOU HAVE A BROKEN FENCE!
RUFF
BARK
WELL, YOU GOT A BROKEN HORN AND A BAD ATTITUDE! WHAT'S IT TO YOU?!
WHAT DID YOU SAY ABOUT MY HORN?!
BARK
BARK
BARK
I SAID IT WAS BROKEN, JUST LIKE YOUR MANNERS!
YOU TRYING TO START A FIGHT? BECAUSE I GUARANTEE—

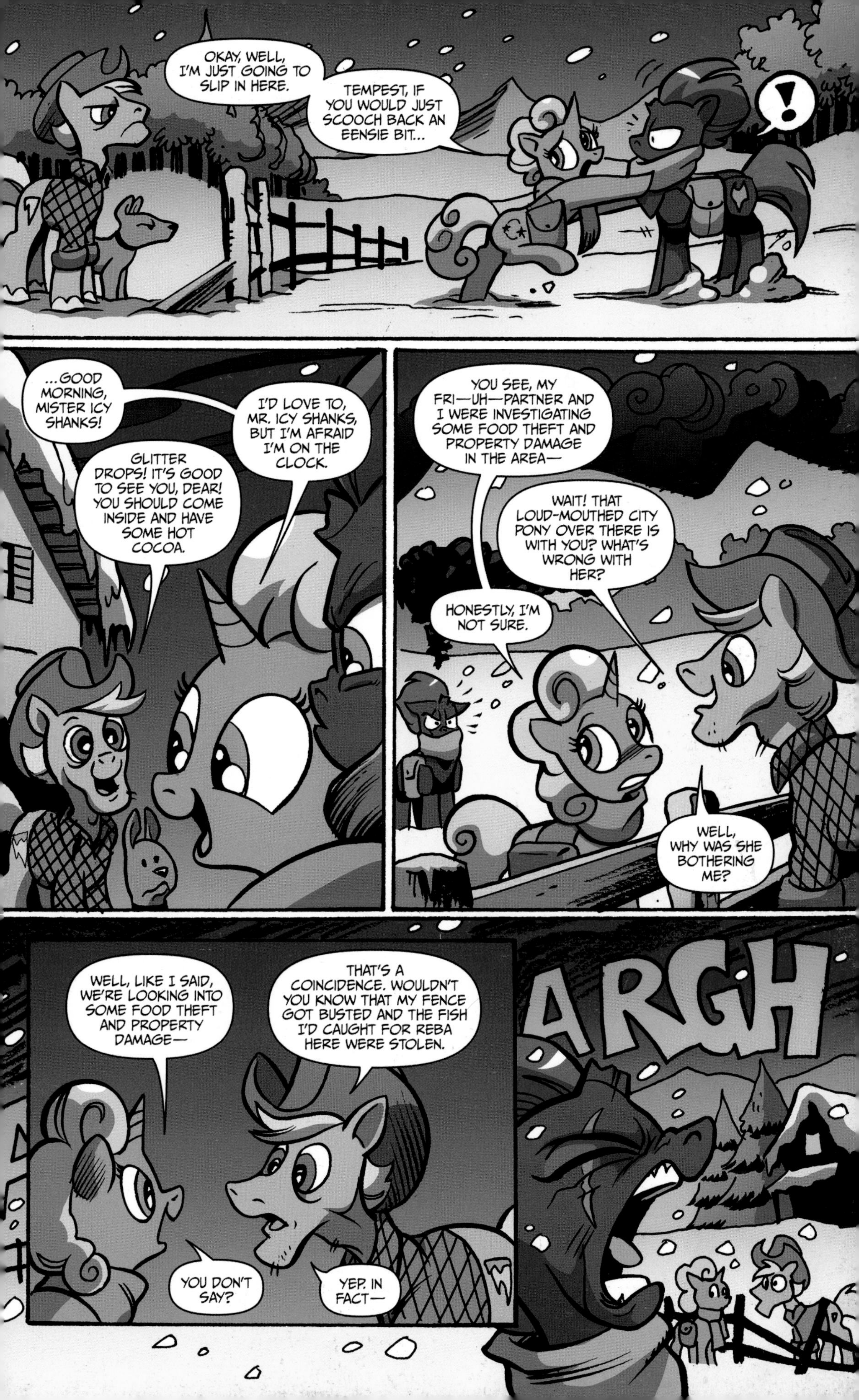
OKAY, WELL, I'M JUST GOING TO SLIP IN HERE.
TEMPEST, IF YOU WOULD JUST SCOOCH BACK AN EENSIE BIT...
!
...GOOD MORNING, MISTER ICY SHANKS!
GLITTER DROPS! IT'S GOOD TO SEE YOU, DEAR! YOU SHOULD COME INSIDE AND HAVE SOME HOT COCOA.
I'D LOVE TO, MR. ICY SHANKS, BUT I'M AFRAID I'M ON THE CLOCK.
YOU SEE, MY FRI—UH—PARTNER AND I WERE INVESTIGATING SOME FOOD THEFT AND PROPERTY DAMAGE IN THE AREA—
WAIT! THAT LOUD-MOUTHED CITY PONY OVER THERE IS WITH YOU? WHAT'S WRONG WITH HER?
HONESTLY, I'M NOT SURE.
WELL, WHY WAS SHE BOTHERING ME?
WELL, LIKE I SAID, WE'RE LOOKING INTO SOME FOOD THEFT AND PROPERTY DAMAGE—
THAT'S A COINCIDENCE. WOULDN'T YOU KNOW THAT MY FENCE GOT BUSTED AND THE FISH I'D CAUGHT FOR REBA HERE WERE STOLEN.
YOU DON'T SAY?
YEP. IN FACT—
ARGH

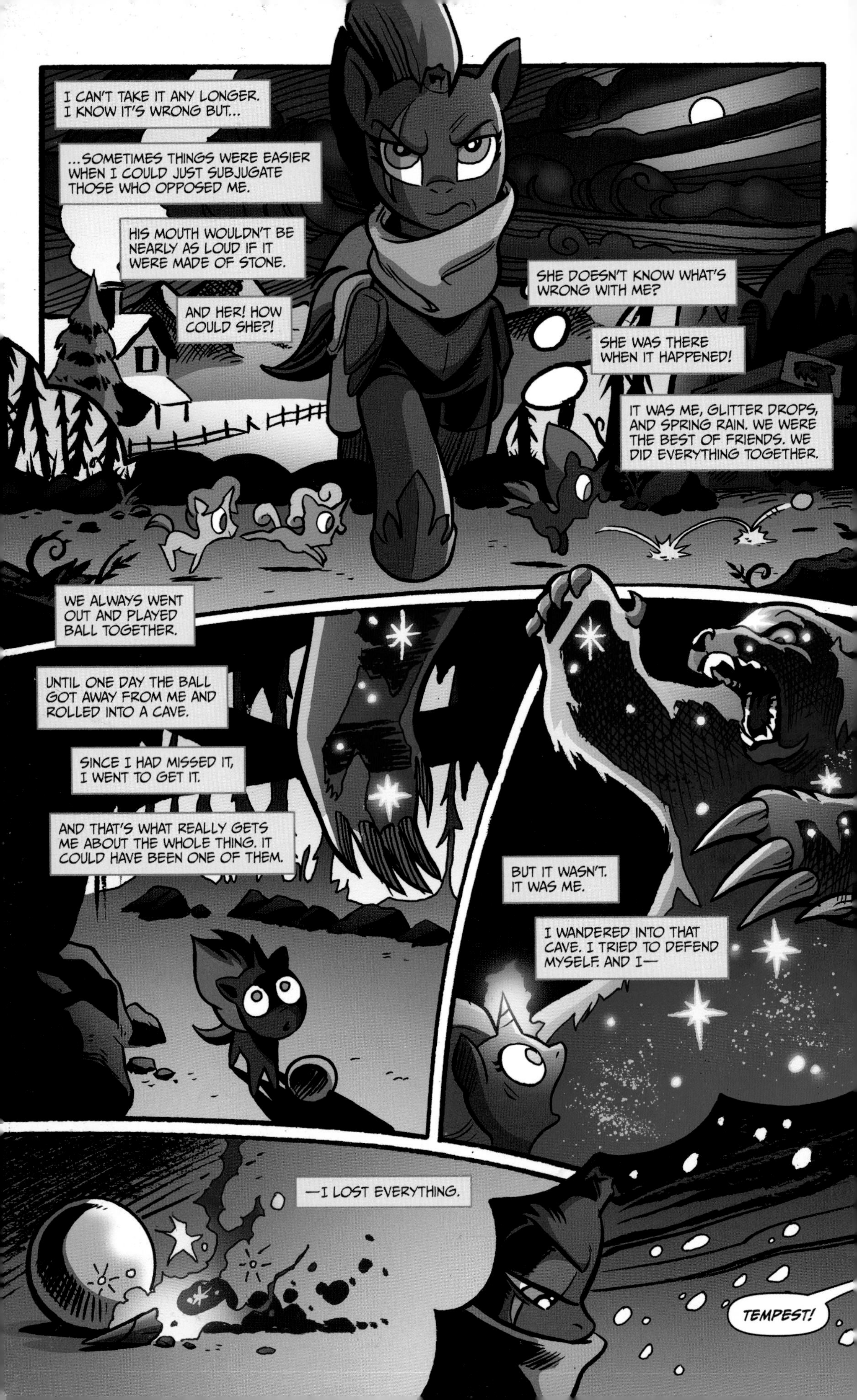

I CAN'T TAKE IT ANY LONGER. I KNOW IT'S WRONG BUT...
...SOMETIMES THINGS WERE EASIER WHEN I COULD JUST SUBJUGATE THOSE WHO OPPOSED ME.
HIS MOUTH WOULDN'T BE NEARLY AS LOUD IF IT WERE MADE OF STONE.
AND HER! HOW COULD SHE?!
SHE DOESN'T KNOW WHAT'S WRONG WITH ME?
SHE WAS THERE WHEN IT HAPPENED!
IT WAS ME, GLITTER DROPS, AND SPRING RAIN. WE WERE THE BEST OF FRIENDS. WE DID EVERYTHING TOGETHER.
WE ALWAYS WENT OUT AND PLAYED BALL TOGETHER.
UNTIL ONE DAY THE BALL GOT AWAY FROM ME AND ROLLED INTO A CAVE.
SINCE I HAD MISSED IT, I WENT TO GET IT.
AND THAT'S WHAT REALLY GETS ME ABOUT THE WHOLE THING. IT COULD HAVE BEEN ONE OF THEM.
BUT IT WASN'T. IT WAS ME.
I WANDERED INTO THAT CAVE. I TRIED TO DEFEND MYSELF. AND I—
—I LOST EVERYTHING.
TEMPEST!

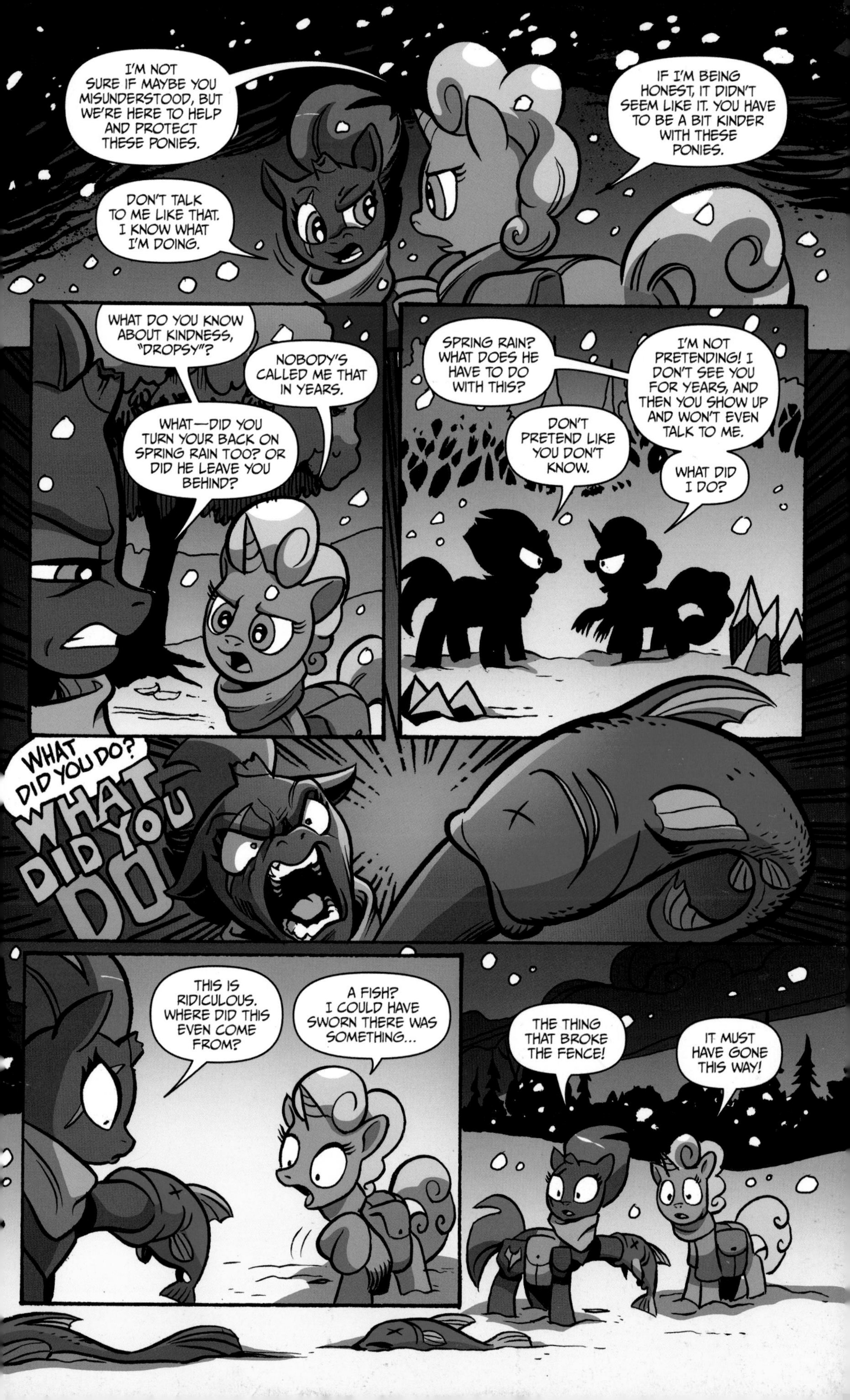

I'M NOT SURE IF MAYBE YOU MISUNDERSTOOD, BUT WE'RE HERE TO HELP AND PROTECT THESE PONIES.
IF I'M BEING HONEST, IT DIDN'T SEEM LIKE IT. YOU HAVE TO BE A BIT KINDER WITH THESE PONIES.
DON'T TALK TO ME LIKE THAT. I KNOW WHAT I'M DOING.
WHAT DO YOU KNOW ABOUT KINDNESS, "DROPSY"?
NOBODY'S CALLED ME THAT IN YEARS.
WHAT—DID YOU TURN YOUR BACK ON SPRING RAIN TOO? OR DID HE LEAVE YOU BEHIND?
SPRING RAIN? WHAT DOES HE HAVE TO DO WITH THIS?
DON'T PRETEND LIKE YOU DON'T KNOW.
I'M NOT PRETENDING! I DON'T SEE YOU FOR YEARS, AND THEN YOU SHOW UP AND WON'T EVEN TALK TO ME.
WHAT DID I DO?
WHAT DID YOU DO?
WHAT DID YOU DO
THIS IS RIDICULOUS. WHERE DID THIS EVEN COME FROM?
A FISH? I COULD HAVE SWORN THERE WAS SOMETHING...
THE THING THAT BROKE THE FENCE!
IT MUST HAVE GONE THIS WAY!

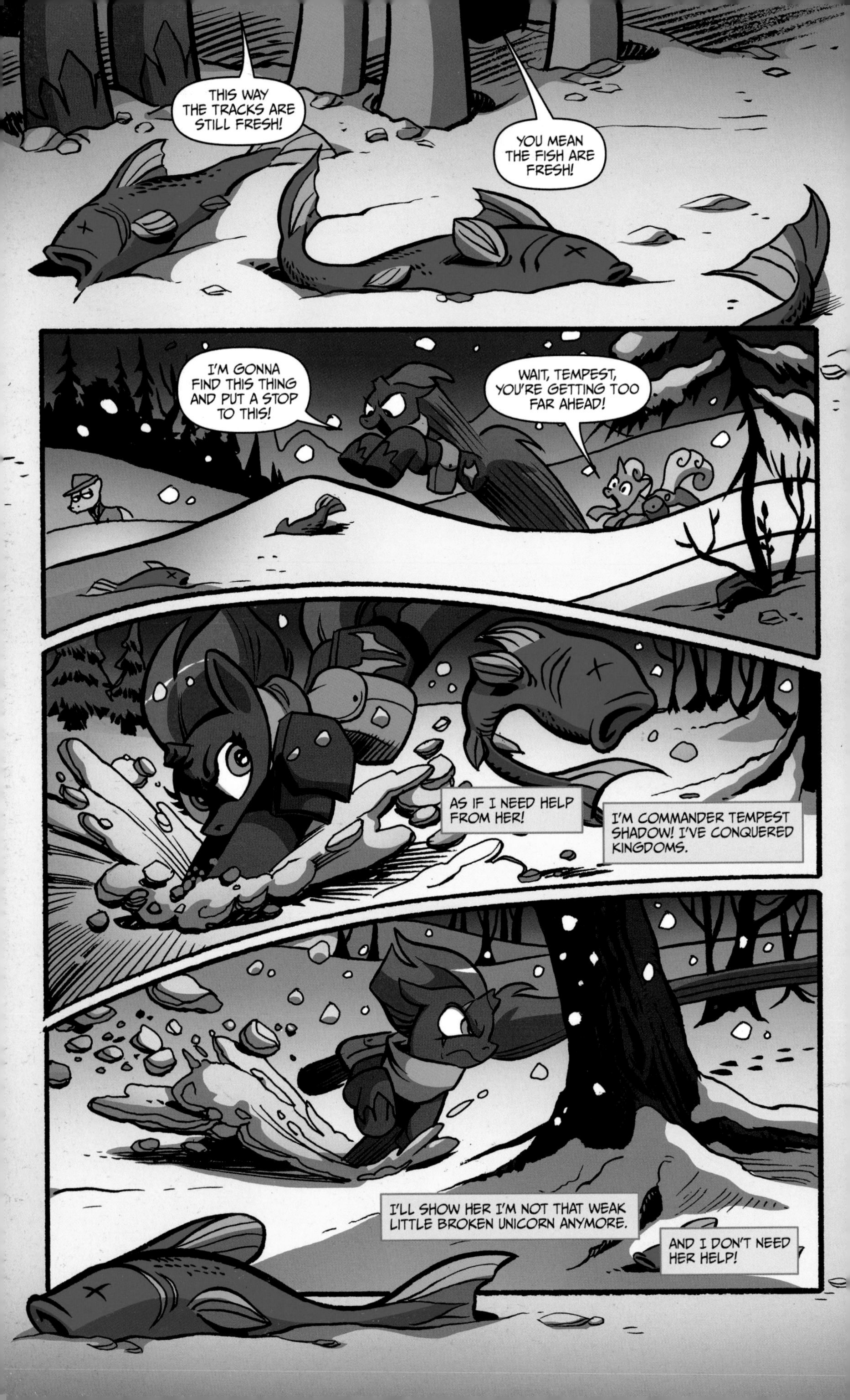
THIS WAY THE TRACKS ARE STILL FRESH!
YOU MEAN THE FISH ARE FRESH!
I'M GONNA FIND THIS THING AND PUT A STOP TO THIS!
WAIT, TEMPEST, YOU'RE GETTING TOO FAR AHEAD!
AS IF I NEED HELP FROM HER!
I'M COMMANDER TEMPEST SHADOW! I'VE CONQUERED KINGDOMS.
I'LL SHOW HER I'M NOT THAT WEAK LITTLE BROKEN UNICORN ANYMORE.
AND I DON'T NEED HER HELP!

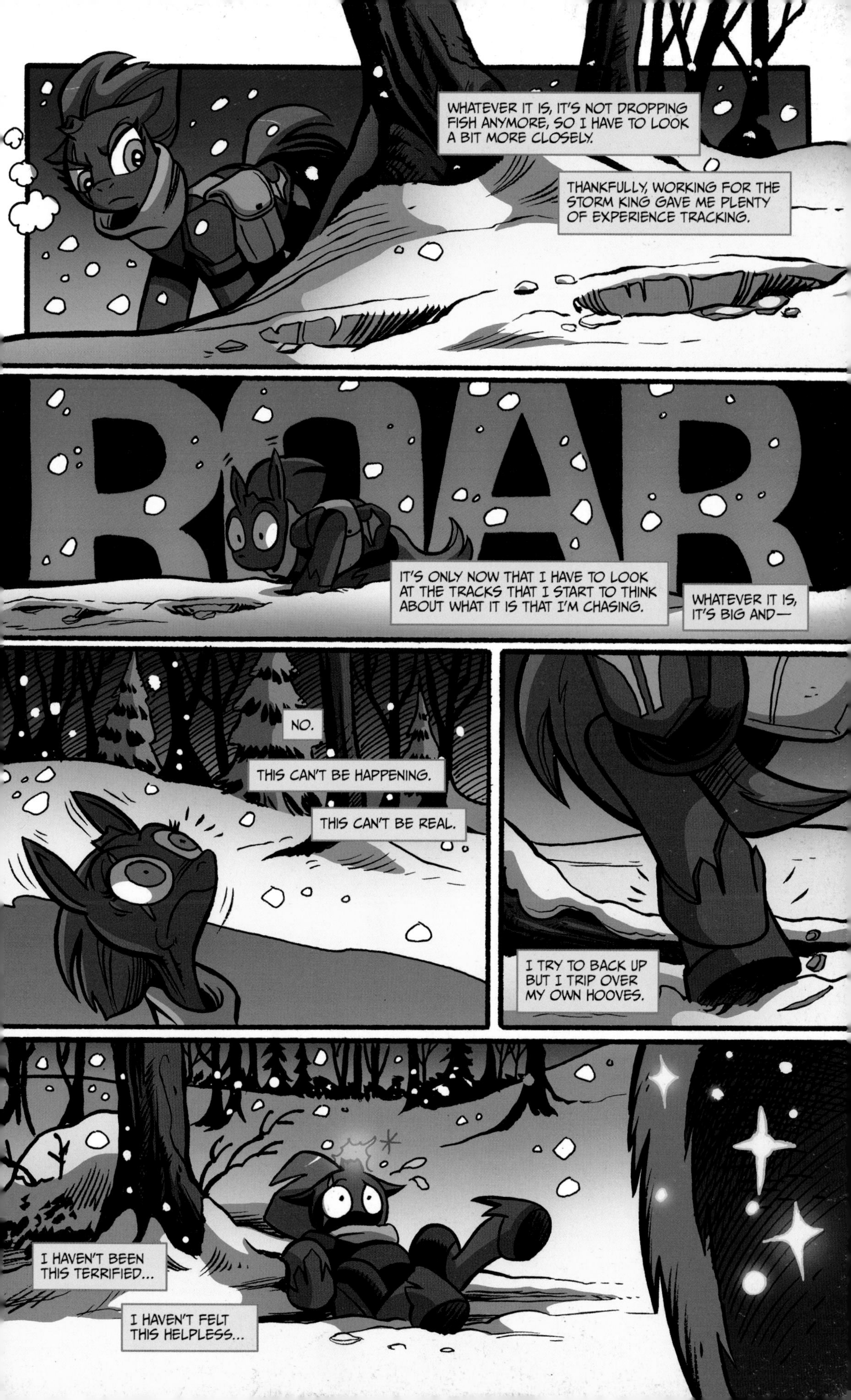
WHATEVER IT IS, IT'S NOT DROPPING FISH ANYMORE, SO I HAVE TO LOOK A BIT MORE CLOSELY.
THANKFULLY, WORKING FOR THE STORM KING GAVE ME PLENTY OF EXPERIENCE TRACKING.
ROAR
IT'S ONLY NOW THAT I HAVE TO LOOK AT THE TRACKS THAT I START TO THINK ABOUT WHAT IT IS THAT I'M CHASING.
WHATEVER IT IS, IT'S BIG AND—
NO.
THIS CAN'T BE HAPPENING.
THIS CAN'T BE REAL.
I TRY TO BACK UP BUT I TRIP OVER MY OWN HOOVES.
I HAVEN'T BEEN THIS TERRIFIED...
I HAVEN'T FELT THIS HELPLESS...

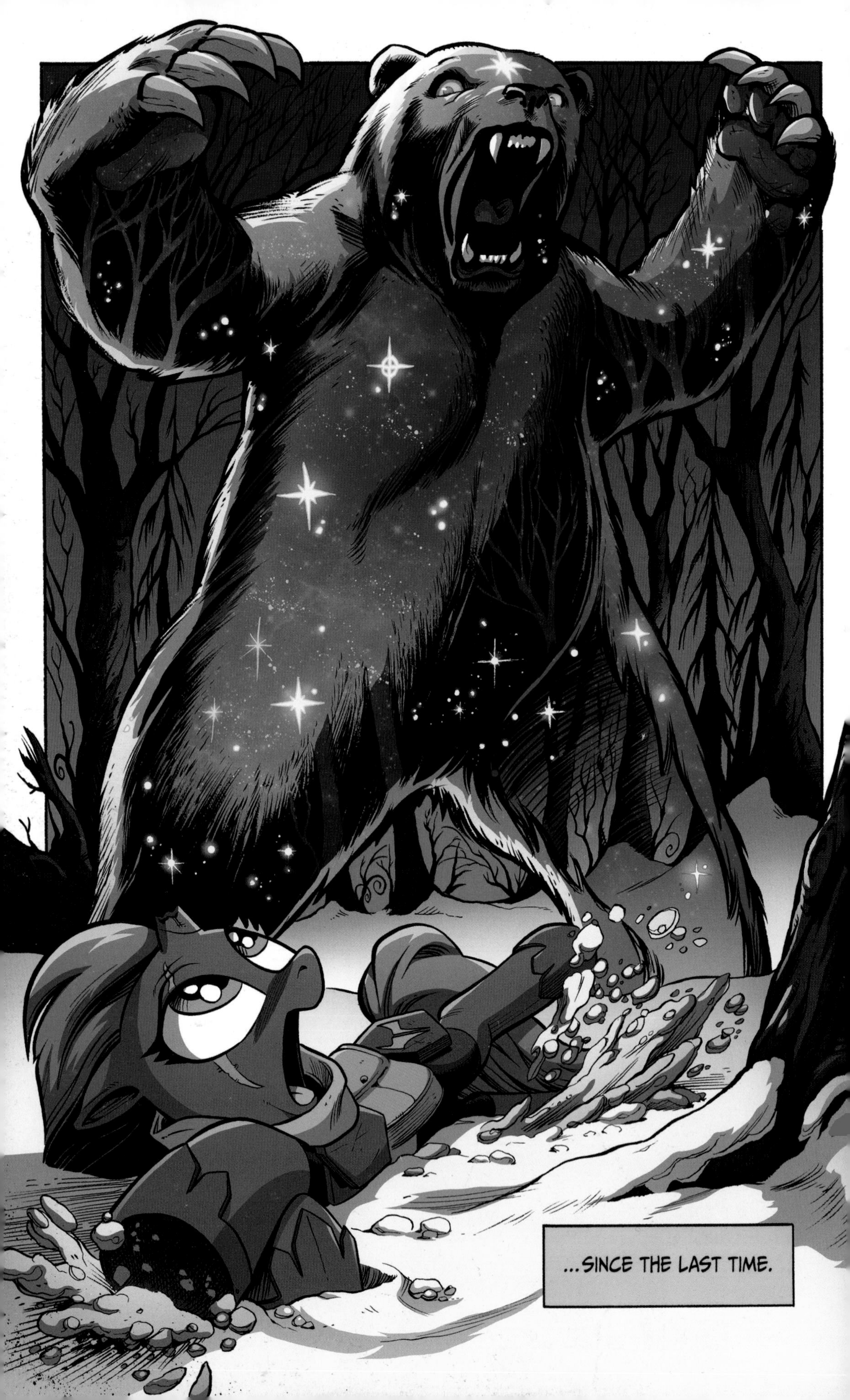
...SINCE THE LAST TIME.

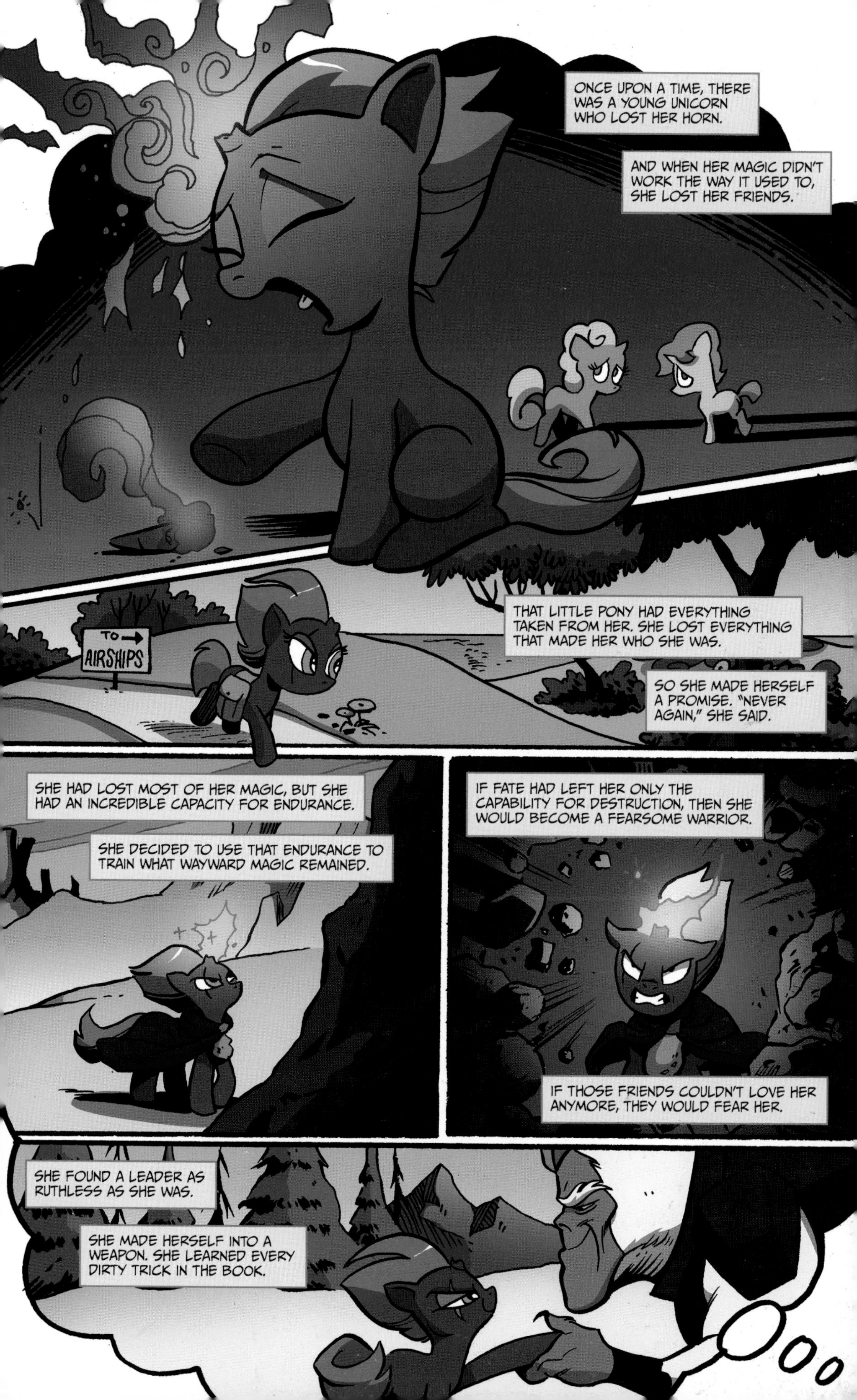

ONCE UPON A TIME, THERE WAS A YOUNG UNICORN WHO LOST HER HORN.
AND WHEN HER MAGIC DIDN'T WORK THE WAY IT USED TO, SHE LOST HER FRIENDS.
TO AIRSHIPS
THAT LITTLE PONY HAD EVERYTHING TAKEN FROM HER. SHE LOST EVERYTHING THAT MADE HER WHO SHE WAS.
SO SHE MADE HERSELF A PROMISE. "NEVER AGAIN," SHE SAID.
SHE HAD LOST MOST OF HER MAGIC, BUT SHE HAD AN INCREDIBLE CAPACITY FOR ENDURANCE.
SHE DECIDED TO USE THAT ENDURANCE TO TRAIN WHAT WAYWARD MAGIC REMAINED.
IF FATE HAD LEFT HER ONLY THE CAPABILITY FOR DESTRUCTION, THEN SHE WOULD BECOME A FEARSOME WARRIOR.
IF THOSE FRIENDS COULDN'T LOVE HER ANYMORE, THEY WOULD FEAR HER.
SHE FOUND A LEADER AS RUTHLESS AS SHE WAS.
SHE MADE HERSELF INTO A WEAPON. SHE LEARNED EVERY DIRTY TRICK IN THE BOOK.

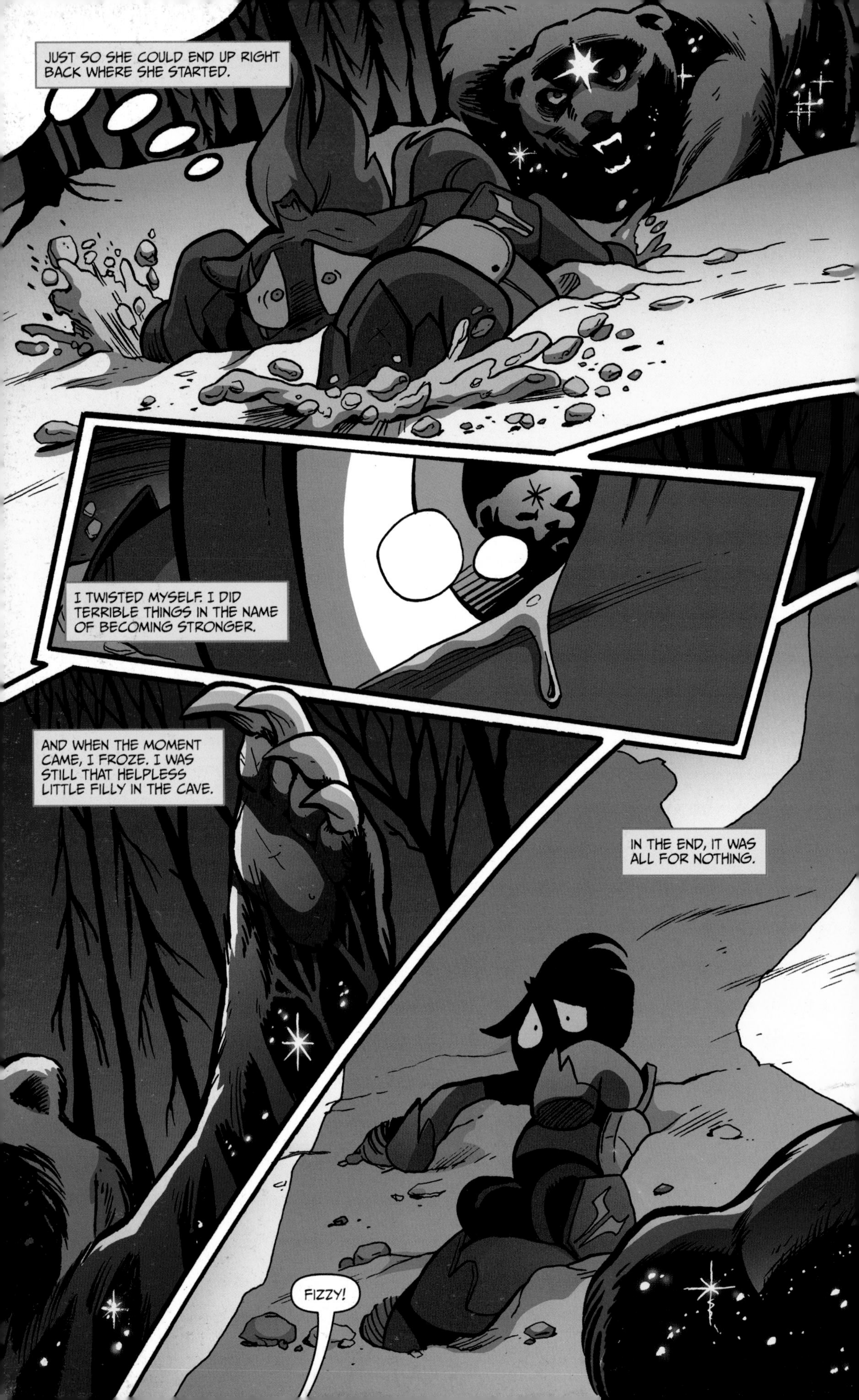
JUST SO SHE COULD END UP RIGHT BACK WHERE SHE STARTED.
I TWISTED MYSELF. I DID TERRIBLE THINGS IN THE NAME OF BECOMING STRONGER.
AND WHEN THE MOMENT CAME, I FROZE. I WAS STILL THAT HELPLESS LITTLE FILLY IN THE CAVE.
IN THE END, IT WAS ALL FOR NOTHING.
FIZZY!

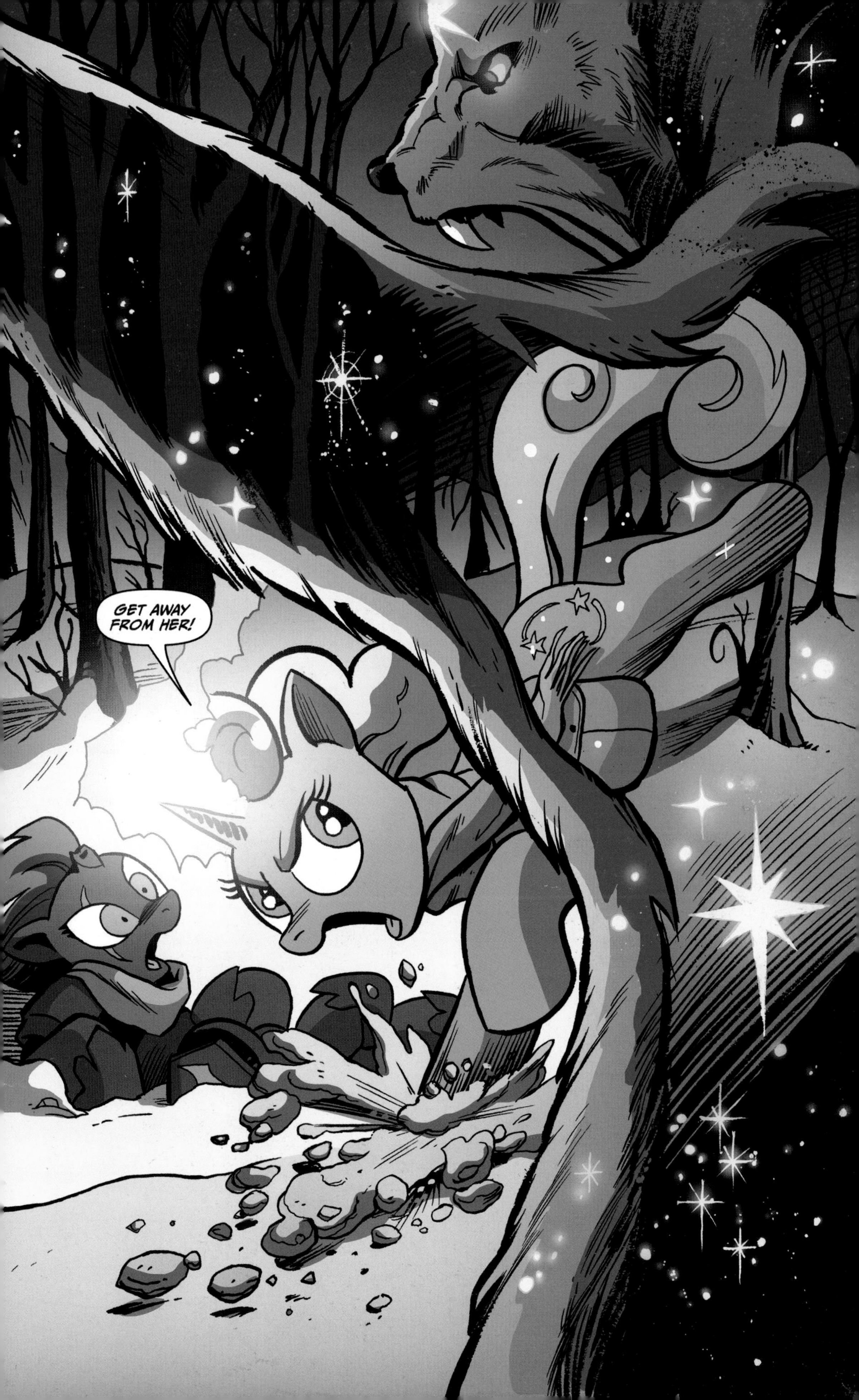
GET AWAY FROM HER!

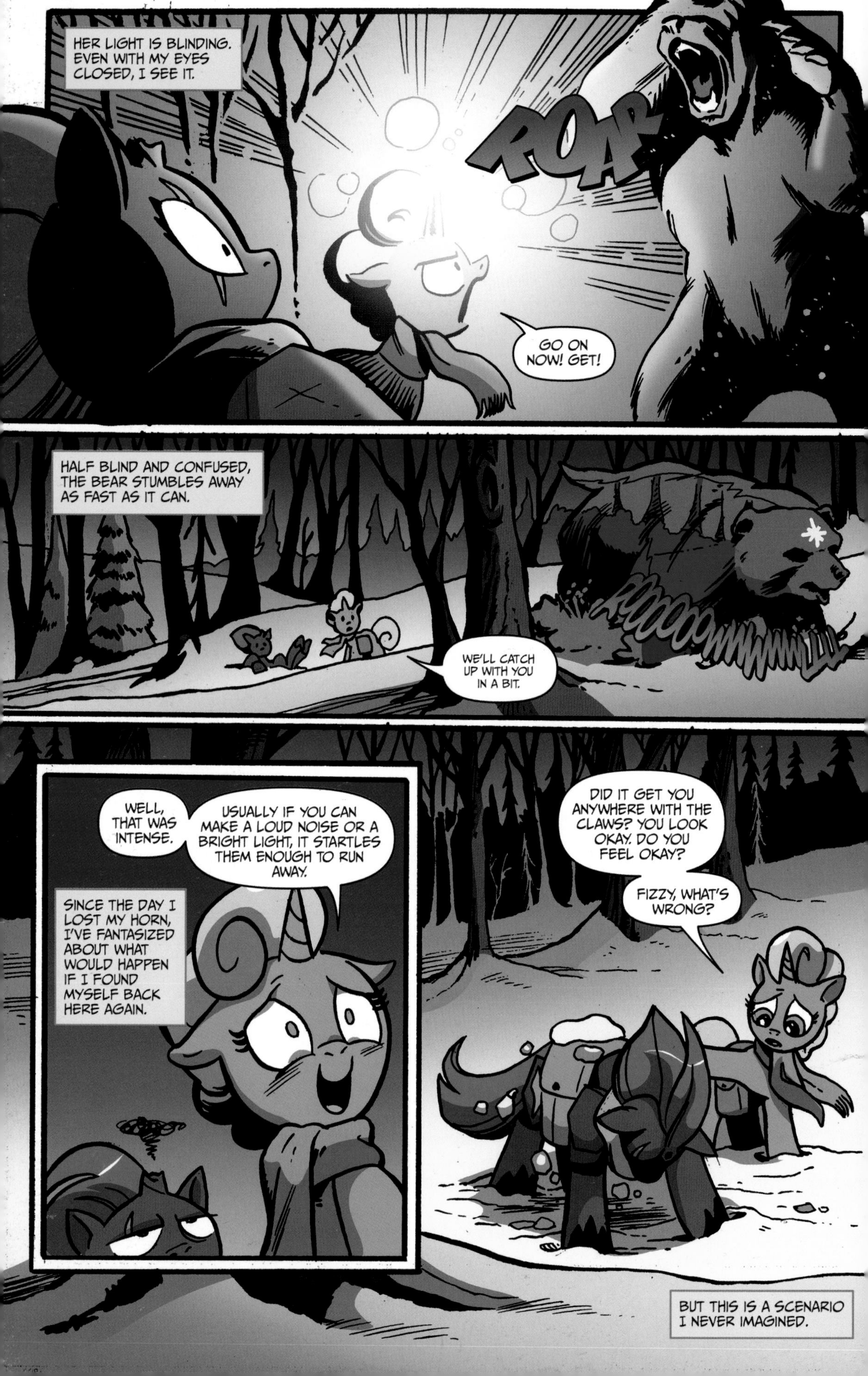
HER LIGHT IS BLINDING. EVEN WITH MY EYES CLOSED, I SEE IT.
ROAR
GO ON NOW! GET!
HALF BLIND AND CONFUSED, THE BEAR STUMBLES AWAY AS FAST AS IT CAN.
WE'LL CATCH UP WITH YOU IN A BIT.
WELL, THAT WAS INTENSE.
USUALLY IF YOU CAN MAKE A LOUD NOISE OR A BRIGHT LIGHT, IT STARTLES THEM ENOUGH TO RUN AWAY.
SINCE THE DAY I LOST MY HORN, I'VE FANTASIZED ABOUT WHAT WOULD HAPPEN IF I FOUND MYSELF BACK HERE AGAIN.
DID IT GET YOU ANYWHERE WITH THE CLAWS? YOU LOOK OKAY. DO YOU FEEL OKAY?
FIZZY, WHAT'S WRONG?
BUT THIS IS A SCENARIO I NEVER IMAGINED.

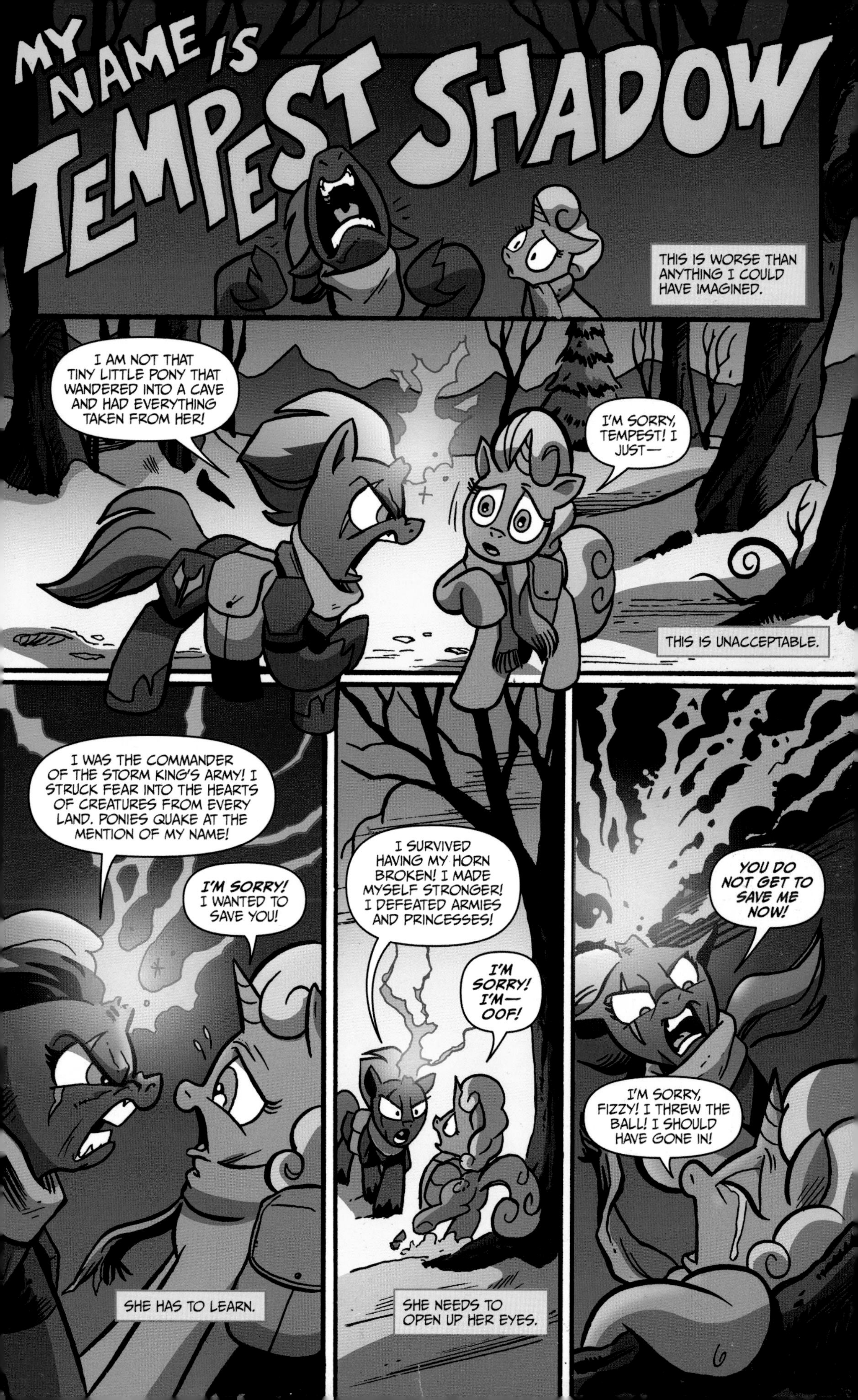

MY NAME IS TEMPEST SHADOW
THIS IS WORSE THAN ANYTHING I COULD HAVE IMAGINED.
I AM NOT THAT TINY LITTLE PONY THAT WANDERED INTO A CAVE AND HAD EVERYTHING TAKEN FROM HER!
I'M SORRY, TEMPEST! I JUST—
THIS IS UNACCEPTABLE.
I WAS THE COMMANDER OF THE STORM KING'S ARMY! I STRUCK FEAR INTO THE HEARTS OF CREATURES FROM EVERY LAND. PONIES QUAKE AT THE MENTION OF MY NAME!
I'M SORRY! I WANTED TO SAVE YOU!
SHE HAS TO LEARN.
I SURVIVED HAVING MY HORN BROKEN! I MADE MYSELF STRONGER! I DEFEATED ARMIES AND PRINCESSES!
I'M SORRY! I'M— OOF!
SHE NEEDS TO OPEN UP HER EYES.
YOU DO NOT GET TO SAVE ME NOW!
I'M SORRY, FIZZY! I THREW THE BALL! I SHOULD HAVE GONE IN!
6

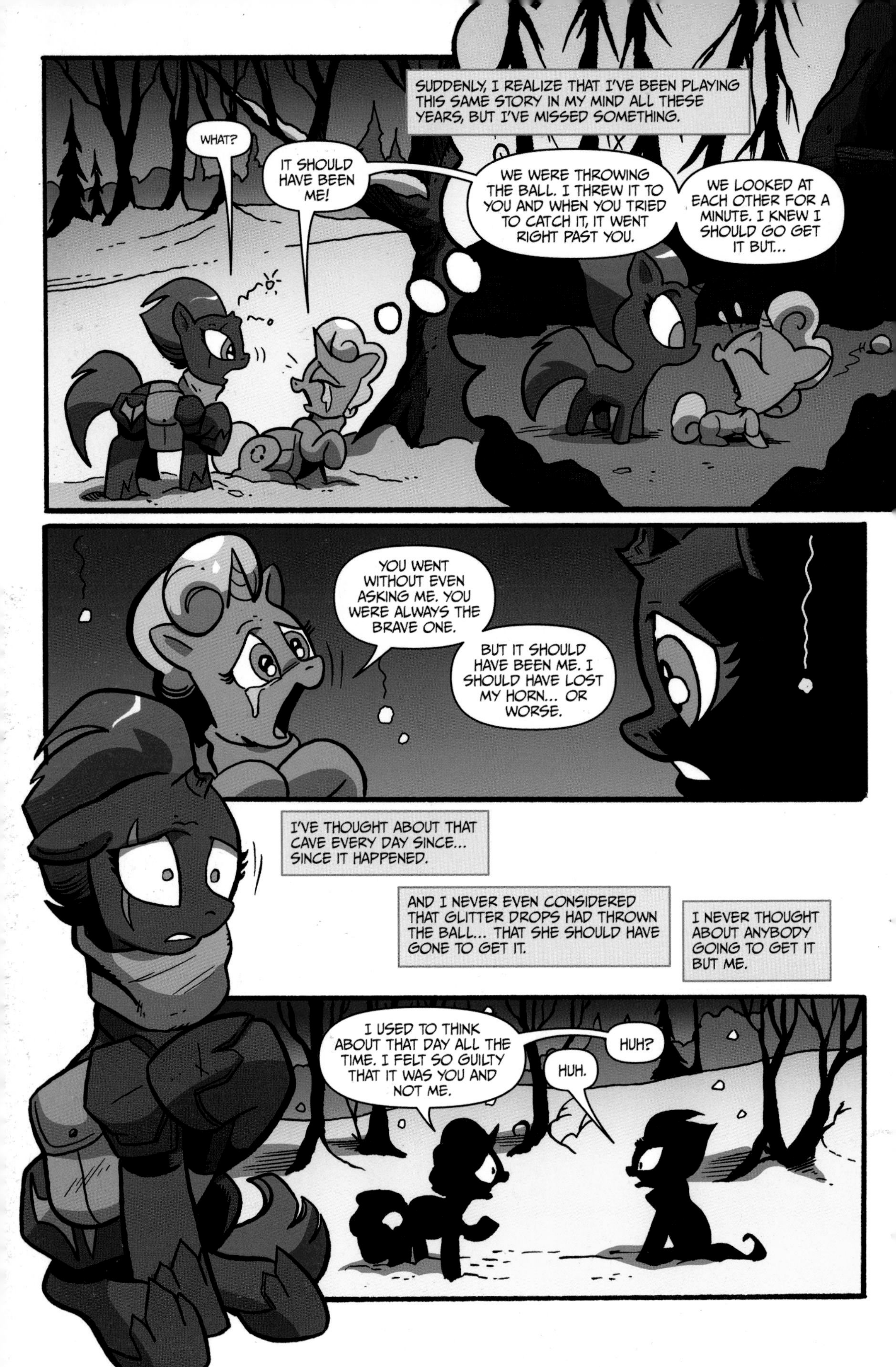

SUDDENLY, I REALIZE THAT I'VE BEEN PLAYING THIS SAME STORY IN MY MIND ALL THESE YEARS, BUT I'VE MISSED SOMETHING.
WHAT?
IT SHOULD HAVE BEEN ME!
WE WERE THROWING THE BALL. I THREW IT TO YOU AND WHEN YOU TRIED TO CATCH IT, IT WENT RIGHT PAST YOU.
WE LOOKED AT EACH OTHER FOR A MINUTE. I KNEW I SHOULD GO GET IT BUT...
YOU WENT WITHOUT EVEN ASKING ME. YOU WERE ALWAYS THE BRAVE ONE.
BUT IT SHOULD HAVE BEEN ME. I SHOULD HAVE LOST MY HORN... OR WORSE.
I'VE THOUGHT ABOUT THAT CAVE EVERY DAY SINCE... SINCE IT HAPPENED.
AND I NEVER EVEN CONSIDERED THAT GLITTER DROPS HAD THROWN THE BALL... THAT SHE SHOULD HAVE GONE TO GET IT.
I NEVER THOUGHT ABOUT ANYBODY GOING TO GET IT BUT ME.
I USED TO THINK ABOUT THAT DAY ALL THE TIME. I FELT SO GUILTY THAT IT WAS YOU AND NOT ME.
HUH?
HUH.

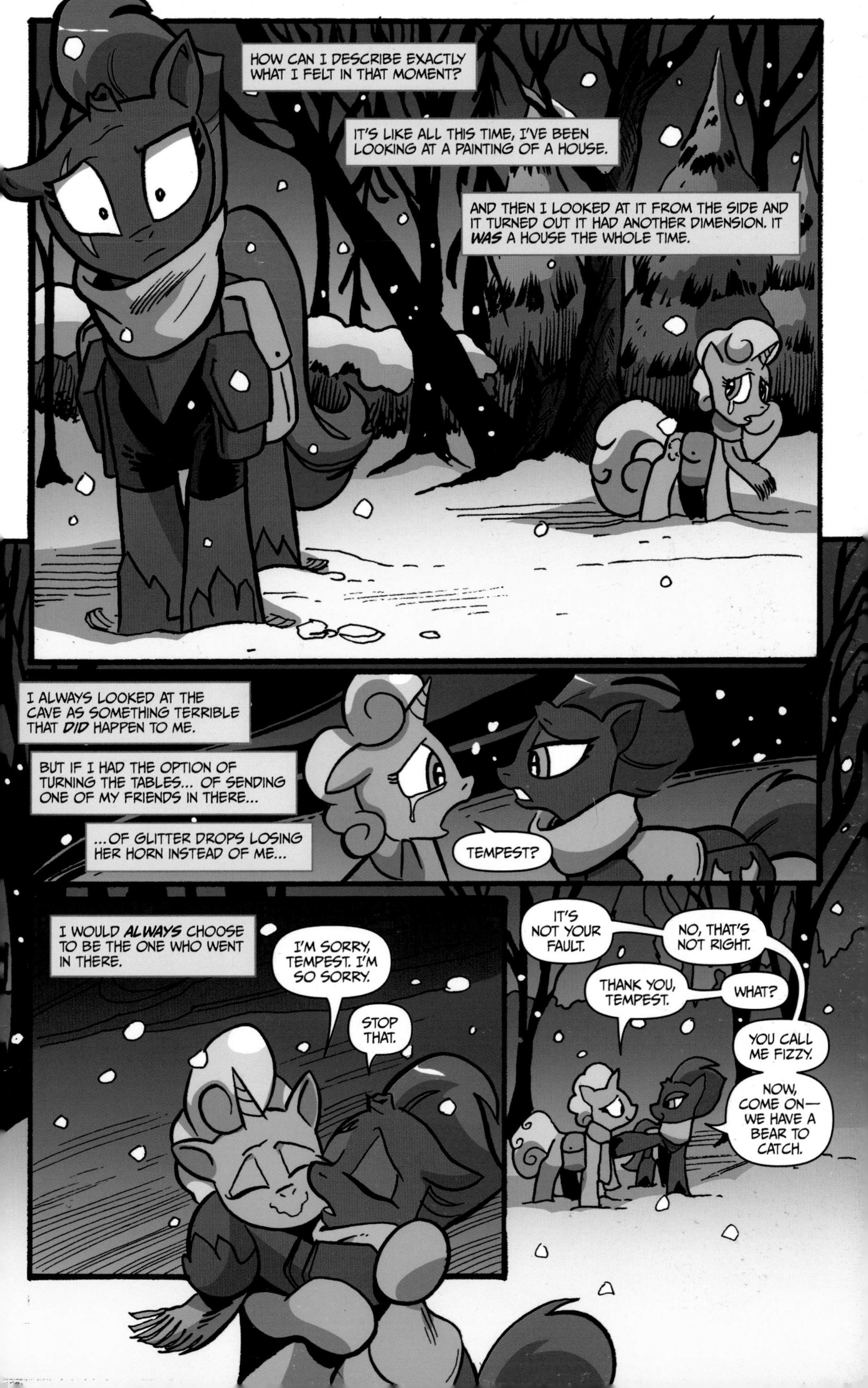
HOW CAN I DESCRIBE EXACTLY WHAT I FELT IN THAT MOMENT?
IT'S LIKE ALL THIS TIME, I'VE BEEN LOOKING AT A PAINTING OF A HOUSE.
AND THEN I LOOKED AT IT FROM THE SIDE AND IT TURNED OUT IT HAD ANOTHER DIMENSION. IT *WAS* A HOUSE THE WHOLE TIME.
I ALWAYS LOOKED AT THE CAVE AS SOMETHING TERRIBLE THAT *DID* HAPPEN TO ME.
BUT IF I HAD THE OPTION OF TURNING THE TABLES... OF SENDING ONE OF MY FRIENDS IN THERE...
...OF GLITTER DROPS LOSING HER HORN INSTEAD OF ME...
TEMPEST?
I WOULD *ALWAYS* CHOOSE TO BE THE ONE WHO WENT IN THERE.
I'M SORRY, TEMPEST. I'M SO SORRY.
STOP THAT.
IT'S NOT YOUR FAULT.
NO, THAT'S NOT RIGHT.
THANK YOU, TEMPEST.
WHAT?
YOU CALL ME FIZZY.
NOW, COME ON— WE HAVE A BEAR TO CATCH.

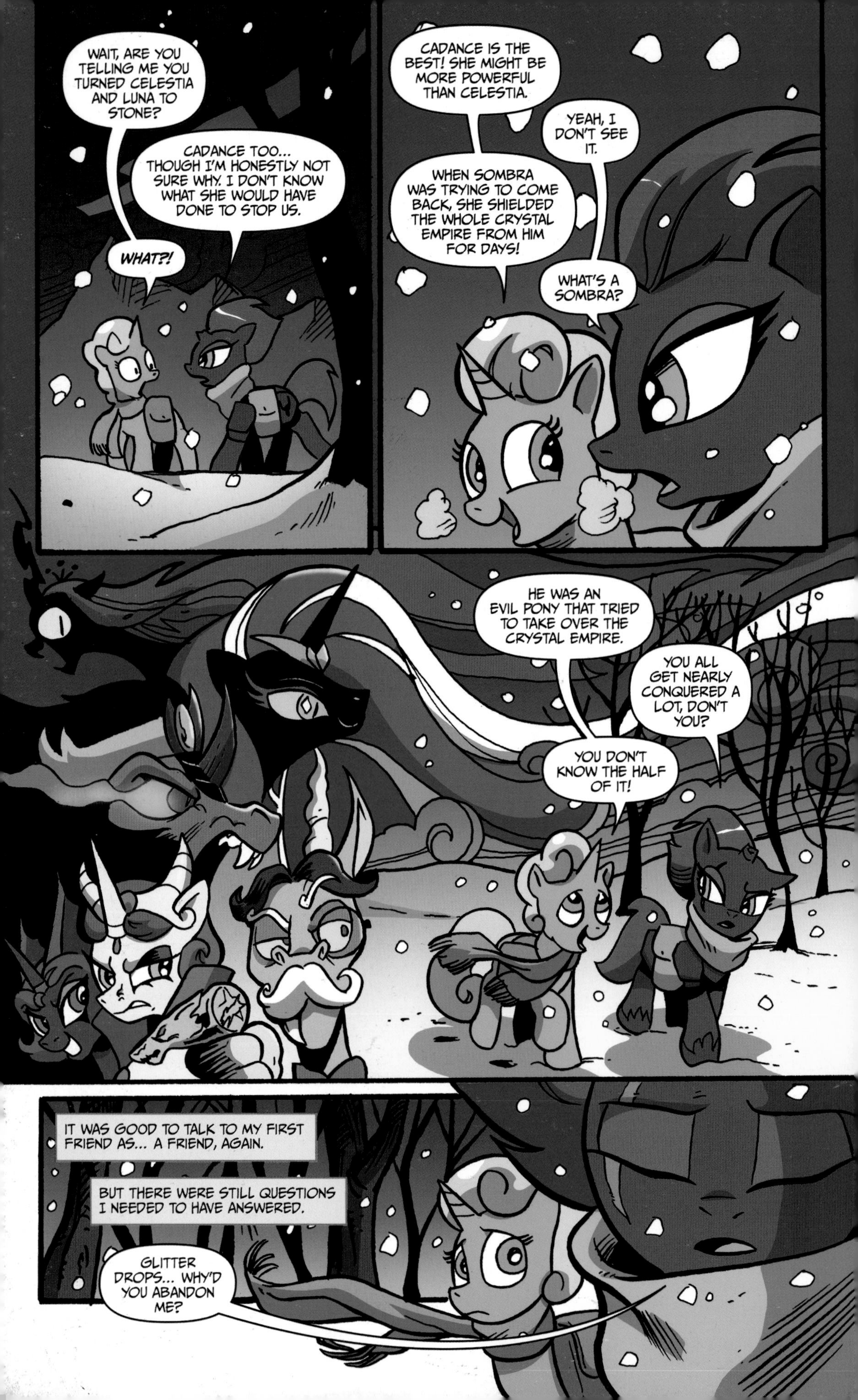

WAIT, ARE YOU TELLING ME YOU TURNED CELESTIA AND LUNA TO STONE?
CADANCE TOO... THOUGH I'M HONESTLY NOT SURE WHY. I DON'T KNOW WHAT SHE WOULD HAVE DONE TO STOP US.
WHAT?!
CADANCE IS THE BEST! SHE MIGHT BE MORE POWERFUL THAN CELESTIA.
YEAH, I DON'T SEE IT.
WHEN SOMBRA WAS TRYING TO COME BACK, SHE SHIELDED THE WHOLE CRYSTAL EMPIRE FROM HIM FOR DAYS!
WHAT'S A SOMBRA?
HE WAS AN EVIL PONY THAT TRIED TO TAKE OVER THE CRYSTAL EMPIRE.
YOU ALL GET NEARLY CONQUERED A LOT, DON'T YOU?
YOU DON'T KNOW THE HALF OF IT!
IT WAS GOOD TO TALK TO MY FIRST FRIEND AS... A FRIEND, AGAIN.
BUT THERE WERE STILL QUESTIONS I NEEDED TO HAVE ANSWERED.
GLITTER DROPS... WHY'D YOU ABANDON ME?

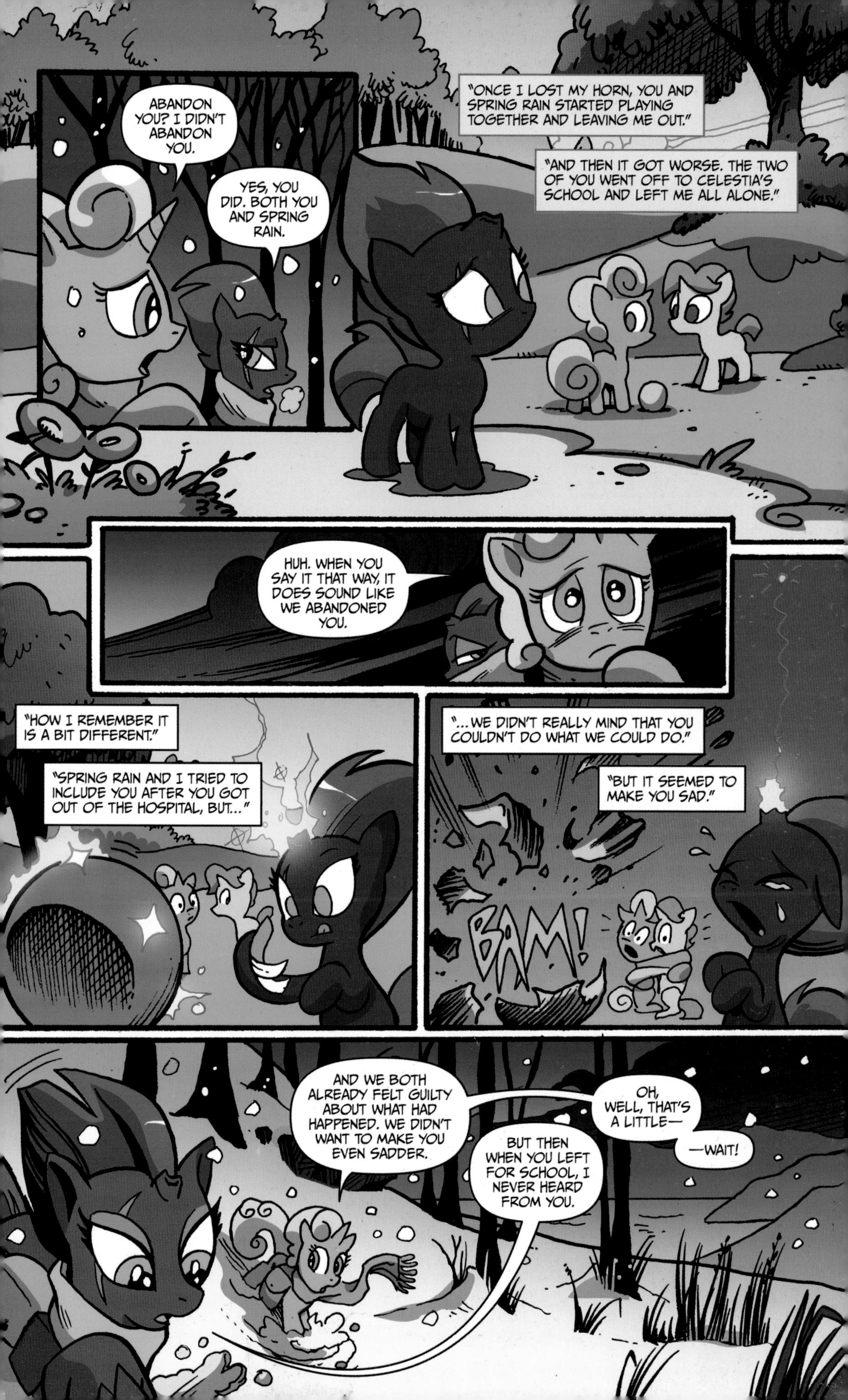
ABANDON YOU? I DIDN'T ABANDON YOU.
YES, YOU DID. BOTH YOU AND SPRING RAIN.
"ONCE I LOST MY HORN, YOU AND SPRING RAIN STARTED PLAYING TOGETHER AND LEAVING ME OUT."
"AND THEN IT GOT WORSE. THE TWO OF YOU WENT OFF TO CELESTIA'S SCHOOL AND LEFT ME ALL ALONE."
HUH. WHEN YOU SAY IT THAT WAY, IT DOES SOUND LIKE WE ABANDONED YOU.
"HOW I REMEMBER IT IS A BIT DIFFERENT."
"SPRING RAIN AND I TRIED TO INCLUDE YOU AFTER YOU GOT OUT OF THE HOSPITAL, BUT..."
"...WE DIDN'T REALLY MIND THAT YOU COULDN'T DO WHAT WE COULD DO."
"BUT IT SEEMED TO MAKE YOU SAD."
BAM!
AND WE BOTH ALREADY FELT GUILTY ABOUT WHAT HAD HAPPENED. WE DIDN'T WANT TO MAKE YOU EVEN SADDER.
OH, WELL, THAT'S A LITTLE—
—WAIT!
BUT THEN WHEN YOU LEFT FOR SCHOOL, I NEVER HEARD FROM YOU.

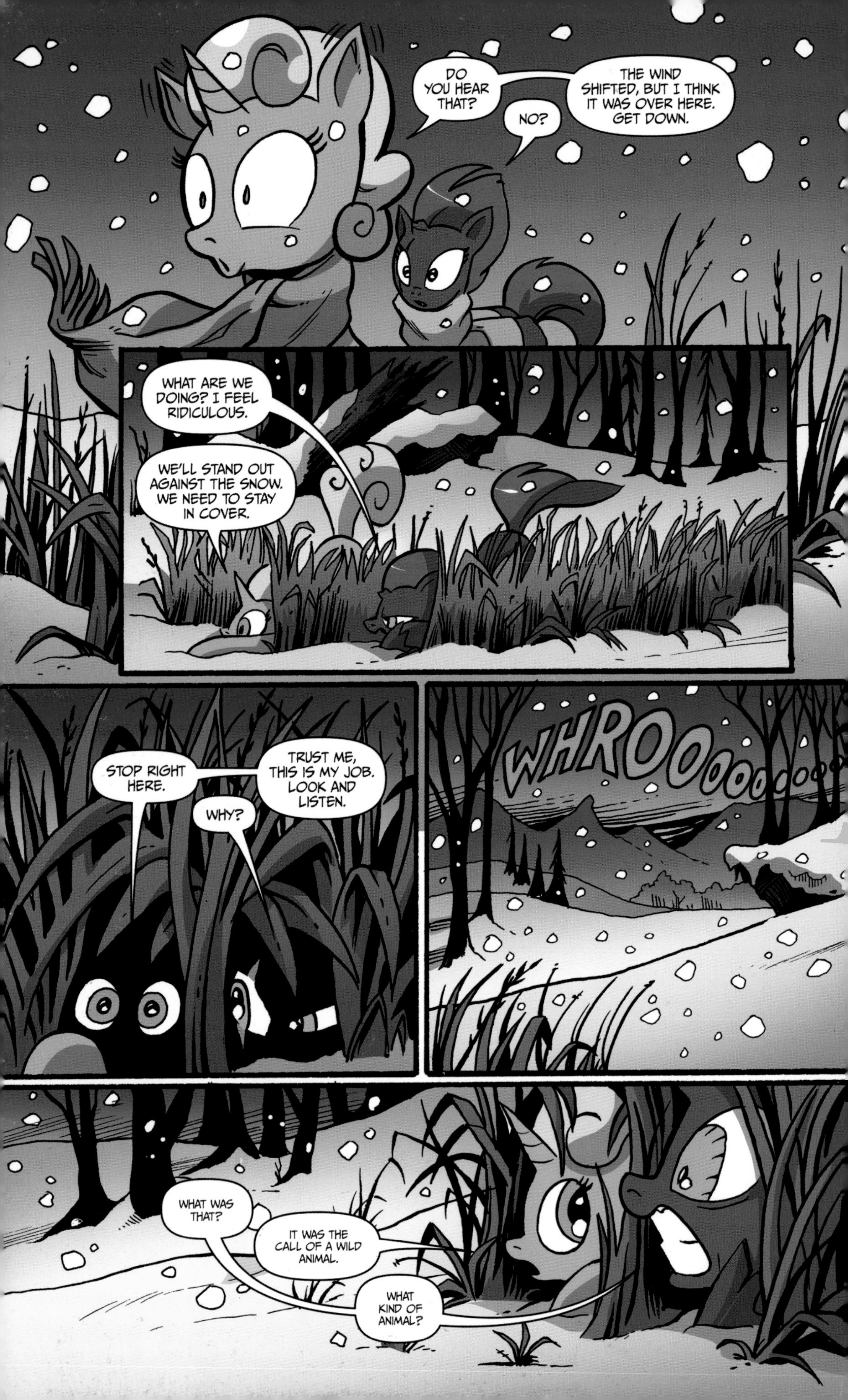
DO YOU HEAR THAT?
NO?
THE WIND SHIFTED, BUT I THINK IT WAS OVER HERE. GET DOWN.
WHAT ARE WE DOING? I FEEL RIDICULOUS.
WE'LL STAND OUT AGAINST THE SNOW. WE NEED TO STAY IN COVER.
STOP RIGHT HERE.
WHY?
TRUST ME, THIS IS MY JOB. LOOK AND LISTEN.
WHROOoooooo
WHAT WAS THAT?
IT WAS THE CALL OF A WILD ANIMAL.
WHAT KIND OF ANIMAL?

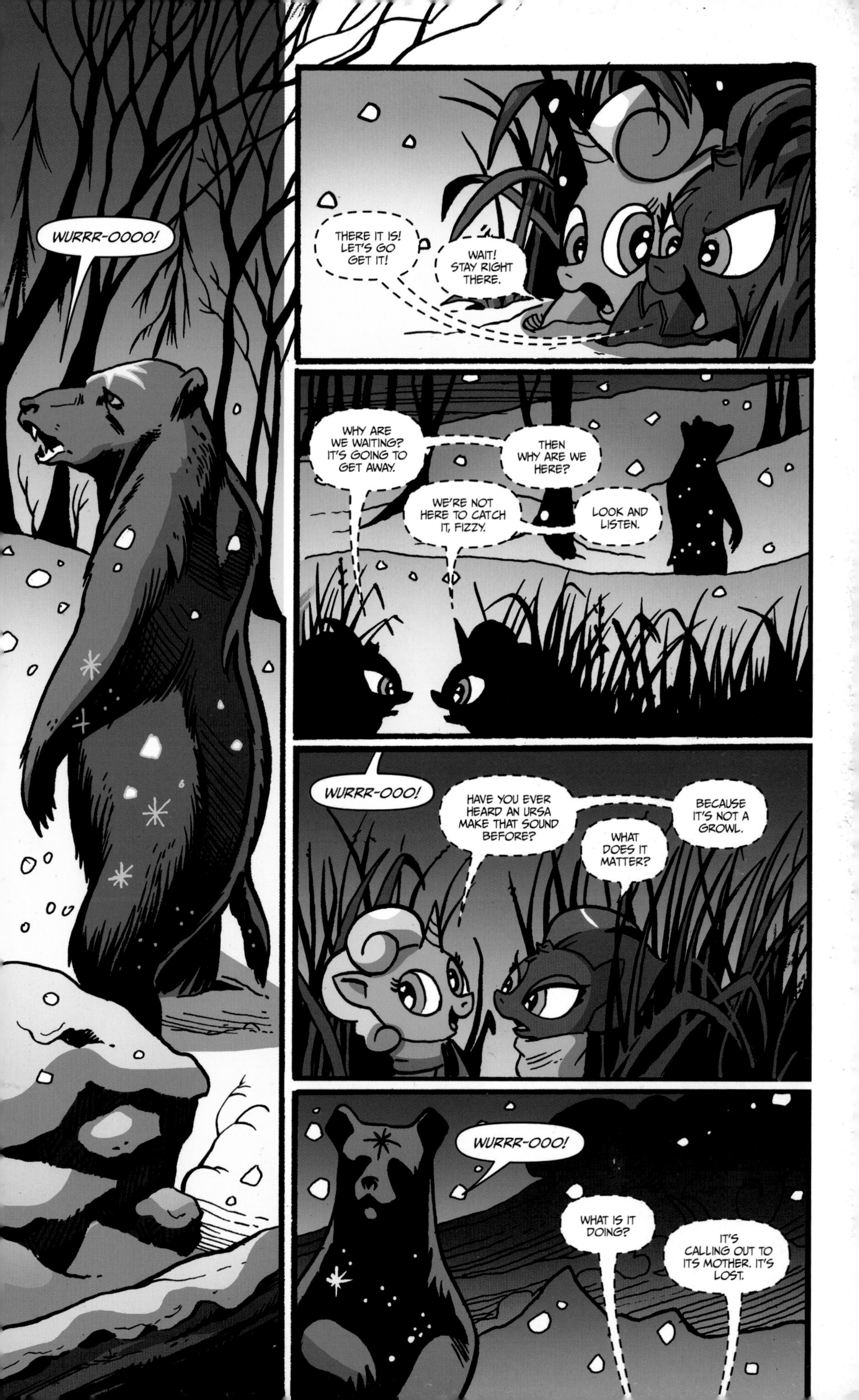
WURRR-OOOO!
THERE IT IS! LET'S GO GET IT!
WAIT! STAY RIGHT THERE.
WHY ARE WE WAITING? IT'S GOING TO GET AWAY.
THEN WHY ARE WE HERE?
WE'RE NOT HERE TO CATCH IT, FIZZY.
LOOK AND LISTEN.
WURRR-OOO!
HAVE YOU EVER HEARD AN URSA MAKE THAT SOUND BEFORE?
WHAT DOES IT MATTER?
BECAUSE IT'S NOT A GROWL.
WURRR-OOO!
WHAT IS IT DOING?
IT'S CALLING OUT TO ITS MOTHER. IT'S LOST.

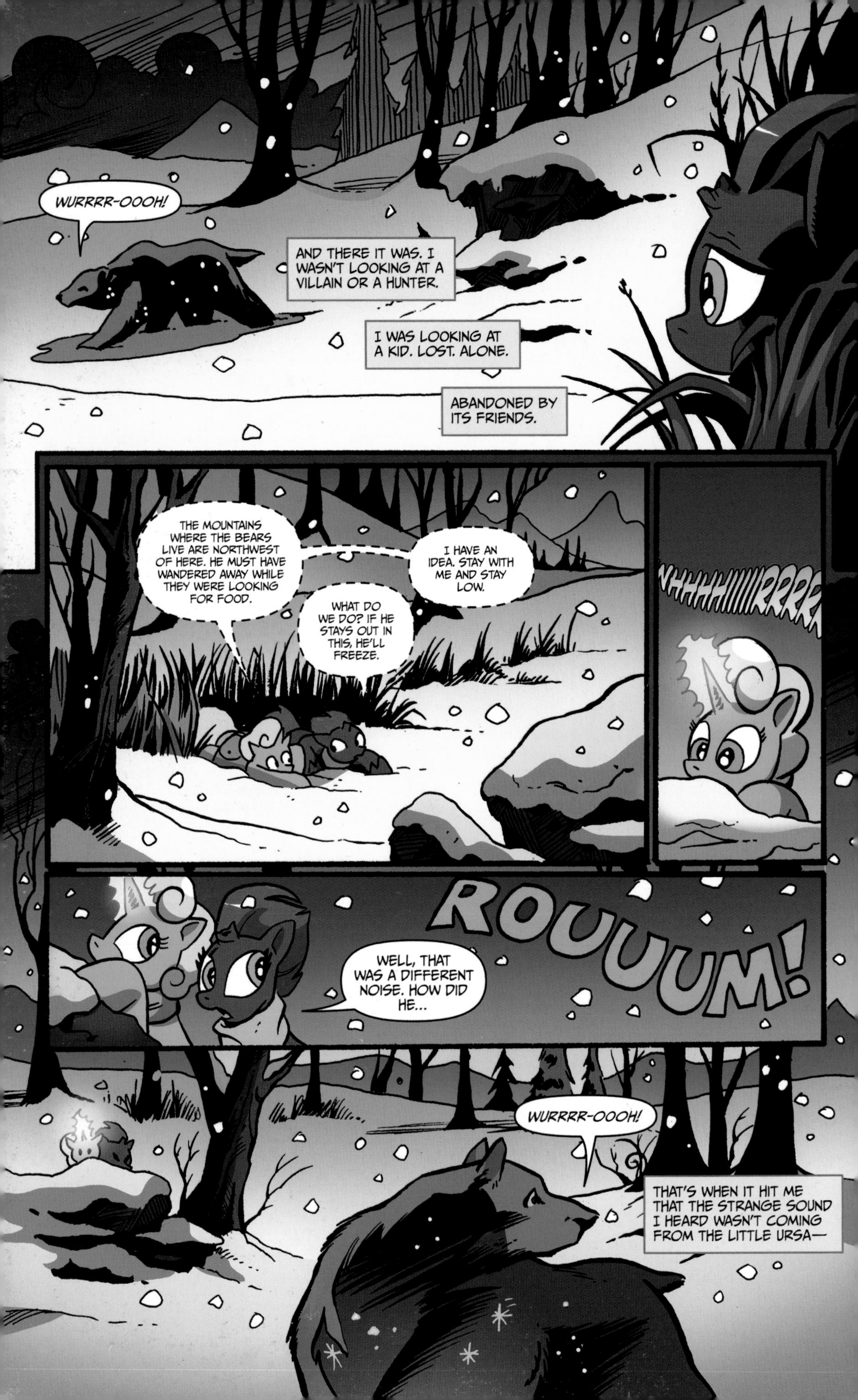
WURRRR-OOOH!
AND THERE IT WAS. I WASN'T LOOKING AT A VILLAIN OR A HUNTER.
I WAS LOOKING AT A KID. LOST. ALONE.
ABANDONED BY ITS FRIENDS.
THE MOUNTAINS WHERE THE BEARS LIVE ARE NORTHWEST OF HERE. HE MUST HAVE WANDERED AWAY WHILE THEY WERE LOOKING FOR FOOD.
WHAT DO WE DO? IF HE STAYS OUT IN THIS, HE'LL FREEZE.
I HAVE AN IDEA. STAY WITH ME AND STAY LOW.
NHHHHIIIIRRRR
ROUUUUM!
WELL, THAT WAS A DIFFERENT NOISE. HOW DID HE...
WURRRR-OOOH!
THAT'S WHEN IT HIT ME THAT THE STRANGE SOUND I HEARD WASN'T COMING FROM THE LITTLE URSA—

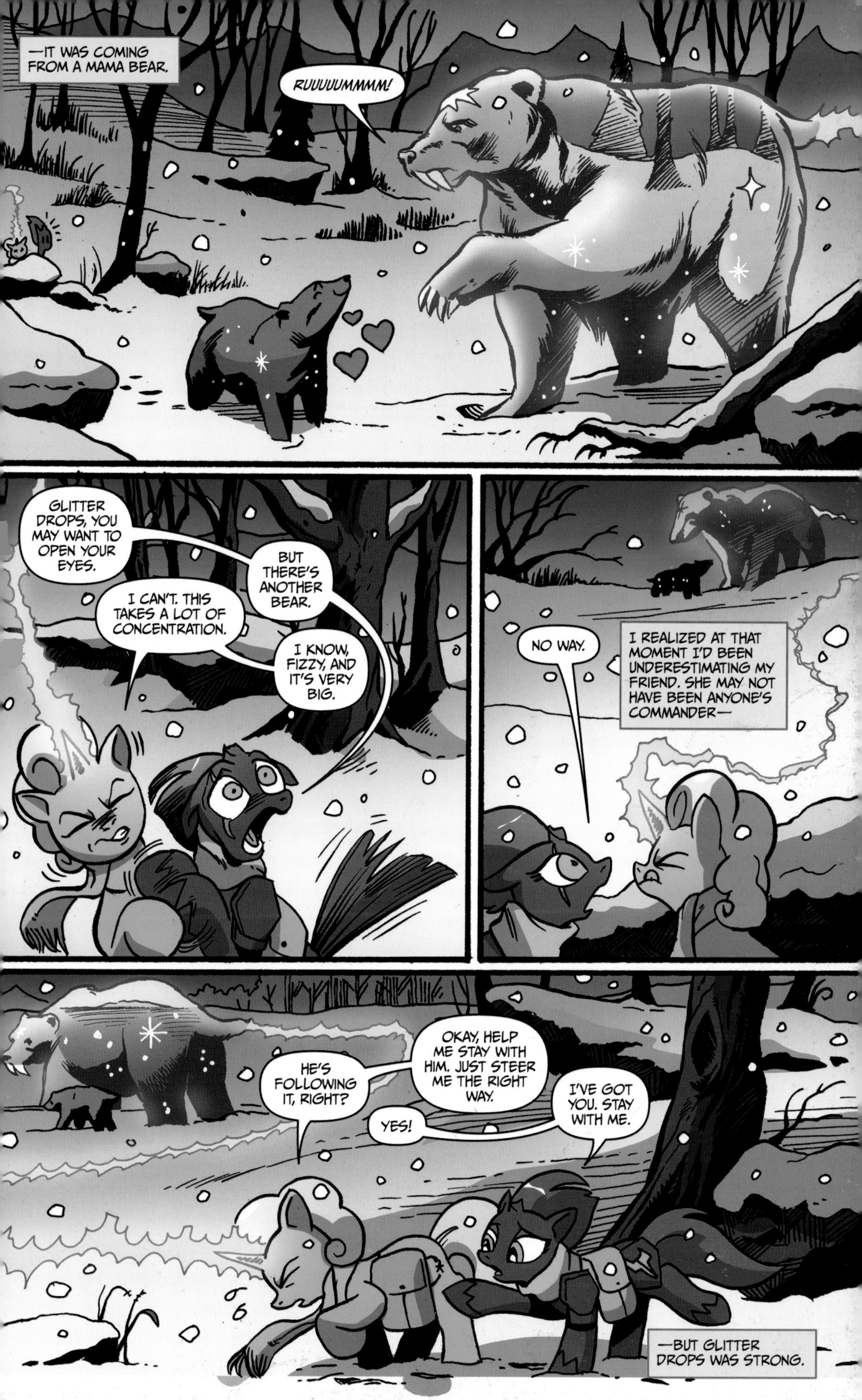
—IT WAS COMING FROM A MAMA BEAR.
RUUUUUMMMM!
GLITTER DROPS, YOU MAY WANT TO OPEN YOUR EYES.
I CAN'T. THIS TAKES A LOT OF CONCENTRATION.
BUT THERE'S ANOTHER BEAR.
I KNOW, FIZZY, AND IT'S VERY BIG.
NO WAY.
I REALIZED AT THAT MOMENT I'D BEEN UNDERESTIMATING MY FRIEND. SHE MAY NOT HAVE BEEN ANYONE'S COMMANDER—
HE'S FOLLOWING IT, RIGHT?
OKAY, HELP ME STAY WITH HIM. JUST STEER ME THE RIGHT WAY.
YES!
I'VE GOT YOU. STAY WITH ME.
—BUT GLITTER DROPS WAS STRONG.

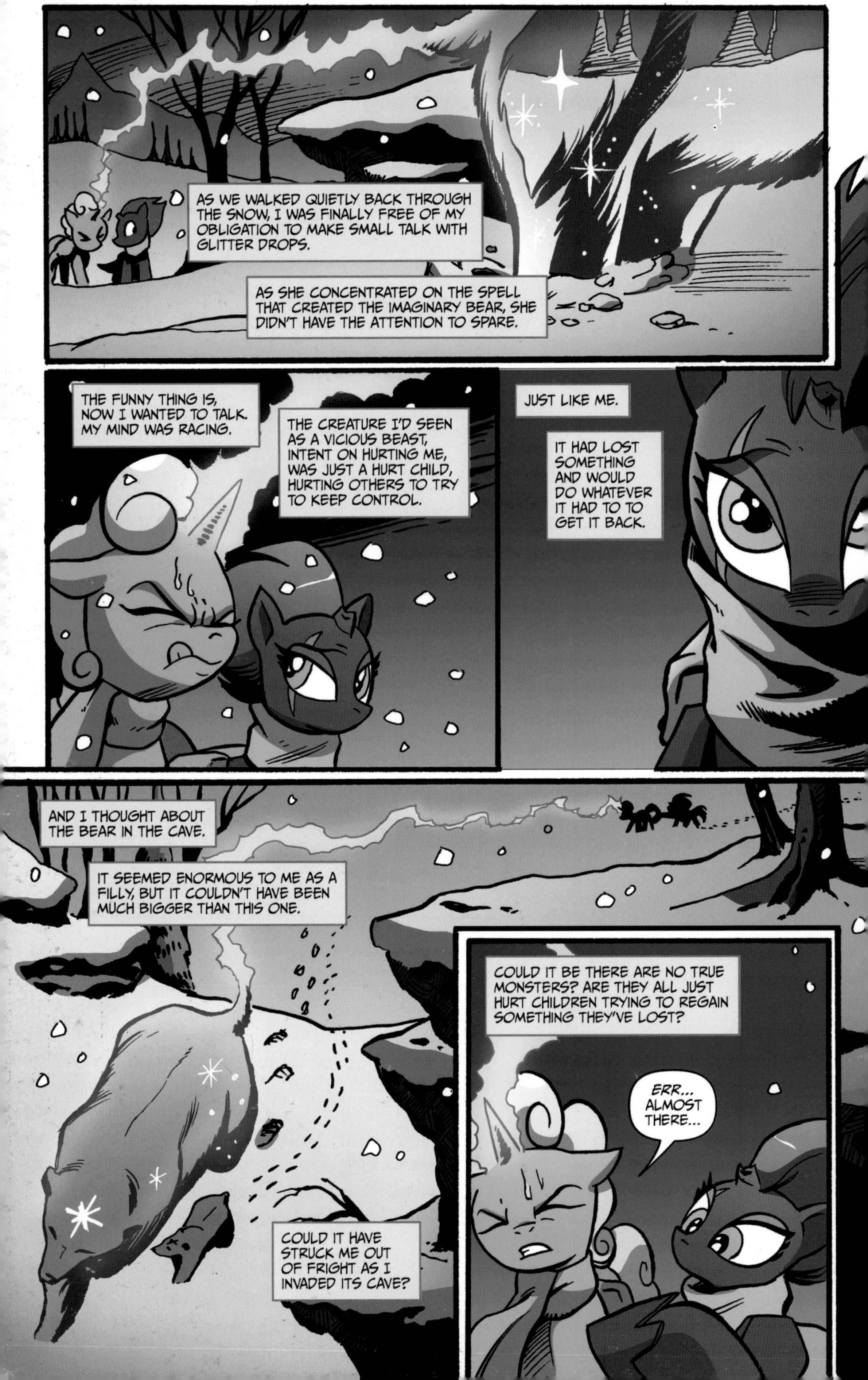
AS WE WALKED QUIETLY BACK THROUGH THE SNOW, I WAS FINALLY FREE OF MY OBLIGATION TO MAKE SMALL TALK WITH GLITTER DROPS.
AS SHE CONCENTRATED ON THE SPELL THAT CREATED THE IMAGINARY BEAR, SHE DIDN'T HAVE THE ATTENTION TO SPARE.
THE FUNNY THING IS, NOW I WANTED TO TALK. MY MIND WAS RACING.
THE CREATURE I'D SEEN AS A VICIOUS BEAST, INTENT ON HURTING ME, WAS JUST A HURT CHILD, HURTING OTHERS TO TRY TO KEEP CONTROL.
JUST LIKE ME.
IT HAD LOST SOMETHING AND WOULD DO WHATEVER IT HAD TO TO GET IT BACK.
AND I THOUGHT ABOUT THE BEAR IN THE CAVE.
IT SEEMED ENORMOUS TO ME AS A FILLY, BUT IT COULDN'T HAVE BEEN MUCH BIGGER THAN THIS ONE.
COULD IT HAVE STRUCK ME OUT OF FRIGHT AS I INVADED ITS CAVE?
COULD IT BE THERE ARE NO TRUE MONSTERS? ARE THEY ALL JUST HURT CHILDREN TRYING TO REGAIN SOMETHING THEY'VE LOST?
ERR... ALMOST THERE...

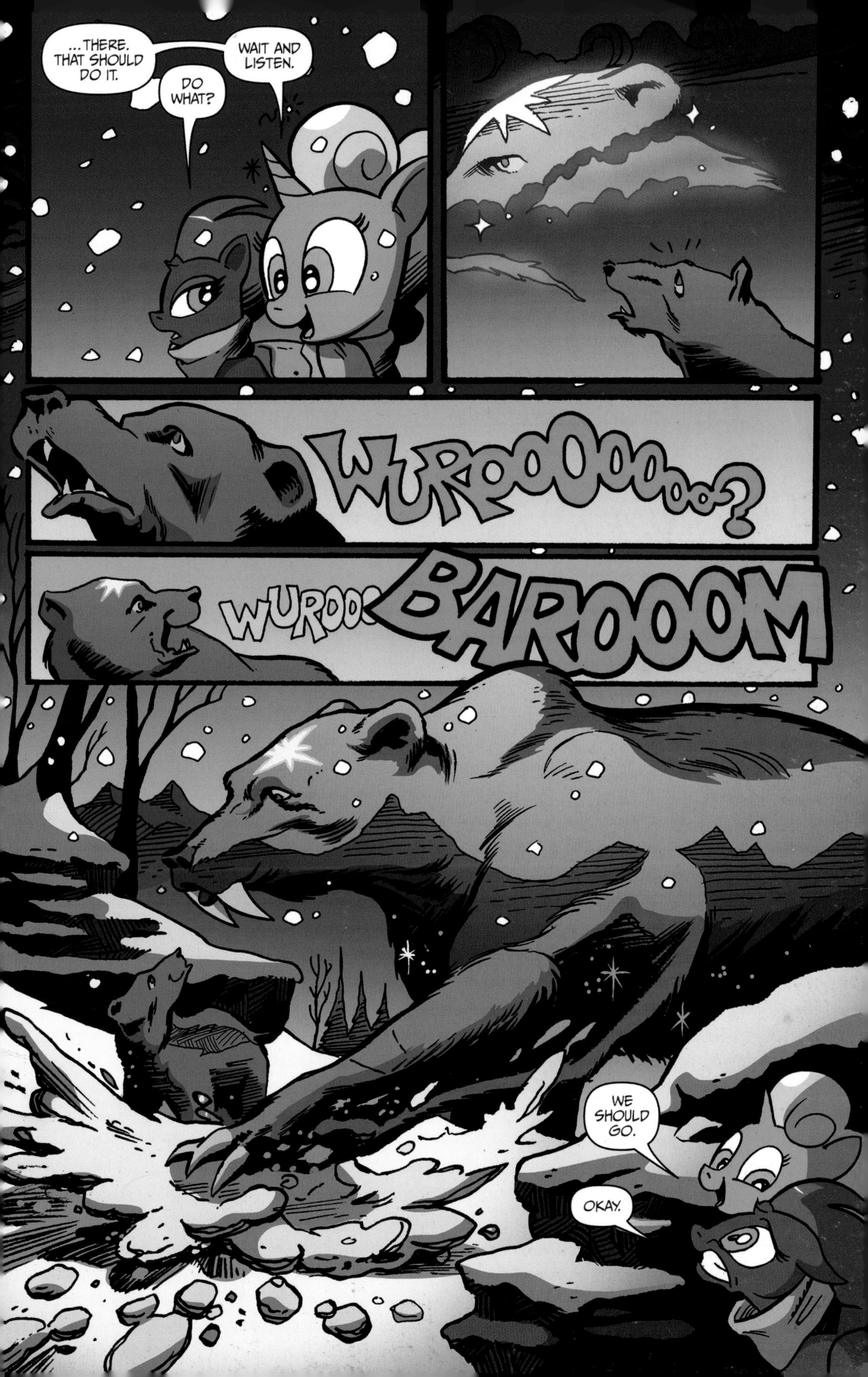
...THERE. THAT SHOULD DO IT.
DO WHAT?
WAIT AND LISTEN.
WUROOOOooo?
WUROO
BAROOOM
WE SHOULD GO.
OKAY.

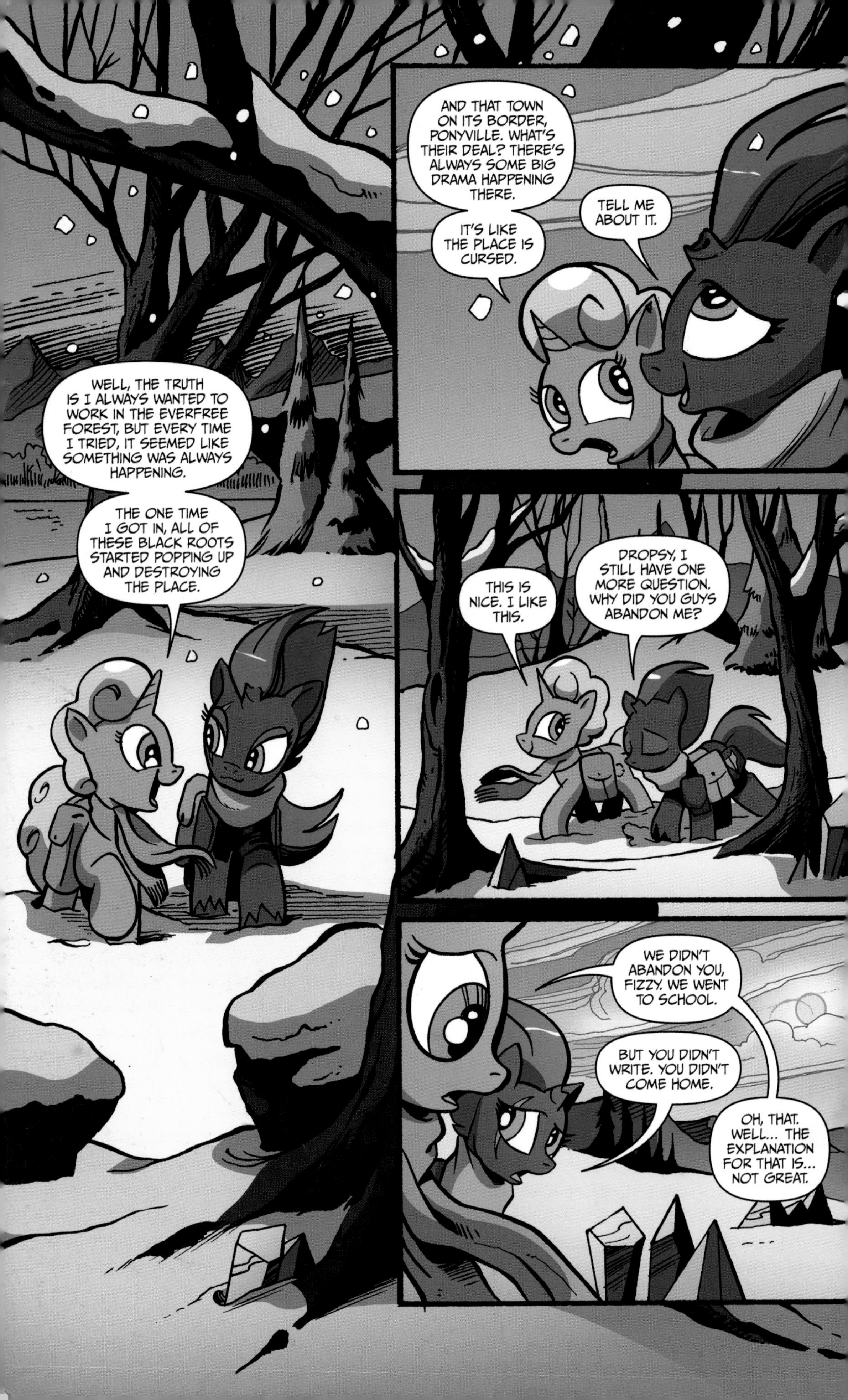
AND THAT TOWN ON ITS BORDER, PONYVILLE. WHAT'S THEIR DEAL? THERE'S ALWAYS SOME BIG DRAMA HAPPENING THERE.
IT'S LIKE THE PLACE IS CURSED.
TELL ME ABOUT IT.
WELL, THE TRUTH IS I ALWAYS WANTED TO WORK IN THE EVERFREE FOREST, BUT EVERY TIME I TRIED, IT SEEMED LIKE SOMETHING WAS ALWAYS HAPPENING.
THE ONE TIME I GOT IN, ALL OF THESE BLACK ROOTS STARTED POPPING UP AND DESTROYING THE PLACE.
THIS IS NICE. I LIKE THIS.
DROPSY, I STILL HAVE ONE MORE QUESTION. WHY DID YOU GUYS ABANDON ME?
WE DIDN'T ABANDON YOU, FIZZY. WE WENT TO SCHOOL.
BUT YOU DIDN'T WRITE. YOU DIDN'T COME HOME.
OH, THAT. WELL... THE EXPLANATION FOR THAT IS... NOT GREAT.

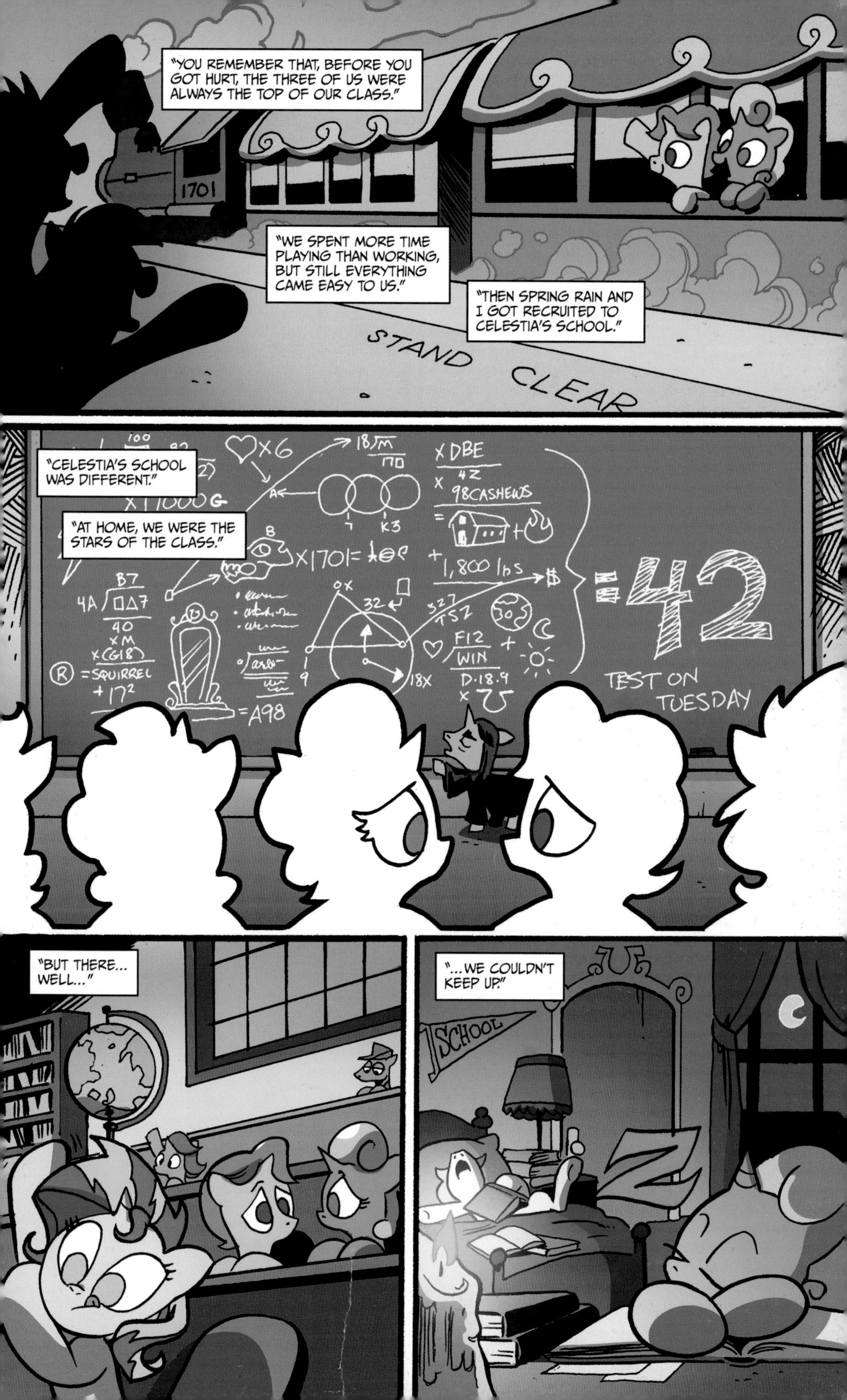
"YOU REMEMBER THAT, BEFORE YOU GOT HURT, THE THREE OF US WERE ALWAYS THE TOP OF OUR CLASS."
1701
"WE SPENT MORE TIME PLAYING THAN WORKING, BUT STILL EVERYTHING CAME EASY TO US."
"THEN SPRING RAIN AND I GOT RECRUITED TO CELESTIA'S SCHOOL."
STAND CLEAR
"CELESTIA'S SCHOOL WAS DIFFERENT."
"AT HOME, WE WERE THE STARS OF THE CLASS."
=42
TEST ON TUESDAY
"BUT THERE... WELL..."
"...WE COULDN'T KEEP UP."
SCHOOL

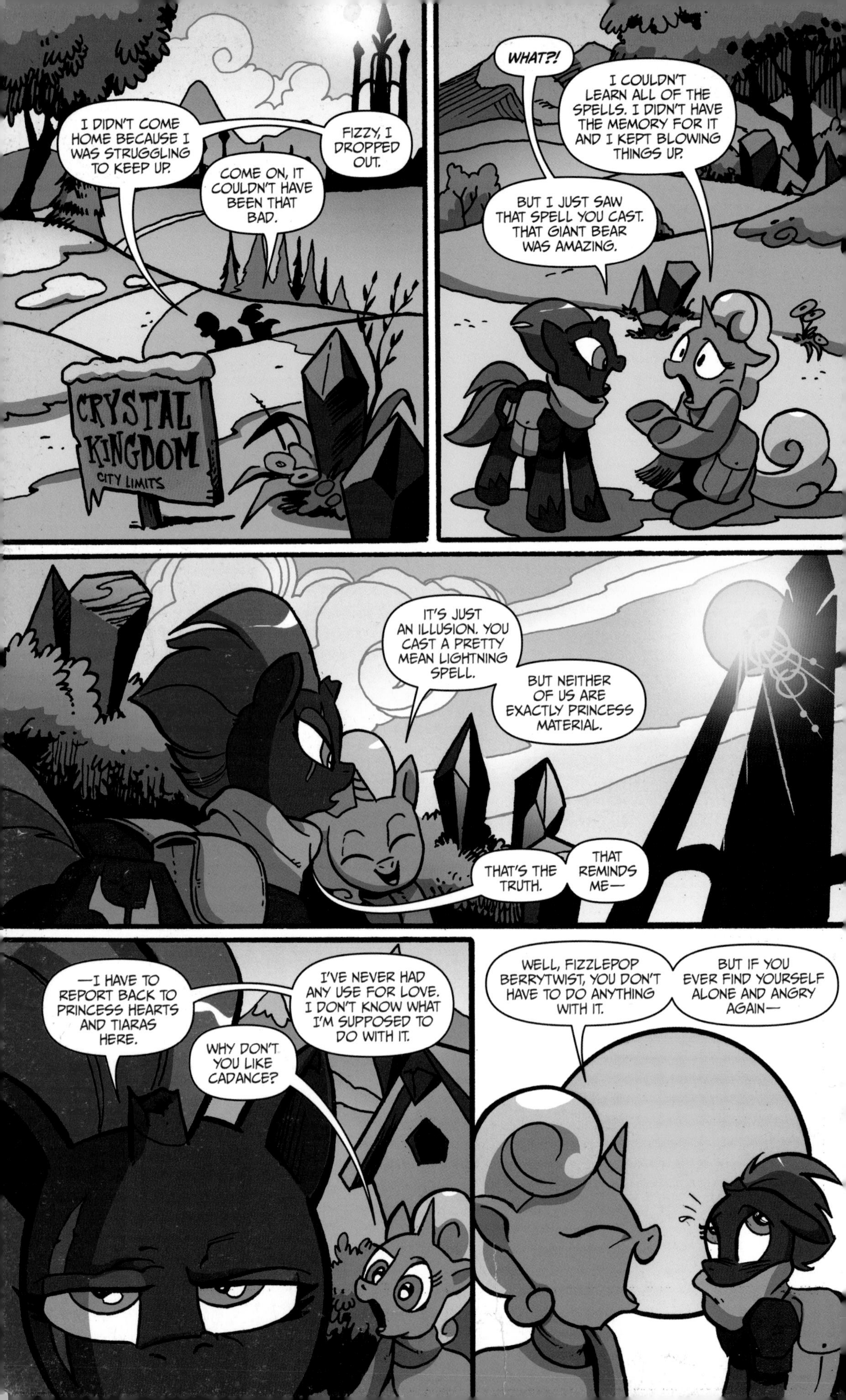

I DIDN'T COME HOME BECAUSE I WAS STRUGGLING TO KEEP UP.
FIZZY, I DROPPED OUT.
COME ON, IT COULDN'T HAVE BEEN THAT BAD.
CRYSTAL KINGDOM
CITY LIMITS
WHAT?!
I COULDN'T LEARN ALL OF THE SPELLS. I DIDN'T HAVE THE MEMORY FOR IT AND I KEPT BLOWING THINGS UP.
BUT I JUST SAW THAT SPELL YOU CAST. THAT GIANT BEAR WAS AMAZING.
IT'S JUST AN ILLUSION. YOU CAST A PRETTY MEAN LIGHTNING SPELL.
BUT NEITHER OF US ARE EXACTLY PRINCESS MATERIAL.
THAT'S THE TRUTH.
THAT REMINDS ME—
—I HAVE TO REPORT BACK TO PRINCESS HEARTS AND TIARAS HERE.
WHY DON'T YOU LIKE CADANCE?
I'VE NEVER HAD ANY USE FOR LOVE. I DON'T KNOW WHAT I'M SUPPOSED TO DO WITH IT.
WELL, FIZZLEPOP BERRYTWIST, YOU DON'T HAVE TO DO ANYTHING WITH IT.
BUT IF YOU EVER FIND YOURSELF ALONE AND ANGRY AGAIN—

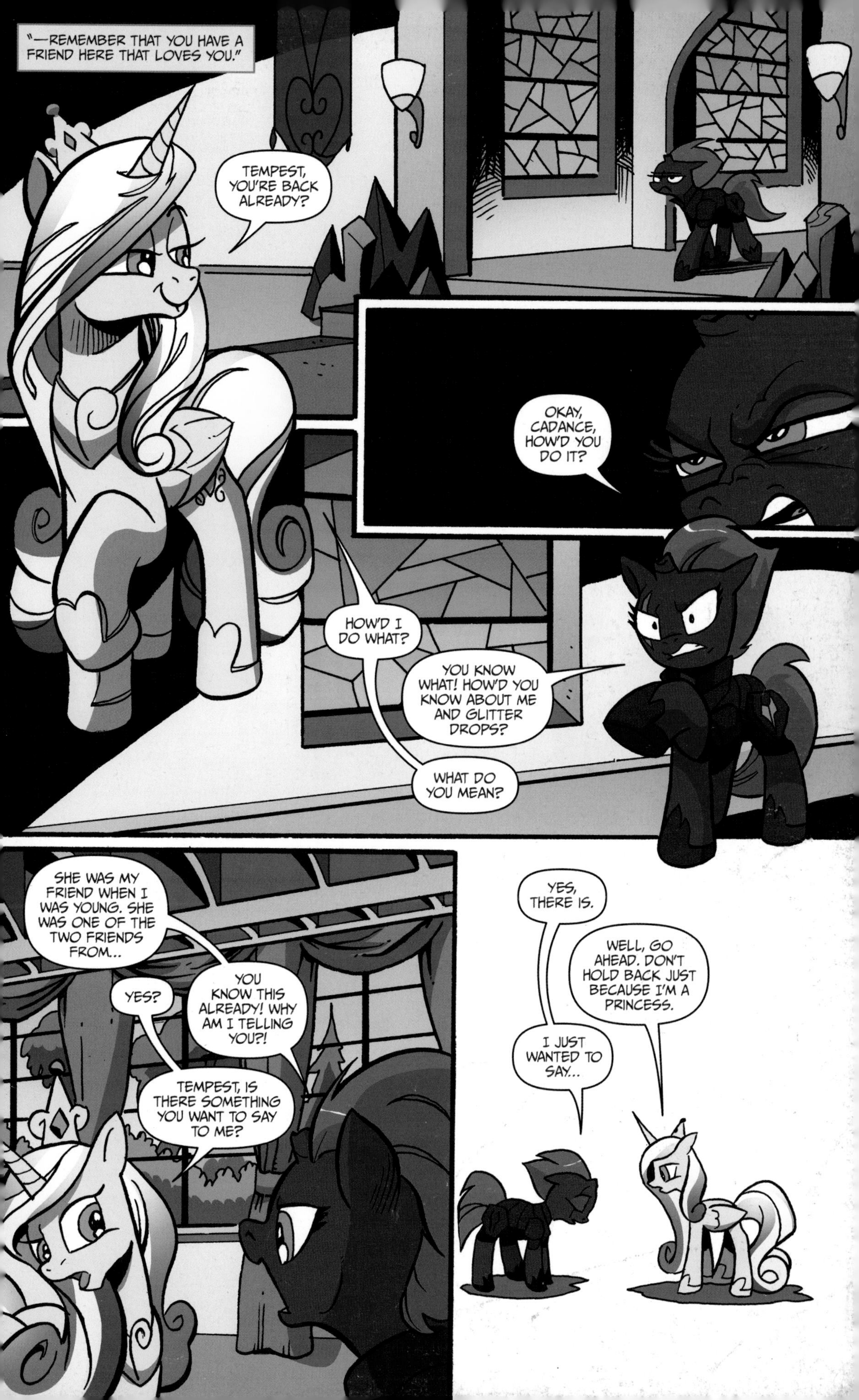
"—REMEMBER THAT YOU HAVE A FRIEND HERE THAT LOVES YOU."
TEMPEST, YOU'RE BACK ALREADY?
OKAY, CADANCE, HOW'D YOU DO IT?
HOW'D I DO WHAT?
YOU KNOW WHAT! HOW'D YOU KNOW ABOUT ME AND GLITTER DROPS?
WHAT DO YOU MEAN?
SHE WAS MY FRIEND WHEN I WAS YOUNG. SHE WAS ONE OF THE TWO FRIENDS FROM...
YES?
YOU KNOW THIS ALREADY! WHY AM I TELLING YOU?!
TEMPEST, IS THERE SOMETHING YOU WANT TO SAY TO ME?
YES, THERE IS.
WELL, GO AHEAD. DON'T HOLD BACK JUST BECAUSE I'M A PRINCESS.
I JUST WANTED TO SAY...

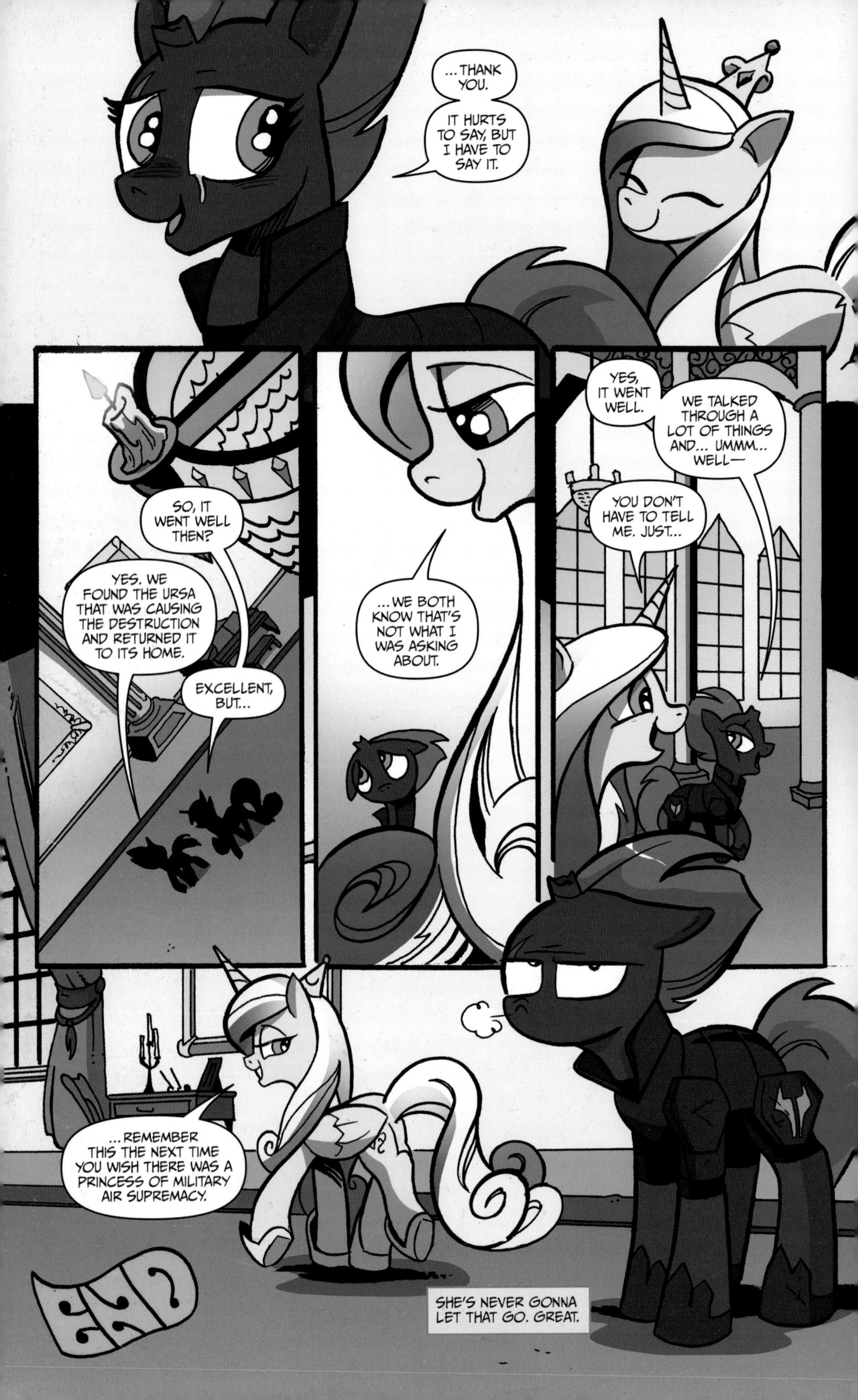
...THANK YOU.
IT HURTS TO SAY, BUT I HAVE TO SAY IT.
SO, IT WENT WELL THEN?
YES. WE FOUND THE URSA THAT WAS CAUSING THE DESTRUCTION AND RETURNED IT TO ITS HOME.
EXCELLENT, BUT...
...WE BOTH KNOW THAT'S NOT WHAT I WAS ASKING ABOUT.
YES, IT WENT WELL.
WE TALKED THROUGH A LOT OF THINGS AND... UMMM... WELL—
YOU DON'T HAVE TO TELL ME. JUST...
...REMEMBER THIS THE NEXT TIME YOU WISH THERE WAS A PRINCESS OF MILITARY AIR SUPREMACY.
SHE'S NEVER GONNA LET THAT GO. GREAT.

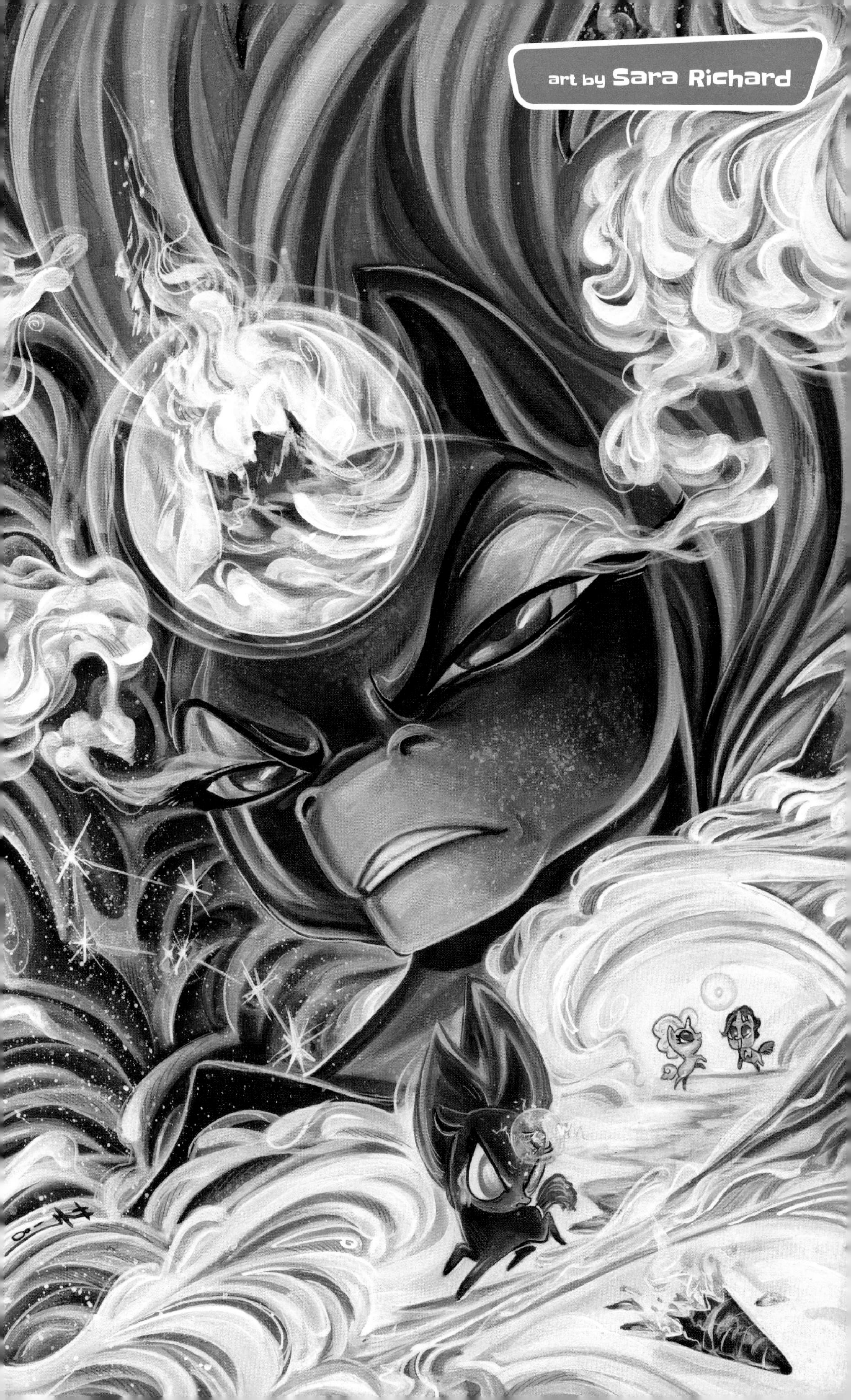

art by Sara Richard

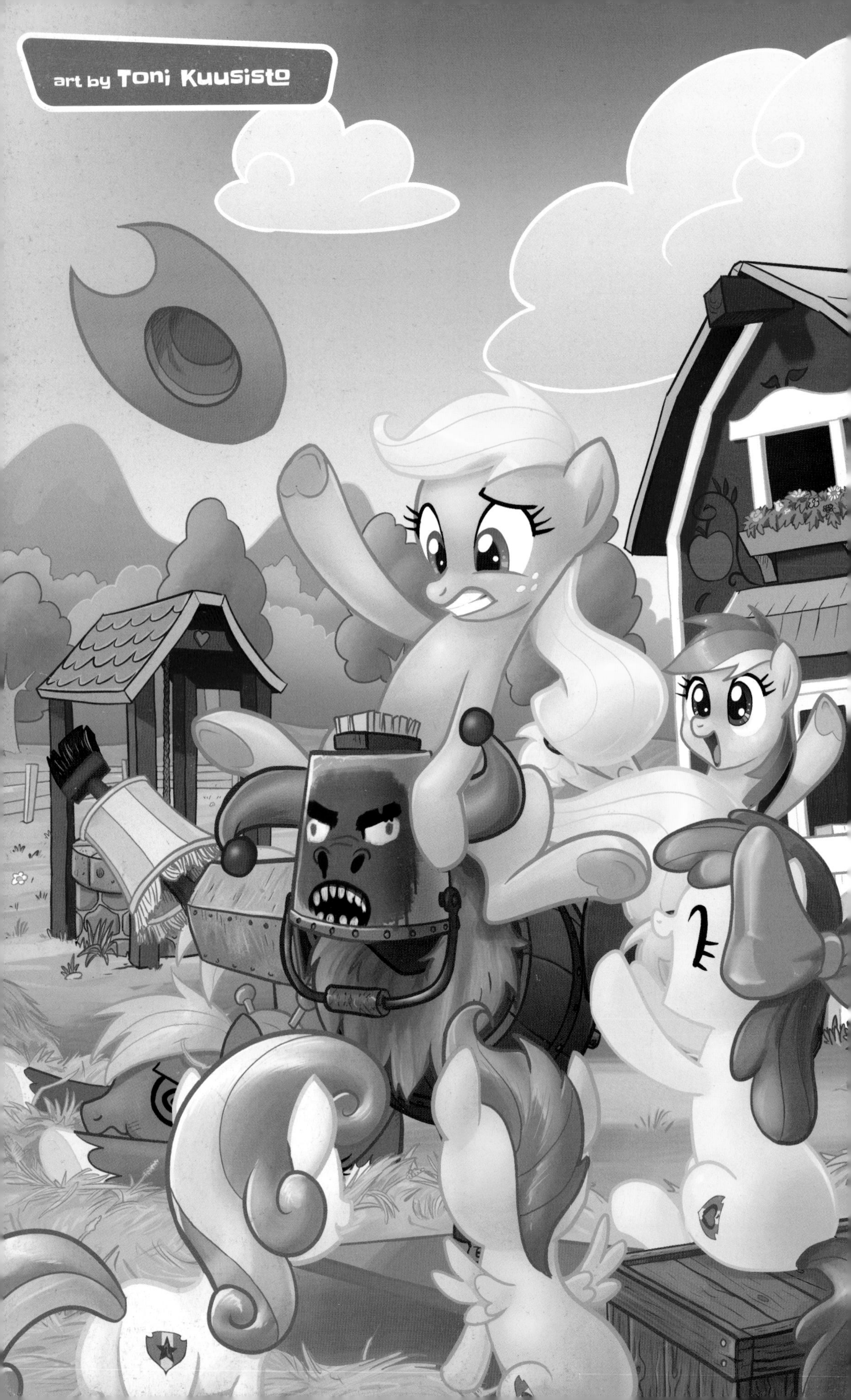

art by Toni Kuusisto

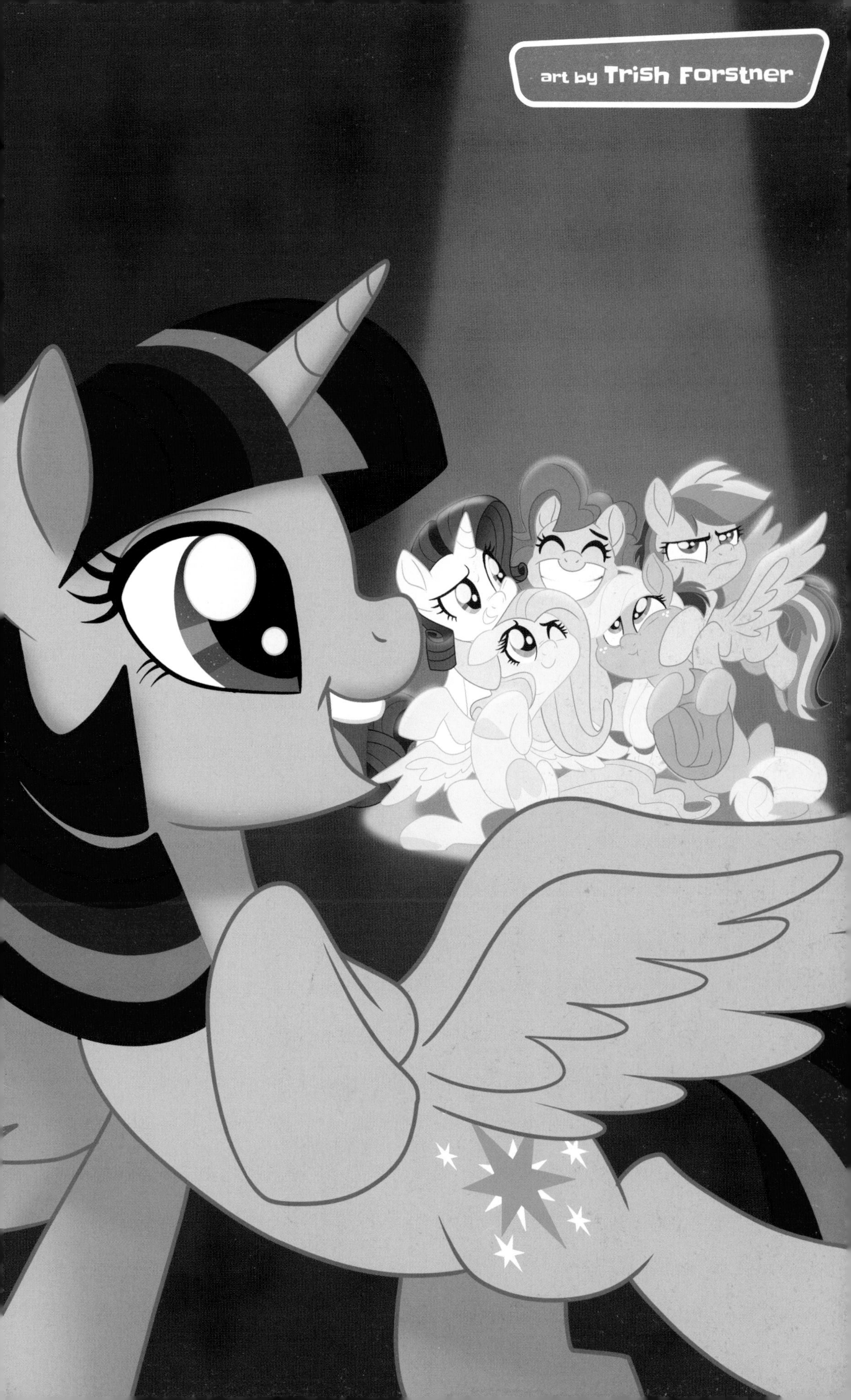
art by Trish Forstner

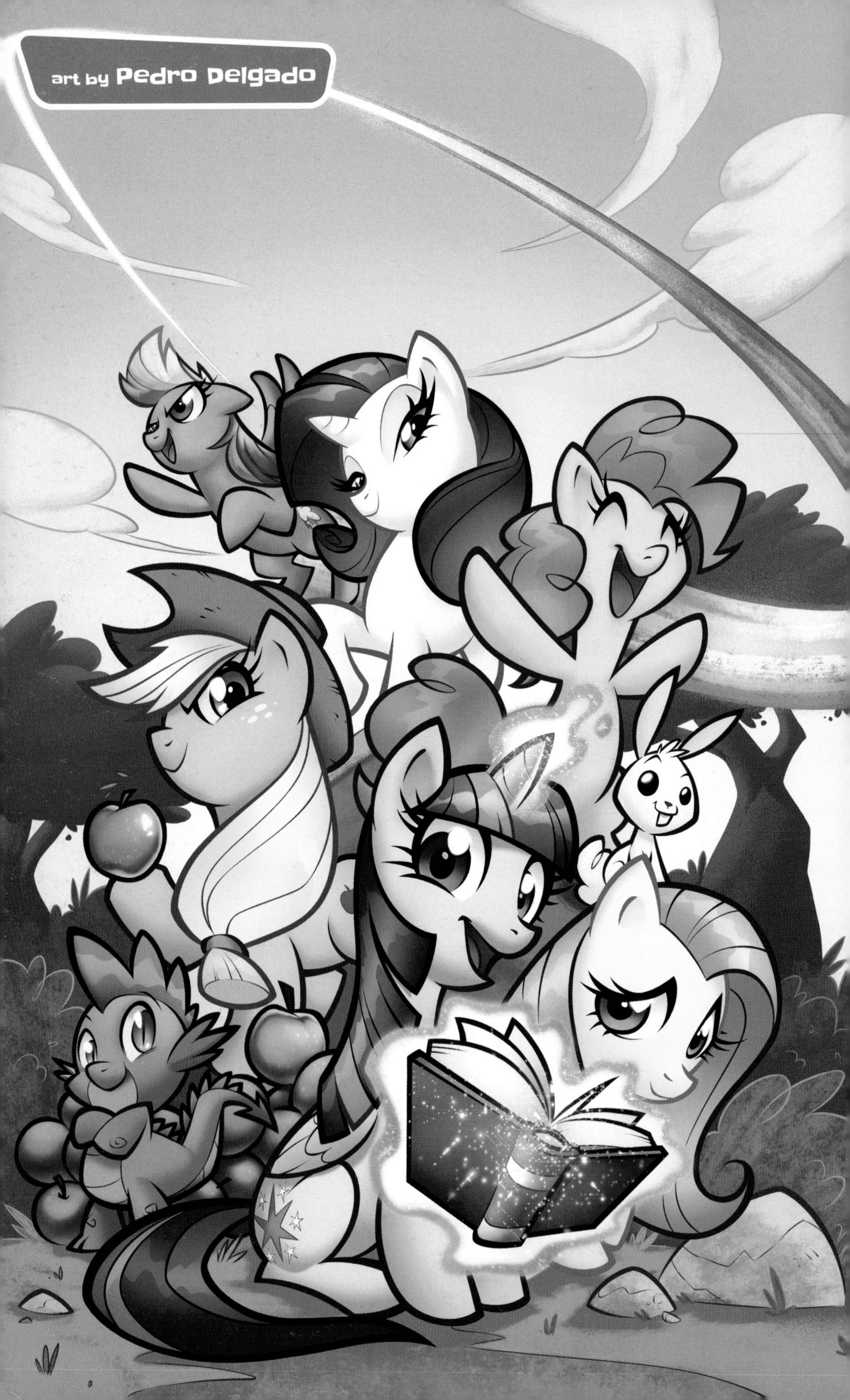
art by Pedro Delgado

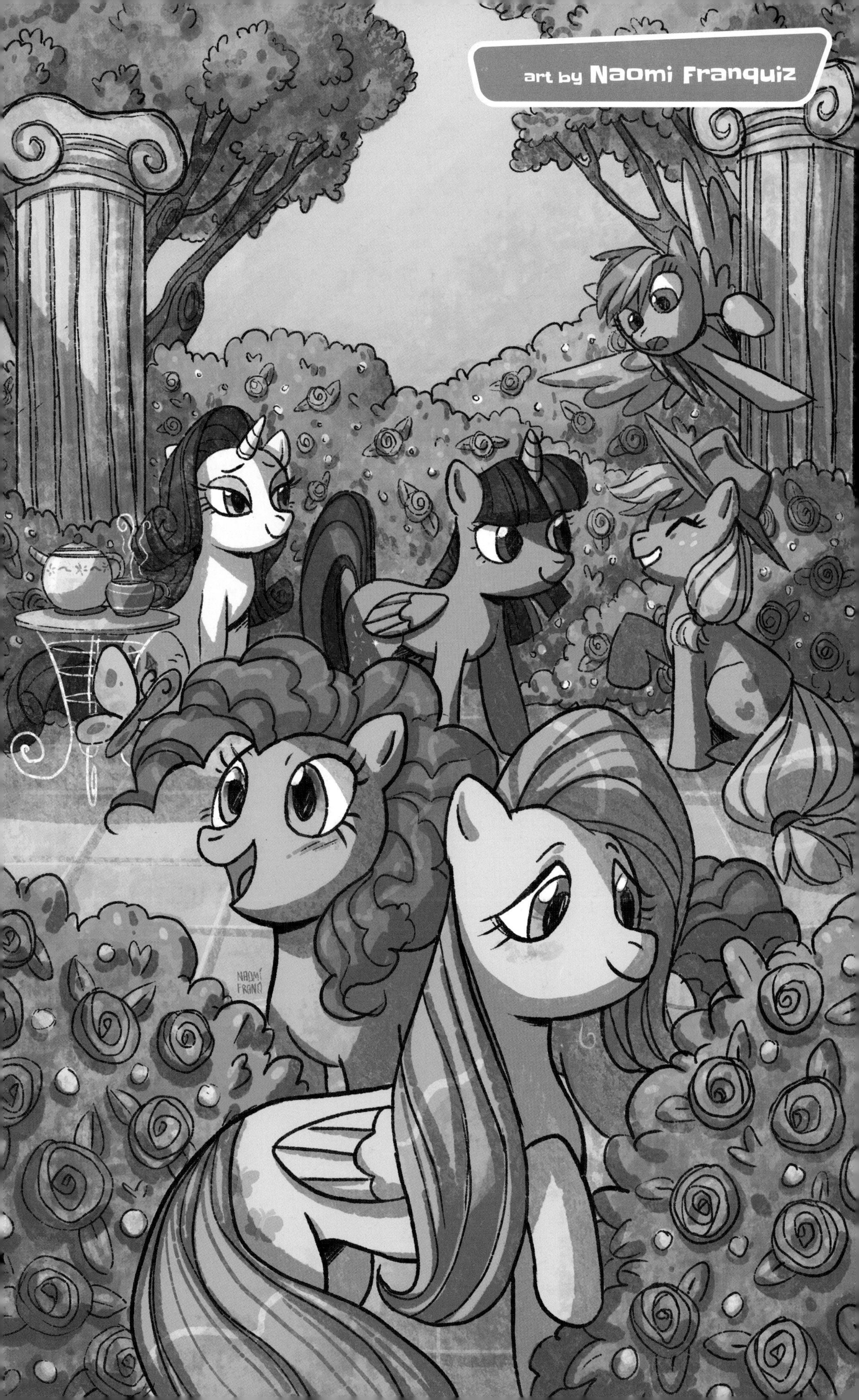
art by Naomi Franquiz
NAOMI FRANQ

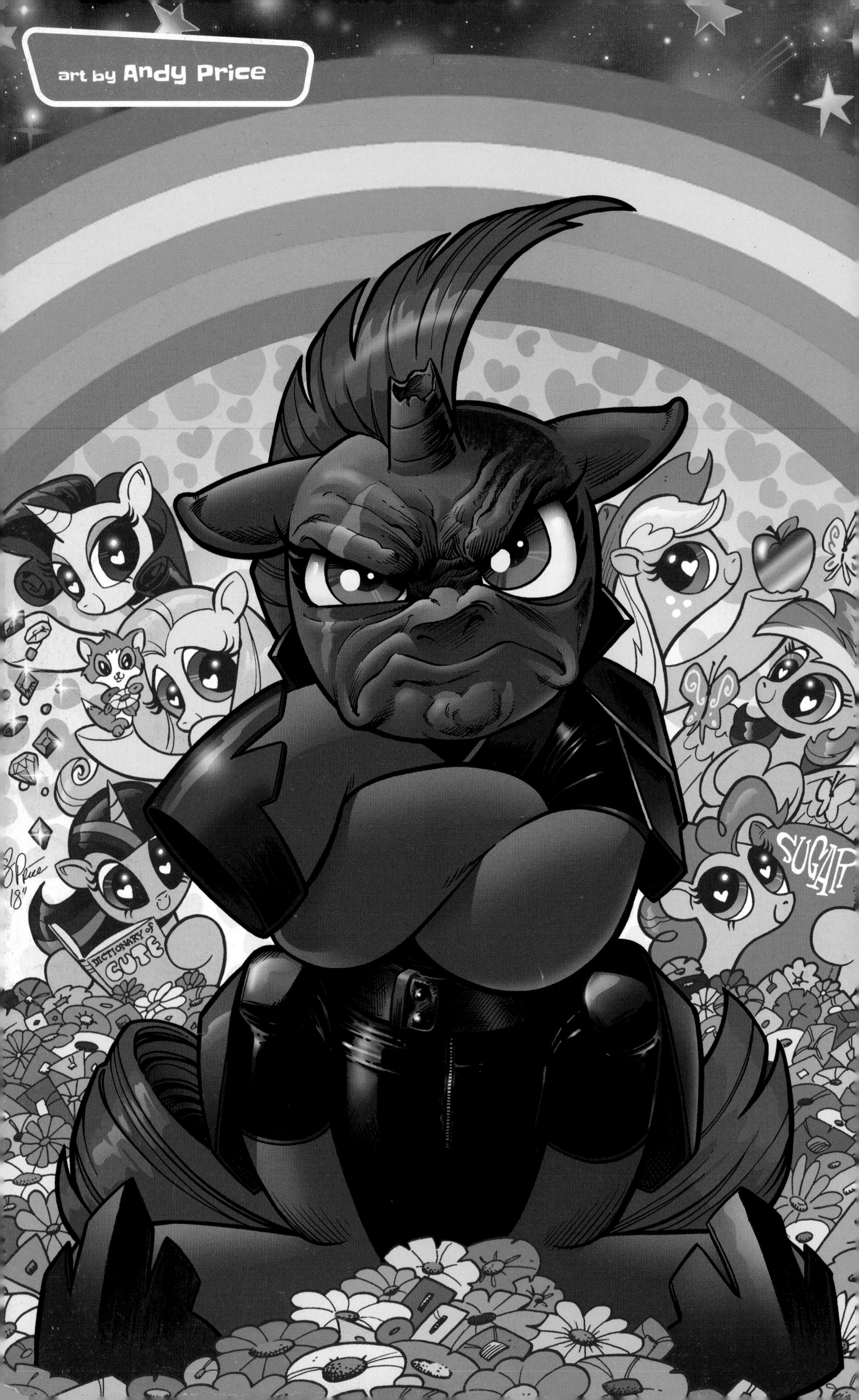
SUGAR
DICTIONARY OF CUTE

art by Andy Price

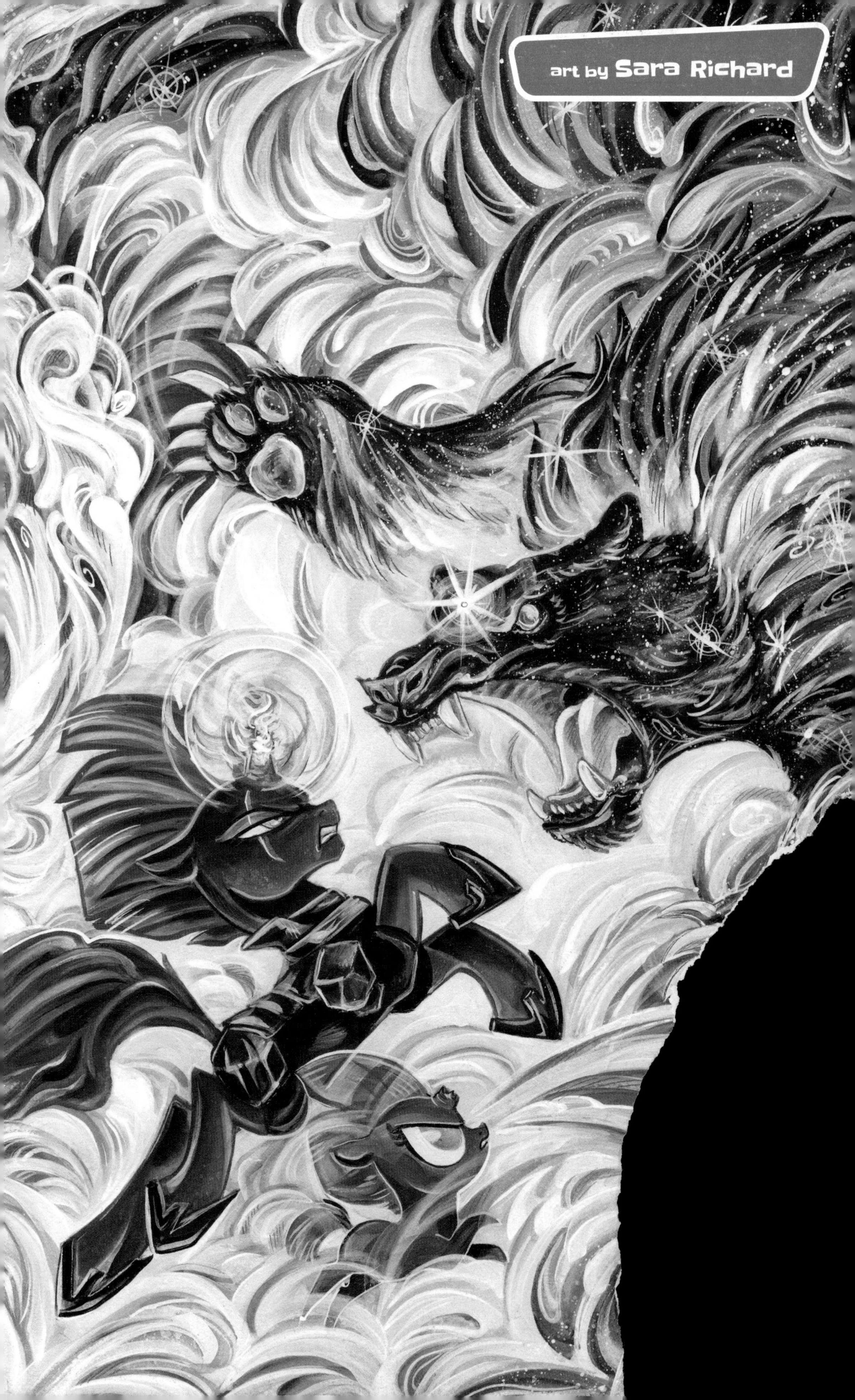
art by Sara Richard

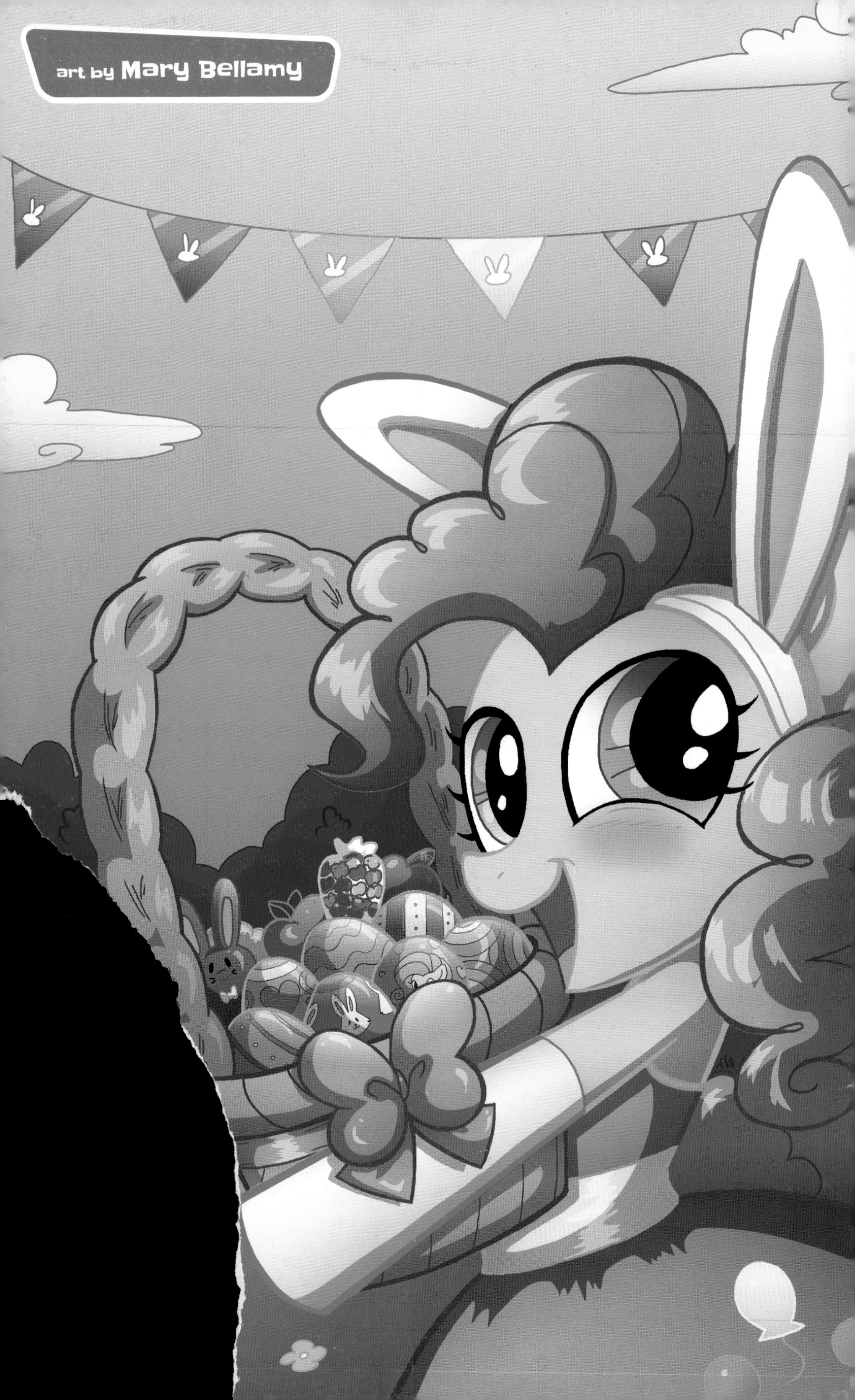

my LITTLE PONY
Friendship is Magic

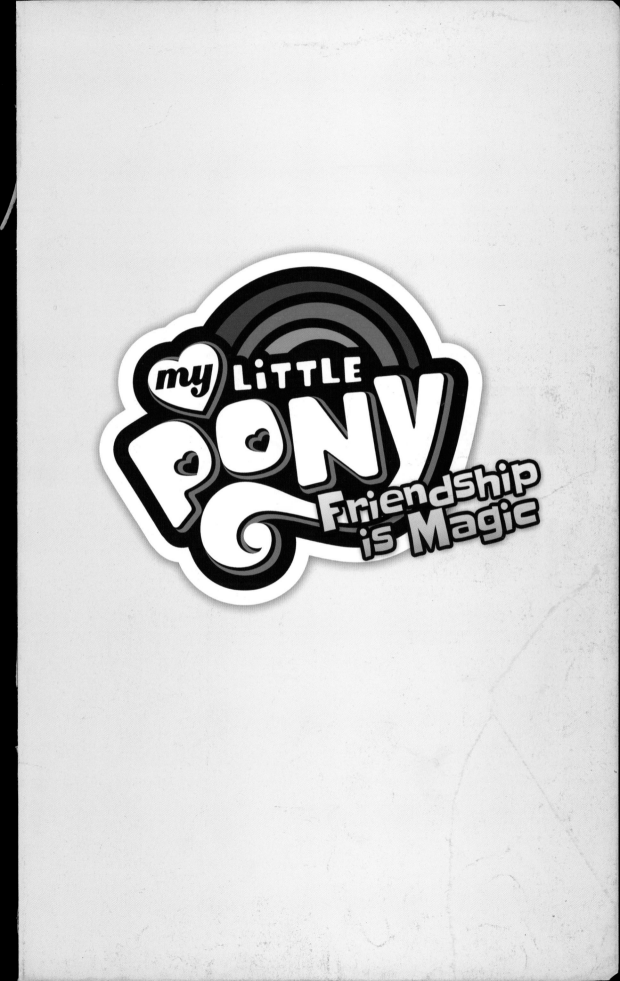

my LiTTLE PONY

| THE ONGOING ADVENTURES OF EVERYONE'S FAVORITE PONIES! | PONIES UNITE IN THIS TEAM-UP SERIES! |

| My Little Pony: Friendship is Magic, Vol. 1 | My Little Pony: Friendship is Magic, Vol. 2 | My Little Pony: Friends Forever, Vol. 1 | My Little Pony: Friends Forever, Vol. 2 |
| TPB • $17.99 • 978-1613776056 | TPB • $17.99 • 978-1613777602 | TPB • $17.99 • 978-1613779811 | TPB • $17.99 • 978-1631401596 |

| SPECIALLY SELECTED TALES TO TAKE WITH YOU ON THE GO! | GET THE WHOLE STORY WITH THE MY LITTLE PONY OMNIBUS! |

| My Little Pony: Adventures in Friendship, Vol. 1 | My Little Pony: Adventures in Friendship, Vol. 2 | My Little Pony: Omnibus, Vol. 1 | My Little Pony: Omnibus, Vol. 2 |
| TPB • $9.99 • 978-1631401893 | TPB • $9.99 • 978-1631402258 | TPB • $24.99 • 978-1631401404 | TPB • $24.99 • 978-1631404092 |